The Revolutionist

Robert M Tucker

Printed in United States of America

The Revolutionist is a work of fiction. Names, characters, places, and
incidents either are the product of the author's imagination or are used
fictionally, and any resemblance to actual persons living or dead, or
locales is entirely coincidental.

In memory of my grandparents who came to America during the early 1900's.

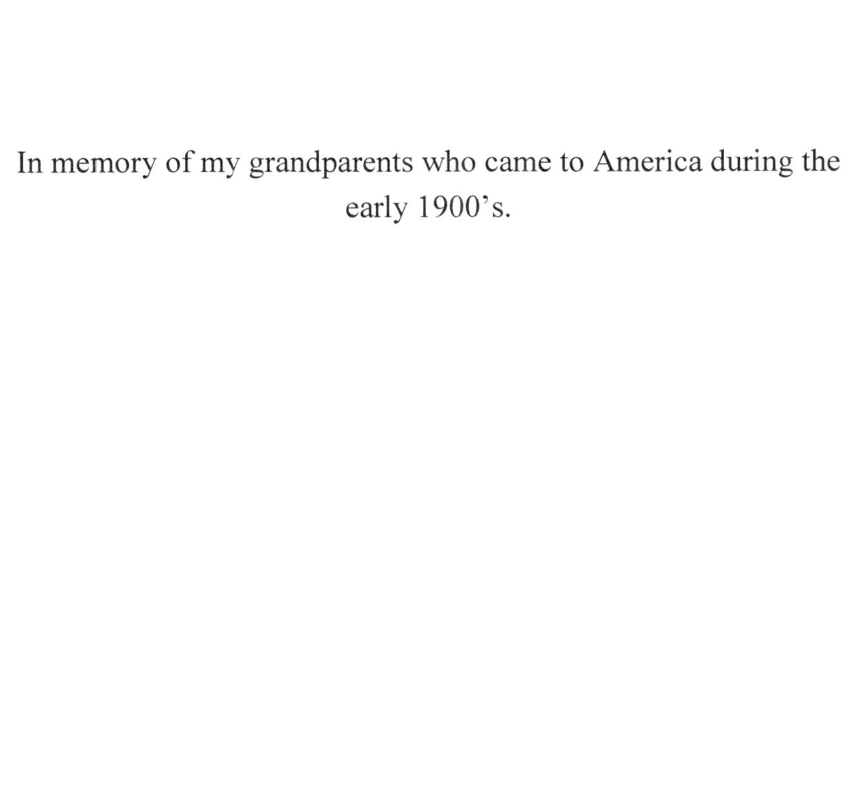

Acknowledgments

My foremost gratitude to Elizabeth Fortin and her colleagues at Tell-Tale Publishing Group, LLC for their response to my work and faith in me as a new author. Your experience, knowledge, and technical and marketing support are phenomenal. A special thanks to Clarissa Yeo for her stunning cover design which captures the spirit of the protagonist and milieu of *The Revolutionist*. A special acknowledgement to Stan Corwin, my friend and mentor over the years for his encouragement and feedback in the development of my novels. A loving acknowledgement to my family for their encouragement and many enjoyable and insightful discussions about writing, publishing, and literature.

"We meet in the midst of a nation brought to the verge of moral, political, and material ruin. Corruption dominates the ballot box, the legislatures, the Congress and even touches the ermine of the bench. The newspapers are largely subsidized or muzzled; public opinion silenced; business prostrated; our homes covered with mortgages; the land concentrated in the hands of capitalists. The urban workmen are denied the right of organization for self-protection; imported pauperized labor beats down their wages; a hireling standing army, unrecognized by our laws, is established to shoot them down, and they are rapidly degenerating into European conditions. The fruits of the toll of millions are boldly stolen to build up colossal fortunes of the few. From the same prolific womb of governmental justice we breed two great classes – tramps and millionaires."

(Ignatius Donnelly – Preamble to the 1892 Populist Program)

TABLE OF CONTENTS

I

Escape

Prologue

Ansel Jaeger looked like an ordinary German citizen on his way home from work. He left the *Commerzbank* exactly on time and moved quickly along Berlin's crowded cobblestone streets to keep his appointment. Only his extended stride gave evidence of the apprehension he tried to repress. He feared the man he was going to meet for the second time.

The first had not been a summons, but what appeared to be a business transaction at the bank. The difference was what was said behind closed doors.

Ansel hesitated at the front door to the office of the *Geheimdienst*, the secret service, located among a cluster of stone government buildings near the Emperor Otto von Bismarck's palace. From here, Rudolf Palm directed the surveillance of the Wohlman family and the gathering of information and evidence that would allow him to make the arrests he so ardently desired.

With great trepidation, Ansel entered the building. He stated his business to a uniformed officer who escorted him to Palm's office.

Palm's slight stature, taciturn expression and ordinary appearance did not dispose anyone to particularly remember him. His only distinctive features were a dense dark mustache that concealed a thin upper lip and a sharply receding hairline that accentuated narrow, widely spaced brown eyes and wire rim glasses snugged at the bridge of a small rodent-like nose.

Ansel stood at attention clutching a leather satchel against his chest as though it were a shield. The satchel contained financial information that would destroy the life of a prominent businessman, Alfred Wohlman.

Palm spoke without looking up from his desk. "Did you bring what I requested?"

"Yes, Herr Director."

Palm glanced at him with an insidious smile. Ansel stumbled forward and placed the satchel on the desk, then quickly stepped back to distance himself from what it contained. Palm opened the bag and lifted out a stack of financial reports and letters of correspondence between the *Commerzbank* and Alfred Wohlman. He began to read, shuffled through the documents, then read more. When he looked up, Ansel trembled.

"You have done well, Herr Jaeger. You have brought me exactly the evidence I need to arrest and execute Herr Wohlman for conspiracy."

Ansel blanched and stuttered. "I am glad to be of service, Herr Director."

"You appear to be uncertain."

"This is difficult for me. I have been employed at the bank for twenty years and never betrayed the trust of a customer."

"Would you prefer to betray me?"

"No, sir, I would not betray you. May I ask what conspiracy? Herr Wohlman is among our leading citizens."

"Only in appearance, Jaeger. He is financing the social democrats in an uprising against the monarchies in Germany and Austria and sowing discord and discontent in other European countries. His influence reaches across borders. We know there are many others involved in his scheme and that they hold clandestine meetings. I'm in search of a list of who they are. The information you have provided will help us identify them and track them down. This," he gestured to the documents, "is a money trail."

"I know nothing about a conspiracy."

For the past three years, Palm had suspected that Alfred Wohlman was a silent financial supporter of the *Sozialdemokrat*, a publication network known as the "Red Postal Service," and the *Sicherheitsdienst* counter intelligence system that identified, analyzed and spied on Palm's own informers and agents provocateur.

Using his merchant business as a front, Alfred was among the hundreds of comrades who smuggled the Zurich published *Sozialdemokrat* out of Switzerland for distribution in other European countries. Their covert activity in Germany broke the law of the *Reich*.

The daring and risky ingenuity of the smuggling system baffled the Imperial German Police who watched for the publications at heavily guarded border posts and through the examination of postal mail. Letter envelopes were among the main distribution methods and large bundles taken across the border in passenger luggage or as freight on boats for further dissemination. The illegal newspaper was also sent from Austria, France, Belgium, Holland, and Sweden.

"Have you spoken to Alfred Wohlman about what you are doing?" Palm continued the interrogation.

"No, sir, not a word."

"That is good, this must always remain a secret between us. It is good you understand, because, of course, you are lying."

Ansel felt the blood rush from his face. "I would not lie to you."

"I know you confided in one of your fellow employees. He is now in a holding cell a few steps down the hall."

"You arrested him?"

"Yes, and since you betrayed me, you are now under arrest. I cannot afford to have any liabilities. As a banker, you must understand that."

"Herr Director, I did not betray you. I brought you what you asked."

"You did not keep silent."

"What about my wife?"

"She will be informed of your traitorous act."

"I am." As he was led away, Ansel looked back to see Palm's lips curl in a tight smirk.

Ansel looked up from where he held his head in his hands in despair. "Not a traitor. I am not a traitor."

He wondered if a guard were going to bring him bread and water. He heard boots approaching outside his cell with determined, forceful steps. A key turned in the heavy metal lock. The door was slowly pushed open on resistant hinges. A tall man with a pock-marked face entered.

"Good evening, Herr Jaeger. My name is Luther Baggot."

Ansel watched in horror as the dark barrel of a shotgun emerged from under the man's greatcoat, aimed directly at his head.

"You will come with me now."

Chapter 1

Berlin   1888

An early riser, Alfred rolled out of bed, taking care not to disturb his softly snoring frau, Anna. A light scent of lavender clung to her from perfume she had touched behind each ear. He leaned over and gently touched his lips to her thinning hair, where the blonde had faded to white. For a moment, he gazed at her cherubic round face, cheeks rosy with sleep. It amazed him that she could sleep so well. He no longer could. He would rise two or three times during the night to relieve himself, and then had difficulty sinking back into a deep slumber.

Lately, he would doze off while sitting at his desk at work and he experienced a noticeable shortness of breath when ascending a staircase or quickening his pace while walking. Anna's *streusels* and sauces over the forty years of their marriage had added to his girth.

Keeping trim had been easy during their younger days when he and his sons would take woodland hikes and go rowing on the Rhine River. He could mark the changes in his physique and gradual decline in energy as his sons grew into manhood and no longer included him in their social outings with their own circle of friends. With one exception, he was relegated to sedentary association with other businessmen like himself who were members of their synagogue.

He had hoped to interest both boys in joining him in his successful mercantile trade and transportation company after completing their university education, but only his eldest son by two years, Kurt, was inclined. Even as a boy, Heinrich had been a scribbler, describing his impressions of life in stories and poems as though born to the writer's art and an appreciation for the aesthetic.

Both his sons had attended *cheder*. Soon after their *bar mitzvah's*, they had moved on from Hasidic tradition to other philosophical and secular interests. Alfred realized that, as a follower of the *Haskalah*, science as a form of faith, he himself had influenced his sons in their choices. Even in his own household, he and Anna did not practice strict Judaic religious tradition.

During his *gymnasien* and, later, university studies in Vienna, Kurt had discovered the emphasis placed on educational achievement, learning and *geist*, intellect, by his classmates and their families. While many of his friends entered the fields of law and medicine, Kurt followed the path of his father into business.

Heinrich gravitated quickly into philosophical and literary studies and produced an outpouring of his own work based on his personal cause against social, cultural, and racial discrimination against the Jewish elite in Germany, and by the Christian Socials in Vienna.

Heinrich wanted to distance himself from being perceived as a privileged artist who was the son of a wealthy businessman. He and other young fin de siècle writers who spent many afternoons and evenings in Vienna's Café Griensteidl reading and discussing each others' manuscripts wanted to take their art in a new direction. They turned their backs on naturalism as an attempt to document humanity without inspiring the passion to do something about its sordid conditions.

Heinrich decided he did not want to be isolated writing in a garret or a tavern, but to be a man of the world, on the dangerous forefront of politics and art that reflected the changing social conditions of the end of a century and the rise of an industrialized world. He wanted to shock, to upset, to cause people to think, question what had gone before and change the unjust and social and economic imbalance. He imbued his writing with styles of modernism, unmistakable symbolism and subjective impressionism while, much like his father, he sought ways to interject himself into the maelstrom of political change.

Alfred poured tepid water from a tall porcelain pitcher into his wash basin. He carefully dabbed a little dampened soap about his face, still clear and unwrinkled as he aged. Looking into a mounted oval mirror, he blinked his blue eyes rapidly to clear a few drops of moisture from the lashes, then patted his skin dry with a clean towel neatly folded on a side table. A few passes with a brush calmed and restored his sleep-skewed gray hair to its normal layered order.

His stomach rumbled at the aroma of pork sausage wafting up the staircase from the kitchen. He slipped off his sleeping gown and, hopping about slightly, thrust his legs into his dark trousers and pulled suspenders up over his shoulders. Even sitting, tugging on socks and shoes had become a mild ordeal since he had to navigate his expanding mid-section. Since he would not be breakfasting with his wife, he decided his undershirt would be sufficiently presentable at the table and that Gustav would not disapprove of his appearance.

Their house servant greeted him with an affable smile as Alfred entered the room. *"Guten Morgan, Herr Wohlman. Kaffee?"*

"Morgan, Gustav, ya, ya."

"Schlaft gut."

Alfred seated himself and glanced at the Berlin Newspaper, *Der Tag*, placed on the side cart near his chair. The main headline read: **Emperor Bismarck Shocked By Comments of Austria Hungary Crown Prince.**

He read quickly down the page and learned that the son of the Emperor Franz Joseph had published scathing and hostile statements toward Germany, favoring a change in alliances by abandoning Germany and Italy in favor of France and Russia.

Alfred found the young man's political position interesting, but unrealistic, since his father clearly aligned Austria Hungary with the iron-fisted rule of Bismarck, the Prussian Emperor.

As he read the article and sipped his coffee between bites of sausage and potato pancakes, out of the corner of his eye he noticed Gustav glancing out the window, then standing aside to escape detection. "Something happening on the street?"

"Policemen are watching the house."

"*Polizei?* How many do you see?"

"Two at the front gate and more along the street."

"Not a good sign." Alfred stood up from the table. "If I am arrested, go directly to the home of my son, Kurt. He will not be at his office for another hour. Tell him he must leave Berlin, get out of the country, and go to Austria. Send a telegram to Heinrich in Vienna. The secret police will be after them both not long after I am taken. Tell my lawyer. Eisenheim may not be able to do anything in this situation, but he can try. I'm going upstairs to wake Anna. Restrain her if she tries to follow me. They will only arrest her as well. You remember our plan?"

"Of course."

"My sons must get out of Europe. Arrangements can be made for Kurt's family to join him later."

"Do you want me to stay with them?"

"Ya, they will need your help. Take care of Anna first. Send her to her sister in Munich. Danke, Gustav. You are one of my family. I'm sorry to see our days end like this."

"As I am. I have many fond memories."

"Go to Kurt now. After I have said my goodbye to Anna, I will leave by the front door just as I always do to find a cab. I won't resist. *Weidersehen.*"

"*Weidersehen.*" Gustav watched Alfred rush up the stairs. With some anxiety, he checked the windows at the rear of the house to see if police or agents waited in the courtyard. The way was clear. He stepped out into the fresh morning air.

Not wanting to appear alarmed in case he was being watched, he walked quickly and purposefully along narrow back streets until he reached the apartments of Kurt Wohlman.

"No, I will not let them take you," Anna sobbed, pulling Alfred down onto the bed with her.

"Anna, *meine liebe*, listen, listen. We have always known this day might come. There is a risk in what we are doing, but it had to be done. Don't worry about me. Think of your sons."

"*Gott im Himmel!* Are they being arrested too?"

"*Nein, nein*, Gustav has gone to warn Kurt. He will join Heinrich in Vienna and leave the country."

"Will I never see my sons again?"

"You will see them again, I promise. When I am out of prison, we will travel to wherever they have gone to resettle. In the meantime, Gustav will arrange for you to visit your sister in Munich."

"But how long will the police keep you?"

"Perhaps a few hours for questioning. Perhaps a day or two. When they find out I don't have any information they want, they'll let me go. Once I'm home again, we'll make plans to leave Germany."

"You are certain about this?"

"Ya, *Liebchen*, this is just a routine investigation. No doubt someone in my company, someone I trusted, tipped them off."

"Who would do such a thing?"

"Someone who is being paid. Germany is no longer safe for any of us. Motteler has to stay in Zurich. If he comes back, the police will arrest him at the border."

"Why can't we just move to Zurich?"

"Until I came under suspicion, I could move money freely to those who needed it here in Germany. For the past five years, Kurt has been making investments outside the country in France, Sweden, Britain, and even America."

"Are Kurt and Heinrich moving to one of those countries?"

"We won't know until we hear from them."

"How much longer before you have to go?"

"I'm giving Gustav a fifteen minute lead. Since the police have been watching me for days, they know my routine. Any longer before I appear, and they will be knocking down the door. I don't want them in the house. They will destroy everything in their search for evidence."

"Wait, wait, let me hold you." She pulled him against her body in a desperate embrace.

"I must go now, Anna. I love you. *Ich liebst du.*"

"*Ich liebst du. Ich liebst du.*" She trailed after him down the stairs. "Can I come and see you?"

"Check with Eisenheim. Gustav will assist you when he returns."

She waited until Alfred stepped outside the front door and closed it behind him. Then she rushed to a window and peered out through the lace curtains past a flowerbox in full bloom with red geraniums. She saw three uniformed police officers stop him at the wrought iron gate. They exchanged a few words. To her relief, they treated him with respect, no force, no violence, as they marched him down the street to a waiting horse drawn police wagon.

Wearing a dark suit and cloak and the black clerical collar of a priest, Jean Guenoc switched the satchel he carried from his left hand to his right and hurried along the back street to catch up with Gustav Weber.

"Gustav, I'm with you."

The older man paused in his headlong rush and glanced at him with surprise. "Jean, we did not expect you until tomorrow."

"It appears I did not arrive soon enough."

"You saw what happened. The police took Alfred."

"I was coming down the street toward the house when it happened."

"I warned Alfred he needed to leave the country for a while, go on a trip, a vacation, but he wouldn't listen. He doesn't always notice what is happening like I do."

"You are his eyes and ears."

"But not his head. I hope he does not pay with it."

"If he did, our revenge would be more than social awareness."

"I would rather we could free him."

"The odds are not in our favor. We cannot walk through prison walls. What will you do with Anna?"

"Her sister is in Munich. It would be best if she go there. At least she will have some of her family around her."

"And you, Gustav, what will you do?"

"I'm one of the family. Where they go, I go. I think Kurt and Heinrich will choose America. I need only to know where and that is where I will be needed."

"You're a good man, Gustav."

"I think of myself as an uncle serving his relatives. I love the Wohlmans as my own flesh and blood."

"We are flesh and blood, Gustav. We are."

"What will you do?"

"I've not met Kurt and Heinrich since they were young boys. They don't know who I am, unless Alfred or you told them about me. I'll follow Kurt and help him to join Heinrich and keep them from harm. It's the least I can do for their father."

"I felt concern about what might happen to them. But now that you will be with them, less so. How will you travel?"

"By steamer down the Danube to Beograd. From there, we'll cross into Croatia and take a ship from Trieste."

"I wish I could be with you."

"We'll meet again, Gustav, somewhere in America." At the sight of a policeman rounding a corner one block away, Jean warned, "Go now. There's no more time. I'll detain that one, ask him for directions." Jean suddenly separated from him and strode away toward the approaching officer, as Gustav ducked down a side street.

Two strong policemen wearing the pointed helmets of the Kaiser firmly grasped Alfred's arms from each side and moved him from the van through the door into the police station. He sensed an urgency in their grip and a sense of momentum that he interpreted to mean they wished to impress their captain and the bespectacled civilian standing next to him.

"You may let him go," said the captain whose red mustache bristled from his nose and covered most of his upper lip.

As the policemen released his arms, Alfred felt like a heavy overcoat had sloughed off his shoulders to the floor. He stood squarely before the police captain and did not give any indication that he was intimidated by the two men who confronted him.

"Herr Wohlman, you are charged with conspiracy against the monarchy of Emperor Otto von Bismarck. We have evidence you have given vast sums to the social democrats and are yourself a member of the social democrats. As you are aware, being a social democrat is against the law in Germany." He turned aside to present the civilian.

"Herr Wohlman, this is Herr Rudolf Palm, Director of the Secret Service and the man responsible for discovering your crimes against the Emperor."

"I'm sure there is no pleasure in our meeting one another," said Palm with a suppressed snear. "I do not have an appreciation for conspirators and insurrectionists."

"I am neither a conspirator nor an insurrectionist, sir. I am a businessman."

"We know who you are and what you have done. There is nothing you can say that will change that. You will be charged with conspiracy and go to prison. But your sentence may be reduced if you are willing to identify others in your organization."

"Before we proceed any further, Herr Director, I wish to have my lawyer present."

"What is your lawyer's name?"

"Florian Eisenheim."

"A Jew like yourself. As a Jew and a social democrat, you have no legal rights. And your lawyer cannot present a case in the high court. If it is determined that he is also a social democrat, he will join you in prison."

"All I have done is send money to Switzerland for the cause of the social democrats."

'Yes, we know of Joseph Motteler. Eventually, we will extradite him, even though he is in Switzerland. He will spend the rest of his life in prison here in Berlin. But you have sent large sums of money to others in different countries, as well."

"I have not made it my business to know who is in the party or where."

"You are not a convincing liar, Herr Wohlman. I know of the list. I'm sure you are aware I have many spies. Very little escapes me. One of your trusted people informed me. What I need from you is where to find the list. Who keeps it? Who possesses it?"

"I have no knowledge of any list."

"I have ways to help you remember."

"So you plan to torture me."

"Only if you refuse to cooperate."

"It isn't Bismarck the social democrats despise, it is you, the man who does his dirty work."

"My position and my services are available to him at his discretion and, of course, upon his orders. I am a reasonable man, Herr Wohlman, not a monster. I'm accustomed to dealing with other reasonable men, such as yourself. You have nothing to fear if you do as you are told."

"If I give up my freedoms, you call that reasonable."

"You are a German citizen, Herr Wohlman, and the Emperor appreciates your business acumen. He appreciates industrious hardworking Jews. They are the foundation for our successful economy and in Austria-Hungary. However, like a good citizen, you must obey German law."

"So you are not going to allow me to have my lawyer present."

Palm smiled. "You may invite him to join you, but once he passes through that door, he will discover it is not in his best interest to be here with you. Rest assured, he will be investigated."

"What is to happen to me now?"

"Captain, show Herr Wohlman to his cell. Provide for his needs."

"Herr Wohlman," said the captain, "please come with me."

Another officer searched Alfred's pockets and patted his trousers down to his ankles, then stood. "Gut."

"This will be your home until other arrangements are made."

Alfred entered the cell and looked at the bare bunk against the wall. "Do I get blankets?"

"Ya, Szweick, blankets and a pillow for Herr Wohlman."

The second officer left and returned promptly with a pillow and blankets, which he handed to Alfred. The captain closed and locked the cell door. "You will be served three meals a day."

"Danke, Captain, danke." Alfred dropped the bedding on the bunk and sat heavily on it. He immediately missed his own comfortable warm bed and his wife.

Kurt Wohlman stepped out of his horse-drawn cab and quickly blended with the bustling people entering and leaving the train station. His heart raced at the sight of police officers, some with Rotweillers and German Shepherds, moving among the ebbing and flowing crowds that parted to allow them a path through and quickly rushed on with their luggage and children in tow to avoid being noticed and singled out for whatever the police might suspect.

Kurt merged with a group of businessmen like himself, bearded and mustachioed *burgers* wearing black homburgs and dark suits and greatcoats. He fit in with them, carrying satchels and umbrellas as they surged to the ticket window against a backdrop of clanging bells and fog horn whistles signaling the comings and goings of smoke-belching trains from the many tracks ensconced in rising clouds of white steam on the chill morning air.

"One way to Vienna," he said to the uniformed ticket master taking *Deutsche Marks* in exchange for the coupons he shoved out from behind his barred kiosk.

Kurt stepped aside and shouldered his way to a news vendor, a teenage boy wearing his slouch hat at a rakish angle, then maneuvered to an empty seat on a bench he spotted in a secluded corner. He sat down, opened his newspaper, *Der Tag*, wide enough to conceal his face and pretended to read while listening for the conductor's call to board.

Rudolph Palm carefully wiped the schnitzel gravy from the corners of his thin sensitive lips, raised his glass of *spatburgunder* red wine and examined its translucent qualities against a gaslight in the street outside the window of the restaurant where he sat at his accustomed table with Luther Baggot.

"Wohlman's eldest son, Kurt, is a fugitive," said Palm. "He was spotted boarding the train early this morning. We know he is going to Vienna to meet up with his brother. The train will be stopped and forced to remain at Herzberg to give you time to catch up on the next train from Berlin. Follow Kurt Wohlman until he leads you to his brother. Other agents and the police will be with you when you take them prisoner. They must not escape, at any cost."

Luther nodded. "They will not escape."

Chapter 2

The Train

Kurt Wohlman did not want to be on the morning train departing from Berlin. He felt driven by the urgency of his father's arrest. The chaos of the day providing for his wife and children and how they must react to this sudden catastrophe in their lives had not allowed him even a moment to consider the risks he himself must undertake. He could not adjust to the thought of being a fugitive. He did not know how to act. Secrecy and furtiveness were foreign to him. His features and appearance were not distinctive. He looked like most bearded *burger* businessmen but he was not a man comfortable with deception.

He carried only one bag with personal toiletries, an extra pair of trousers, silk cravat, and a few changes of socks and undergarments. As of that moment, he did not know how far he would have to travel or what his needs would be. That the lives of his family could suddenly be thrown into such an upheaval outraged him. He desired revenge of some kind, but knew it was not available to him. He would gladly have paid an assassin to end Bismarck's rule.

Managing the vast operations of the railroad, freight forwarding, and shipping company, he had no direct involvement in his father's political affairs. He had attended a few gatherings disguised as glee clubs and gymnastic societies and listened to discussions at the dinner table and over late night cognac and cigars. He knew that clandestine meetings took place at safe beer halls and inn locations unknown to him. The secret police constantly watched him and his family. He suspected that spies worked as employees in his own company, but had no way to identify them, no proof of their disloyalty.

He understood the rise and spread of the social democratic movement and their need to operate as an underground society to promote economic and political objectives. The police had destroyed socialist trade unions. The *Fachvereine* craftsmen could never discuss political matters at meetings or in their trade journals.

As a manager of thousands of German workingmen and women in the family's far flung company, Kurt had a different perception of their political role. They lived and worked in advanced industrial cities throughout Prussia, Austro-Hungary, Italy, and France and were not inclined to be radicals and anarchists. Revolution was not of interest and not on their minds. The weakness of the movement was further undermined by police infiltration of cells and conclaves and arrests and imprisonment of its leaders.

His father had said the social democrats wanted to distance themselves from the anarchists to avoid being associated with acts of violence, since, under socialist law, the government termed anarchism a radical version of social democracy that raised the voice of the proletariat, the suffering masses, the persecuted and oppressed.

Kurt believed in the cause of the social democrats, but first and foremost in his mind was that he had a family to support and a business to run. He and his father had expanded their international forwarding business into southeastern and western Europe and were establishing sea transport from Fiume and Triest in Croatia.

Kurt had learned entrepreneurial skills from his father. A creative strategist, Alfred had purchased the shipping agency of the French Eastern Railway and began the practice of consolidation, combining a number of small shipments into single railcars. The first combined freight shipments of wine, cognac, cosmetics, and fashions from Paris to Vienna in 1873 established a progressive marketing trend.

Alfred's promotion and sale of railway forwarding services led to a succession of contracts including with the Great Eastern Railway in London. He negotitated a contract with the *Hessische Ludwigs-Eisenbahn-Gesellschaft* and a contract with the *Chemins de fer de Paris à Lyon et à la Méditerranée*, based in Paris. This expanded his operations for importing goods from the seaport at Marseille.

He established an office in Munich to serve the Bavarian railway in 1886, the year he brought Kurt into the firm. Kurt had expanded traffic through Bavaria to the Danube ports. River transport on the Danube was a major artery of commerce from Germany to the Black Sea. Kurt had built a fleet of nine tug boats, 36 barges, and with branches in Linz where the Elbe joined the Danube River, and in Vienna, and Budapest.

The success of river traffic gave Kurt the incentive to move into sea transport. He had followed the same pattern as his father with the rail business, negotiating agency contracts with shipping companies.

It did not take Kurt long to recognize that freight companies could not meet his demand for transportation. He advised his father to establish their own shipping company for trading with Great Britain. The new shipping line started on the route from the Adriatic Seaports Trieste and Fiume to Glasgow, Scotland. Soon a regular schedule of seven steamships traveled between Trieste,

Fiume, London, Liverpool, and Glasgow. Kurt then expanded his contracts and agencies with other shipping companies, and founded a line for sea traffic from the Adriatic to the United States.

Kurt knew Bismarck would seize all the company's financial and capital assets in Germany and government bureaucrats would run the business and benefit from all that he and his father had built over the years. He began to plot how he and his brother, Heinrich, would take back what was rightfully theirs once they had established themselves in America.

His skin tingling with paranoia, Kurt watched several other male passengers with suspicion as they boarded the train at the *bahnhof*, the first stop of the evening. He averted his eyes and pretended interest in a news copy of *Der Tag* left behind on a neighboring seat by a departing traveler.

Darkness gradually nudged out the blue and orange hues of dusk, as though the train were steadily penetrating the wall of night. Brief glimpses of warmly lit villages flashed past Kurt's window, bringing a lump of sadness to his throat. At this hour, he would be sitting down to dinner and teasing and laughter with his wife and three young daughters. He could see their smooth fair skin and expressive faces rosy with enthusiasm. If any harm came to them, he vowed he would join the anarchists. He would gladly kill anyone in the monarchy if harm came to his family.

As time crept on, hunger overcame his anxiety. He rose from his seat and made his way along the aisle in the direction of the dining car.

The man with a scruffy unshaven face who sat several seats away had boarded just behind him back in Berlin. Although he wore a rumpled suit and no hat, his rough countenance reminded Kurt of a peasant, but he was curious about the man's black collar identifying him as a priest. Kurt did not believe he could be a spy. Their eyes met and the man lowered his chin in a brief nod.

The barely muted blast of iron wheels grinding on steel rails gave Kurt pause as he stepped into the vestibule between the two cars. There was something vaguely familiar about the man. Perhaps they had met sometime years ago, but Kurt could not place him. He continued through the next car crowded with passengers. A few had opened picnic baskets and were eating bratwurst sandwiches and drinking from bottles of wine.

He passed through the dining car door into an eruption of cigar smoke and conversational noise. Two white-jacketed waiters balancing trays gracefully sidestepped each other on the balls of their feet as though in a dance. Kurt spotted an empty table just being evacuated by a man and his wife and assisted the woman by sliding back her chair.

"Frau."

"Danke."

He stood by the claimed chair and waited for the table to be cleared before seating himself. Fresh linen, utensils, glasses, and a menu were placed before him.

"A glass of *riesling*, please." Kurt quickly read the limited choices on the menu and settled for potato soup and *sauerbrauten*. A year ago, the thought had occurred to him to investigate the business possibilities for passenger comfort and travel services. Arranging for the movement of people proved to be just as profitable as shipping freight.

The vinegar seasoning carried the right spiciness to his taste. He ordered a bottle of *mosel* to wash it down. Upon the return to his own car, he observed his fellow passenger had entered the dining car unnoticed behind him and was devouring a schnitzel smothered in potatoes and gravy and *kohl*. Again they exchanged nods.

Relaxed from the heavy meal and the wine, Kurt settle back onto his bench seat. The passing blur of barely illuminated night images from distant farm homes and the pressing proximity of evergreen forests lulled him into a doze.

A sudden rough shaking of his left shoulder pulled him from the depths of sleep. He looked about disoriented and could not immediately remember where he was or why. He was surprised to see his fellow passenger from across the aisle bent over him. The man's low urgent tone sharpened Kurt's focus.

"Herr Wohlman, you must bring your bag and come with me now. We must leave the train at once."

He heard a long whistle and sensed the train slowing as it prepared to stop at the dirty yellowish light refracted the length of the station platform framed in his window. The additional sight of a cluster of uniformed helmeted police with two German Shepherds and a Rotweiller caused him to sit up with a sharp grunt. He stared at the man's face. "Who are you? How do you know me? Are you with the police?"

"I'm a friend of Gustav and your father. I'll explain later. But we must leave the train now before they board and find you."

Kurt scrambled up out of his seat, grabbed his bag from the overhead rack and stumbled after Jean Guenoc's parting figure. He caught up to Jean at the vestibule.

"Here! This way!" Jean shouted back to him.

They descended the few metal steps to the bare ground on the side of the train away from the station platform. They could hear the dogs barking and snarling at the tension of the situation and distracting noise and steam from the train.

"Hurry! Stay with me!" Jean walked quickly toward the rear of the train, then abruptly angled away from the tracks to conceal their movement behind a storage shed. "They can't see us. Now, run!" Jean set a long-legged pace that left Kurt breathless until they stopped within a small woods.

At the station, police boarded the cars at all doors and began their search. Their sudden threatening appearance and the savagery of the attack dogs terrorized the passengers. A woman screamed and her child cried, sensing her fear. Passengers held up their baggage as shields or scrambled up onto their seats and stood against the windows.

"What do you want?" the conductor asked. "Who are you looking for?"

None of the male passengers matched the news photograph and description the police had been given. They held up the train for an hour until they were satisfied that Kurt Wohlman was not on board. They then gathered on the station platform and conjectured as to what might have happened, how he might have escaped, or if he had even been on the train at all. It was too late to search the nearby streets and houses. They decided their fugitive had slipped out on the other side of the train and would now be running on foot into the night. The police decided that instead of rousting the local residents out of bed, they would wait until morning to interrogate them and see if anyone had rendered aid.

Upon regaining his breath, Kurt asked. "Thank you for saving my life. Who are you?"

"Jean Guenoc. I worked in the society as a social democrat for your father in Paris. I was on my way to Berlin when he was arrested. Gustav sent me to look after you. He thought you might need help. And so you did."

"And I thought you were the police."

"As you can see, they have been watching you closely; and I have been watching them."

"What about Heinrich? What about my brother? I was supposed to meet him in Vienna."

"So you shall."

"How will we get there? The trains are being searched."

"There are other ways to travel. We will find one."

"What of our mother?"

"Gustav will take her to Munich to stay with her sister."

"I wonder if we will ever see her again."

"Time will tell."

Kurt nodded. "Time is everything."

"Everything and nothing. It's what we do with it."

Kurt did not know what to make of this man who had suddenly appeared and saved him from arrest and imprisonment and now strode along beside him in the night. "Vienna is a long walk."

"It's good to have a sense of humor."

"It seems we're at their mercy."

"We have to be smarter and take opportunities where we can find them." Jean suddenly stopped and looked back in the direction they had come through an outlying ghetto of a small town.

"What is it?" Kurt tried to see or hear whatever it was that held Jean's attention.

"No dogs. They aren't coming after us." Jean started walking quickly toward the town.

"What are you doing? They could still be there." Kurt stumbled after him.

"We'll find out."

Kurt's eyes teared from coal dust mingled with sweat coursing down from his hairline over his brow. His confusion and disorientation coalesced into a surge of rising anger that he worked hard to repress. Jean Guenoc had saved him and was here to help him. Kurt's anger was at people and forces beyond this town and the night. It was against his own impotence to stop them.

The orderly existence he had known as a husband and father and businessman had been destroyed and torn asunder. In his mind, he cast about for an anchor to which he could attach himself and sort out his options. He did not want to lose all that he had because of an absurd difference in political philosophy. Yet, now here he was, a fugitive stumbling after a stranger in the middle of Germany in the middle of the night.

He gathered in the gossamer strands of his wandering mind and forced himself to focus on the situation that confronted them. Jean moved quickly toward the train and stopped in the shadow of the passenger car from which they had recently escaped. He stooped down to view the station platform across the undercarriage. He saw no policemen's boots and no dogs.

The engine belched a cloud of black smoke at the stars and white steam hissed from the brakes.

"They're gone," said Jean. "The train is about to leave. We can get back on board. Follow me, quickly." He grasped a handrail and pulled himself up onto the steps to the inter-car platform. Looking back, he extended a hand to Kurt and assisted him up the steel steps onto the vestibule.

"We should not appear to be together," said Jean. "The police don't recognize me and we want to keep it that way at least until we reach Vienna."

As the train lurched ahead with a clang of couplings, they balanced themselves against the forward motion, pulled open the door, and entered the car. To Kurt's relief, the conductor was not in sight and none of the other passengers took notice of them as they returned to their original seats.

Trembling from stress, Kurt took several slow deep breaths to calm his beating heart. At the first opportunity, he would ask Jean how he became involved with his father and Gustav. He struck Kurt as being a rather mysterious and powerful figure, in charge of his destiny. He did not think he would be able to sleep again that night, but was mildly surprised to be awakened by the warmth of sunrise on his face through the passenger car window.

He gazed out at the rolling foothills of farm country through which the train was passing beginning a slow labored climb toward an alpine terrain. He glimpsed far away vast dark blue peaks and sensed the train was running parallel to the distant snow-encrusted crest. Their geographical proximity gave him a sense of where he was. He had traveled this same route many times before on business trips to Vienna. He knew he was now near the Bohemian border, which was an auspicious sign that he and Jean might arrive in Vienna undetected. They had traveled south from Berlin through the towns of Lauchhammer, Meissen, and the city of Dresden and were headed for Prague.

The sunrise instilled in him the hope that all things would turn out well for the family. Other passengers around him were waking up, stumbling down the aisle and waiting in line to use the commode, then going to breakfast in the dining car. As the doors opened and closed, the culinary evidence of hot pastries, bacon, and *kaffee* drifted back to him in aromatic snatches.

Kurt watched a mother and her young girl and thought of his own wife and three daughters. He envisioned Marissa's luxurious wavy brown hair, glowing high cheek bones, and grayish-green cat eyes that bewitched him with her challenging and coy expressions.

They had met quite by accident at a salon gathering hosted by a friend of his mother. The event of the evening was a small chamber orchestra playing works of Schubert, Liszt, and Mozart. What caught his attention was that she was a violinist and the only woman among the group of musicians. Other than in private salons, women were barred from playing in public as professional musicians. To do so violated the cultural norm of being wives and mothers. Musicianship was left to the men.

Bringing her a glass of champagne from a tray carried by a passing waiter, he approached her and complimented her on the excellence of the orchestra's interpretation of Schubert's quintet. "It is a shame the composer is so underrated. He is an astounding musician of great range and talent."

"You seem knowledgeable about his work. Are you also a musician or, perhaps, a patron?"

"A patron. I'm sorry to say I don't have a musical bone in my body, but the love and appreciation of music."

"Then I think we might get along quite well. I'm an amateur compared to these gentlemen."

"Not to my ear. Your solos were exquisite."

"Perhaps you would like to learn a little more about theory."

"With you, Madame, it would be my pleasure."

At the Herzberg station, the conductor announced that the departure time would be delayed by three hours. Jean noticed two men who roused his suspicion board the train. Wearing dark suits, long cloaks and hats, they entered the car from the station platform where they paused to stretch their legs and smoke a pipe. As they scanned the other passengers, their gaze came to rest momentarily upon Kurt, which immediately alerted Jean. He detected the bulge of pistols under their coats – secret police. He signaled to Kurt to follow him to the vestibule.

"There are two detectives on the train. They are now seated together at the front of this car. I'm sure from their actions they have identified you and will probably make an arrest when we reach Prague."

"What should I do? What can I do?"

"Nothing. Just go about your journey as normal. Don't signal that you are aware of them. Ignore them. I will take care of them. Now, we'll go back separately to our seats, you first."

"When?"

"I'll tell you later. You will not be involved."

Kurt returned to his seat. A few minutes later, Jean re-entered the car from the vestibule and, with a polite nod to a fellow gentleman passenger, took his own seat.

Jean watched and waited for an opportune moment. Eventually, every passenger had to make a pilgrimage to the commode. When the first detective rose from his seat, turned toward the rear of the car and shook his trousers, Jean read the telltale sign of discomfort. He waited for the man to walk past him, then maintaining a discreet distance, followed him to the back of the car.

"Monsieur." Jean delivered a quick precise two finger punch to his throat, which caused the detective to collapse into his arms. Jean immediately removed the man's hidden pistol from its shoulder holster and jammed it into his own belt. "The time for departure has come, Monsieur. Sorry for the inconvenience."

Outside the rear of the car on the vestibule, the sudden rush of air revived the man, who realized he was being supported by his attacker now holding him at gunpoint.

"The time has come for you to leave the train, Monsieur." Jean stared down at the man's eyes bloodshot with fear and his pulsating nostrils and nervously twitching mustache, reminding Jean of a seized rabbit.

Poised on the vestibule steps, the detective contemplated the ground rushing past and the hazards of leaping from the moving train. Looking ahead, he saw a grassy embankment that he hoped would provide a soft landing.

"A piece of advice, Monsieur. If I push you, there is a greater danger of you being hurt. If you jump of your own free will, land with your knees bent and roll your body. There is much less chance of being injured."

As he leaned outward, the wind jerked the hat from his head and swept it into the wake of black smoke billowing over the top of the train. With a sharp cry, the detective leaped. As he crashed against the ground, his chin and mouth connected hard with the jarring impact from his knees. He heard the crack of dislocation from his jaw moments before an electric jolt of pain wrapped itself around the back of his head and he was rolling and rolling into a deep dark unconsciousness.

After twenty minutes, the second detective looked toward the back of the car wondering what had happened to his partner. Unlike the scrawny build of the first man, as he lurched up from his seat, the tall second man appeared to have well-muscled bulk and weight, which would make him a formidable opponent. Jean noticed that the scars and severe pock marks on the left side of his rugged face gave evidence that he was accustomed to fighting.

He blundered through the rear door, looked about, then stepped back inside. Pushing on the commode door, he found it open and empty of any passengers. With great consternation, he lunged back through the rear door outside onto the vestibule and pondered whether his partner had continued on into the next car for some reason. His body suddenly tensed at the cold end of a pistol barrel pressed against the back of his neck.

"Do not turn around, Monsieur. Do as I say and you will live," Jean's low menacing voice purred in his ear.

"What have you done to my partner?"

"The same thing you will do, Monsieur. He stepped off the train many kilometers ago."

"What! You threw him off a moving train?"

"Not at all, Monsieur. He leaped of his own volition. I assure you he is not harmed, perhaps momentarily lost."

"Let me assure you that if I leave this train, you will go with me."

Jean cocked the pistol. "Then you will go as a dead man." He saw the detective's right hand sliding into his coat for his pistol. "Bring your gun out very slowly and throw it off the train. My bullet is only a split second from entering your brain."

"You will pay with your life for doing this." The detective cast his gun into the passing brush.

"Use the handrail to brace yourself on the steps. I will give you a few moments to select where you will jump. Be thankful we are not on a trestle. Your partner survived. You can do the same."

"You're a priest. How can you do this?"

"Without guilt."

"Then you're a charlatan."

"Non, Monsieur, Bismarck is a charlatan. We are not standing out here to discuss politics. It's time to jump."

"May you burn in hell!"

"That is not likely. I'm an agnostic. I don't believe in such a place."

The man extended his foot out into the rushing space below the bottom step.

"You hesitate," said Jean. "If I have to push, you will be off balance and could break a limb upon landing. The best way is to tuck in your knees and roll and absorb the shock."

"So you have experience at this, a train robber. You have done this before."

"Many times. I give you to the count of three, Monsieur. *Einz, Fie, Drei.*"

The man leaped, his cape flowing upward and outward behind him like the massive wings of a large predatory bird. Jean heard his loud curse as he struck the ground, then he was lost in the rapidly fading distance.

When Jean re-entered the car, Kurt asked, "What do you think we should expect?"

"I would guess they will be waiting for us in Vienna. That is where your brother is."

When the Frenchman had forced Luther Baggot to leap from the moving train, a bone (the femur) in Luther Baggot's right leg snapped from the impact of his hitting the ground. What enraged Luther as much as the broken leg was that he had concentrated on following the instructions given by the Frenchman for a safe landing. He vowed that if he ever encountered the Frenchman again, he would kill him on the spot. But first, he had to get himself out of this predicament of being lost somewhere in the forests far south of Berlin.

He decided that retracing the route north by following the tracks, he might come across his partner who, hopefully, would be in a better condition than he. Since he couldn't put any weight on his injured leg without sending searing jolts of pain all the way up his back into his head, he hobbled about to find a sturdy fallen branch for support.

After staggering along the track bed for two miles with frequent stops to rest, he came upon a dirt wagon track that led to a small rural village. He paid a farm boy to ride on horseback to Dresden to deliver a message to the chief of police, who dispatched a coach and mounted patrol to the village. Luther learned that his partner had not been injured in his leap from the train and had walked twenty miles back to Dresden.

Chapter 3

Vienna

Wet stone grazed her smooth cheek as Sophie Rose leaned in to peer around a tall front column of the main Vienna University building onto the *Ringstrasse*. She did not see a sign of his movement anywhere through the curtain of light rain that diffused the glow from the gas street lamps stretched like posted sentinels along the border of the great city square, the heart of Vienna. The broad avenue of massive architectural structures of Roman, gothic, baroque and renaissance styles housed the parliament, municipal government offices, the university, and the theater.

At this late hour, a line of cabs and carriages at the entrance of the *Hofburg Theater* waited for patrons to emerge. Horses shook their harnesses and stamped their hoofs on the cobblestones in uncomfortable resignation to the chill damp air. Sophie watched the sporadic movement of the vehicles deployed in all directions along the wide boulevard. Couples linked arms and walked quickly to disappear down side streets. A sudden burst of loud laughter from a small cluster of young men, university students, caught her attention, but Heinrich was not among them.

Her pulse quickened with the thrill of real danger and suspense, not at all like the staged dramatizations of the operas and operettas in which she performed. She preferred this reality, the expectation she had felt when they first met in the costume department, the cogent nearness of his body and breathe engaging her in a false embrace, a charade to escape the notice of the secret police who followed him.

"Just pretend I'm one of the actors, your lover." He had draped himself in a sweeping cape from the rack of costumes and planted a plumed cavalier hat on his head before encircling her with his arms and planting his mouth firmly against hers. Her eyes searched his daring young face and she responded with a passion that surprised him. But after all she was a pretender, an actress, a diva in the opera company and this incident was life imitating art.

Their ruse diverted the two plainclothesmen racing backstage. Having lost sight of their fugitive, they left Sophie and Heinrich to their romance in the stage wings. Believing he had departed by the exit door into the side alley, they continued to run after him in an illusionary chase.

That Heinrich had not appeared at the appointed time told Sophie that he was being followed. An extension of the German Chancellor Bismarck's spy network, the secret police had been watching his comings and goings and hoped to catch him in a political gathering of the *sozialdemokrat*, social democrats, that would result in his arrest and extradition to Germany for trial and imprisonment. Although Franz Joseph, the Emperor of Austro-Hungary, did not outlaw social democrats in his country, he did cooperate with Bismarck under the alliance of their monarchies.

Because of the social democrats fierce political criticism, Bismarck had brought legal proceedings against them, accusing them of high treason. Although he was a wealthy Jewish merchant and financier in Berlin, Heinrich's and Kurt's father, Alfred Wohlman, identified with the revolutionary forces that Otto Von Bismarck called the pariah of German society.

Going back to 1875, Bismarck issued a penal code for inciting classes of society against each other or attacking the institutions of marriage, family and property. The Prussian state then crushed the Social Democratic party on the grounds it violated the law of associations and challenged the beliefs and values of German society.

In a loud session of the *Bundesrat*, the *Reichstag* had passed and proclaimed, "This anti-socialist bill will repress social democratic activities and destroy the labor movement. We will shut down their meetings and outlaw the publication and distribution of Social Democratic newspapers, pamphlets, and books by fining and imprisoning anyone caught in promoting those activities. The *polizei* are authorized to arrest and deport citizens thought to be dangerous to public security and order."

Jean signaled Kurt to follow him out onto the vestibule between two moving passenger cars where they appeared to be engaged in casual conversation.

"I need some information about your brother," said Jean, "a description, where he lives, whatever you can tell me."

"He's a taller more handsome version of me," Kurt grinned.

Jean's eyes twinkled in appreciation of the humor. "Also, we need a way to avoid detection by the police."

"I know this route," said Kurt. "I've traveled it many times on business over the years. If we're going to be met by the police in Vienna, we should get off the train in Klosterneuberg. It's a few kilometers north. We can enter the city under cover of darkness by coach."

"We should not go directly to your brother. The police will be watching him. When we arrive, take me to where he lives, I will follow him and make the contact. Can you arrange for the three of us to travel from Vienna on the river?"

"I'll go to our office of operations at the main dock. We have three steamships and seven barges that make regular trips up and down the Danube."

"What stops are made?"

"Bratislava, Budapest, a few small towns. Once we reach Beograd in Slavonia, we will no longer be followed and we can go by train to Trieste and book passage to England. From there to America."

"You're an embarrassment to us all," Sophie's brother, Stefan, had accused her in one of their many private altercations. Stefan would unceasingly attack her on this point when they were in the presence of their mother and father. He hoped they would side with him against her and persuade her to support his campaign. Since she was an admired personality of the Viennese theater, her endorsement would gain him votes.

"Your association with your Jewish friends is ruining my career," he ranted. "Everybody thinks I'm like you, just because we share a family name." He was vying for a position on the city council in the third curia. Sophie would have none of it. As a liberal, she distanced herself from Stefan's political ambitions and alienated herself from her family.

Until she was enrolled in the *gymnasien*, she had not fully recognized the social and political separatism that existed and influenced her life. All of her choices had been made for her, except the gift of her voice.

Although as a child she made friends with other girls, she was not allowed to socialize with the ones she admired, the young

Jewish *madchen*, who read books and talked about philosophical subjects beyond what she and children from the families of her own class were told to ignore. "You do not have to concern your mind with such drivel, her father told her. We are German *hausherren*, the highest class. We have wealth and serve the Emperor."

She remembered as a small girl skipping alongside her father's imposing, slightly corpulent figure when he allowed her and her brother to accompany him on a tour of the palace court to his chambers. She fidgeted impatiently for most of two hours while expected to sit quietly nearby and watch and listen to business negotiations between her father and vendors and bankers who did business with the court. He was an economist and an accountant, who boasted to his family about the great sums of money for which he was responsible on behalf of the Emperor Franz Joseph.

A favored son, Stefan showed his interest by later asking questions that demonstrated he had been listening to the discussions, whereas Sophie had received solicitous smiles and a pat on the head. She had decided then and there that she had no tolerance for bureaucracy, but her father was not affected by her lack of appreciation for his stature and position. She was, after all, only a girl who would become a young woman and marry a man of suitable rank in society. His mother, Emma, would groom her for that eventual role, just as she had her three older sisters, who were well married and established in Viennese society with children of their own.

Emil, had been greatly relieved when Stefan was born. He could relate to a son, but had always been aloof with his daughters, as long as they were compliant. Sophie, however, confronted his authority from the time she was a small child and often refused to submit to his will. He thought he perceived in her behavior an enjoyment in thwarting him. As much as he carried on with boisterous threats, he never raised his hand against her.

Her admiration for her uncle, Helmut, an officer of the fashionable Hussars, a position reserved for the sons of aristocratic families, aggravated Emil, but lessened his concern for Sophie Augusta Rose until he learned she was going to the royal riding academy on a regular basis where Helmut was teaching her to ride like a man. He was an excellent horseman and swordsman, as well as a dashing cavalier for the ladies who sought his favor at court receptions and balls.

His humor, laughter, and gusto captured his niece's imagination and drew her away from the dull limited existence she saw that lay before her as a woman of the leisure class. Upon seeing her uncle and his brigade practicing maneuvers on horseback and hearing the clash of metal, snorts and trumpeting neighs amid the rumble of galloping hoofs, she pronounced, "Had I been born a man, I would become a Hussar."

She loved the theatricality of their blue and red uniforms, plumed helmets and fine young faces sporting mutton chops and sweeping mustaches. The realities of battle, booming canon, screams, death cries, blood and carnage, were unknown to her, but the rush of charging men and horses excited her. To Sophie Rose, at an early age, life was theater. She cast herself in imaginary roles on the stage of her own imagination.

Her parents and other girls who were her classmates in school did not quite know how to relate to her. She could not tolerate mundane discussions and preoccupations with fashion and pretense and self-importance. She would speak her opinions and pointedly attack and embarrass girls from the bourgeoisie she did not like, especially when she overheard them gossiping about Jewish students. She discovered and savored conflict in being an advocate and protector. In so doing, she alienated members of her own class, who thought her strange and came to fear her wrathful attacks, especially when she burst into an operatic tirade, actually singing at them. She wore her loneliness as a badge of her individualism.

Her mature voice became her trademark. Within a year of her joining the church choir, the music director at St. Stephens had her singing solo leads from works by Bach and Handel and Mozart. Her lilting crystal clear soprano voice soared upward into the vaulted gothic ceiling.

It was in such a church setting that the director of the Vienna Opera heard her and brought her into the company to train for roles in productions of works by Rossini, Puccini, Verdi, Mozart, and Strauss. After two years as an understudy, she was cast as the lead soprano in *La Boehm* and delivered a performance that overshadowed all others.

When interviewed by journalists from the *Neue Frei Presse* and *Neues Weiner Tagblatt,* she explained how closely she identified with the tragic heroine, because she, Sophie Augusta Rose herself, was a true Bohemian.

At the age of eighteen, she became the talk of Vienna. Hostesses competed for her attendance at salons and receptions. Well-to-do bachelors sought her favor without success. Offers of marriage were turned down. Her parents struggled with the dilemma of pride at her achievement and fame, and her public notoriety.

Her position as a leading performing artist coupled with the upper *bourgeoisie* status of her family allowed her the freedom and transparency to move back and forth effortlessly between the classes of Viennese society.

She attended balls at the palace alone, never on the arm of an escort. Young men lined up for the privilege of dancing with her. She was equally at home among the crowd of dignitaries in their formal military uniforms, swelling orchestral waltzes, the ballroom erupting with a flood of dancers whirling and flowing smoothly across the massive marble floor as though their ballooning gowns were elevated on air.

The *bourgeoisie* women viewed her as too independent, too modern. Although they were cordial and complemented her on her opera performances, their gossip at teas and salons rumbled with disapproval of her preference for bohemian company. She enjoyed the companionship and impassioned talk of impoverished artists, musicians, poets and struggling novelists and playwrights in the *kaffee hauses, bierlokals, and weingartens.*

She herself took an apartment in the opera district next to the *Schwarzenberplatz,* a highly desirable residential area symbolizing the social divide between the impoverished Jewish artisan tenements and the wall to wall neo-Renaissance structures inhabited by wealthy Jewish businessmen, textile manufacturers, doctors, lawyers, and their families. Her parents had to endure criticism from matrons and others of their class. "How can you allow your Catholic raised daughter to live among even affluent Jews?"

The Queen was an exception to this social undercurrent. She did not begrudge the daring ingénue of the operatic stage her free spirit. Elizabeth envied her and chaffed at the constraints of her royal marriage to the Emperor, Franz Joseph.

The volatile Elizabeth despised receptions and balls and was most at home out riding her white thoroughbred mare or trekking through the countryside on arduous hikes followed by her ladies in waiting trailing in horse-drawn wagons.

An accomplished horsewoman herself, she first saw Sophie Rose putting a Trakehner stallion through his paces in the dressage ring at the riding academy. What struck the Queen was that Sophie wore men's breeches and sat astride rather than using a woman's conventional side saddle.

Owing to its Thoroughbred ancestry, the Trakehner was Sophie's mount of preference. Of rectangular build, with a long sloping shoulder, good hindquarters, short cannons, and a medium-long, crested and well-set neck made him ideal for the strength and intricacy of dressage. The head was finely chiseled, narrow at the muzzle, with a broad forehead. The breed possessed a strong, back and powerful hindquarters and was known for its "floating trot" - full of impulsion and suspension.

The Queen saw Sophie on two other occasions, one taking her horse over fences, and the third time leaning low over her her horse's neck in a flat out run across a mountain meadow.

"There, but for a difference in birth, go I," she thought.

"The Queen and the Emperor have an odd sort of marriage," Sophie's father told her once as they sat before the fireplace in his library sipping a post prandial cognac. "He has sired children, yet he and the queen live apart for long periods of time. She really doesn't care for Vienna. She prefers Corfu, because it is warm and the skies are drenched with sun when we have rain here in Vienna. She also has a fascination for mythology, which is why she has her palaces built to look like Greek and Roman temples.

"Did you know the actress Katherine Schott is a very close friend of the Emperor? She visits him at his hunting lodge. It is not known for certain if she is a lover or just a friend. Their relationship is a topic of conjecture in the court. For a man of the highest powers, he has family problems like anyone else. The court gossip is that the Queen can't stand her mother-in-law and that's why she stays away from Vienna as much as possible."

Sophie stifled a yawn. Her father's gossip of the Royal Family bored her.

Stefan had two purposes in paying frequent visits to his father in the royal court offices, to be noticed and to gain information that he could parlay back to Karl Leuger, the leader of the Christian democratic party. Other than any intelligence Stefan could provide him, Leuger did not particularly care for the insincere fawning young man whose main interest was in promoting himself. He saw Stefan as merely a syncophant, a hanger-on with few capabilities as a politician, despite his studies in law. But lower level staff were necessary to Leuger to accomplish menial and mundane tasks and to support him with their admiration.

Leuger was a demagogue who oozed great personal charm and had a much admired political astuteness. Stefan emulated Leuger's use of anti-Semitic slogans that appealed to his lower middle-class constituency. Anti-Semitism was common to Austrian public life. As the leader of the Roman Catholic party, the Christian Socials, Lueger had created a mass political movement playing on the fear Viennese artisans and shopkeepers had of Jewish capitalism and the business competition from their more efficient factories and retail distribution networks. His platform was that Jewish business was a "threat to the Christian social order."

Stefan openly blamed the Jews for his lack of parliamentary access as a politician. But mostly, he blamed his sister, Sophie

Rose, for her romantic relationship and public support of an outspoken Jewish university student, Heinrich Wohlman.

Heinrich's uncompromising antagonism often got him into trouble with professors in classes dominated by students from the elite bourgeoisie. In one such lecture on the economy of Germany and Austria, Heinrich was in a boil at the assigned reading of a violently anti-semitic book by a University of Berlin professor, Eugen Dühring. The book's title was enough to push Heinrich over the edge of classroom protocol and decorum, *The Jewish Question as a Race, Morals and Cultural Question.*

Heinrich would not allow his own professor, Bruno Taafe, a soft balding imperious academic, a self-proclaimed authority in his field, to proceed with his lecture. Heinrich accused the professor of being unable and, thereby, refusing to respond to Heinrich's challenge of the validity of Dühring's assertion.

"On what proof, on what authority does he claim that Jews are a racial group that can never be assimilated or Christianized? His book is nothing but pure political propaganda for bourgeoisie elites who are threatened by Jewish competitors in the job market. You try to exclude us from teaching in the universities and technical institutes. The League of German Nationalists (*Deutschnationaler Verein*) has called for a campaign against Jewish influences in the economy and political life, as well as in intellectual life and the arts. They try to persuade Viennese busnessman that Jewish speculators and bankers are the cause of their downfall.

"You bar us from joining the *Burschenschaften* student fraternities, because we aren't Aryan enough for you. We don't have your pure German blood and questionable moral qualities and therefore, cannot mingle in your exalted social circles. I have many Jewish friends. They are writers, artists, philosophers, musicians, bankers, doctors, and lawyers that have raised Austria and kept her afloat for years, and I prefer their company."

"I imagine you would, Wohlman, since you are a Jew. Your kind tend to stick together."

"You, Professor Taafe, are a disgrace to your profession. Instead of offering intellectual insight, you try to program us with this tripe." Heinrich slammed the book to the floor and spit on it.

"Jewish spittle is not tolerated in my classroom, Wohlman. Go and wallow and spit with your Jewish friends. You have no place here. You should not even be here."

"You are a racist and a bigot, Taafe. Let it be known to the people of Vienna that Professor Taafe is not one of the intelligensia. He is a racist and a bigot."

"Are you quite finished with your immature tirade? Your classmates are here to learn, not watch you carry on with a childish Jewish tantrum. You are done here, Herr Wohlman. You may not continue in my class. I am giving you a failing mark."

"To me, sir, it is a mark of pride and honor." With head held high and an expression of dignity amid the boos, hisses, and whistles of his classmates, Heinrich had walked out of the classroom.

As the train slowed and approached the Klosterneuburg station, Jean clutched his bag and leaned against the window to see who might be waiting on the station platform. He glanced across the aisle at Kurt, who also had his bag in hand and waited for a signal from Jean, in the event they would have to move quickly to get off the train.

A small gathering of men and a few women watched the chugging, smoking engine pass and the trailing cars line up with a screech of brakes against steel and hissing clouds of steam.

Jean did not see anyone in uniform, but did not rule out the possibility of undercover police in the crowd and others hidden inside the brick-walled baggage warehouse area of the small station. He had decided that exiting the car by two different doors would make it more difficult for anyone watching to identify them. He assumed that by now his and Kurt's description would have been conveyed by the two police agents he had forced to jump from the train. He conjectured that their arrival would be expected in Vienna, not before reaching the city.

As instructed by Jean, Kurt positioned himself at midpoint in the line of disembarking passengers and continued to conceal himself among them, as they dispersed and went their separate ways.

For several minutes, Jean disappeared in the other direction and did not immediately meet up with him. Pulling his hat low over his eyes, Kurt walked quickly to where the hansom cabs were lined up on the street. He dodged just under the snuffling nose of a tall gray and maneuvered to keep the horse's large body as a sight barrier between him and the train station.

A moment later, a cab pulled up beside him and stopped. The door swung open and Kurt saw Jean seated inside. He climbed in and Jean swung the door shut, reached out an arm and rapped on the side of the door for the driver to proceed. Kurt and Jean listened to the steady chop of hoofs pulling them away from the vicinity of the station. The fading whistle of the train behind them sent a message that they had escaped detection.

Jean had given directions that the driver take them to a livery stable where they hired a closed coach to travel the remaining distance to Vienna along the high road through the upper slopes of Kahlenberg and Leopoldsberg on the edge of the Vienna Woods.

They arrived at night. A light rain was falling. Heavy horse and carriage traffic carrying revelers moved along the *Ringstrasse*. Jean leaned out the window and instructed the driver to stop near the *Hofburg* Theater, just another carriage in the line at the entrance. .

Jean signaled and hired another cab to convey them to the neighborhood where Heinrich lived. Kurt pointed out the location of Heinrich's apartment, then continued on to the waterfront offices of the Wohlman Steamship Company. From an observation point, Jean watched and waited for Heinrich to appear.

Jean's unexpected voice from the shadows surprised the young man.

"Heinrich. Heinrich Wohlman."

Heinrich stopped and stared toward the dark cave of an alley. "Who are you? Who's there? Show yourself."

Jean edged forward just enough so that the light from a gas lamp barely illuminated him. "Jean Guenoc. I have news of your father."

"You're a priest. What did they do to him? Did Bismarck have him killed?"

"Then you received the telegram from Gustav."

"How do you come to know Gustav?"

"We are old friends. It is because of Gustav that I'm here."

"But you're a priest."

"Don't let my collar mislead you. We will learn of your father when we next meet up with Gustav."

"Where?"

"In America."

"I don't understand."

"I'll explain later. Your brother is waiting for us at the dock. We must go."

"I can't just leave without saying goodbye to someone very dear to me."

"A woman."

"A very beautiful woman."

"We have little time. We go on board tonight. The boat leaves at dawn."

"I must see her. I'll send a message with a trusted friend to meet me at a wine garden."

"That is too open and public. The police are trying to find you. They've been after us since we left Berlin. Do you have another place?"

"Yes, on *Olinstrasse* where my friend lives, in the ghetto."

"Can he bring her to you?"

Heinrich nodded. "She knows him. It is a little dangerous, but she is not deterred by such things."

"Then I'll be nearby. Undercover police may be watching you. They are hoping to arrest you and your brother together. That's why you and Kurt cannot see each other until you're on board. Gustav sent me here to help you."

"He has looked after me ever since I was a boy."

"I know him well. Take us to where your friend lives. I'll follow and stay out of sight."

With rising anxiety, Heinrich set off at a quick pace along architecturally well appointed streets to where the living conditions transitioned into a massive conglomeration of tenements occupied by impoverished Jewish artisans and their families. Although he cast occasional glances over his shoulder, he never caught sight of Jean.

He wondered who this man was who seemed to be a priest, but perhaps wasn't. "Don't let my collar mislead you." The words hung in Heinrich's mind. Jean Guenoc, he said his name was and he knew Gustav and obviously his brother, Kurt, and he knew of their father in prison. Jean's strange sudden appearance and rendering orders had catalyzed Heinrich into an action for which he did not feel prepared. But the urgency of his situation was unmistakable. Their lives had been sabotaged by Bismarck and his secret police. He and his brother must escape.

He turned down *Olinstrasse*, a narrow side street barely illuminated by dim lantern and candlelight cast out through dirt encrusted windows onto the cobblestones. There were no numbers. The shops and apartments were known only by the names of the residents within. He stopped at one of them and knocked on the door. It was answered by a middle-aged Yiddish woman wearing a headscarf and peasant dress. Heinrich murmured a quick greeting and asked for admittance to speak with his friend.

As she left the *Ringstrasse*, Sophie was surprised and alarmed to be met by Heinrich's friend, David Jettel, a young musician who played the clarinet at Yiddish weddings and had ambitions to one day play in an orchestra.

"What is it? What has happened to him?"

"Nothing, Sophie. Don't be alarmed. He sent me to meet you and bring you to him. It's merely a change of plans. He can tell you."

David took her arm and led her through the dim back streets of the city to where he lived with his parents.

As they came through the front door of the little shop on *Olinstrasse*, Sophie ignored the squalor and went directly into Heinrich's open arms. "Don't say anything else. Just explain."

"Thank you, David," Heinrich first acknowledged the young man for his service. "You are a true friend." Then in a voice filled with tension, he spoke to Sophie. "I'm going to meet my brother, Kurt, he just arrived from Berlin. He has been traveling to escape Bismarck's secret police. They arrested my father and now they're after Kurt and me. I could not meet you at the *Ringstrasse* tonight, because I had to evade the police. I received a telegraph from home. My father has been arrested and put in prison. He is too old to endure torture and will likely die. In his letter, Gustav said the baton has been passed to my brother and me. We will travel on the Danube south, then overland to the Adriatic."

"I'll go with you," said Sophie without a moment's hesitation.

"I'm not asking you to come with me, dear Sophie, not like this. My brother and I are going to America."

"Are you saying goodbye then? We'll never see each other again?" She reflected on their brief romance, making love in her apartment, Heinrich's preference to live in the Jewish ghetto.

"Unless you want to join me at a later time."

"I have nothing to keep me in Vienna. How would I ever find you?"

"In our network, I have people who can get a message to you."

"No, I'll go with you now."

"You're a famous person. You'll be recognized. I don't want to endanger you."

"I'll not hold you back and I am going with you. I don't have to remain hidden, which will be to your advantage. Where will I meet you and your brother?"

"On the waterfront at the main dock at sunrise. There's a steamship."

"Where will you stay tonight?"

"Near the river."

"At sunrise then." She kissed him fully on the lips, then turned with a rush of her skirts.

"David will go with you." Heinrich raised a hand at his friend. "Make sure she gets home safely."

David nodded with a sad smile. Heinrich had always felt somewhat sorry for the young man with his dark sprung curls and mild expression.   He was not in the least aggressive or assertive, qualities he needed to advance himself in the music world of Vienna. "I'm sad to see you go. Maybe someday, I can come to America."

"Maybe someday."

Chapter 4

The Danube

The smoke from morning fires sifted from tall chimneys in wispy tendrils blending with the gray prelude to dawn. A thin stream of people began to stir from their shops and apartments into the streets to bring Vienna out of sleep.

Carrying a large carpet bag and with a leather trunk in tow, Sophie struggled through her front door and called out to an urchin bent on scavenging his breakfast.

"You, boy, *schnell* get me a cab from the *Ringstrasse* and three guilders are yours. You can buy your breakfast."

The boy waved he understood and ran off, returning a few minutes later with a horse and cab in tow. She paid the boy to remain long enough to assist her in hefting the trunk to the driver, who positioned it behind him on the roof of the cab.

"To the wharf," she instructed.

"Ya, Fraulein."

The horse pulled the cab at a brisk trot along the cobbled street, took the turn to the *Ringstrasse* and headed south along the boulevard through the sparse morning traffic of cabs, light coaches and carts and wagons.

Approaching the waterfront, they penetrated a fog rising from the river partially concealing a long row of warehouses and shipping offices that lined the wharf. Keening seabirds that had migrated inland swarmed overhead swooping in and out of the whitish tendrils where two steam ships and a tug and barge nudged the algae-encrusted pilings.

Sophie called to the driver to stop before the Wohlman shipping office and warehouse. She stepped out of the cab and the driver clambered down with her trunk. As soon as the cab pulled away, a plainclothes police officer walked over to her from a cavernous warehouse door where stevedores were transferring freight to one of the steamships.

"*Guten Morgan, Fraulein* Rose. Planning a little trip?" He barred her way.

"*Guten Morgan*, excuse me, please. I must buy my ticket."

"Why are you leaving Vienna?"

Her haughty imperious glare did not intimidate him. "You are being impertinent. It is no business of yours. I'm performing in an operetta in Budapest."

"We're looking for a friend of yours, a Heinrich Wohlman. He was recently seen in your company."

"Perhaps you are looking in the wrong place. Do you see him with me now?"

"Do not get surly with me, *Fraulein*. I can take you in for questioning and you will be detained. Your understudy will have to sing in the operetta for you. I'm certain the audience would rather see you appear on the stage."

"I have many friends who are writers and musicians. Herr Wohlman is among them, but he and I do not often see each other unless there is a gathering at a *kaffee haus*. We have no personal attachment."

"He was seen a week ago leaving your apartment - late at night."

"So you have been spying on me. I will have the Emperor speak to your supervisor. You expect me to know where he is at this moment? Herr Wohlman has been writing a libretto for me for an opera in development by Johann Strauss. You may have heard of this composer."

"Indeed I have Fraulein, but your answer does not satisfy me. We believe you met with Herr Wohlman in the ghetto last night."

"Believe what you want. My boat is departing shortly. I do not have time to satisfy your curiousity. If you want to know more about the opera, I would suggest you call on Johann Strauss yourself. *Guten Morgan, mein Herr.*"

She shoved past him and marched through the door of the shipping office with indignant strides to purchase passage, completed the transaction, reemerged accompanied by the agent who carried her trunk, and went on board. Upon glancing back, she saw the police officer conferring with two men in plainclothes who had stepped out of another of the waterfront buildings.

As Sophie crossed the gangplank onto the main deck, she was greeted by a member of the crew who looked vaguely familiar, especially the twinkling blue eyes. *"Wilkommen, Frauline Rose."*

Take away the beard and yes – "Heinrich, is that you? How clever."

"Jean's idea. He is the clever one. Were it not for him, my brother and I would be on a train to prison in Berlin. May I show you to your stateroom?"

"Of course, *mein Herr*. Are your quarters close by or do we share a bed?"

"The accommodations are according to your choosing."

"After I see the stateroom, I'll let you know."

Heinrich gestured for her to precede him forward along the deck. His gaze followed the long flow of her skirts. "It is the first door on the right, *Fraulein*. Next to the boat captain, you have the finest view."

"Most thoughtful of you, *mein Herr*. Do we have fair weather?"

"As fair as you, *meine Liebe*."

"Aren't you a bit familiar for a member of the crew?"

"Consider I am being nothing more than a gracious host at your service."

"That may not give you privileges. I never sleep with sailors, you know."

"The thought never occurred to me, *Fraulein*. I have a bunk in the crew's quarters below deck."

"Are you remaining disguised for the entire journey?"

"Only until we are out of sight of Vienna. The ship's captain tells me we will be putting in to dock at three towns along the way before we reach Budapest."

"How many days?"

"Three. It gives the police time to figure out where we've gone."

"So we are fugitives until we reach America?"

"Let us hope not. Still, we have to be cautious until we're out of the country. Rudolf Palm's spy network extends everywhere."

"Who is Rudolf Palm?"

"To me, the most despised man on the face of the earth. Bismarck's chief of intelligence and the secret police. He is the one who put my father in prison in Berlin."

"Well, soon you'll be beyond his reach."

"It seems there are men like that anywhere you go."

"There are also good men like you and your brother."

"I think we are in the minority. Corruption and power are the way of the world."

"I would like to believe love is the way of the world."

"When I'm with you, the other fades away. I'm glad you chose to come with us."

"Think of what we're doing as an adventure, the two of us together."

"It is an adventure at that."

"So you are aware, the captain has invited us to dine with him this evening."

"How elegant."

"Kurt said Herr Schuler has been a riverboat captain with the company for fifteen years."

"Then good hands are at the wheel."

"Indeed."

The cook served a Hungarian goulash heavily laced with strong paprika accompanied by a bold red wine. The white-bearded captain shared stories of his days piloting steamers on the Danube. He complimented Sophie that he was honored she graced his ship. Other passengers had acknowledged her during the day and her presence lent a special significance to their journey.

Jean prowled the deck, surreptitiously watching male passengers for any sign of suspicious behavior, then took a position in the wheelhouse where he could have a clear view of the river traffic in all directions.

Influenced by the flow of wine and conversation, Jean relaxed at dinner and told of his early years as a Jesuit priest in the French colony of Vietnam in Southeast Asia and how Buddhist monks had taught him martial arts.

"Who would believe that those humble gentle souls in their saffron robes who led lives of prayer and personal denial could be such fierce and stealthy combatants. With the expenditure of minimum effort, a point of pressure could paralyze and incapacitate. They taught me to use the intent and momentum of an attacker against himself. They also taught me the beliefs and values of their religion that caused me to leave the Christian faith."

"Are you a Buddhist then?" Sophie asked.

"I share their value of life, but no, after ten years of working under French imperialism, I became an agnostic."

"Yet," said the captain, "You still wear the collar."

"It often allows me entry where I might not otherwise have access. It has served me well in the underworld of political intrigue."

"Will you be going to America with us?" asked Sophie.

"Yes, my life and work are linked to the Wohlman family."

"For which I, for one, am truly grateful." Kurt raised his glass of wine.

Heinrich and Sophie raised their glasses in acknowledgement.

Later, that night, under a clear star-studded sky, Heinrich and Sophie strolled about the deck and paused to rest their arms on the railing as they overlooked the wake shimmering from the running lights of the boat. The pumping of the steam engines below kept the ship in a steady glide down the center of the river.

"So what plans do you and your brother have?" asked Sophie. "What will we do in America?"

"Several years ago, our father transferred five million dollars to an American banking company in New York, the Morgan bank. He saw the direction Bismarck was going with Prussia and it did not bode well for our company and our family. Just before father was arrested, Kurt was in correspondence with Henry Philips, our investment manager at the Morgan Company."

"Are you going to live in New York City?"

"No, Kurt has been gathering information about what is happening in America and determining what and where our best opportunities would be. Since we're already in the freight and shipping business, we decided to continue over there, but in Chicago. It is the hub of railroad traffic and the Great Lakes provide the inland shipping routes from the mines and forests of the North. We'll re-establish our business in Chicago."

"What about the company here in Germany and Austria-Hungary?"

"If it has not already been stolen from us by Bismarck and his lackies, it soon will be. Fortunately, Father diversified and distributed his holdings to other countries, as well, Sweden, Norway, and England, where the social democrats have a following. We might continue to do business there, but we'll start in Chicago. Kurt was told there are no barriers or regulations in America. The financial barons are ruthless and have no ethics, but we'll soon be one of them," he said and grinned. "We can learn their nefarious ways and use them to our own advantage."

"Do you intend to become ruthless like they are?"

"No, our family is not like that. Father and Kurt are fortunate to have made the kind of money they have, but they came by it honestly. We'll continue our political work in America."

"Do you believe Jean will stay with you?"

"I assume so. He is now a hunted man here and in Germany."

"Yet being hunted doesn't seem to concern him. He has no fear."

"He is an unusual man."

Approaching the city, the town of Buda appeared on the right bank and further, the tan neo-Gothic arches and buttresses of the *Orszaghaz*, Parliament Building, met the river like an extended wall on the left. As the steamer passed under the first of three bridges and entered the harbor, the captain angled the boat across the current toward the main wharf. Standing at his usual position in the wheelhouse near the captain, Jean noticed three detectives and six policemen waiting for the steamer to reach the dock.

"We can't put in here."

"Why? What is the problem?"

"Those men are waiting for us."

The captain looked at the gathering. "Police."

"They know we're on board. What's the next town on the other side of the river where you can dock?"

"We don't have a scheduled stop until Dunajvaros, a day's travel."

"Can you put in at a small town south of Budapest where there is a dock?" asked Jean.

"If the dock is large enough and the water is not too shallow for the draft of the ship. I can't risk running aground."

"We would not ask you to risk that."

"I'm sure I can find a safe landing."

"We'll leave the boat and you can come back to Budapest with the other passengers," said Jean. "When the police question you, tell them we forced you at gunpoint. It won't hurt for them to think we are armed."

The other passengers raised cries of protest as the steamship surged past the city.

Five miles downstream, the captain maneuvered the boat to a much smaller dock than the wharf at Budapest. He dealt with the complaints of irate passengers while two other crew members assisted Kurt, Heinrich, Sophie, and Jean ashore with their baggage. Jean and Heinrich each grabbed a handle of Sophie's trunk and they set off into the town.

"There are no railroads from here," said Kurt. "Not until we reach Beograd. From there we can go all the way to Trieste."

"Then we'll need a horse and wagon," said Jean. "As soon as the police know where we went ashore, they'll come after us with a mounted patrol. Do you know the condition of the roads along the river?"

"Likely not good, mostly traveled by peasant carts."

"What's the next town?"

"Dunajvaros."

"We'll follow the river, then hire a scow at Dunajvaros and sail to Beograd. We'll look like other merchant boats and should not be recognized."

Passengers embarking and disembarking from small boats such as keelboats, tugs and scows were not an unusual event to the inhabitants of the village, but a steamship had never pulled in to the main dock before and raised the curiosity of the local constable. Schmidt was at that moment leaving his stone and thatch roof cottage and walking down the narrow main street after taking his mid-day meal of sausage, cabbage soup, black bread, and beer served him by his wife.

He watched the four strangers, two strong-looking men carrying a trunk between them, accompanied by a third man and a beautiful woman wearing traveling clothes and without a headscarf. From their manner, clearly, these people were not peasants, but the circumstances of their sudden appearance on the main street of his village prompted questions in his mind. He raised his right hand both as a greeting and a signal to them to halt.

"*Guten Tag mein Herrs und Fraulein.* I am the constable here," he tugged at the lapels of his frock coat to reveal a badge underneath attached to his vest, "but do not be alarmed. The steamship has never stopped at our village before. Perhaps I can be of assistance."

Jean immediately suspected the man's actual purpose in seeking information, but saw in the sincere snub-nosed face fringed by a short tufted reddish beard and mutton chops a straightforward simplicity of purpose.

"*Danke, Herr*, thank you. We are in need of a horse and wagon. Can you direct us to the nearest livery?"

"There is only one, at the other side of the village, *Das Pferdplatz*, next to *eine Bierlokal.*

"*Danke*, you are most helpful. We will be on our way."

"*Bitte*, please wait." The constable pointed toward the river. "The ship is turning back to Budapest."

"We have left the ship under special circumstances," Sophie intervened. "I am the diva, Sophie Rose, and these gentlemen are my escorts. I'm on a special journey and we wanted to avoid drawing attention in Budapest."

"Ah, yah, Sophie Rose. I have heard of you, but have never seen you on the stage."

"Upon my return, I will be sure you have tickets and accommodation in Vienna at my next performance."

"Such an honor, schone Fraulein, such a great honor. Wait 'til I tell my *Frau* who I met today. She will be amazed. I will take you to the livery stable."

"I'm sure we can find our way," said Jean, but we welcome you as our guide."

"*Kommen, Sie*, follow me." Puffed with self-importance, the constable led them down the street as though he were the grand marshal of a parade.

At the livery, Kurt quickly dispensed with the transaction of purchasing a sturdy horse and harness while the constable chattered on about the privilege of serving the great opera singer, Sophie Rose.

An hour later, Kurt and Heinrich bounced uncomfortably in the back of the flatbed wagon while Sophie sat up front with Jean, who expertly handled the reins in guiding the willing and patient brown horse along rough sections of the dirt road. A recent rain had left patches of mud, causing Heinrich and Kurt to have to jump down and put their combined weight against the rear spokes and wheel rims to dislodge them.

A red and gold painted sunset dyed the bend of the river at Dunajvaros. Jean pulled the wagon off to the side of the road, unhitched the horse from the wagon tongues, removed the harness, and turned the animal loose in an adjacent field where it lowered its head into the tall grass to graze. Tossing the harness into the wagon bed, Jean said, "Someone will come along and claim them."

Weary of the road, they trudged on into the town and searched for an inn where they could wash away the dust and refresh themselves and spend the night.

The next morning, Jean and Kurt walked to the small harbor in search of a scow. Many traveled inland rivers as the main transport vessel for coal, metal, logs and other cargo. Jean knew that in the event they might have to change course to some other river to escape detection, the flat bottomed scow could navigate shallow waters and could be beached for loading and unloading. The dark-bearded, swarthy sun-bronzed owner of the boat had agreed to take them on board for a fair price and only if he could continue to ply his trade along the river. Jean agreed and offered to act as crew, since he was well experienced with sails and rigging from his days navigating waterways in Southeast Asia.

The next week passed without incident or signs of pursuit, as they sailed with the downstream push of the current, making stops at Mohacs, Vukovar, and Novi Sad, ending their journey at Beograd, the confluence of the Sava and Danube Rivers.

Upon disembarking from the scow, they went directly to the station and purchased tickets on the next train to Trieste.

Chapter 5

Croatia

The passenger cars were packed with a cross section of cultures and nationalities, Serbs, Hungarians, Slovaks, Croats, and Montenegrins, men wearing fez's or burnooses, decorative vests and billowing white pants tucked into Cossack style boots, women wearing head scarves and wrapped in woolen shawls, tucking in their long gray or black skirts to make room for another on the hard bench seats.

Kurt commented that the railroad here was not as developed as those in Germany, and Austro-Hungary, no luxuries, no cushions, and only a rough imitation of a commode with a drawn curtain at the end of each car.

As for meals, if you wanted to eat at all, the fare was whatever you carried on board, which accounted for a range of meat, cheese, and ripen fruit odors released from cloth wrappings to be consumed with copious bottles of wine that set the vituperative tongues and comments of some of the men muttering, and in some cases, calling out insults to other passengers of a different ethnicity or religion.

Sophie, Kurt, and Heinrich shared one such bench and Jean occupied an aisle seat a few feet away next to an Islamic Albanian woman, who was uncomfortable being so close to a strange man that their hips and thighs actually touched. She prevailed upon her husband to change positions with her, which he did dutifully, then fixed a threatening stare on Jean as though he had sexually offended the man's wife.

Before they boarded, Kurt had cautioned his companions of the political and ethnic volatility they were likely to encounter. "Kosovo is in a state of anarchy. The Albanian tribes are committing genocide against the Serbians for their attacks on caravans. They want to exterminate them. They're attacking and pillaging Serb villages, raping the women and burning their homes. The Muslims want to get them out of Kosovo. Bandits will stop at nothing. They've even taken to robbing passengers on the train."

There had been grievances over agrarian rights and heavy taxation against the Albanians propagated by Serbian politicians and in Herzegovina by the Montenegrins. The conflicts surged back and forth, but there was no political or military movement from Vienna. The Emperor Franz Joseph did not want to send in an occupation army and risk a war with his Russian ally who supported the Serbs.

Viennese political alliances with Germany and Russia and conflict with the Turks in Constantinople were not foremost in their thoughts, as Kurt, Heinrich, Sophie, and Jean began their journey to Trieste, but they could not escape the influence of those forces.

That reality began with the screeching of airbrakes and the resistant slide of steel wheels on iron rails. The undercarriage of the cars slammed against the couplings and set the coaches swaying so violently that several passengers were thrown from their seats.

Before the train had completely stopped, two bandits, each brandishing a pistol and a saber burst into the car from the doors at both ends setting off screams and wailing among the women, who clutched their belongings and leaned away from the aisle. As they shouted out their commands to hand over jewels and money, the bandits paused briefly at each bench while desperate hands scrambled among coats and shawls and loose clothing to come up with meager offerings to avoid the thrust of a sword.

The rank odor of horse mingled with sweat and smoke and garlic rolled off the raiders like an aura. As the first man came abreast of his bench, Jean flew up out of his seat, surprising and catching him off guard. A pinching grasp of his wrist caused him to drop the pistol, which Jean snatched out of the air as it fell and fired a single shot into the man's chest, sending him careening backward down the aisle, dropping his sword.

Jean snatched up the saber and fired a shot at the second man leaping over his fallen partner and rushing toward him. The bullet caught him high in the shoulder and half spun him around, but did not stop him. The downward sweep of Jean's blade that cut off his hand still clutching the pistol did.

With arterial blood spewing from his wrist over the nearest passengers shrieking in terror, he continued his howling charge and took a broad swipe at Jean, who parried the blow and returned with a precise slash that severed the man's head from his shoulders. The bloody head with mouth still wide in a now silent scream and black eyes solidified in a death stare landed in the lap of a woman who went berserk and fainted.

Jean grabbed the head by the curly dark hair and flung it out an open window. He then dragged the bodies to the nearest door and hurled them out into a mountain chasm bordering the tracks.

Yovan Boskovitch, the leader of the Albanian bandits, suddenly paused in his self-congratulatory success on having stopped the train on a narrow curve. The engineer was forced to slow to a crawl so as not to derail and free fall into a neighboring abyss to jagged rocks and a rushing stream several hundred feet below. The bandit leader's only concern was that the narrow roadbed left scant room for his men to maneuver their horses alongside the line of cars. So he had decided that the boarding would be staged on foot with the six members of his gang erupting from the rocks and boulders hugged by the passing train.

The first two at the front boarded the engine cab and commandeered control by poking a pistol in the ribs and suggestively resting the sharp edge of a saber blade against the throats of the fireman and engineer.

Yovan suddenly saw the severed head of one of his men catapaulted out an open window and roll end over end down into the gorge to be followed by two bodies through a door of the central passenger car. Moments later, he heard shots fired and a third man clutching his blood soaked leg careened out of the car and fell off the train steps.

Realizing there was a formidable opponent on board the train, Yovan shouted to his two men holding the engineer and fireman hostage. As the two bandits leaped from the cab, stray shots kicked up stones at their heels. They beat a hasty retreat.

No further danger threatened the train on the remaining tiresome journey through the southern Balkan valleys to the Dalmatian coast. At Trieste, Jean continued to exercise caution on the chance that Palm would have guessed their point of debarkation and posted agents to watch for them. They boarded without incident and the large ocean-going steamship set out against a steady wind-blown chop across the Adriatic and south along the Italian coast.

Although, Rudolf Palm had assigned agents and Luther Baggot to watch Kurt's family, with the help of the secret society of social democrats, they slipped away undetected, smuggled out of Germany to France, then England. Other than in shipping records, the last trace of the Wohlman name was in Hull, England, where they had boarded a ship to America.

Knowing that he was going to die in prison and wanting to throw Palm off the trail of his family, Alfred Wohlman suggested the existence of a list of society members of social democrats that was maintained anonymously in Sweden. Unintentionally, his innocent attempt to thwart Palm, put Luther Baggot on the trail of the Josephson family. Shipping records showed they had immigrated to America ten years ago. He reported back to Palm, who paid him to track them down and bring him the list.

"And what would you like me to do when I find them?"

"Kill them. Kill them all."

The order was gratifying to Luther, who enjoyed killing. Killing was in his blood which was why he had become a soldier in Bismarck's army. There had been ample opportunity to invoke violent death on enemy soldiers until he had suffered his own nearly fatal wound, a gunshot to the face. His disfigurement had reinforced a desire to take the lives of other humans in a like manner. Shooting his victims in the face became his trademark.

II

Rivermen

Chapter 6

Against The Grain

A framed photograph taken of them in the summer of 1898 hangs in the historical museum at St. Cloud, Minnesota. It shows Newt Josephson's sister, Julie, his boyhood friend, Aaron Peet, and Newt standing among a posed group of loggers in front of the Frazier River Mill. The green tinged copper title plate at the bottom of the picture elicits a bemused smile --- *Rivermen.*

Because of the coveralls and wool shirts and work boots and caps they wore, an observer could not detect that Julie was a girl. They didn't hire girls or women, not even to cook in the lumber camps. Logging was considered a man's job.

Julie pretending to be a boy presented more of a problem than keeping her hair cut short, her voice pitched low, walking square, and never screaming when she was afraid, or crying when she got hurt.

Newt supposed they had the honor of being included in the photograph, because they were the three youngest members of the crew. He was the oldest, sixteen. Aaron was fifteen.

At the time, they had no better means to make a living and they were on the run from a man who wanted to kill them.

Newt had not seen his sister for one month since he and Aaron had moved to their own place on Chicago's west side. So it was with great surprise that a nun from a Catholic religious order showed up at his door late one cold winter night with a manuscript she had been instructed to give him.

"My name is Sister Pavalek," she said. Your sister asked me to bring this to you." She handed him a book-sized packet wrapped in a thin leather hide.

He invited her to come in and have some coffee or tea, but she was tense and nervous and kept glancing back into the shadows.

"I dare not," she said. "I may be followed and he mustn't find this manuscript. Also, your sister said she didn't want you pulled into the investigation."

"Investigation? What investigation? What has happened to her? What has she done?"

"I honestly don't know, sir. I can't explain. She stayed with us for a short while. She needed a sanctuary, then said she was going back. I don't know where. Just before she left, she entrusted me with her manuscript and requested that I deliver it to you for safekeeping. That is all I know."

"Did she say anything about where she was going?"

"No, she did say she didn't want to endanger us."

"What do you mean, endanger?"

"The sisters, sir. She didn't want to endanger the sisters at the convent."

Newt grasped the leather wrapped volume and peered at the nun's white oval face framed by her cowl giving the appearance that it hovered detached from the dark shawl and robe concealing her body.

"Have you read this?"

"No, it has not been opened. It is not my place to know what it contains and she never told us what her trouble was."

"Do you have any idea where she's gone?"

"I'm sorry, sir. I do not. She just said she was going back. She said the manuscript would help you find her."

"Who's following you?"

"She didn't say his name. She feared he would discover she was hiding in the convent. And now, I must go. I wish you and your dear sister well." She started to move away.

"Wait. Where is the convent?"

"In the German sector. Her parting words were to tell you to read the manuscript. Goodbye, sir." With a rustle of her long garb, she hurried down the dark street, dimly illuminated by gaslights, and merged with the night.

Newt waited a moment to see if anyone followed her or would come to his door, which he then promptly closed and locked. As he turned, he saw his friend, Aaron, watching with curiosity etched in the knit brow of his sleep-drawn face.

"Who was at the door?"

"Something has happened to Julie."

"Julie?"

He nodded. "I don't know who this person is. She said Julie had been hiding at a convent and brought me this manuscript that Julie wrote. We haven't seen her since we moved here."

"Is she in trouble with the law?"

"That's not likely, but something else is happening. I don't have a good feeling about it."

"What do you think it is?"

"I don't know. A nun brought me this." He hefted the manuscript.

"It's late."

"Ya, but I want to read some of this."

"We have to get up early for work. I'm going back to bed."

"Goodnight."

"Goodnight."

Newt was also weary after a long day at the shipping company, but the strange delivery during the dead of night peaked his curiosity, especially when it involved the perilous ventures of his sister. He poured a cup of hot black tea and sat down at the kitchen table with the manuscript before him.

He unbound its leather package and began to read.

Their mother once told Julie and her brother that life was a great adventure and they should go out and experience it. "Let nothing daunt you," she encouraged in her intense energetic way of thrusting her blonde head forward so that they could see the taut cords of her neck. She was not a frail woman.

Their father said that being married to their mother was the great adventure, at least for him. And in many ways it was for the children as well. Although their personal adventure was unexpected, perhaps that was what adventures were intended to be.

"It's important for you to see many faces in many spaces," she told them. But where they established their home, there were not many faces, and only one large endless space, the Minnesota prairie.

The world as seen through the eyes of a small child is quite astonishing. Everything is new and unexpected, because a child has no expectations but to be fed and nurtured. The tumultuous sights and noises of life are absorbed through all the senses and churn in a kaleidoscope in a miraculous brain that sorts it all out in a meaningful way.

Over time, Julie came to understand how different influences splinter that kaleidoscope in a multitude of directions with profoundly different results in how they lived their lives and the invisible forces that pushed them. There were forces that she struggled against then and continued to do so during her later years.

Although she and her brother were born in Sweden, their parents brought them to America when they were small children of three and five. They settled on a one hundred acre farm they purchased in north central Minnesota near the town of Brainerd. Their closest neighbor, the Peets, lived a mile away down a rutted dirt road that made for a jolting ride by horse and wagon during the mud season and a smooth ride by sleigh during the winter.

Aaron Peet was the second eldest of five children, four brothers and one sister. They were Newt and Julie's only friends. They often did not see each other for great stretches of time except when the Peet children began coming to their house for home school. Ingrid Josephson had been a teacher back in Oslo.

Not many children continued beyond the sixth grade in America. Girls were not normally allowed to even go to school. They were to learn domestic tasks and prepare for their future roles as wives and mothers.

An educated woman was not considered desirable for marriage, since she would be prone to think for herself and disagree with her husband. That behavior in a wife would not be tolerated. As Julie heard it spoken in the wedding ceremonies in the Lutheran church at Brainerd, the wife must obey and submit to the will of her husband.

Of course, she was raised to not believe any of that nonsense, because her mother did not. Ingrid was an educated woman and had graduated from the *gymnasium* in Sweden. She was a free thinker, but she wasn't dangerous to Julie's father. Fortunately for him, he was a free thinker too, although from time to time, they did have lively arguments just for the mental and verbal exercise. Even if he didn't believe in the opposing position, Olaf would make a challenging case for it. "I'm being the Devil's advocate," he told them.

Julie thought that at least he was a non-threatening kindly Devil.

"Debates are just a kind of thinking game," he explained, as they sat in their wooden rocking chairs out on the porch sipping lemonade during a warm summer evening. Caressed by a clover-scented wind off the prairie, the close-knit family enjoyed the occasional repartee which belied their lonely existence.

"But I can get myself in trouble with your mother. She's very good at logic and can take apart any argument I make. For example, when I asked your mother to marry me, she said I had to present her with a convincing argument for her to accept my proposal. If I had failed, the four of us would not be sitting here now. I did fail the first time, but not the second. I learned my lesson."

"What did you tell her?" asked Julie.

"The first time or the second time?"

"The first time."

"The first time, he was miserable," said Ingrid.

"You mean he felt bad?"

"No, he was terrible at trying to convince me."

"Actually, I did feel miserable."

"Which was a good thing for you. You enjoyed yourself far too much. I thought you didn't have a serious bone in your body."

"Proposing marriage doesn't have to be serious. It should be fun, you know."

"Believe me, children. It's a serious moment, a major turning point in your life."

"What did you say?" asked Newt.

"I said that she was be lucky that I was proposing marriage to her and that I had a whole long line of *flickas* who were hoping I would propose to them, because I was such a handsome man and wonderful in every way."

"Oh, listen to him brag," said Ingrid. "I just saw him as a braggart and not so wonderful. The two things he had talent for was drinking beer and dancing."

"You have to admit I was a great dancer in my younger days," said Olaf.

"You were also a great drinker and a great talker, mostly about your own opinions."

"We often shared the same opinions," said Olaf

"And just as often did not," Ingrid raised her cup of lemonade.

"And what did you say?" Newt asked his mother.

"I just laughed and told him to find himself a *flicka* who was equal to this *flicka*. I also told him to go jump in the ocean."

Newt and Julie burst out laughing. "You told him to go jump in the ocean?"

"I did. I most certainly did."

"And I did," said their father.

"You jumped in the ocean?" Newt was astounded.

"Let me tell you, it was very cold. I thought I was going to drown. As a matter of fact, I was planning to drown myself if your mother refused to marry me."

"It's a good thing you didn't," said Julie, "or we wouldn't be here sitting on this porch."

"Most certainly," said their mother. "By the way, your father would never drown himself. He didn't have the gumption. He would miss out on having so much fun with all his *flickas*."

"Is that what you thought?" asked Newt.

"Well, to be honest, I did think about what I would miss, but I wanted to do the fun things with your mother, not with somebody else."

"Would you have drowned yourself, if she said no," asked Julie.

"Oh, I was in such despair at the time, I could have drowned myself."

"Your father is full of horse droppings," said Ingrid. "He is overly dramatic about such things just to impress you how much he loved me."

"And I did love her." He glanced at Ingrid's facetious scowl. "I still do love her as much and more as I did then. Do you know where the more comes from?"

"Where?" asked Julie with a grin, almost knowing the answer.

"The more comes from having you and Newt as our lovely incredible children."

Julie and Newt nodded in agreement.

"But what did you say the second time?" Newt persisted.

"I don't know that it's important anymore," said their father. "I mean, after all, we got married and here you are, here we are, talking on the porch."

"No! No!" Newt and Julie chorused. "You have to tell us! You have to tell us!"

"Should I tell them?" Olaf asked his wife with a wink.

"Just be careful you don't embarrass yourself with the truth. After all, they have put you up on a pedestal for all these years."

"Tell us! Tell us! Tell us!"

"All right, it's time to let out the truth. Here is what I said. On bended knee, I told your mother that I would be honored and blessed to become her husband because she, and I emphasize the she, was such a loving and beautiful woman and her intelligence was superior to mine. I had a difficult time saying that, but I did, and subsequently, came to realize it was true. Your mother is much more intelligent than I am, although I have my moments."

"They are few and far between," said Ingrid.

"Few and far between they may be, but they do occur."

"Do you ever agree on anything?" asked Julie.

"Rarely, but probably on most things," said their mother.

"What does that mean?" asked Newt. "That doesn't say you agree on much of anything."

"We agree to disagree and then we move on," said Ingrid. "An expression of a single opinion doesn't stop the world. It's only an opinion. There are millions of opinions, as million as there are people. It's only the collective opinion in the best interest of the majority that makes a difference, that gets anything done, that moves society forward. That's where your father and I agree."

"Actually, we agree on many more things, like when to milk the cows and harvest the wheat and feed the chickens and feed the kids."

"We aren't like chickens," Julie retorted.

"You're more demanding than chickens," said their mother. Those are practical things we agree on to live from day to day, Olaf. I'm talking about what is intangible in the lives of people. We both know that."

"Of course, I just want our children to know, as well."

"They will come to know. They will live it."

"They will live it." Her mother's words returned to Julie again and again.

Julie and her brother enjoyed the debates as a kind of intellectual sparring which established Julie's foundation for engaging in controversy. This ability served her well, as she in later years grew out of childhood and became a young woman.

In the end, her mother and father always agreed to disagree, but it never ruined their relationship. They thrived on discussion and hungered for information not easily attained in their remote circumstances far out on the windswept plains of Minnesota.

Whenever their father, Olaf, would make the long trip to St. Cloud, and a few times all the way to St. Paul, he would return with a trunk filled with books and old copies of newspapers and McClure Magazines which introduced his children at an early age to leading free thinkers and journalists of the time. Susan B. Anthony, Elizabeth Cady Stanton, Lincoln Steffens, Emma Goldman, and Ida Tarbell were held up to them as the vanguard of progressive social reform.

Such exposure was their indoctrination in beliefs and values that had much to do with their lives.

As a child of three, Julie remembered a damp chill and dense fog when her family boarded the ship during one early morning in Stockholm. The high keening of gulls and other seabirds whirling and caroming above the stacks and masts was the significant impression that remained with her about the voyage. The pressing crowd of dark-clothed immigrants in steerage was the second. And she remembered the smell of unwashed bodies, decaying fish and the clanging of a large brass bell in the salt air.

She remembered being carried incessantly by either her mother or her father. They rarely set her down when they were out on the shifting tossing deck for fear she would wander off and blithely slip overboard between the rails.

Olaf kept her brother tied to him by a short length of stout rope with a double loop around Newt's waist. Newt hated the rope. He quickly became bored and whiney and Olaf had to take him for frequent walks like a dog and restrain him from charging toward the bow of the ship where glistening plumes of sea spray spumed and spread like evanescent chilling feathers.

Newt was always brave and daring and oblivious to fear. He welcomed challenges and scoffed at Julie's concerns when they were growing up. She loved and admired him and thought of him as her protector.

The trans-Atlantic crossing extended for many days. The sea was rough, but not stormy, and tossed the ship about, promulgating endemic sickness and trips to the rail by green-faced men and women.

Julie never fussed or cried and her parents ensured that she and Newt did not go hungry and did not eat rotten food. They had packed cured meat, dried fruit, and several loaves of bread that they quickly consumed. Then they relied on hard biscuits and limes. The last milk Julie and Newt had was breakfast at the Whaler Inn at the Stockholm harbor. A bottle of fresh milk was among the first purchases their father made when they stepped ashore in America after processing through Ellis Island.

It was several years before Julie and Newt understood why their parents had left their home country. Although it was really more Ingrid's idea, their parents simply explained they wanted a better life for all of them and America had beckoned. Julie was later to question what illusionary advantages they thought they were pursuing and hoped to discover. For the betterment of their lives was short-lived. But people didn't know or think about such things when they set out in a new direction.

Most people did not think of work as an adventure, but the Josephson family did. Even as children, Newt and Julie worked much of the time alongside their parents. Newt was outside more often with his father chopping wood and helping feed and milk their six dairy cows. They were soft brown Guernseys with enormous gentle dark eyes. During the summer, their tails whisked violently at swarms of flies attracted to their odorous hides.

When Julie became five, her father began teaching her how to milk the cows. Once, she wandered too close and the wide-hipped bovine's whip-like tail lashed across her face and sent her rolling into a pile of fresh manure. Her stinging eyes were swollen shut for two days and she was confined to the house where she stumbled around like a blind person. Her mother applied warm compresses soaked in prairie herbs and Epsom salt. She relied on her own forms of medical treatment, since the nearest doctor was seventy miles away in St. Cloud.

Julie's childhood belied who she had become. In retrospect, what she had done astounded her. As a small child, she had never been daring and adventurous like Newt.

Her brother had pale blue eyes that stared at the distant horizon with a soulful intensity that made him seem transfixed by some eminent event of either hope or catastrophe, depending on the swing of his imagination. His steady gaze and prominent set features capped with a short mane of wild blonde hair gave him the heroic visage of his Viking heritage.

Juxtaposed with Newt's light appearance and blazing swiftness, his friend, Aaron, was a dark counterpart who lacked

Newt's godlike features. Aaron's brows cowled his brown eyes as though to conceal their emotional expression. His slight body appeared lean and stringy in contrast to Newt who had inherited the size and strength of his parents. Aaron's thick black curls capped his head and crawled down the back of his thin neck into his collar like a furry pelt.

Julie would follow Newt and Aaron when they hiked off to a small nearby lake to fish for bass and trout. They brought along an extra cane pole for her, but she was squeamish and a little terrified of the fat night crawlers they would dig up from the loamy soil. She was convinced that the first one she touched bit her and she dropped it with a loud squeal.

"Worms can't bite you," Newt explained laughing. "They don't have teeth."

"That one does," She insisted pointing at the twisting, curling serpentine creature. "He does. I could feel his teeth."

"Those aren't teeth. That's just his skin."

"It's not. It's not. My skin doesn't bite."

"He has a different kind of skin so he can live under the ground."

"How do you know? Do you talk worm talk?"

"No, father told me. He knows about these things."

"He doesn't know everything."

"You shouldn't say that. Father is a smart man. If you read as many books as he does, you can be smart too someday."

"I'm smart. I know things."

"Yes, but there's a lot more you don't know, little sister."

"Okay, but I'm smart. Mama told me."

"You are for your age."

"Someday, I'll even be as smart as you. Smarter."

"Well," he grinned at Aaron. "You'll have to work at it."

"Will you put the worm on my hook?"

"Aaron can do it. I need to get my line out in the water."

"Aaron," She held out her line with the dangling bare hook. "Will you help me?"

Aaron nodded grimly, scooped up the fallen worm desperately trying to escape into the porous soil. Julie watched intently while he speared the slimy squirming body onto the curved barbed hook.

"Are you hurting him? It looks like you're hurting him."

"Worms ain't like us. They don't feel nothin'."   He showed her how to extend her line out into the water. "Watch the cork. When it goes under, you know you got a fish."

"Will you help me when I catch one?"

"Yeah."

So she watched the cork and quickly grew bored when she did not receive the immediate gratification of seeing the cork bob under the surface. She noticed that Aaron and Newt weren't catching any fish either.

She was sitting in a pool of warm sunlight on a bed of soft golden grass that lay flat on the slight incline of the bank to the muddy edge of the lake. A slight breeze rippled the surface in a mesmerizing way. Within a few minutes, her mind succumbed to an overwhelming lethargy and she fell asleep.

The next year, having graduated from handling worms, Newt taught her how to shoot a rifle at small targets made from sticks and stones.

"But I don't want to kill anything," she protested.

"You never know when a wolf might come into the yard," laughed Newt. Packs of wolves roamed the outlying prairies and occasionally preyed on settlers' livestock.

She practiced diligently and demonstrated that she had a natural eye and was able to manage the long rifle quite well, since she never missed, to Newt's pride and dismay that she was a more accurate marksman than he.

One day, a lame wolf did come onto the property and went after the chickens running loose in the yard. Accompanied by the dogs, Newt and his father were working out in the fields and her mother had made a trip on the wagon into town.

Julie grabbed the rifle, stepped outside into the back yard and put a bullet into the wolf's head as it tried to make off with a struggling chicken clutched in its jaws.

When Newt and their father came in late that afternoon, they were pleased at her diligence and amazed at the size of the wolf. They noticed that his back right foot had been caught in a trap at one time, which accounted for his lameness and diminished ability to hunt large wild game.

Hemmed in by hundreds of European immigrants surging down the gangplank seeking a new life in America, Luther Baggot momentarily felt displaced. He had not come to these shores in search of work or wealth or a way to re-establish himself in escaping the repression and poverty of the 'Old Country' he repeatedly heard described by his fellow passengers. He had come as a hired bounty hunter to find and kill people.

The irony of his task did not occur to him that he had been sent from a country ruled by a fascist monarchy to a country that espoused individual and political freedom.

Tracking and finding Olaf and Ingrid Josephson in Minnesota had required some ingenuity. He decided on the ruse of pretending to be one of the social democrats. As he told relatives of the Josephsons back in Sweden, he was on a mission to help them in their cause. His lie had lead him to St. Cloud, Minnesota.

At St. Cloud, he inquired about meetings of social democrats, then believably convinced the local organizers that he was trying to find his relatives, the Josephsons.

His first response from a crusty old Swede was, "There are a lot of Josephsons in Minnesota. More Swedes here than trees."

He checked land grants of homesteaders to find their names and the location of their farm on a state map. Mounted on a black stallion purchased in St. Cloud, he rode to Brainerd. Giles Hansford, The proprietor of the general store in the small rural town, was his final unwitting source of information.

The day he rode the ten miles out onto the prairie to their farm was the day that Ingrid and Olaf were driving their team of horses and wagon into town for food staples, coffee, rice, and beans, and other supplies. Seeing them coming from the distant house and barns toward the dirt track that served as a road, he rode off out of sight onto a wooded hill and looked at them through his spy glass. Biding his time, he waited until they were headed towards town then followed them. Just before they reach Brainerd, he forced them to halt at gunpoint.

"I know who you are, Ingrid and Olaf Josephson. I have tracked you all the way from Sweden."

Olaf stood up on the dash board. The reins dangled from his fingers. "Who are you?" He stared at the man's scarred disfigured face which gave him the appearance of being demonic.

"I hunt for anarchists. You were conspirators with Alfred Wohlman in Berlin. The Chancellor Otto von Bismarck had him arrested and put in prison. Before he died, he named you among the leaders of the movement and said you were in possession of a list we have wanted for a long time. I'm an agent of the Chancellor's secret police sent to find you."

"The name of Alfred Wohlman is not familiar."

"Given some persuasion, he named you. He knew you quite well. You made many trips to Berlin to collaborate with him. We know this about you. You are lying, Olaf Josephson."

"You tortured him?"

"No, but I watched."

"We came to America to get away from people like you."

"And, after a great deal of effort, it has taken me two years to find you. You must have been important to Chancellor Bismarck and to the director of police to send me this far from Germany. We know you escaped arrest in Sweden by coming to America." He clicked the two hammers of the shotgun into position. "Things have changed in Germany. You being social democrats is of less interest to us now. The Director sent me here for personal reasons, and I have my own."

"If we had a list, we'd give it to you."

"*Herr* Wohlman said he gave you the list. Even if you don't tell me, I'll find it. I'm looking for certain people on that list for what they did to me."

"I swear to you we don't have any list."

At the shotgun blast, the team of horses bolted. The combination of the devastating impact and the recoil as the wagon lurched forward, thrust Ingrid and Olaf backwards into the clattering bed. Strings of blood and ravaged tissue and erupted eyeballs rendered their faces unrecognizable.

After a half mile run into town, the winded horses slowed. A man dashed out onto the main street and waved the team down with shouts of "Whoa" and grabbed the side reins, pulling them into a turn that half dragged him in the dust but broke their momentum as others rushed to subdue the frothing animals.

The sight of the dead man and woman sickened the gathering bystanders.

"Who are they?"

"I know 'em. I know their horses. That's Olaf and Ingrid Josephson."

"Jesus and Mary, who the hell would do this?"

"Someone get the sheriff."

"Someone bring the coronor. He's got to get 'em into pine boxes. We can't let their children see 'em like this."

"There was a stranger come through town this morning. Anyone know him?"

"He came into the store asking the whereabouts of their farm. Ugly lookin' bastard. All dressed in black and he was ridin' a black horse."

"Did he give his name?"

"Said he was a relative."

"Think he did this?"

"Had to be him."

"Those poor children."

"What'll become of 'em?"

From the moment Newt and Julie learned of the murder of their mother and father, each memory gained in value and importance. Some years would pass before Julie realized the insidious and powerful forces that caused their untimely deaths and set her on a path of vengeance.

In the beginning, what she wanted to destroy more than political and corporate greed was the man who had ended her parents' lives and cut her childhood short. She was thirteen at the time they were killed. In 1898, most children were cast into the maelstrom of labor at her age, but her parents held different values, especially when it came to an academic education. This too had been abruptly terminated along with their love and the security they provided. Newt and Julie weren't ready to go out into the world on their own, but they had no choice.

Chapter 7

Dead Wood

The two coffins landed with a heavy dull thud in the dust of a small side street outside the mortuary in Brainerd. One was slightly longer and contained the corpse of Olaf Josephson. They were made of rough unfinished pinewood still dripping with the sweet acrid scent of resin. The logs had been recently cut.

Julie stared at the whorls and patterns in the wood that were once the vessels that carried nutrients from the soil up through the roots and trunk and out the branches to the leaves conversing with the sun and air, giving the tree its life. She thought it ironic that the now dead wood housed the bodies of her mother and father.

Within a short time, she would witness the destruction of acres of living pine trees converted to dead wood for construction and fuel and other uses that supported life and did not contain death.

When Sheriff Anders Karlsson rode out to the farm to tell Newt and Julie their mother and father had been killed, Aaron's father, Timothy Peet, had driven his double team and wagon back to town with Aaron and the two children to claim their parents. They ached to see their mother and father one last time, but the coroner refused their tearful request.

"I'm sorry, son, little daughter." The coroner had sealed the coffins. "They can't be opened." He thrust an ink-smeared yellow document at them.

"Can't you do something?" Newt appealed to Timothy.

"It's best you remember them as they were in life," said Timothy. "Think of your happiest days with them. Seein' 'em now will only make it worse for you."

Julie would never accept the finality of their death without some explanation, without knowing why. "But who killed them? Why did somebody kill them? They never mean't anybody harm. They loved us." She was on her knees, bawling like a calf. Her tears pearled in the dirt.

"Don't have no information on that," said the coroner. Timothy scanned the death certificate. "You didn't write nothin'."

"Doesn't the sheriff know?" asked Newt.

"You'll have to take it up with him," said the coroner, his Adams apple bobbed with nervousness. He didn't like to be confronted. "Just done my job."

"We'll talk about this later," said Timothy. "Let's carry 'em home."

Because they were denied a final look, Julie tried to imagine what must have happened to them and that perhaps they had been disfigured in some way. Such an image interfered with Timothy's advice and became a festering sore in her mind that drove her toward a future she never intended.

"We have to arrange for their burial," said Timothy.

"Can we bury them at home?" Newt asked.

"Yes." Timothy's stout body stooped at the front end of mother's coffin. "Boys, get the feet. Lift together."

Wiping the snot drooling in a stringy web from the tip of her nose, Julie watched them heave and shove the two coffins into the flatbed wagon. She didn't understand why Newt wasn't crying, but he always had a way of holding in his feelings until some other time when he would express them in private.

Newt and Julie rode in the back, Aaron up on the seat with his father. They watched the receding freight train pull away leaving clouds of steam and pulsing black smoke and the haunting whistle's cry in its wake. The brisk prairie wind swept the smoke over them as though the dark spirits of their mother and father enshrouded them with a final farewell.

Eventually their tears dried, as Julie watched the two coffins shift and jerk absorbing the shock of the rutted hard dirt road through the iron rim wheels. She imagined her parents were still alive erupting within their narrow confines shoving and pounding to be released. She wanted to shout, "Mr. Peet, Mr. Peet, stop the wagon! We have to let them out! They're trying to get out!"

But it was only a scene she created in her mind and allowed her to reconnect with them in spirit, because she was unwilling to accept their physical non-existence and let them go. She would never let them go.

She imagined that they stopped the wagon and Mr. Peet pried open the coffins with a hammer and chisel. Her mother and father sat up and climbed out whole and unharmed with broad smiles on their beneficent faces, and they encircled their two children in their arms.

She felt someone shaking her shoulder. She woke up standing at the center of the road behind the now stationary wagon and looked into her brother's eyes. Their parents had faded away into the sun and tossing wheat fields.

"Julie, Julie," he was shouting at her. "Wake up! Wake up! What happened to you?"

"Where are mother and father?" They were with us, right here.

"You were just having a dream. That's all. A dream."

She looked wildly about at the sameness of the fields surging and roiling in wind-driven waves to the horizon. She saw the black tail of one of the two horses lift and he defecated a shallow pile of greenish-brown manure that stained his rump. Julie inhaled the sweet acrid smell rising into the air as her brother lead her back to the wagon and lifted her up onto the flatbed. As she sank down between the two coffins, a wood splinter pierced the web of skin between her left thumb and forefinger. She endured the sting and discomfort. A moment later, Mr. Peet clucked to the team of dark bay horses. The frayed end of the whip snapped in the air over their backs and the wagon jolted forward. They continued their journey home.

The trek took the remainder of the day. They arrived well after dark. With the exception of some bread, dried buffalo meat, and a jug of water, they had eaten nothing since supper the night before. They had not washed except at the water pump. Their anticipated weekly Saturday night bath supervised by Mother would never happen again. Their clothes had absorbed the sour odor of grime and sweat. Cleanliness was far removed from their concerns.

Julie listened to the rattle of reins against leather harness and the chop of the horses' hooves on the road as they turned in at the lane leading to the house, bone white under a hovering pale moon. Their two herd dogs, Bruno and Oberon, came racing toward them without raising a bark and trotted alongside the wagon until it halted at the water trough near the barn. The two horses plunged in their noses and drank with loud sucking sounds.

Julie heard the dairy cows lowing their hunger from the barn. The dogs had brought them in from the pasture at sunset, but there had been no one home to feed them. After Mr. Peet and the boys had lifted the coffins from the wagon and placed them on the ground near the front porch steps, they all went to the barn to feed and milk the six cows and feed the two draft horses, Mel and Nell, Percherons. With mother and father gone, the farm had become Newt's and Julie's responsibility.

Before going into the house, Julie scattered grain for their Guinea rooster and small flock of hens that were tightly penned to ward away foxes and prowling coyotes. She lit a large kerosene lantern and started a fire in the cast iron wood stove.

Through the kitchen window, she heard the harsh snorts and grunts of the hogs, as Newt and Aaron poured slops into their trough. The team of horses still attached to Mr. Peet's wagon neighed at the scent of hay and grain from inside the barn. The day was at an end and they were communicating their hunger. She saw Mr. Peet walk steadily from the barn carrying two wooden buckets filled with oats. The horse's nostrils flared and fluttered with guttural snorts of anticipation.

With all the animal hunger going on around her, Julie thought it strange that she felt none. It occurred to her that even with death, life circumvented and continued around them oblivious to the natural course of events. She drank a dipper of water from the small metal hand pump at the sink and considered how woefully inadequate and forlorn she was. She depended on the strength and knowledge of her mother and the positive steadfastness of her father. She and Newt were left only with memories and what they had taught them. They were no longer children but they must get on with their lives.

Mr. Peet returned the empty grain buckets to the barn, then walked to the back door with Newt and Aaron and came into the kitchen. They stared at her standing at the sink.

"I don't feel hungry," she said.

They settled on the rough wooden chairs at the table.

"Aaron and me'll come back in the morning to help you bury your ma and pa," Mr. Peet spoke more directly to Newt and barely glanced at Julie, sparing her that reality a little longer she surmised. "We'll talk later about what it might be best for you to do."

"We can run the farm," said Newt.

Mr. Peet nodded. "Well, son," he spoke to Aaron, "time for us to head home." He rose and Aaron and Newt followed him outside. Newt stopped halfway out in the yard. Julie watched from the window as Mr. Peet and Aaron climbed up to the wagon seat. Mr. Peet grasped the slack reins, slapped them gently against the horse's rumps and turned the wagon away from the water trough. Newt raised his hand, then slowly lowered it as the clop of the horses' hoofs and squeak of an axle in need of grease faded to silence.

Newt turned and came back inside the kitchen. Brother and sister stood and stared at each other for a short time. "I'm not hungry either," he said. "We should go to bed."

Julie nodded. He handed her the lantern. "You goin' to the Johnnie house?"

She nodded and went out the back door and crossed the yard to the outhouse. The stench of decay rising through the floorboards made her want to retch, but she had nothing but water in her stomach that came up with a rush and spewed over the ground at her feet. She wiped the corners of her mouth with her sleeve and back of her hand, then stepped inside to do her business. She left the door open so the moonlight would supplement the light cast by the lantern.

She returned to the house and she and her brother stumbled through the semi-darkness to their bedrooms. She paused at the open door of their mother's and father's room and envisioned them asleep in each others arms, but the prim bed linens and quilted coverlet were tucked and unwrinkled.

She set the lantern on her side table, then removed her boots, socks, pants and shirt and tugged on her sleeping gown over my head. She extinguished the lantern light and stared down from her second floor window at the two coffins in the moonlit yard waiting for morning.

The high yipping howls and wails of coyotes pulled her leaping from her bed to the window. Guarding the coffins, the herd dogs barked and snarled at a pack of their bretheren slinking about at the outer edge of the yard drawn by the smell of death.

A moment later, a gunshot roared from the porch beneath Julie's window and sent the canine shadows running, melting into the darkness. Newt stepped out and gave each of the dogs a pat on the head. Their grayish brown bodies wriggled at the praise. As Newt reentered the house, they curled up in attitudes of alert sleep next to the coffins. They knew who was inside.

Three shovel blades stabbed the dark soil turning up loamy bites alive with twisting pink worms until two symmetrical piles crested at the lip of two deep scars in the prairie earth. The odor of Olaf's and Ingrid's decomposing bodies was leaking through the wood. They could not remain above ground any longer. Julie did not want her memory of them to be associated with the smell of rotting flesh. She had to walk away. Both her hands wiped at her flood of tears as she ran past the wagon and the horses peacefully grazing.

Hidden from the others by tall wheat grass, she threw herself to the ground in uncontrollable rage and sorrow. She would never see them again. They would never again hold her in their arms against their clothes and bodies scented with garlic and cooking herbs and hay. Hereafter, those smells and the odor of pine wood became the most significant in her life.

She did not return to the graves, but watched from a distance as Mr. Peet and the boys lowered the two coffins into their final resting place, easing them down with thick ropes.

After the last shovelful smoothed the elongated earthen humps, she walked back to help Mr. Peet and the boys seal the graves by piling rocks scavenged from the field into two mounds to prevent clawed animals from digging in search of the bodies. In time, the coffins would disintegrate and their mother's and father's flesh would merge with the earth through the digestive tracts of bacteria and insects, leaving only their bones. Despite what the preacher had once told them, she had to believe their spirits would have moved on to a good place, wherever or whatever that might be.

She owned only one dress which her mother had made for her for when the family occasionally went to a church social in Brainerd. For all other occasions, she wore coveralls or trousers and acted like a boy. Attendance at those enjoyable functions made up for the fact they didn't go to church services on a regular basis, which irritated the preacher. Mother and Father told them they didn't care for the doomsday messages the preacher fired off like a cannon every Sunday morning. He stopped trying to convince the Josephson family they were in spiritual jeopardy after father told him their spirits were just fine and didn't need constant reminding.

They rode in the wagon the short distance back to the house. Newt and Julie climbed down and stood at the front porch.

"I'll come by to see how you're getting along," said Mr. Peet.

Julie and Newt nodded. "Thank you, sir," said Newt. "We could not have done this without you."

Mr. Peet gently shook the reins and the team set out at a slow respective walk. Aaron looked back at his friends until the wagon had progressed far down the lane. They did not raise a hand in farewell.

Newt and Julie silently set about the tasks they had inherited. Newt went to the barn and harnessed and hitched Mel and Nell to continue plowing and seeding corn where he and his father had left off. Julie made the kitchen her domain and applied what her mother had taught her in baking bread and pies and preparing simmering rabbit and chicken stews supplemented with tomatoes, potatoes, onions, and turnips from their garden. She recreated the cooking aromas of her childhood and, therefore, memories of her mother.

A few days later, she saw the Peets' horses and wagon troddirg up the lane to her house. A third horse, Aaron's cow pony, was tied to the rear of the wagon. She left off hoeing weeds in the garden and ran to the barn to call Newt, who was sharpening a plow blade with a rasp. "Peets comin'!" He dropped his tools and they walked out into the yard to wait for them to arrive.

Mr. Peet looked down at them from the wagon seat. "Doin' all right?"

"Better'n we thought," said Newt.

"Your ma and pa taught you well."

"They did," said Newt. "They taught us well."

Aaron climbed down from the seat and walked around to the back of the flatbed wagon where he pulled out a duffle bag, untied his horse and led him over near Newt and Julie.

"Aaron's goin' to move in with you a while. We talked about it. I got other hands at home and we decided you could do with some help," said Timothy.

Sudden smiles transformed Newt's and Julie's somber faces. "We got a place for ya," said Newt, his voice cracking with gratitude.

"I won't stay but for a cup of coffee," said Timothy stepping down.

With a quick nod, Julie turned and ran back inside the house. She kept the large metal pot brewing on the cast iron stove just like her mother always had. Within minutes, she was back with a steaming crockery cup and handed it to Timothy who sat resting on the front porch steps.

He sniffed deeply of the aroma and slowly drank the fortifying black liquid with lip-smacking slurps. "Good as your ma's."

Julie blushed in appreciation. Timothy gazed off in the direction of the graves whose humped mounds peered slightly above the prairie grass.

"Went to Brainerd," he said, "and asked around about what happened."

Julie waited expectantly to hear what he had to say.

"Don't want to upset ya. You've had enough come at ya."

He paused and took another sip of coffee.

"Heard talk I don't like."

"About mother and father?" Newt stood straight and solid before Mr. Peet. Julie sat on the porch step next to him and gazed intently at the profile of his aquiline face.

"In a way yes and in a way no."

"How can that be?" she asked.

"Has nothin' to do with them bein' killed, but it does have to do with your farm."

"What about our farm?" Newt's voice suddenly sounded deep and concerned, like father's.

"If someone comes out here to see you, don't do nothin'."

"Who would come out here to see us?"

"Can't say for sure. There's talk that us small farmers might be in for trouble. Not the first time railroad's made a land grab."

"The railroad wants our land?"

"Maybe not. Depends on where they want to run a trunk line. It's all about movin' wheat and cattle and freight charges. Fear is we could all lose our farms in these parts."

"They can't take away our farms," said Newt. "They're bought and paid for."

"Your ma and pa and me don't own the land outright. Bank does. We have to pay the bank."

"Pa always had money to pay the bank. We have a good farm. Julie and I can sell our wheat and pay the bank."

"Bank has their own way of lookin' at business when it comes to getting' what they want, or what someone else wants."

"Who is that?"

"Business – railroad, farms, meat packers, lumber, ore."

"Lumber? Ore?"

"Up north. Railroads go to the source."

"They can't take our farms. This is our lives out here."

"It is that. Nothin' might happen. When there's talk, best to be warned and not surprised."

"What if someone does come?"

"Send Aaron to get me. That's why he brought his horse."

Julie's body twitched with a surge of insecurity. She had to get up and move away from Mr. Peet, just because he was a harbinger of another imminent catastrophe.

Mr. Peet rose from the steps and handed her his empty cup. "I thank you for the coffee. Aaron's a hard worker and a good lad."

"We're glad to have him," said Newt. "He's our best friend."

Mr. Peet placed a firm gentle hand on his son's shoulder, climbed up onto the wagon seat, and turned the team about. He set off down the lane to the dirt road and did not look back.

"Leave your duffle on the porch," said Newt. "We'll put up your pony in the barn."

Julie watched them walk across the yard to the barn and was left alone holding Mr. Peet's empty cup.

Chapter 8

The Assassin

"Since your mother and father are no longer alive, the ownership of the farm reverts back to Morgan Guarantee and Trust. We hold the mortgage and, as children, you cannot continue to maintain the payments."

They were seated in the kitchen. The rising heat of the afternoon did not nearly match the heat of anger Julie was feeling. She was about to explode. She didn't understand how her brother could just sit there so accepting and not say anything.

As soon as the entourage of three men in black suits had driven their light team and carriage up to the house, Julie knew who they were and what they intended to do. She ran out the kitchen back door and across the yard to the barn where Newt and Aaron were cleaning the harnesses they used on the Percherons to til the fields.

"Strangers comin'," she said. "The ones Mr. Peet told us about."

"I'll go get my father," Aaron leaped up from where he sat on a weathered wooden bench. He dashed out to the paddock and brought in his horse. "How close are they?"

"Just turned in from the road." They heard the neighs of horses. "Sounds like they're at the house."

Aaron quickly saddled and bridled his quarter horse, vaulted onto his back, and with a grunt of encouragement to the animal, they shot out of the barn and were headed down the drive to the road just as the bankers pulled their wagon to a stop in the front yard. Greatly surprised, the intruders craned their heads to look after the flashing sprint of boy and horse. Within a minute, they were chased by a rising dust cloud churning upwards from their energetic charge along the distant road.

Newt and Julie knew intuitively not to let these men dominate them. They must meet them and stand firm. Julie wanted to prevent them from crossing the threshold. Newt could have gone inside and brought out their father's rifle, but that would have caused more problems. The bankers would likely return with the sheriff.

"We need to hear what they have to say," she muttered to Newt. "We don't have to sign anything. That's what Mr. Peet said. We'll just tell them that Mr. Peet is coming to help us out."

"I know what I'm going to say," said Newt. But as it turned out, Newt said nothing, because he had not expected to hear what Fergus McConnell from the Morgan Guarantee and Trust told them. McConnell's face reminded Julie of a rodent that had just crawled out of a hole somewhere.

"Your parents did not leave a will transferring ownership to their children. You have no recourse but to pack a few belongings and move out. The house and barn and the land and livestock now belong to the bank." He thrust an official looking document onto the table top. "This transfer of deed explains it."

They had waited for Aaron to return with his father before all of them went into the house. Mr. Peet had not taken a chair, but remained standing protectively between Newt and Julie like a lawyer without an argument. She could tell from his face that he would like to do something to the three men with their officious mustaches and gray mutton chops and expanding girth that rendered them an intrusive physical domain. Julie imagined that if she poked their guts with a knife, a hissing stink of hot air would escape their bloat. But she could do nothing.

"They need a few days," said Mr. Peet. "They can come stay with my family. We'll take them in."

"We'll give you 'til noon tomorrow. Just don't move any of the stock over to your farm or the sheriff will throw you in jail for rustling."

"We can take our dogs and cats," Julie spit from between clenched teeth. "They aren't stock."

"The dogs and cats can go with you."

"And the furniture," said Mr. Peet. "It don't come with the house."

"Not sure about that," Mr. Holderman looked over his shoulder at his lawyer, who muttered something unintelligible into his ear. Holderman rested his gaze on Mr. Peet. "Personal belongings are okay, but the furniture stays with the house."

"What you gonna use it for," said Mr. Peet. "Kindling?

Holderman scrapped back his chair. "By noon tomorrow. We'll be here with the sheriff to make certain there are no transgressions."

Nothing more was said. Julie listened to their boots trudge a cluttered resounding path across the resisting wooden floor to the door. Then they were out in the day and climbing back into their carriage. Julie and Newt were powerless against them. They possessed a document of their own making that had destroyed the children's lives as they had known them and was a plan that took away what was rightfully theirs with the finality of their parents' coffins.

From that moment on, Julie promised herself she would find out how such a thing could happen. She would dedicate herself to bringing down the men who had done these things to them. The vastness of what she discovered would do everything to crush her.

She sat in the wagon bed next to a leather trunk filled with the books that their mother and father had collected over the years. The trunk reminded her of a third coffin that contained another segment of their lives. Only she could open this one and remove and read stories and other written works that linked her to their spirit and memory and who they were and what they meant to her and her brother when they were living. The trunk and what it contained eased the thought, but not the reality, of their decaying bodies.

Newt and Julie had visited the graves for one last time before boarding the wagon to travel with Mr. Peet and Aaron to their home. They had also had a difficult time of corralling the half dozen cats who wanted nothing to do with leaving the farm rich in mice and prairie dogs. Only the one Julie had named Moth, because of her gray and white mottled coloration, allowed herself to be coaxed to sit in her lap as she often did purring into the long evenings on the porch.

The dogs did not give leaving a second thought. The wolfhound, Oberon, who had intimidated many coyotes and the black retriever, Bruno, would follow them wherever they set out to travel. They leaped into the back of the wagon bed without hesitation and nestled up against Julie and Moth.

As they expected, the conditions were crowded when Newt and Julie moved in with the Peets, an already large family of five children. Newt shared a bed with his friend, Aaron, and Julie shared a bed with Aaron's oldest sister, Beth.

She and Beth had always been friends before this disruption of their lives. They both liked books and the discussion of ideas that hovered beyond their reach out there in the world, but touched their lives through the selection of what her parents had packed into the trunk. Beth and Julie devoured the contents of those books by sunlight and candle light. But Julie did not shirk her chores.

As guests of the Peet family, Newt and Julie wholeheartedly contributed their labor to the mutual well-being of them all. Newt worked in the barn and the fields as he had with his father and Julie joined the girls harvesting crops, canning fruits and vegetables for the winter, quilting and sewing garments, and preparing daily meals.

Mrs. Peet, June as she encouraged Newt and Julie to call her, was not as energetic as their own mother had been, but she was as silent and steadfast. She rarely spoke, which surprised Julie, since her mother had talked incessantly about ideas and what needed to be done on a day to day basis.

Another characteristic she noticed was that nobody in the Peet family argued with her. Her mother and father had encouraged Newt and Julie to argue with them. They said argument was part of the learning process. Sometimes they expressed disappointment if their children didn't challenge them.

June Peet was the foundation of the family. Her husband never made decisions without consulting her. If she didn't know enough about a situation, she would insist that Mr. Peet bring home more information before she arrived at a conclusion. But once her position had been established, there was no turning her around.

Unlike Julie's mother and father, she was not a free thinker. She believed that people should just settle for what was given them. Trying to better oneself beyond the confines of their station in life was to be discouraged, since the effort would result in pain and suffering and dismal failure. Better to trust in the Lord and pray for salvation that you would be rewarded in the next life.

Given her preferences, she did not entirely discourage enjoyments offered in the present life, so long as they were overseen by a presiding parent. She allowed the children to play and sing and dance and enjoy good food.

Four of the Peets were boys, but Beth had the advantage of being the oldest. Aaron was next in age. With Julie becoming one of the family, Beth had the opportunity to share confidences about subjects she could never discuss with her mother, who kept her busy with daily domestic tasks. Julie's help provided Beth with a respite from laboring dawn to dark, then crawling exhausted into bed.

As they lay in bed one night, she said, "I don't want to become like my mother. I love her, but I don't want to become her."

That Sunday, they had gone to church in Brainerd. After the service, well meaning adults had approached Newt and Julie to express their condolences at the loss of their parents. What they said caused Julie to cry. Beth grabbed her arm and pulled her away. They ran down the dirt street and suddenly Beth's laughter converted Julie's tears to laughter.

"What are we doing?" Julie sputtered.

"We're running away."

"We can't run away," Julie shouted.

"Yes we can! Yes we can! We can travel around the world!"

Gasping, they finally stopped at the railroad depot. There wasn't a train in sight.

"We can't do this," Julie laughed. "There's not even a train."

Beth looked up and down the track. "If there was a train, would you go with me?"

Her serious intent caught Julie off guard. Beth thought she had pulled Julie away to cheer her. Julie looked at her lovely face. Her wide brown eyes rode the bridge of her slender nose like a balance and crinkled slightly downward at the outer edges in bemused friendship. And although she claimed she didn't want to be like her mother, she had her mother's thin determined mouth and long straight dark hair with unruly strands that curtained her face during strenuous effort. Her ethereal body reminded Julie of a swan coasting across the surface of a still lake. She had been named after her grandmother, Elsebeth, who had come to the Minnesota prairie in 1846 as a young pioneer woman, married a farmer, and raised seven children.

"Maybe, if there was a train," said Beth, "We could just get on it and go wherever it would take us. The day will come when I will leave," she said. "I cannot think of living all my life here."

Julie nodded. They turned and walked back to the church yard.

"What were you doing?" her mother asked. "Where did you go?"

"Julie was feeling sad," said Beth. "Those people were making her feel sad."

"Oh, we'll be going back home now."

They walked to the horses and wagon.

Beth was a dreamer. The books from Julie's parents' trunk opened up thoughts and views she never knew existed and she wanted desperately to go out and see that world.

After four months, she and Julie had worked their way through the books and essays to the bottom of the trunk. There they discovered a list of names..

"What are these?" Beth lifted out five worn pages and held them up to the window light so they could more easily read them. "Do you know these people?"

"No, I've never seen this before. Mother and father never talked about it."

"Some of these are foreign names."

"They must have known them from somewhere else."

"I don't recognize any of them," said Beth. "They don't have farms around here and they don't live in Brainerd."

"Father often made trips to St. Cloud and brought back books and pamphlets that he stored in the trunk."

"Maybe these people are free thinkers he knew in St. Cloud."

"No one ever came to see us, but Mother and Father always talked about meetings when he came home from his trips."

"What did they say?"

"They talked about what was in the pamphlets and that the movement was growing."

"What do you suppose that means?" Beth thumbed through one of the pamphlets.

"I don't know. They never told us."

"Did you ever read these before?"

"Not 'til I came here. Father kept the trunk stored in the attic. He told Newt and me not to go looking in it. He said these were his special papers."

A few of the pamphlets were written in Swedish, but most were in English. Nevertheless, the girls didn't understand to what they referred. These were not topics or incidents in their past lives their parents had discussed with them.

One was an essay against a law prohibiting agitation and disobedience that had been passed in Sweden and was directed against socialism. Another, a social policy measure including a law that forbade the employment of women in mines during the first 4 weeks after giving birth. There was one about a law to protect workers against accidents at work. A law document from 1891 described state support for voluntary health insurance, which meant nothing to them. There was a pamphlet to introduce obligatory insurances against accidents and to fund retirement.

Another was a series of demands regarding social issues to shorten the workday, and a reform of the franchise law by the *Landsföreningen foer kvinnornas rösträtt* (Union for Women's right to vote).

There was also a pamphlet on agnosticism, that the existence of God could neither be proved nor disproved.

The longest one was a thick document on *Plans For A New Social Order*. Beth and Julie had not read this publication.

Timothy and June Peet assimilated Newt and Julie into the family as though they were their own children. Beth and Julie developed a loving sisterly bond. They shared secrets and dreams of what they would like to become and made up stories together. At night, they would fall asleep in each others' arms. They also took delight in both nurturing and teasing Beth's three younger brothers.

Although Julie loved them all, little Max, the youngest, was her favorite. He was five years old and projected an excited fascination with everything in his small world, despite the fact he had been born deaf. No one could explain why, not even the doctor that Mr. and Mrs. Peet had taken Max all the way to see in St. Cloud.

Because he lived in a world without sound, Max used his hands, arms, face, and body to express himself in a dynamic way. Beth and Julie never failed to understand him for simple and obvious things. They tried to figure out a way to teach him to read and write by having him imitate the drawing of their letters on a slate that named objects in the room and animals out in the farm yard.

High-pitched exaggerated noises erupted birdlike from his mouth agape in his attempts to talk. He must have remembered sounds from the time before he became deaf. The girls helped by having him watch their lips and tongues and feel their breath when they held his hand up to their mouths and expelled air in forming a particular word.

Of the three younger boys, Julie would have to say he possessed a pure beauty in his smooth perfectly featured face that glowed with an inner energy. His doting mother rarely cut his thick blonde curls, so they grew down the nape of his neck and he could have been mistaken for a girl.

The next oldest was Elmer, a miniature version of his father. At ten, he dressed like him and followed him around like a faithful dog desiring only to please and be noticed. Timothy Peet responded in kind with his gentle manner of teaching and imparting information so that Elmer was able to learn skills in raising crops and livestock.

In contrast, June Peet had to constantly remind her rebellious thirteen year old, Claude, who seemed bent on displeasing everyone, to mind his manners. Claude appeared as rough as he talked and acted and was occasionally challenged by older boys who misjudged his strength and speed of his fists in fights that took place behind the church or the general store when he and his father went to town for supplies. His blunt features and tousled mop of brown hair did not deter the attraction of town girls who were drawn to his shameless flirting and feats of strength as much as by the daring expression in his iridescent gray green eyes.

One day, Beth and Julie were out feeding chickens in the yard when they saw a horse and rider turn up the lane from the road and proceed at a brisk canter the half mile to the house. The rider was dressed in a black business suit and wide-brim hat and handled the fast black stallion with ease. As they drew closer, Julie noticed how the sun glistened off the horse's shining coat and, for a moment, glimpsed the holstered gun belted to the man's waist as the corner of his coattail flipped back in the wind.

Beth shouted. "Mama, there's someone coming to the house."

"Get inside at once! Hurry! Hurry!" June shouted from the back door. As the girls rushed inside, she said, "Go to your room and stay out of sight. Don't let him see you."

"Why?" asked Beth. "Why do we have to hide?"

"Don't ask questions. Where's Newt?"

"Out in the fields with Aaron and Mr. Peet. They're putting up hay."

"Move quickly now. Go."

"What is it, Mama? Who is that man?"

"He was in town asking about Newt and Julie. Giles Hansford told your father when he was buying supplies."

Beth and Julie ran down the short dark wooden hallway to the room they shared and crouched low beside the bed. Their window fronted the house. They raised their heads just enough to see over the top of the bed and caught glimpses of the approaching horseman through the rising and falling muslin curtains lifted like billowing sails by the stiff autumn breeze.

The rider stopped his blowing horse in the yard, but did not dismount. His eyes searched in the direction of the barn and out toward the fields, then returned to the house. Partially covered by an ominous dark beard, the left side of his face was reddened and pock-marked, like it had received a blast of bird shot. His penetrating blue eyes seemed to possess beyond normal sight that gave Julie chills. He wore a dull burnished gold badge pinned to the left side of his vest. A rifle was tucked deep into a saddle scabbard on the right next to his dusty black boot. Julie thought it odd that he wore only one rowled spur on his left boot.

He called out. "Anyone here! Anyone home!"

The girls could not see, but could hear the front door squeak open as Mrs. Peet stepped out onto the wooden porch. She did not at first say anything, but waited for the man to speak.

"Mornin' Ma'am. I'm told the surviving children of Olaf and Ingrid Josephson live here now."

Mrs. Peet maintained her silence.

"May I ask your name?"

"State your business."

"I'm Luther Baggot, an investigator for the Pinkerton agency on an errand of private business."

"Then you have no business with me or those children. They have done nothing to break the law."

"That is not my purpose. My employer wishes me to speak to them about a list of names important to the company. A search was made of the vacated Josephson house and it was not to be found. The information is important to the company."

"Of what company do you speak?"

"I am not at liberty to share that information since this matter is of the highest confidence. I have a question I would like to put to the children."

Julie could barely breathe. "It's him," she choked.

Beth looked at her.

"It's him. I know it's him. He killed mother and father."

"How do you know? How can you be sure?"

"He wants the list. They were killed because of the names on that list. I'm sure of it."

"The ones in the trunk?"

"Yes." Julie leaped up and ran from the bedroom down the hall across the living room and slammed through the front door out onto the porch.

Startled and horrified, Mrs. Peet., waved her back, but Julie ignored her.

"You want to see me!" she shouted. "I'm here!"

"Are you Julie Josephson?"

Julie jumped the four steps to the ground and snatched up three stones which she flung with all her might at the horse who shied and reared with such sudden force, it nearly unseated his dark clad rider, but Luther Baggot quickly brought the snorting hoof flailing animal under control.

"What do you think you're doing?" Luther roared at her.

Hot tears rushed down the girl's face and blurred the man and his horse. "You killed my mother and father."

"I did not kill them. I'm looking for the man who did. Your mother and father had a list. The name of that man is on it."

She did not trust what he said. Since Luther Baggot was hired by a private company, she could not believe his interest in the names on the list were to find her parents' killer. If there was a name, then she would want to discover that for herself. Although she could not explain why at the time, she sensed the list had a far different purpose. She also questioned why, if Luther Baggot already knew the name, what reason did he have for wanting the list.

She reached for another stone, but Mrs. Peet restrained her and pinned back her arms.

"I don't know about any list," Julie shouted. "Mother and father never told us."

"I want to see what you took from the house," said Luther.

"We took our clothes and dogs and a cat."

"There were documents, writings, and pamphlets."

"I don't know about anything like that. They never showed us anything like that."

Luther stared at her as though he could see straight through her. Without him having to say, he knew she was lying.

"Julie Josephson, you cannot deny a request from the law."

"I don't know who you are, just because you have a badge."

"Do not doubt me, child. You will be dealt with severely."

"That's enough," Mrs. Peet interrupted. "You have no reason to threaten her. She told you what she knows. She would not lie to you. Her mother and father were protective of their children. They would not tell them what they didn't need to know."

"Which leads me to you, Mrs. Peet. What might you and your husband know about a list?"

"Nothing. What is it you're seeking? Who would be on such a list that a Pinkerton agent must possess it for a company whose name cannot be revealed?"

"I am not at liberty to tell you any more than what I have. I'm on the trail of a killer."

"We cannot be of help to you, sir. I bid you a good day. It's best you ride on."

Luther stared hard at them, assessing what they didn't say more than what they had told him. "You have not seen the last of me." He abruptly wheeled his horse about and galloped back to the road.

Mrs. Peet released Julie's arms and looked down at her. "That was a brave and foolish thing you did. I don't trust him either. He's a violent man. I fear he may return and do us harm. Do you have knowledge of a list?"

Julie shook her head. If she did not know about the list, then she would be clear of its association. She would have to warn Beth to never mention the existence of the list.

"This has to do with your mother and father," said Mrs. Peet. "He might believe we are part of whatever it is they've done."

"What could they have done that they were murdered?"

"I don't know, child. And I don't want to know. I just don't want any harm to come to my husband and children. I'm afraid you and your brother will have to leave us."

Stunned, Julie stared up at her unrelenting expression. "We are not a danger to you."

"No, but that man is. He's an assassin."

"Do you believe he killed mother and father?"

"I have only my suspicion which is not enough to condemn him. Perhaps there is a grain of truth in what he said."

"But my brother and I don't have a list."

"Then let it be. But that man will not rest 'til he finds it. Therefore, you and Newt must move on."

"To where? Where can we go? What can we do?"

"We'll talk it over with Mr. Peet tonight."

"Do you believe me, Mrs. Peet?"

"I believe you."

"I want to go with them," said Beth.

"That is out of the question," her mother retorted.

"But why are you letting Aaron go.   I'm the oldest."

"You are also a girl and you are needed here at home."

"It's unfair. Aaron helps father."

"We're near the end of the harvest season," said Mr. Peet. "Aaron has reached a time to seek a life outside of the family."

"As I have," argued Beth. "I'm not a girl any longer. I'm a young woman."

"With no prospect of marriage."

"And that is the only reason I can leave, if someone proposes marriage?"

"You are being noticed in town," said Mrs. Peet.

"Noticed? I don't care to be noticed. I wouldn't marry any man within a thousand miles of here. I don't want to live the rest of my life on a farm. There's a whole world out there I want to see."

"Newt and Julie and Aaron are going where they can escape the Pinkerton man and find work," said Mr. Peet. "They aren't going out to travel the world. That life is only for the very rich."

"What work can they do that I cannot?"

"There's work available in logging camps up north," said Julie.

Beth's burning eyes roamed directly from her father to her friend. "What work do they have for girls and women?"

"Julie will have to find other work, perhaps as a tutor or maid," said her father. "The logging camps don't hire women and girls. It's a man's work."

Her glance shifted to Aaron and Newt. "They are not yet men."

"They will soon become men. They are young and strong. They can already do a man's work."

Beth's face clenched as firmly as her mother's. "You can prevent me now, but one day, I will leave, and not on the arm of a suitor." With a violent swish of her skirt, she whirled and stomped out of the room.

Mr. Peet would transport them by horse and wagon to Brainerd the next day. They would take the morning train to St. Cloud, and then a trunk line into the North Country forests. That night, after Beth had fallen asleep, Newt and Aaron and Julie secretly devised a plan for her.

Chapter 9

Running

It was the end of autumn, after the harvest, which Newt and Aaron had helped bring in. The days were growing shorter and the weather had turned noticeably colder, especially at night. Mrs. Peet had brought down quilts from where they were stored in the attic trunks to keep mice from burrowing into the material and making nests. After a day of airing in the sun and wind, she covered each of the beds in the house with their multi-colored patterns.

Their images in Julie's thoughts merged with the tearful farewells among the Peets and her own private parting with Beth, who vowed she would follow her friend.

Clouds of black smoke billowed back over the length of the train and swirled down past the passenger car windows that presented them with a shifting panorama of golden wheat fields and endless blue sky until they entered the lakes and northern forests of Minnesota.

Julie pondered what had brought them to this place and why their mother and father had left their homeland. Now, with their lives cut short, victims of the society in which they had sought freedom and opportunity, they lay silent under its earth.

As Newt and Julie were growing up, their mother and father had told them about their decision and why they chose to settle on a farm out on the prairie, with the exception of one important matter that Julie would not learn about until sometime later. A law against agitation and disobedience had been passed directed against socialism. Their parents had come to America so their father could avoid being thrown into prison. Newt and Julie had inherited their legacy and now they were running from the same oppressive political forces.

For several years, Olaf and Ingrid Josephson had profited in a small way from cultivating and harvesting wheat needed to feed the flour mills in Minneapolis and St. Paul. Most of the wheat came from "bonanza" farms hundreds of miles to the west on the endless plains of the Red River Valley. Ranging from 3,000 to 30,000 acres, these huge commercial farms used fleets of harvesters and armies of workers to gather their crops.

Railroads linked the farms and mills and also carried the food and supplies that the men and women living on the single-crop bonanza farms needed to live.

The St. Paul, Minneapolis, and Manitoba Railway (StPM&M) owned the bulk of the wheat trade and operated a thousand miles of track across the Minnesota and Dakota plains.

The slowing of the train followed by a sudden jolt and clashing of railcars woke Julie from a sound sleep only to discover they had stopped somewhere surrounded by a dense forest in the dead of night. A kerosene lantern threw a dirty yellow glow across a patchwork of rough wooden planks that served as the station platform. There appeared to be no one in sight, as though the station master had left the light burning inside the small square shack for the arrival of the train and gone home to bed.

The conductor, a small balding man with tufts of gray hair at his temples, came down the aisle and poked at Newt and Aaron, who had also fallen asleep. He saw Julie's eyes were already open. "This is your stop," he said.

"What's the name of this place?" she asked with a yawn.

"Don't have a name, but it's close as you kin get to the McClatchie Lumber Company by train. You have to either walk or go by horse and wagon the rest of the way."

She peered out the window. "How often does anyone come here?"

"Never stayed long enough to find out. Git yer bags and climb down. Train moves on in five minutes."

They lifted their bags and bumped each other shuffling sleepily along the aisle to the connecting vestibule between cars, then stretched down the metal steps to the ground. They crossed the planks to the station house and were met by the pungent odor of cut pine as they pushed open the door.

There was a single rough hewn wooden bench against the far wall next to a stone fireplace. The coals had been banked, but continued to offer a subdued glow if one moved in close enough. A hand-carved pendulum clock hanging on the wall behind the station agent's desk marked the hours. They had arrived just a few minutes past midnight. They would not see anyone until morning.

An explosion of steam followed by a clash of gears and grinding of wheels informed them that the training was moving on. Left standing in silence, they peered at each other in the dim light. "Best we get some sleep," said Newt. "Julie, you can have the bench."

"Don't think it will be softer than the floor," she remarked.

They spread out near the fireplace to share its waning warmth and used their carpet bags as pillows. The hard wooden floor pressed in against the weight of their bodies, but they ignored the discomfort in pursuit of needed rest.

Julie's sleep was restless and plagued with dreams of threatening dark shapes that engulfed and tried to smother her, as she lay trapped underground in a coffin. Her moaning awakened Newt and he gently touched her shoulder. "Julie, Julie, you all right?"

She came up gasping out of the black depth. Her eyelids flicked open and she stared at his stolid reassuring young face. "I'm glad you're my brother," was all she could say.

He kissed her on the forehead and she promptly fell back into a pleasant sleep.

Dawn angled through the tall pines, crept through the dirt-stained latticed windows and splattered the floor with spots of sunlight. Julie woke to this mosaic, raised her head and looked around.

Newt and Aaron still slept soundly. A cacophony of singing and squawking jays drew Julie from the floor to the door. Her stomach rumbled with hunger and she felt a desperate need to relieve herself. Glancing outside, she noticed a worn narrow path that led to an outhouse across the rutted dirt road.

As she entered the little shack, the clean clear pine scent of the surrounding woods was replaced by the acrid scent of frozen human waste rising from under the two-hole bench seat. She was gratified to see that paper had been provided, albeit containing an occasional thin splinter of wood that required removal before the paper was vigorously applied.

When she returned, Newt and Aaron were awake stretching and yawning. "We wondered where you went." Newt scratched his tousled head.

"Across the road. There's paper."

"I'm hungry," said Aaron. "Where can we get something to eat?"

"Have to follow the road. See where it takes us."

"Someone must come here," Julie said. The lantern had gone out.

"Let's get to it," said Newt, heading for the door.

"There's two holes," She informed them.

They grunted in acknowledgement and, jostling each other, walked quickly across the road to the path. She loved them both.

While she waited, a family of quail came scooting around the corner, their tiny feet scuttling them along like a miniature train. They caught sight of her and took to the air in a scattershot of drumming wings and were gone as abruptly as they had appeared.

With the exception of birdcalls, the chatter of jays, and the drilling vibration of a distant woodpecker, the forest was silent and a little foreboding. Julie wondered how far along the road they would have to go until they would find a settlement. She briefly searched the area hoping to find a berry patch. Even a meager breakfast would do.

A clear stream gurgled from low in the underbrush. She followed its sound around the side of the station and discovered a hand pump with a dipper and bucket. She cranked the heavy metal handle up and down several times producing a thick steady stream of cold pure water gushing from its spout. She filled the metal dipper and drank deeply of the mineral flavor. Then she scooped water on her hands and washed her face, gently touching the area around her neck where there used to be hair. Beth had cut it short the night before they left the Peet family. Mrs. Peet had been suspicious, but she didn't ask questions. It was clear she wanted them gone from the house. She didn't want to think of Julie actually trying to work in a logging camp.

She was waving her hands around in the air to dry them, when Newt and Aaron returned from across the road and sampled the water from the pump.

"We need to talk more about this. We can't call you Julie anymore. We have to get used to calling you by your boy's name, Joel. It's close enough to Julie you can remember it. The other thing is you need to stop walking the way you do and walk like Aaron and me, square and straight ahead. Don't sway your butt the way you do sometimes."

"I don't sway my butt. I have never swayed my butt."

"Lately, we noticed there's a little sideways motion. And you need to carry your hands and arms stiff and straight. You need to look strong, not like the first big wind'll knock you over."

"Like this?" She locked her arms and wrists ramrod down against my sides.

"No, we don't look like that. They have to hang natural. Just don't turn your hands out and if you point at something, do it like you mean it."

"I always mean it if I point at it."

"And another thing, when you get excited, your voice goes up. You need to keep it down in your throat. So from now on, you have to practice these things. Do it as we walk along, and we'll tell you if you look and sound like a boy."

"I've always looked and sounded like a boy. There's always been boys around me and I do what boys do."

"Well, except you helped mother in the kitchen and when you're with Beth, you act different."

"How do you mean?"

"Girly. You act girly."

"We are girls, you know."

"But you can't be a girl now, not for a long time, if we expect to have work. And you have to learn to piss standing up."

"I can do that already."

"That's good. Okay, we need to start walkin' so we can get someplace where there's food and we can find work." Julie dropped her voice an octave, but the effort caused her to cough.

They went inside the station house for their bags, then trooped back out setting a swift pace along the ruts and gouges of the wagon track.

"Walk in front of us so we can see you better," commanded Newt.

"You don't have to watch my butt."

"Yes, we do. We'll tell you if it moves sideways."

She moved out ahead of them and concentrated on taking long straight strides and swinging her arms firmly at her sides. Her butt did not move from side to side.

The settlement wasn't much to look at; but after a five mile walk through the woods, they were glad to find the log structure of the general store, a barn and three nearby cabins. Thin spirals of white smoke rising from stone chimneys raised their spirits, knowing that they were about to encounter human life. They noticed a corral occupied by three shaggy-coated horses and three milk cows. A shed afforded shelter to a flock of chickens. A sow and her half-grown piglets rooted about a recently filled trough. A boar hog snored with flatulent shivering of his distended pink and gray flesh, oblivious to the facts of the morning.

As they went up the steps of the general store, Julie tugged her boys cap lower over her forehead to partially shield her face. A grizzled, balding man rose from his wooden chair behind the counter. He wore a leather apron over coveralls and a woolen blue shirt. His thick hands and fingers splayed on the counter top supporting his solid bulk as he leaned forward, gray eyes peering inquisitively at them through metal-rimmed lenses.

"Where you boys from?"

Julie was gratified that he did not recognize her as a girl. Although her face was refined in its features, her nose was wide enough with a slight tilt and she could harden her expression in a surly manner to pass for a boy.

"We came in on the train from St. Cloud last night," said Newt.

"Figured as much. Not another way to get here 'less you're on horseback."

"No horses," said Aaron. "Had to leave 'em."

"Come off a farm?"

"West of Brainerd," said Newt. "We're lookin' to work at the mill."

"Mmh."

"How far is it?" asked Newt.

"Five miles up the road."

"We can walk that."

"Supply wagon comes in later this morning. You can ride back."

"We're hungry," said Aaron. "Can we buy food?"

"Save your money. My missus is makin' breakfast first cabin by the barn. She'll feed ya. Tell her I sent ya over. 'Bout how old you boys be?"

"Sixteen," said Newt. "Aaron here is fifteen. My kid brother's thirteen."

"Not much meat on 'im, but there's work in the camp."

"I can pull my own," Julie said, lowering her voice with an effort.

"Mmh. Head on over there. Just left the table a mite ago."

"Thank you, sir," said Newt. "If there's anything we can do to help you 'til the wagon comes, we'll be glad to oblige."

"Might have a chore or two. Go feed your hunger first."

They filed out of the store and along the dirt track to the cabin. When they were safely out of the proprietor's hearing, Julie said, "He thinks I'm a boy."

"Don't be over confident," said Newt. "You have a lot of people yet to fool."

"It's better if you don't say much," said Aaron. "Your voice can give you away."

"I made it sound lower," she said.

"I could hear girl in it," said Aaron.

"I am a girl."

"Not anymore," said Newt. "From now on, you're Joel. Don't even think about being a girl. Just think like a boy so you don't lose your concentration."

"I am thinking like a boy. I've been with you two more than anyone."

"Shush now. There's a window open. She could hear us."

The cabin door opened within a moment of Aaron's knock to reveal the ruddy kind face of the proprietor's wife. Her small hands wiped berry-stained flour on her white apron protecting a light blue gingham dress. From her expression, she must have thought it strange to suddenly have three visitors from the middle of the wilderness. Her twinkling blue eyes rested on Julie just a moment longer than the others, bringing a quick smile and flash of white teeth to her weathered countenance. Julie lowered her head. The wife appeared to have spent as much time in the out of doors as in the kitchen. Pushing back a stray wisp of gray hair from her forehead, she greeted them with, "So what brings you three lads to me doorstep?"

"We were at the store," said Newt. "Your husband sent us to have breakfast."

"Breakfast, did he. You do look famished. Come in. Come in. Mind you scrape your shoes. Don't need mud on the floor."

"Yes, Ma'am. Thank you, Ma'am. Kind of you, Ma'am." They brushed past her into the warm kitchen.

"Manners, you have. Good upbringing by your mum and dad. You come on the train?"

"Last night, after dark," said Newt. "We slept at the station."

"Come off the farm? Most your age do."

"Are there others at the mill like us?" asked Aaron.

"Have been in the past, but they moved on. Some stay for all their working days. Grow old, then go back to the farm or move to the city. My Walter was a riverman for twenty-five years. I married him on the condition he save his money to set up the store. At the end of the month, he turned his earnings over to me and I'd give 'im saloon money. Set yourselves down at the table there. Hot cakes, pork, and eggs are the order of the day. Name's Melissa. Worked at the hotel in Pinedale 'til Walter brought me to the camp. You passed through Pinedale on the train. Small place then. Not much bigger than the settlement here. I was the cook at McClatchie for seven years. Not a place to raise children. I took my two boys back to Pinedale and they'd see their pa once a month. Didn't want to be rivermen when they come of age. Went off to the city. Don't know where today."

Melissa talked incessantly about her life while she served them breakfast. They were not compelled to contribute and she didn't ask them any personal questions. She missed her sons and complained that once they were gone, they had not returned to visit or ever written her a letter to inform her of their condition. At the conclusion of the meal, she encouraged them to feel welcome any time if they needed a respite from working at the logging camp. They thanked her for the ample hot breakfast that left them feeling plump and lazy and returned to her husband at the general store.

Under his amused eye, Walter enlisted their services by having them restock shelves with canned goods and sundries from the last supply train delivery. Newt and Aaron hefted numerous fifty pound sacks of sugar, salt, and flour in the back room storage area while Julie counted, shelved, and tabbed supplies from wooden crates that Walter opened with a wedge and hammer.

When they were finished, he asked them, "You outfitted for the weather at the camps?"

They didn't know to what he was referring, so Newt said, "We figger they'll give us what we need."

"Not clothes they won't. You got to bring your own. Come over here."

They lined up at the wooden counter and he brought out woolen pants and heavy socks and coats. "Mackinaw," he said. "Without these, you won't last a week when the snow falls. Mackinaw'll keep you warm and dry. Here, try these on. And you're gonna need good boots. What you're wearin' is for when you ain't workin'."

They pawed through the pile of clothes, removed their farm boots and pants and tried on the Mackinaws for size. The smallest was a little roomy for Julie, but she would make do. The smallest size boots were slightly large for her. By wearing two pairs of thick wool socks, she could shuffle along in them. This way of moving contributed to how she was to portray herself as being slow and a little dull when they arrived at the logging camp. Thanking him profusely, they bundled their new belongings into rucksacks Walter gave them.

At noon, the supply wagon from the McClatchie logging camp arrived and Walter introduced them to the driver, Mitchum Hardie, an ebullient little man not taller than Newt and Aaron. Melissa fed them all a noon meal before they headed up the road deeper into the forest. Mitchum's endless string of stories about his life since he came over from Scotland as a boy reinforced their deceptive sense of well-being, especially for Julie. She was accepted and known as Joel Josephson.

Chapter 10

Loggers

The McClatchie lumber camp unexpectedly startled the eye like a series of dark carbuncles on the shore of the Frazier River. With the exception of a few scrawny pines, the area surrounding the six log buildings and a barn and blacksmith shop was denuded of trees long since harvested and floated down the wild river by drivers to a distant sawmill where the battered logs became lumber.

A sharp wind grabbed at the gray smoke billowing from the stone chimney of a shanty at the center of the compound. A large number of pigs roamed freely near the woods and open areas of the camp. Some waited, grunting and snorting at a log trough in a large pen for the next slops to come from the kitchen. The pen neighbored to a smokehouse where many of their kin and they themselves would be butchered, cured, and hung by steel hooks.

As their wagon approached on the uneven road winding out of the forest, Julie's nose twitched at the aroma of spiced meat commingled with freshly baked pies and bread. They would eat well.

She felt self-conscious and was constantly on guard that anyone would perceive her as being other than a boy. As a consequence, she was quiet and stand-offish. Within a few days, she heard comments from the men that she was either not friendly or maybe dull. Newt explained that Joel was shy and dim and didn't know how to talk much. He said that this had happened when their mother and father were killed.   Julie took his characterization of her as a cue for how she should act for as long as they were in the camp, or at least in the company of the loggers and rivermen, who showed no sympathy. They had all come from hard times of one kind or another.

"What'd you *cadge* us here, Mitchum?" These were Jack Moulton's, the foreman, first words of greeting. "Welcome to the shanty," he said. "Snow's comin' and we got plenty a work ahead. Glad to have ya."

His penetrating dark eyes brooded over them in a grim and haughty way. Like most of the other rivermen, his stocky body was as solidly square as the beard that framed his grizzled wide cheeks. A blue woolen cap pulled down to just above his small ears completed his resemblance to a bear. Thereafter, Julie was always a little fearful of him and tried to avoid him, thinking that he was suspicious of her from the beginning.

"This here's the cookery," he waved his arm to the log building where Mitchum had stopped the wagon. "Mitchum'll show you to the sleeping camp. Got your turkey, I see," he referred to their bulging duffle bags. "That's good. That's good. Must know somethin'. What you don't, you'll learn fast enough or go packin'. After you get yourselves into the sleeping camp, we'll talk about what crew to put you on. Two of ya look like you got some meat on ya. How old are you?" He spoke directly to Julie.

She lowered her voice. "Fourteen, sir."

"Fourteen? Don't look much older 'n ten or twelve. Makes no difference. Lot of us started when we was nippers. Mitchum, take 'em over to the sleep camp so they can get ticked up."

"Boss." Mitchum jumped down from the driver's seat and said, "Since you got a ride, gimme a hand here and help the cookees unload, he referred to two young men with their white shirt sleeves rolled up who had emerged from the cookery cabin.

Newt, Aaron and Julie left their turkeys in the wagon and tugged at flour sacks at the tailgate. Julie could not begin to lift one herself, so Aaron assisted her in her red-faced efforts. She managed to move one bag into the root cellar to every two of the others.

The sharp darting eyes of Tomas LaPier, the head cook, glanced up at them from his array of pots and pans at one of the two large wood-burning stoves. Twelve loaves of bread had been set to rise on a rack above them. The peppery aroma of simmering beef stew and wood smoke overpowered the room furnished with five split log dining tables and benches that sat twenty men each. A large hand pump provided well water used to fill metal sinks.

"More mouths to feed I see. How many?" he shouted.

"Three," the tall, slender cookee with thinning blonde hair by the name of Myles Bennet called back from where he was dropping a heavy sack from his shoulder. "Young'uns, by the look."

"Eat just as much. Size don't matter. What crew is Jack gonna put 'em on?"

"Didn't say as yet."

"So where you hail from?" The flash of white teeth grinned at the newcomers from his Gallic features, a prominent Roman nose and close-cropped dark hair.

"Minnesota," said Newt. "We lived on a wheat farm."

"Ah, so would I think. Straw hair and blue eyes. Swedes, are you not?"

"We came from Sweden with our mother and father when we were small."

"Now you run away from home to become lumberjacks, eh?"

"No, our mother and father were killed."

"Oh, I am sorry for you. The world is a hard place. How did it happen?"

"An assassin," said Newt. "They were murdered."

Tomas and the others shook their heads in sympathy.

"It is a bad way to die," said Tomas. "You are welcome here. We will be your family."

"It smells good," said Aaron.

"Our food is the best, even when you are out in the bush."

"I'm not Swedish," Aaron felt the need to distinguish himself.

"You look like a Polack," said Myles.

"I don't know where my mother and father are from."

"What's your last name?"

"Peet."

"Peet, huh, sounds like they were from England. Ain't that where them peat bogs are?" Myles laughed at his little joke.

"I don't know about peat bogs."

"They burn that over there instead of wood."

"My mother and father never told me."

"Well, that means you ain't a Polack. Anyone comes from Europe is a Polack. Don't matter if they're German or Russian. We just call 'em Polacks and they like it fine."

"Workin' together is the important thing," said Mitchum. "Don't matter where you come from or where you been. Let's get your ticks."

Newt, Aaron, and Julie followed him outside and crossed the compound of hardened stony earth to the sleeping camp. Mitchum pushed open the heavy wooden door and they entered the rectangular building with a sharply canted roof to deflect the heavy weight of snow that would press down on it all winter. The center of the room was clear and open to allow for the unobstructed movement of a large group of men. Two steel drum boxed wood-burning stoves radiated heat and several coal oil bracket lamps hung from hooks on cross beams cast a shadowy yellow illumination against rows of double-tiered wooden bunks along the four walls. A well pump and a metal sink trough filled half of one end wall next to a storage section.

"Most of the crew sleeps here," said Mitchum. "Teamsters have their own camp near the barn. Stays warm in here, even when it gets down to twenty below. Logs are double-caulked. That's how we put up every camp."

"Is there more than one camp?" asked Newt.

"MacLatchie has three on the Frazier and Pike Rivers and the mill fifty miles down at Lake Wanatchee. Bit of a town sprung up there too. General store and two hotels. MacLatchie hisself has a big house there, like you find in the city. River widens out at the south end of the lake enough for a steamer to come up the channel from Saint Paul to the mill. Makes the trip every two weeks except in winter. Lakes and most of the river's under ice."

He stood at the center of the room and swung his arm in a wide gesture at the walls. "Any bunk you don't see a blanket on is free to take. Ticks are stuffed with straw. You can get more from the barn if you want to soften 'em up. Bag of hay for a pillow unless you want to roll up a blanket, but you only get two until the temperature drops. Then we ration out a third. Heavy wool, but most sleep with their Mackinaws on when it gets that cold."

Newt and Aaron and Julie scanned the bunks in search of three close together, mainly for her protection. They found them along the wall farthest from the stove. They were late arrivals and had to take what was left. They claimed them by piling their turkeys on the straw and tick mattresses. Julie's bunk was between Aaron's and Newt's.

"Blankets are over here." Mitchum walked the length of the floor to the opposite end where additional ticks and blankets, lanterns and tools were stored. The number of pikes and axes in that area would expand as the crews came in later for the night.

They each selected two of the thick wool blankets smelling slightly of must and the absorbed scent of pine wood. A rat scuttled away and slipped from sight down a hole in the floor where it cornered at the wall.

"Ah," Mitchum expelled a loud breath. "Need to patch that over, but I'll drop a morsel touched with arsenic down there to get the beastie. Put your blankets on the bunks and I'll show you the rest you need to know. I'm the chore boy for this camp. Keep the stoves going and the lanterns lit and ready. I tell you when to sleep, lights out, and when to wake up. Nine o'clock on work nights and ten on Saturday night. Got a fiddle player on the crew and one plays a hell of a mouth organ. Couple others do spoons and a washtub. Fiddle man can play a saw too. You'll hear it on Saturday night. I keep the place clean. Got a tub to wash clothes. Ain't often in the winter though. Too damn cold and they freeze solid. Have to thaw 'em out inside. Gotta do your long johns from time to time, which takes us to a most important and holy place."

He laughed as they followed him outside to a twelve foot long and six foot wide lean-to shanty set out at the edge of the compound. "Don't need to tell you what this place is for. You can smell it for yourselves."

Their senses were stung by the rising ammoniac odor of decomposition emanating from a deep trench over which stretched a long pole wide enough to sit on and another to lean back against to avoid falling in.

"I keep it supplied with toilet paper 'til we run out. After that, it's newsprint and straw from the barn."

Julie was immediately worried how she would be able to use the outhouse in privacy. She would have to plan her visits when only Newt and Aaron accompanied her to stand guard and warn her if someone was coming. To her misfortune, when the foreman learned that both Newt and Aaron were skilled in handling horses, he made them teamsters and they had to move out and bunk in the second cabin next to the barn.

Supper was an hour away and logging crews began to straggle in from the bush. The three friends waited outside and watched nine teamsters drive their draft horses, Percherons and Belgians, huffing and snorting, hooves chopping up clods of earth, to the barn to have their harnesses removed, be fed and rubbed down, and bedded for the night.

Other loggers carrying sharp axes, crosscut saws, canthooks, and the river drivers with their long pikes materialized out of the woods like a small army of medieval warriors wearing the loose slovenly gray clothing of European immigrants. Newt, Aaron, and Julie were pleased that they looked just like them.

"Hey, young fellows, movin' in, I see. Need someone to shine my boots." Laughing, Charlie Brandt removed his slouch cap exposing a shiny bald head and tossed it to Julie. She reacted quickly and managed to catch it. "Charlie Brandt, you can be my personal valet."

A few other men laughed. "You need a valet, fat man," called out Helmut Haas, a muscular German with sweeping long blonde mustaches. "You can't bend over to tie on your own boots without turnin' red as a cherry." Helmut's mischievous expression expanded into a wide grin that graced Julie as he trudged past. *"Parlez vous Francais,* boy? Charlie says he wants to be waited on by a French valet when he strikes it rich."

"What's a valet?" Julie asked, eliciting an explosion of laughter from the men crowding into the doorway.

"A rich man's servant," an anonymous voice trailed back to her from the group.

"You need to wipe his arse, throw out the chamber pot, and help 'im put on his clothes in the morning 'cause he's too damn lazy to do it hisself," someone shouted, bringing on another wave of laughter.

"Charlie'll bend over for ya so you can do the honor. Can't reach around there hisself no more." More muffled laughter came from within the building.

Julie was left holding Charlie Brandt's cap and didn't quite know what to do with it since he had gone inside. She didn't imagine he meant for her to keep it, since she was already wearing one of her own. They seemed like such a friendly lot she couldn't be certain. "What should I do with this?" she asked Newt.

"Give it back."

"Alone?"

Newt glared at her in disbelief. "Act like a man," he muttered with his head lowered so as not to be overheard by a few stragglers who smiled and waved at them. "And don't forget your name."

"I won't."

Feeling great trepidation, she pulled open the door and went inside with Newt and Aaron right behind her. They stood near the cast iron stove and observed and listened to the men storing their tools and crisscrossing the room to their bunks where they removed their Mackinaws and sat or lay back on their ticks while exchanging comments and humor about the days work. She noticed Charlie Brandt's heavyset frame descending onto his bed like a slowly falling tree.

"Go over to him," whispered Newt, giving her a sharp nudge.

She shuffled across the wooden floor in her oversized boots, drawing notice to her manner of walking. After her comment about the valet, she imagined they were now thinking she was slow and dull witted, which she hoped was for the good. Approaching Charlie's mountainous belly, she extended his cap.

"Sir, I already have a cap and won't need yours."

His bewhiskered face slowly turned toward her with a mixture of bemusement and scrutiny. "You had any schooling, boy?"

Julie shook her head. "My mother taught me to read and do some numbers."

"Did you really think I meant for you to keep my cap?"

She again shook her head. "That's why I'm returning it."

He studied her for several moments, then reached out and took the cap and rested it centrally on his stomach. He looked back at her and the narrow squint of his bushy gray brows lifted in concert with his grin. "Don't listen to them others. They are just havin' fun with ya as am I. No man here is another man's valet. We all pull our own weight. As you kin see," he patted his belly, "I'm carryin' a lot of it. You come here to be a logger and, by damn, we'll make you into a logger."

"Thank you, sir."

"You are graciously welcome. You are a different kind. We will take that into our consideration. I notice you call me sir. I like that. It's a sign of respect. No one other of these man jacks calls me sir. Of course, I have my own names for them, but they take 'em in good spirit. That's the point. What's your name, young fellow?"

"Joel Josephson."

"Well, Joel, you and me are friends. You call me Charlie."

"Thank you, Charlie."

"You could teach us all some manners. Your mother and father raised you to be a good boy, I see."

"They were both killed."

His sympathetic gaze forced her to turn aside.

"I am indeed sorry for you, Joel. When you come of age, you'll remember well your time at this camp."

She nodded.

"I'll ask the foreman to assign you to my crew."

She smiled.

"Good to see a smile. That's good."

She turned away and her self-conscious glance took in the other men watching her, some with amusement, others with expressions of doubt and disapproval.

"Don't want 'im on the handle end of an axe close by me," said a swarthy dark bearded logger pulling off his caulked boots. "Might let go. Don't want to be in his sightline."

"More 'n likely cut off his own foot," hooted another. "Shouldn't have a slow head in the camp. Danger to all of us."

Anger and embarrassment seared Julie. She felt the heat rise in her face which must have been obviously glowing red, or so she thought. Yet she could not say anything in retort. Her only recourse was to prove she was worth becoming an accepted and respected member of these men. Charlie Brandt would help her and Newt and Aaron, but the burden of proof lay upon her thin shoulders. Back on the farm, she had occasionally split kindling for mother's cook stove. But that was small pieces of soft wood, whittling twigs compared to the giant trees these men brought down.

She wanted to rail against them, but they would have laughed and ridiculed her away like dust into a corner. She wondered why they had centered their attention on her and made no mention of Newt and Aaron. But the boys appeared to be bigger and stronger than she. She guessed it was the loggers' false perception of her being dull-witted and slow and they probably feared she might let her work partner down.

Chapter 11

The Specter

Walking his stallion along the short main street of Brainerd, Luther noticed curious stares from conventionally dressed men and women who quickly averted their eyes and hurried on as he looked in their direction.

He had returned to track down the Josephson children. His plan was to induce a collective opinion and instill fear among the sparse population of Brainerd that would encourage speculation about the killing of Ingrid and Olaf Josephson.

Luther had grown up in a rural village in Germany and knew that people in small towns talked among themselves and reinforced common beliefs and opinions. He had sensed their suspicion by their reticent manner and avoidance during the two days and nights he had spent at the small Brainerd Hotel and Saloon after being confronted by Mrs. Peet. He had hoped the children might show up in town, but they had moved on and the Peets would not disclose where. He determined to force the issue in his own unique way.

The curved shoulder muscles under the stallion's glossy black hide drove the legs and hoofs with piston precision, chopping the dirt street and raising puffs of dust feathered by the long fetlocks. The thick tail switched and the broad rump sashayed to the animal's powerful

rhythm.

Luther rode up and down the main street three times to establish his presence and reinforce his image.

He stopped at the hotel, dismounted, and loosely wrapped the ends of the braided leather reins around the wooden hitching rail worn smooth by years of use. He walked slowly and deliberately up three steps to the boardwalk and paused. His right thumb nail ignited a match head to light a thin cigar. A trail of smoke arced from the extinguished match in its descent to the dirt. His breath released a grayish-white puff as he entered the hotel.

Rolf Amundsen, the proprietor, visibly stiffened at the sight of the man dressed in black coming through the door. Rolf was not normally superstitious, but Luther's distorted pocked face and penetrating blue eyes unnerved him, as though this alien rider had come out of nowhere and appeared to be a denizen of the underworld.

Ever since the killing of Ingrid and Olaf Josephson, the pastor at the Lutheran church in Brainerd had pronounced from the pulpit that the coming of this stranger into their lives was a sign of the Lord's displeasure.

"Olaf and Ingrid Josephson were not people of God. They did not come to church. They did not pray. They did not read and believe in the gospel. The Lord has punished them and now He is challenging us to cleanse our souls and our community. The appearance of this man is a sign. He is from the Devil. With prayer and devotion, we must cast him out from our midst."

Then, miraculously, Luther and his horse vanished. Hans Hoogman, the smithy at the livery stable, had arisen the next morning to discover the black stallion missing from its stall. He had rushed to the hotel, entered, and cautiously and quietly inquired of Rolf, "Did the bastard leave? His horse ain't at the barn."

"Come down here at the crack of dawn. Said he was goin'. Took some coffee is all."

Hans nodded his enthusiasm, then next went to the sheriff's office with his information. "He's gone!" he shouted to Anders Karlsson. "The damn killer's gone!"

As the news had spread throughout Brainerd, the pastor and his flock congratulated themselves for their devotion and gave thanks to God for his "Divine intervention." Now, one month later, the sudden reappearance of the evil left them fearful and confused as to what further they must do.

Wringing his hands in anguish and frustration, Pastor Abraham Hokansson paced the empty aisle of his chapel.

"The people of the town expect me, with the intervention of God, to protect them from such dark influences in their simple lives," he confided to his pious wife, Edwina, who pretended to hang on his every utterance even though she had heard them again and again over the ten years of their childless marriage. She had settled for the security and domination he provided her and accepted that obedience was her station. She had a roof over her head and food on the table. That would suffice.

Abraham was at a loss as to why his prayers had not been answered. Not believing in the reformed church, he was not accustomed to its reason and logic in explaining earthly manifestations. Why had the merciless killer returned to invade their lives? The pastor knew he must find an answer and it must come from God.

He delivered his emotionally charged Sunday sermons with a pugnacious red-faced vehemence that cowed his congregation and swept away all doubt that Divine inspiration came from the Word of God and that every word contained in the Bible was His Word.

"The Holy Scripture speaks through the prophets and is the Word of God and carries His full authority. Every doctrine of the

Bible is the teaching of God. Every single statement of the Bible demands your acceptance. Every promise of the Bible calls for your faith and trust in its fulfillment. Every command of the Bible is the directive of God Himself and demands your observance. The Bible tells you all that you need to gain salvation and live a Christian life."

After two such Sunday diatribes, Olaf and Ingrid Josephson and their children had stopped coming to the church. When Pastor Hokansson confronted them during one of their trips to town to purchase supplies, Olaf had explained that he and his family respectfully disagreed with the pastor's liturgical and theological position.

"We are realists," said Olaf. "We consider the existence or non-existence of a Higher Being, in whatever form or force that might be, through scientific and philosophical logic, not blind faith in a document written and interpreted by men."

"For such blasphemy, you will all surely burn in hell."

"We don't believe in hell, Pastor Hokansson. Hell is created by man, by what he does. There is nothing spiritual about it. There is no such physical place of eternal fire. That is just an artistic representation, a myth just like all religious myths."

"Nothing good will come of this. You will know the wrath of the Lord."

"Good day, Pastor. We have heard quite enough." Olaf turned away from the discomfited man's fuming simian face and followed his wife and children into the general store.

Rolf did not know what to expect as Luther approached the counter. Despite his threatening appearance, he had acted in a cordial manner toward him and his wife, Katrina, who cooked and served the meals, changed the beds, cleaned out slop buckets and provided general housekeeping. Their conversation had consisted of a minimal exchange of gruff pleasantries and ordering food and drink. Rolf hesitated and wiped his hands on the stained apron he wore when tending bar for guests and local patrons, regulars who came in for a whiskey or a beer. He felt vulnerable and defenseless against the imposing man. Luther looked and walked like a gunfighter. Rolf did not want to show disrespect by wearing the apron if Luther were going to sign the register as a guest, but neither did he want to encourage the man to stay by being overly receptive and polite. He touched the top of his head where his hairline receded to baldness and lowered his gaze. He decided he would not remove the apron.

"Will you be staying with us again, Mr. Baggot?"

"Yes, I'd like a room at the front where I can see the street." Luther's deep guttural voice and German accent underscored the importance of the view.

"You're the only guest we have, so you have your choice of rooms."

"I'll take the same as last time, if you remember."

Rolf nodded and gestured to the ink pen standing upright in its well. "I remember." *How could I forget, he thought.* "Will you be stayin' for more than one night?"

"I haven't decided. It depends on how things go."

Rolf trembled inwardly at the thought of what those "things" might be. Under other circumstances, he would inquire about the business of a guest in a friendly way, but did not dare pry into the affairs of a man like Luther Baggot.

"Wife's cookin' up a pot roast for dinner, if yer interested."

"I am. I recall she served a fine stew when I was here before."

"'Trina does have a way with food. I'm the proof." He patted his stomach and flashed a brief sheepish grin. Seeing that Luther was not responding, he turned quickly to retrieve the room key from one of several metal hooks on a wall board behind him. "Here you are, sir. I do prefer advance payment, if it ain't no trouble."

Luther reached into one of his saddlebags and brought out a roll of one-hundred dollar bills, peeled off three, and dropped them on the counter top. Rolf glanced up at his face. "That's too much. Room ain't but two dollar a night. That gives you a bath."

"This is to pay for your silence."

"My silence?"

"While I am here, the townspeople will see me. They do not need to hear about me from you. Do we have an understanding?"

Rolf tugged at his knobby nose and clutched his gray beard to still the shaking of his other hand. "We have an understanding."

"*Sehr gut.* I will take my horse now to the livery." Luther snatched up the key and started toward the door.

Rolf fingered the bills. "'Tis kind and generous of you, sir."

"Kindness and generosity are not in my nature," Luther called back. "No one should think I am kind and generous." He pushed open the door and stepped outside.

A great sigh bordering on a moan escaped Rolf. He noticed his robust wife standing at the kitchen entrance. "He came back," she worried a gray strand that had worked its way loose from her bonnet of thick hair that had once been the color of golden wheat.

"He came back."

"What you suppose he wants?"

"I guess we'll know soon enough. Look what he gave me." He held up the bills. "All this money. Doesn't want us to talk about 'im. So don't say nothin'."

"Not me. He's a scary sort."

"That he is. He's gonna want to eat yer pot roast tonight."

"You told him?"

Rolf nodded. "He says yer a fine cook."

"Long as it keeps his hand off his gun."

"I'm thinkin' maybe he sees us a little different than the rest. But a dog don't shit where he sleeps either."

"Time for dinner, Schwarz, and a warm stall." Luther patted the great horse on his thick neck, untied the reins from the hitching rail and looped them up to the horn of the black, hand-tooled leather saddle. Inserting his boot into the near stirrup, he mounted with a lithe swing of his right leg inches above the animal's hind quarters and settled his lean body into the deep cantled seat. A light touch of the rein cued the black into an easy striding walk in the direction of the stable. Luther softly hummed the melody from his favorite Viennese waltz, *The Blue Danube*.

Hans Hoogman stepped away from the open wide double doors to greet him. "Saw you ride into town, Mr. Baggot. Didn't know if you'd be stayin', but I got a stall ready for your black. Nice thick straw, clean timothy and alfalfa. You want me to grain 'im like before?"

"*Danke* for your hospitality, Hoogman." Luther dismounted. "Give him double grain. We have been a long time on the road from St. Cloud. He worked hard and deserves more."

Hoogman nodded. He still wore his leather apron. Being both a farrier and owner of the livery increased his business. "Want me to check his shoes?"

"*Ya, Das ist gut.* If he needs shoes, make them. I will pay you now." Luther handed him three one-hundred dollar bills from his bankroll. His horse should have equal to or better treatment than Luther's own.

Hoogman stuffed the bills into the pocket of his coveralls under the apron. His face, ruddy from hours of bending over a hot forge, cracked into a wrinkled smile exposing straight white teeth through the concealing bush of his brown beard. He watched Luther remove the saddle and take the shotgun and saddlebags, leaving the bedroll tied under the cantle.

"You at the hotel?"

"Ya."

"Need your black in the mornin'? It's Sunday, you know. Town's quiet. You can rest easy 'fore you move on."

Luther nodded and began walking up the street.

"When you want 'im?"

Luther called back over his shoulder, "In time for church."

Hoogman thought the answer to be a strange one. With a shrug, he led the massive stallion into the livery barn. The horse neighed at the smell of his kin and the sweet aroma of oats and hay.

His shotgun cradled across his lap, Luther sat alone in his room and watched the street where several men sporadically appeared in horse-drawn wagons or on foot to congregate in the saloon downstairs. He had taken an early meal, savoring Katrina Amundsen's pot roast, reminding him of goulash from the old country.

After a suitable time, allowing the patrons to drink their beer and whiskey and conjecture about his return, he rose from his chair.

The gathering of men in the saloon went silent at his appearance, slowly ascending the wooden staircase. The metallic ring of his left spur resounded like the warning of a belled cat stalking its prey. Without looking at the men, he sat at an empty table apart from them and signaled to Rolf for a bottle of whiskey. He poured and raised a glass to the curious gathering hunched against their tables and trying desperately not to stare at him. Eventually, intimidated and suppressed by the suffocating tension that descended over them, with a light scraping back of chairs, the regulars left the saloon and took their comments and conversation out onto the street suffused with the fading glow of dusk.

Even after ten years, the need for revenge burned in Luther's mind. He remembered gazing out at the rolling foothills of farm country through which the train was passing beginning a slow labored climb toward an alpine terrain. He glimpsed faraway vast dark-blue peaks and sensed the train was running parallel to the distant snow-encrusted crest. Their geographical proximity gave him a sense of where he was. He had traveled this same route before on trips to Vienna. He knew he was now near the Bohemian border. He had traveled south from Berlin through the towns of Lauchhammer, Meissen, and the city of Dresden and was headed for Prague.

Other passengers around him were waking up, stumbling down the aisle and waiting in line to use the commode, then going to breakfast in the dining car. As the doors opened and closed, the culinary smells of hot pastries, bacon, and kaffee drifted to him in aromatic snatches.

After twenty minutes, Luther looked toward the back of the car wondering what had happened to detain his partner. Unlike the scrawny build of the first man, as he lurched up from his seat, Luther boasted evenly distributed bulk and weight, which would make him a formidable opponent. He took little notice of the Frenchman wearing a clerical collar, but the Frenchman was clearly watching him. The scars and severe pock marks on the left side of his rugged face gave evidence that he was not a stranger to fighting.

He blundered through the rear door, looked about, then stepped back inside. Pushing on the commode door, he found it open and empty of any passengers. With great consternation, he lunged back through the rear door outside onto the vestibule and pondered whether his partner had continued on into the next car for some reason. His body suddenly tensed at the cold end of a pistol barrel pressed against the back of his neck.

"Do not turn around, Monsieur. Do as I say and you will live," the Frenchman's low menacing voice purred in his ear.

"What have you done to my partner?"

"The same thing you will do, Monsieur. He stepped off the train many kilometers ago."

"What! You threw him off a moving train!"

"Not at all, Monsieur. He leapt of his own volition. I assure you he is not harmed, perhaps momentarily lost."

"Let me assure you that if I leave this train, you will go with me."

The Frenchman cocked the pistol. "Then you will go as a dead man." He saw Luther's right hand sliding into his coat for his pistol. "Bring your gun out very slowly and throw it off the train. My bullet is only a split second from entering your brain."

"You will pay with your life for doing this." Luther cast his gun into the passing brush.

"Use the handrail to brace yourself on the steps. I will give you a few moments to select where you will jump. Be thankful we are not on a trestle. Your partner survived. You can do the same."

"You're a priest. How can you do this?"

"Without guilt."

"Then you're a charlatan."

"Non, Monsieur, Bismarck is a charlatan. We are not standing out here to discuss politics. It's time to jump."

"May you burn in hell!"

"That is not likely. I'm an agnostic. I don't believe in such a place."

The man extended his foot out into the rushing space below the bottom step.

"You hesitate," said the Frenchman. "If I have to push, you will be off balance and could break a leg upon landing. The best way is to tuck in your knees and roll and absorb the shock."

"So you have experience at this, a train robber. You have done this before."

"Many times. I give you to the count of three, Monsieur. Einz, Fie, Drei."

Luther leaped, his cape flowing upward and outward behind him like the massive wings of a large predatory bird. The Frenchman heard his loud curse as he struck the ground, then he was lost in the rapidly fading distance.

Ever since the incident on the train, Luther hated and despised religion and all things religious. He associated them with the Frenchman, who had been a false cleric. To Luther, all religions were false, fantasies for people to attempt to explain what they could not understand.

Luther lived on the regular large infusions of cash wired to him by Rudolf Palm from his villa in Florence, Italy. Palm's purpose had changed from finding and stopping social democrat leaders to protecting his financial interests from the return of the Wohlman brothers. Under the reign of Chancellor Otto von

Bismarck, Palm had forcibly taken over the company owned by the Wohlman family and embezzled millions of dollars to support his opulent life in Italy.

The change suited Luther, since his purpose was to one day find the Frenchman who had forced him to jump from a moving train. Luther and another detective had been assigned to track down and arrest the two brothers, Kurt and Matias Wohlman, as they fled from Germany and Austria. Luther fantasized how he would cause the Frenchman to die in a like manner, only under the iron wheels. If he could locate the Wohlman brothers, he knew the Frenchman would be near by. He suspected that when they came to America, they had changed their identity. The list was the key to finding them.

On Sunday morning, Luther rode to the church. He left his horse tied to a wooden cross in the neighboring graveyard where, with soft snuffling breath, the animal nibbled at the grass.

There were no laggards about the yard, only horses and wagons at hitching posts.   All in attendance had gone inside. Pastor Hokansson had begun braying his sermon heard clearly through open windows along the walls. His voice choked to an abrupt halt at the moment Luther, cradling his shotgun on one arm, entered the chapel. He remained standing, silhouetted in the open door.

People's heads turned to follow the Pastor's gaze and a universal gasp seized the congregation. Parents shielding their children rose from the benches and herded them to the side of their aisles. Their only escape was through the front door blocked by the specter of evil.

"You, sir!" the pastor shouted out. "You may not bring guns into the house of the Lord! You have no business here! You are not welcome here!"

"Is that why you call Christian charity, turning away a stranger?"

"We know who you are! You do not deserve our charity! What do you want from us? We have done nothing against you! Why are you here?"

"If you think about it, you will know why I am here."

"I do not play games with an agent of Satan."

"This is not a game. I am here for a purpose."

"What is your purpose?"

"You will come to know it."

"How? How can we know if you don't tell us?"

"Try praying to the Lord. Perhaps He will tell you."

"The Lord does not speak to us of the likes of you!"

A slow smile spread from his mouth until the facial scars prevented it from going further. "You call me an agent of Satan. Do you think your Lord does not speak to me?" Luther stepped back through the doorway onto the porch riser and disappeared from view.

Pastor Hokansson left his pulpit and strode down the main aisle. The skirt of his cassock whipped the nearest benches as he passed. He stopped at the door and looked out into the sunlight. He saw Luther mount his horse, glance once at him, then ride back into town.

The sheriff, Anders Karlsson, was the only man to follow him after crowding his wife to the wall with the other parishioners.

Abraham spoke without looking at him. "You are the law here, Anders. You must do something to stop him."

"I think that will be to give him the answer he's looking for."

Abraham turned his head sharply, taking in Anders' doleful face accentuated by long handlbar mustaches and blue eyes squinting as though continually looking into the sun. "Do you know?"

"I suspect I know. I saw what he did to their mother and father. I just don't have the proof. It had to be him. There's no one else who would kill them like that."

They watched the Peet family clamber quietly onto their wagon. Timothy wasted no time urging the team to carry them out of town at a brisk trot.

"If he must pursue the children, then it is the obligation of Timothy and June Peet to tell him where they've gone, before we fall victim to another act of evil," said Abraham.

Anders did not relish the task that had been thrust upon him. He respected the Peet family for the good-hearted homesteaders they were. They tended to keep to themselves and look out for their own, but supported the community at large. That afternoon, he rode out to the Peet farm. When they saw him coming up the lane to the house, they clustered on the front porch, as though expecting him.

"Tim, June." He touched his hat brim, then dismounted. Holding the reins, he spoke upwards to them from the ground. "Don't like what I been asked to do, but has to be done."

Timothy muttered to June, "I'll take care of it," and walked down the four wooden steps to stand side by side looking out to the fields with their backs toward the gathered family.

"Nobody holds you to blame."

Timothy nodded.

"What the man wants is a list. He believes the Josephson children have it, wherever they've gone."

Timothy again nodded.

"You know where they've gone?"

"North – lookin' for work in a loggin' camp."

"Lots of those up north."

"Lots of those."

"Could be he'd never find 'em."

"Could be."

"So I'll just tell 'im that's all we know," said Anders

"Don't want 'im to come out here lookin' for somethin' more."

"I'll tell 'im that's all we know."

"Thank you, Sheriff. Spare us from what others might think."

"We have to look out for each other."

"That we do."

"Thank you, Tim. You're a good man."

"Once you've had your say, best to stay clear of 'im."

Anders nodded. He looped the reins back to the saddle and remounted the bay. With a second touch to his hat brim in acknowledgement of Timothy's wife, he turned and put the horse into a lope back to the road.

"What did he say?" asked June.

"He'll tell 'im what he knows. That's all. The man'll go after 'em, but might never find 'em. Lots of lumber camps in the north."

"That there are."

Upon his return to town, Anders wasted no time and went to the hotel. He tied his horse at the rail and went inside. "Where's his room?" he asked Rolf.

"Top of the stairs."

"I'm goin' up."

"Don't draw on 'im."

Anders shook his head. "Just words."

Rolf watched him slowly climb the wooden stairs as though ascending a gallows.

Anders knocked at the door. Luther waited inside. He called out, "Enter!"

Anders slowly pushed open the door. The two dark holes of Luther's shotgun barrels stared at him. Luther was sitting in his chair. "What is it you want?"

"I'm here to speak for the townspeople."

"Have they prayed?"

"They have prayed."

"And what did the Lord tell them?"

"Timothy Peet said you went out to his farm the last time you came to Brainerd. He said you are looking for some kind of list."

"Do you know who has the list?"

"He was not certain, but he thinks the Josephson brother and sister might have taken it with them."

"And where did they go?"

"He didn't know and no one else in town knows."

"How unfortunate for the town."

"There are hundreds of logging camps in the northern woods. They could be at any one of them. We have no way of knowing."

"But I have ways of finding them."

"The people of this town are innocent. I ask that you do not bring them harm."

"No one is innocent. The pastor tells them that every Sunday. So they should not be surprised at what can happen."

"We have met your demand. We have told you what we know."

"And for that, I thank you."

Anders hesitated.

"Is there anything else?"

Anders slowly shook his head.

"Close the door as you leave. Remember, the shotgun will be aimed at your back."

Luther left his black stallion tied a block away and stalked along the line of trees and shrubs fencing the boundary of the church property and cemetery. Swaying in a fierce wind, the high bare branches of tall elms splintered the rising moon in the autumn sky sending down shards of pale light that enmeshed the church, vestry, and adjoining house in disparate, quivering shadows.

To his satisfaction, Luther noted that the buildings were constructed of wood. Had they been stone, he would have sent fire through the windows. He carried two containers of kerosene purchased that morning at the general store, one for the house and one for the church. The proprietor had sold the kerosene to him with great trepidation, but dared not refuse him. Luther's boots crunched on the gravel drive. He stepped off onto the lawn and paused to listen for a dog's bark. The silence urged him on.

As Luther encircled the house twice, pouring kerosene along the foundation, He envisioned the sleeping clergyman and his wife. How unsuspecting they were that he was sending them to hell.

The carriage horse nickered a low greeting as he entered the barn. He would spare the horse. He released him from its stall and drove him outside into the yard where it nibbled at the grass. Luther grabbed an armload of straw and returned to spread wisps intermingled with dry leaves over sections of the kerosene. He then prepared the church for immolation in the same manner and considered the barn.

Touching a lighted match to each line of fuel surrounding the two buildings, he waited for a few moments to watch the flames lick upwards into the painted wood soaked in linseed oil which added a catalyst to spread the fire in an explosive climb that simultaneously enveloped both structures. It struck him as oddly poetic that he was destroying the holy house of a man of the cloth. He thought of himself as the Devil's man, paying the pretentious pastor a visit.

Walking quickly away back down the street to his stallion, Luther did not hear the screams from within as the pastor and his wife, wearing nightshirts, raced out into the yard and gaped at the flames consuming their chapel.

"We will build a new church and a new home," proclaimed Abraham. "We will show God that we are worthy of his blessings. No man, woman, and child living here in Brainerd or from the surrounding farms may shun the church of the Lord again or we will cast them out just as we have cast out the evil that was visited upon us. We forgive Timothy and June Peet, for they have done their duty to send that specter of evil on his way."

The next day, Timothy took Beth by horse and wagon to the train station. She had convinced her mother and father that she must warn her brother and Newt and Julie Josephson that Luther Baggot was coming for them.

Chapter 12

The Bush

Julie's first lesson did not proceed well. It did not proceed at all. Beginning with the moment she lifted a heavy axe and could not raise it above her shoulder and bury the steel head into the trunk of a thick tree without it leaping free of her grasp, she was doomed to failure. She imagined the axe possessed an independent life of its own, much as an untrained wild horse and sensed that she was a novice it could dominate.

Her efforts elicited snorts of amusement from other men in the gang, but Charlie waved them to be quiet and to not ridicule her.

"He'll chop his foot a'fore he cuts any bark," said Bill Shelly, a tough lean axeman with a narrow scar that traversed his lined weathered face from the corner of his right eye to his lips. "This is what the slip of a blade can do," he pointed to the healed wound with the skin stretched taunt between the jagged cut and his nose on one side and his jaw on the other, which gave him a lopsided appearance. "The boy ain't big enough or strong enough for this, Charlie," he referred to the gang foreman.

"We'll find work for you, boy," he said with a kind gruffness as he took the axe from her frail grasp. "Lot to be done. If you ain't right for the bush, they can use you in camp. For now, you watch and learn. Next time, we'll pick a smaller axe. You can cut trails and peel bark. Don't take a lot of strength. I know that. You can be a chickadee. Grab that shovel and dig away the brush. If we don't clear trail, we can't move a load."

"Thank you, sir." Julie took the shovel he extended to her. "I'm sorry." Crew members who were chickadees dug the brush out to create trails to the trees and also shoveled aside horse dung. Not many wanted to work as a chickadee. Loggers and rollers and teamsters were the coveted positions on the gangs.

He nodded down at her. "A man can only do what he can do, lad. Time will tell." He turned back to the other four men and Julie's brother standing on the heavy wooden cross bench of the log sleigh. Newt had proven himself at once in handling a team. "Okay, move out!" called Charlie.

Newt whistled and shook the reins. Those on foot trudged after the sleigh and matched pair of dark bay Percheron geldings. Their breath smoked in the cold morning air. The steel surface of the wooden shoe runners screeched along the frosted trail as though it were snow instead of dirt. After about a mile, the trail ended, blocked by a dense stand of hemlock.

Helmut Haas was the chopper in Julie's gang. He selected a pine with a large diameter and circled it once to determine in which direction he would cause it to fall. Bill Shelly and the other two loggers, Arnold Scott and George Hardie, both just a few years older than Newt, chose other trees and started peeling and spudding the bark. With their axes, they ringed the trees at the base around the roots, then again four or five feet higher, split the bark and pulled off the butt sheet.

Julie watched Helmut do the same on his tree. Stacking the bark aside, he swung his gleaming honed axe five times biting into the base of the tree that jettisoned wood chips into the air like small tan projectiles taking flight. Within minutes, he had the tree notched and pointed in the direction it would fall. Bill Shelly and Arnold Scott moved into position with a large crosscut saw. A spit of red Chum tobacco streamed from a wad in Arnold's bulging right cheek as he fell into the rapid rhythm set by Bill. The ringing saw blade sent its vibrating hum out into the surrounding forest.

An explosive crack cut Julie's space as though lightning had struck and the tree began to lean and sway over the notch. As the saw passed through the base on its journey to the other side, the felled giant toppled forward with a crashing roar, ripping and tearing through the branches of its neighbors rending havoc and filling the air with a swirling dustcloud of cones and needles and shredded bark until its final thunderous blow against the earth echoed, fading away through the forest.

George Hardie immediately pushed his stout solid frame in among the dense foliage of the fallen tree and began limbing, cutting off the branches close to the knot at the trunk. When he had finished, he and Bill Shelly, who was the top loader, and Arnold Scott, placed spiked skids at an angle against the sleigh and rolled the log upward onto the sleigh using cant hooks to leverage it into location.

After the load reached a height of about four feet, Newt unhitched the team and led the horses around into position to pull the logs up onto the pile using a decking line. This was a chain attached to the log at one end and passed through a pulley lashed to a tree at the other. The tailing end of the chain was attached to a separate double tree of the harness so the strength of the horses could be used to pull the log up onto the next level of the load. The top loader worked the log into position using his cant hook.

Julie watched the gang repeat this routine twenty times until the men had a pyramid of massive logs lashed to the sleigh by chains using a looping pattern that caused the weight of the topmost logs to press down on the lower logs in the pile.

The crew needed a break by midmorning. They had been rousted awake an hour before dawn, by Mitchum Hardie, the choreboy. Newt hung canvas nosebags on the horses so they could have grain. One of the cookees, Myles Bennett, arrived right on time with a horse-drawn pung, a large box containing pots and pans and hot food. The foreman, Jack Moulton, called in three other gangs working nearby to take a meal with Julie's crew. They gathered around to receive large helpings of meat and beans and potatoes on metal plates, mugs of strong steaming black coffee that burned her mouth and caused her eyes to water. She watched the men slurp it down like they dipped a cold drink from the well. After the first time, she ducked her head so they wouldn't notice her tears. Bill Shelly teased her saying, "Either you gotta be crying 'cause the food tastes so bad or it tastes so good. Which one is it?"

Julie shook her head. "I'm not crying. The food's good. I'm not used to the coffee so hot."

"Ya hear that, Myles? Yer coffee's too damn hot for the kid. Makin' 'im cry real tears. Ya should be ashamed of yerself. Next time, blow on it afore ya serve the lad."

His comment raised a general round of guffaws that turned Julie's face red with embarrassment. The last thing she wanted was to have any attention called to her for a sign of weakness. She saw Newt give her a warning look from where he and Aaron were sitting on a nearby log together.

Aaron was a teamster on a neighboring gang. When they returned that night, he and Newt would be moving from the logger's camp to sleep in the teamster's camp and Julie would no longer have them close by to look out for her. Her biggest problem was timing her visits to the outside toilet so that her sex would not be detected. It helped to have Newt and Aaron with her to avoid suspicion, but also to stand guard and give her a warning if someone approached.

Another worry was spotting blood once a month. Newt supplied her with feed sacks to fashion a cloth tucked under her long johns between her legs. She had to go out in the woods and bury these as they became soiled. Because they were on the rough side and sometimes contained remnants of grain, they tended to chafe and cause a rash during her brief spells.

The days of hard work passed quickly and Julie was glad to climb bone weary into her bunk among the sweating sour stench of odorous men and their cacophony of snores. She was asleep before nine when Mitchum would come through to turn down the lanterns and shout that all talking must cease at nine o'clock. There was a round of final tobacco juice projectiled in the numerous spittoons near the bunks. A boot would come sailing through the air at anyone who continued to talk.

Working as a chickadee, Julie was constantly chopping and clearing brush and noticed the increasing strength and resiliency in her arms and legs and stomach. From time to time, she rode on top of the load with Newt as he moved the logs along the trail to a log dump at the top of a hill near the river, where they would be held until the spring flood.

Until then, only a few light snows had fallen. The first heavy winter storm caught the crew five miles from the camp. The cold gray dawn had been eclipsed by a steadily darkening sky and a rapid drop of the temperature to below freezing. The howl and rattle of the wind caused the horses to toss their heads and stamp the hard ground. They were anxious to return to the warmth and security of their barn.

"We'll head back after we dump this load," said Charlie.

The members of the gang followed along behind the sleigh to the site where Bill Shelly and Arnold Scott released the logs from their restraining chains onto the dump skid. Diminishing light and a skein of hard-driving snow slanting across the clearing slowed the work. By the time they were ready to move on, they couldn't see the road, but they followed the horses who knew the way. The animals pushed on with their large nodding heads thrust into the wind and white drift that clung to their manes and long eyelashes.

Their trek to the compound took an hour. The storm rendered it nearly invisible. Rather than going directly to the sleeping camp, Julie stayed with Newt and Aaron to help with their teams. They unhitched just outside of the barn and led them into the eight foot wide runway directly to their stalls. They quickly closed the large doors that swung open on forged steel hinges.

She helped remove the harnesses and hang them on wall hooks. Then she and the boys fed hay and grain to the accompaniment of rumbling knickers and trumpeting neighs. They rubbed the horse's coats dry with grain sacks and curried down the animals intently chomping and grinding their food.

As they were about to leave and cross the compound through the blizzard to the cookery, Roy Ludgate came stamping in, slapping the clinging snow from his mackinaw with his cap. His leather apron extended down the front of his legs to his boots.

"Beast of a storm," he said. "Ain't cuttin' logs tomorrow with a howler like this." He peered at them from behind his dense black beard and thick bushy brows that threatened to conceal his eyes. "Need to sharp shoe 'em tomorrow. Roads'll have ice." He turned away and walked back out into the storm.

Newt and Aaron and Julie linked arms to keep from being separated and lost in a drift to perish in frozen death. At that moment, she loved her brother and Aaron, their dear childhood friend more than anyone or anything else in her life. She was just grateful to be there with them. They did not see her look up at each of them and grin as they struggled their way toward the beckoning warm yellow light in the windows of the cookery.

They pushed and walked through the open door into a riot of heat from the stoves and noise and laugher from the men who were in a celebratory mood at the prospect of a party and sleeping extra hours the next morning because of the storm.

Julie licked away drool from the corners of her lips at the aroma of pork and potatoes and beans and cinnamon flavored apple pie that hung in the boisterous air. Six or seven bottles of whiskey had been produced from somewhere and were being sampled and passed from mouth to mouth up and down the long tables. Even the foreman, Jack Moulton, did not look askance or order a cessation of the festivities. Julie saw him tip a bottle that was thrust to him and drink at some length to the cheers and hosannas of the men.

She, Aaron, and Newt went over to the sinks to wash the grit from their hands. Grabbing plates, cups, and utensils, they passed along the serving line to receive large helpings of food and coffee, then managed to squirm in side by side on one of the benches. Within moments, a bottle of whiskey was thrust on the table before them. Aaron and Newt did not hesitate to take a swallow. Julie's lips touched the open rim with a tentative sip that caused her throat to burn and close up with a gagging cough.

She heard laughter, but no one made a point of ridiculing her. She noticed that somehow Aaron and Newt had managed to not have a similar violent reaction, but they were madly stuffing potatoes and gravy into their mouths to still the searing descent of the whiskey down their gullets.

Within moments, she experienced a rush of elation and raised a shout that brought curious looks at her from Aaron and Newt, followed by nods of approval. She did see Charlie Brandt laughing at her and nearly falling over backwards off the bench where he sat several places down on the other side of the table.

By the time the men finished eating, the musicians of the camp had brought their instruments and were tuning up at the center of the dining hall where everyone focused their attention with great expectation.

Through the haze of after supper pipe tobacco smoke wafting in somnolent gray layers into the rafters, she saw a logger making adjustments on his fiddle, another stroking a slightly curved vertically held cross-cut saw with a homemade bow, a third huffing and puffing a mouth organ, and a forth rattling sticks and spoons on a large upturned metal drum and a few small hollowed logs and pails.

Then Myles Bennett, the cookee, stepped forward and burst into song with an amazing tenor voice that silenced the chatter and caused everyone's eyes to rivet upon him. But within a minute, all the men were clapping and stomping and, for those who knew the words, joining in.

The shantyman's life is a worrisome one
Though some call it free from care.
It's the ringing of the axe from morning 'til night
In the middle of the forest fair.
While life in the shanties, bleak and cold
While wintry winds do blow
As soon as the morning star does appear
To the wild woods we must go.
All you jolly fellows, come listen to my song; It's all about the pinery boys and how they got along. They're the jolliest lot of

fellows, so merrily and fine. They will spend the pleasant winter months in cutting down the pine.

Some would leave their friends and homes, and others they love dear, And into the lonesome pine woods their pathway they do steer.Into the lonesome pine woods all winter to remain, 'waiting for the springtime to return again.

Springtime comes, oh, glad will be its day!. Some return to home and friends, while others go astray. The sawyers and the choppers, they lay their timber low. The swampers and the teamsters they haul it to and fro.

Next comes the loaders before the break of day. Load up your sleighs, five thousand feet to the river, haste away. Noon time rolls around, our foremen loudly screams, "Lay down your tools, me boys, and we'll haste to pork and beans." We arrive at the shanty, the splashing then begins, The banging of the water pails, the rattling of the tins. In the middle of the splashing, our cook for dinner does cry. We all arise and go, for we hate to lose our pie.

Dinner being over, we into our shanty go. We all fill up our pipes and smoke 'til everything looks blue. "It's time for the wood, me boys," our foreman he does say. We all gather up our hats and caps, to the woods we haste away.

We all go with a welcome heart and a well contented mind. For the winter winds blow cold among the waving pine. The ringing of saws and axes until the sun goes down. "Lay down your tools, me boys, for the shanties we are bound."

We arrive at the shanties with cold wet feet, Take off our overboots and packs, the supper we must eat. Supper being ready, we all arise and go For it ain't the style of lumberjack to lose his hash, you know. At three o'clock in the morning, our bold cook loudly shouts, "Roll out, roll out, you teamsters, it's time that you are out." The teamsters they get up in a fright and manful wail:"Where is my boots? Oh, where's my pack? My rubbers have gone astray."The other men they then get up, their packs they cannot find. And they lay it to the teamsters, and they curse them 'til they're blind.

Springtime comes, Oh, glad will be the day! Lay down your tools, me boys, and we'll haste to break away.The floating ice is over, and business now destroyed. And all the able-bodied men are wanted on the drive.

With jam-pikes and peaveys those able men do go Up all those wild and dreary streams to risk their lives you know.On cold and frosty mornings they shiver with the cold, So much ice upon their jam-pikes, they scarcely them can hold.

Now whenever you hear these verses, believe them to be true. For if you doubt one word of them, just ask Jack Moulton's crew.

During the song, the men roared and stomped and clapped their approval. Two jumped up and danced a jig together.

Julie could not believe she was hearing such a beautiful voice coming out of that tall thin man. A combination of the pungeant food, whiskey, the heat of the cookery and the camaraderie of the crowd responding to the music caused a surge of joy and well-being to well up inside her.

Her original sense of trepidation melted away like wax on a burning candle. Although she wasn't a riverman yet, she could at least count herself among them. They were courageous, steadfast, and noble.

At the conclusion of the song, the cookery erupted into a deafening roar of "bravo bravo" and applause that rivaled the howling wind of the storm smashing against the stout log walls. They were all safe and secure against the outside world and Julie felt this impression even more so as the whiskey bottle passed for a second and a third time around the table and she tipped it to her lips that had gone numb with the fire that passed into her belly.

A few years later in her life, she would learn how to imbibe wine in a lady-like manner. For now, there were no ladies and she was not a lady. She was Joel Josephson, the logger, who resided within the company of loggers and rivermen.

Without hesitation, Myles transitioned into a mournful ballad with such melancholy supported by the player of the mouth harp and the fiddle that tears sprang from Julie's eyes and washed unabashedly down her reddened cheeks. It helped her to notice that others were crying or trying to hide their sudden expression of emotion.

Events began to blur after that. She remembered Charlie confiding in her that she reminded him of his daughter, Maude. "Don't take offense," he said. "I know you ain't no girl, but you're a loving and timid sole like my Maudie. She was slow like you, but she didn't live past ten years afore the Lord took her. Died of pneumonia. She meant more to me than my own life. I would have traded mine for her to still be alive. The both of you would have been good friends."

Mitchum did not call out the time for bed that night. He, too, was taking sustenance and joy from one of the bottles being passed up and down the length of the cookery.

Julie saw Aaron's eyes rolling in his head, as he and Newt staggered out into the storm to flounder their way to the teamster's sleeping camp. At their departure, it suddenly dawned on Julie that she was left to her own resources as to managing the trek to the outdoor toilet. She could not make the journey with someone other than Newt and Aaron and risk the discovery of her sex, and she certainly could not venture across the compound on her own.

The storm would devour her. She decided the next best possibility was to slip unnoticed out the back door of the cookery.

In a drunken stupor, divesting herself of her mackinaw, shucking her suspenders, dropping her trousers, and unbuttoning and shoving down her long underwear became an ordeal.

She sensed that someone must have been watching her, for she did not remember waking. Had she remained asleep in the snow, she would have never awakened and would have been discovered half naked and frozen the next morning. She suspected Charlie had brought her in and trundled her fully clothed onto her bunk. If he noticed Julie was not the boy she pretended to be, he never divulged that knowledge to her or any other.

Thereafter, when she was working with the crew clearing roads out in the bush, Julie noticed he took special care to ensure she did not endanger herself, but he continued to address her in a rough manner as one of the men.

Chapter 13

Ice

The storm did not abate until late the following day. Upon awakening, Julie's head pounded from her indiscretion of the night before and her stomach churned with a need for food to neutralize her queasiness. She stuffed herself with flapjacks smothered in butter and molasses and a side of salt pork washed down with cups of hot coffee before venturing to the stables across the piling drifts burying the compound. The frigid air seared her nostrils and she quickly wrapped her wool muffler across her face, leaving only her eyes exposed and tearing from the cold.

She found Newt and Aaron lining up their team horses in the shop, accessible to the barn, to be shod with caulked shoes by Roy Ludgate, the blacksmith. He had the front leg of one of Newt's big Percherons bent at the knee and tucked into the leather apron across his lap. Julie watched him clinch off the old shoe, then, using a curved hoof pick, dig out the dirt lining the V-shaped frog forming the center part of the sole. He rasped the hoof smooth with a long heavy file raising a slight odor of decay by reducing the material of the hoof's edge to a fine powder. The horse nibbled at Roy's back with its rubbery soft black lips.

He moved to the forge behind him and, using a pair of long metal tongs, extracted a newly formed caulked shoe from the flickering glowing charcoal kicking up a small shower of sparks. His hammer struck ringing blows shaping the metal that he thrust with a scalding sizzle and explosion of steam into a vat of cold water to temper it.

After checking its shape against the bottom of the animal's hoof, he thrust the shoe back into the forge, then shaped it for a perfect fit. From an array of long horse shoe nails clenched in his teeth, he affixed the shoe by driving each nail from the bottom up through the outer shell of the hoof and clipped off the exposed tips.

He gently lowered the leg and fresh shod hoof to the ground, patted the animal on its thick muscular neck, and moved to the other side to work on the next hoof. He hummed a recurring tune in a deep basso voice which reassured and calmed the horse. After two hours, all four horses had been newly shod under his adept hands.

As the temperature dropped, within a week, Julie noticed the river transformed to stillness sealed over with sheet ice. She knew it wasn't thick enough to walk on, because she could see surging air bubbles through the gray frozen structure. Once the ice was sufficiently a few feet thick, the teamsters could drive their horses and sleighs up and down the river as a road. The caulks on the horses would prevent them from slipping and losing their footing.

Two weeks later, Jack Moulton, the foreman, ordered test holes to be cut along two miles near the shore and at the center of the river. He granted his approval and the teams and crews cadged and skidded more logs from the woods and made more trips given the quick access from the main camp. The harvest grew so rapidly that additional log dumps were established at spaced intervals along steep areas of the bank where the logs could be skidded downhill into the river after the spring thaw.

Using her smaller ax and shovel, Julie continued to clear side brush and work with Charlie Brandt's gang. There was less road work to be done, since a tank crew would go out the night before and plough the snow aside on the trails. Then they would fill a sealed wooden tank from barrels of water taken through a hole blasted in the river ice. The tank was mounted on a sleigh and dispensed water as it was pulled by a team of horses. The water instantly froze to create a roadway of slick ice over which the sleigh runners could pass with ease.

Julie's task was to fill small holes gouged out by the sleigh runners after they passed. Five or six of the chickadees were shoveling snow and giping or fixing holes as fast as they appeared. Once grooves were established by repeated passing along the road, the sleighs would stay in the tracks.

Charlie told her that after two or three big freezes, the ice was solid enough to hold the weight of a team and a sleigh filled with logs. Because they could use the frozen river as a road, Jack Moulton ordered the crews to increase the size and height of the loads by adding logs that towered two and three times above the teams.

Julie was standing on top of one of the banks at a log dump that overlooked where an iced side road connected to the new track. She saw Aaron drive his team off the trail out onto the ice and head down the center of the frozen river channel. Then she heard the heart-rending crack before the ice began to break.

Aaron instantly tried to guide the team away from the area and back toward the bank, but it was too late. The ice separated in massive chunks and the load sank into the frigid water, the weight pulling the horses down. They thrashed and neighed, their eyes rolling in terror at the weight and the freezing current pulling them under.

Aaron leaped from the top of the descending log pile which managed to momentarily stay afloat. He staggered and crawled across the surface of the ice in an attempt to reach the animals. He slipped into the water with them and frantically pulled at the fastenings of their harness to free them, but they were going under too fast and the loaded sleigh was closing over them from behind. Aaron would be crushed and forced downward with the animals unless he escaped from the widening hole.

Helmut Haas and Bill Shelly came shouting and running along the bank. They scrambled out onto the ice, dropped to their stomachs and crawled as close as they could to the jagged edge of the opening, and extended their canthooks to within Aaron's reach. He managed to grasp one and Bill pulled back and dragged him to where he could reach over the edge of the hole where Helmut dragged him out by his arms.

Aaron gasped and cried in anguish as he watched his beloved team disappear in a churning froth of bubbles, smothered by the tonnage of logs pressing them down to their death.

Julie ran along the bank and crossed the river upstream to meet Aaron and his rescuers on the opposite side. Aaron shook in spasms from his near drowning. Ice formed on his clothing and his skin took on a blue pallor. He was unable to move.

"Got to get him to a fire and out of these clothes," said Bill.

Being the larger of the two men, Helmut hefted Aaron over his shoulder and, with Bill supporting him, struggled up the bank to higher ground.

"Build a fire!" he shouted to the gathering bystanders. "Build it now!"

Julie followed closely and gathered up cut branches wherever she could find them in the snow to contribute to the life-saving fire. She saw a logger swing his ax to bring down a small pine and chop out the punk for kindling.

Helmut and Bill peeled off Aaron's boots and clothes and wrapped him in their own mackinaws as the makings of the fire came together and the sticks and small logs converted to flames. Helmut rubbed and massaged Aaron's limbs to restore his circulation. His teeth chattered uncontrollably as he struggled to breathe.

Other loggers built up the snapping crackling blaze until Helmut and Bill were holding him in a crouch before a roaring bonfire. Until she tasted salt tears at the corners of her lips, Julie didn't realize she was crying.

Once the crews returned to camp that evening, Jack Moulton announced that the frozen river would no longer be used as a route to haul logs.

Aaron remained bedridden for three days and was looked after by Myles Bennett, who fed him hot soups and herbal concoctions whose ingredients were known only to himself. Newt and Julie visited their dear friend each night until the call by Mitchum Hardie for lights out.

Aaron's greatest concern and sorrow were for the team of percherons he had lost. He felt responsible for their drowning, even though Jack Moulton explained it was beyond anyone to know the ice would give way. He said he regretted ordering that the crews build larger and heavier loads and blamed himself for the incident.

When he recovered, Aaron did not have a team to drive, so he asked if he could work as an assistant with Roy Ludgate, the blacksmith. Roy was more than glad to have him.

"Climb on up!" Newt shouted from the driver's rig to his sister.

A cloud bank had blocked the brief warmth of the afternoon sun, causing a rapid drop in the temperature to below freezing. Her legs, arms, and back stiff and sore, Julie welcomed the ride back to the camp at the end of the day. She did not realize Beth was there until Aaron rushed from the blacksmith shop at hearing the horses and sleigh pull up to the barn. Before they even stepped down off the runners, he said, "My sister's here. She came with Mitchum on the supply wagon from the railroad."

"What did you tell her?" Julie asked, looking fearfully around.

"She knows not to call you by your real name."

"Why did she come? How did she know where to find us?"

"I wrote a letter home."

"You didn't tell us."

"No, I'm sorry. I just wanted to let mother and father know we're okay. But there's something else."

"What is that?"

"The Pinkerton man, Luther Baggot, came back with others and searched the house for that list."

"Did she say they found it?"

"No, she hid it in the barn. She brought it with her. She said Baggot is trying to find us."

Julie stared at him. "Where is Beth now?"

"The cookery."

"She won't be able to stay here. What could she do?"

"I talked with Jack Moulton. He said she can work in the cookery and she can wash clothes for the men."

"Where will she sleep? She can't bunk in the same camp with the men."

"They're giving her the spare room in the cookery. There's a bunk in there. I got her a tick and blankets."

"You're sure she won't forget to call me Joel?"

"She knows."

"Okay, I'll help put up the horses and then we have to go over there together." Julie paused. "Didn't she think that man might follow her?"

"She said she did not see him when she went to the station."

"We have to be careful," cautioned Newt. "Just because we don't see him doesn't mean he won't find us. He could just ask the railroad agent back at Brainerd."

"The station agent doesn't know," said Julie. "We could have gone anywhere. Why does he want those names so much he would come after us?"

Their boots crunched along one of several intersecting pathways that had been trodden down across the compound and gave evidence of common foot traffic patterns. Elsewhere, the snow formed a series of waist-high walls.

As they entered the cookery, Julie saw Beth ladling potatoes and beans next to large hunks of moose venison on a line of tin plates. What struck her first was the usual rush to the tables was not happening. The line stalled at the serving counter as the loggers stared in wonderment at this young, beautiful, dark-haired female apparition that aroused instant emotions of hearth and home and creature comfort of another kind.

Beth did not seem to be put off in the least by their rough appearance, but smiled graciously and nodded at their guttural comments of gratitude and the occasional expression of, "And ain't you a beauty," And "Hope you come to stay awhile."

"Shouldn't be here," growled another beard. "Camp ain't no place for a woman."

"She's a welcome change from lookin' at yer ugly mug."

Laughter passed up and down the line, as the men huddled along.

"Where you come from, Ma'am?" asked another. "Maybe you know my sister."

"I came here to work," Julie heard her say, "and to be with my friends."

"I'll sure as hell be yer friend. I'll be yer friend for life."

"That'd be a short life for you," called out another. "She wants a real man."

"You wanna take this outside?"

"No, I wanna eat dinner. Besides, she's spoken for."

"Well, that's the worst news I've heard all day. You got a feller, have ya, little lady?"

Beth flashed a wide grin.

"Anyone we know?"

She shook her head and her hair shimmered in the lantern light. "No, I'm sorry."

"Don't be sorry for him, miss. He don't deserve anyone near a beauty as you."

The anonymous comment elicited more laughter and the poor man moved on.

Then Julie was standing in front of her across the serving bench.

"Jul - Joel, Joel Josephson, how nice to see you again, and my good friend, Newt. Aaron told me you were working out in the bush, but I would see you at dinner time."

Julie nodded and conjured up a weak grin.

"We missed you," said Newt.

"Looks like a lot of us miss the likes of her," said Charlie nudging in behind them. "Jack told me there was a woman in camp. Didn't believe it 'til I saw you with my own eyes. It's true and I think we'll all be the better for having a womanly influence in our midst."

"There you go," shouted someone from the long table. "Charlie'll treat you like his long lost daughter. Won't leave any time for the rest of us. He'll talk yer ears off."

"Well, it's good that I'm an eager listener," said Beth. "You must be Charlie."

"That I am," said Charlie. "So Joel and his brother, Newt, here are your friends, I gather; and I heard Aaron's your brother."

"That's so," said Beth. "We lived on the neighboring farm back in Brainerd."

Julie stole a glance at Charlie at his reference to Newt and her being brothers. She wondered if he was telling her in a subtle way he knew she was Newt's sister and was keeping that secret or if he hadn't really discovered her identity the night she collapsed unconscious in the storm.

Newt and Julie did not have the opportunity to talk privately with Beth until later that evening after she finished washing dishes and pots and pans with Myles Bennett, who soon discovered the scullery maid was an appreciative audience and a songbird, as she came to be known a few years later. They heard them harmonizing when they returned to visit with her over cups of hot steaming black tea.

"Did your mother and father let you go or did you have to sneak away in the night?" Julie asked.

"No, after that Luther Baggot and his men forced their way into the house, they smashed and tore open chests and cupboards, but they couldn't find what they were searching for. Baggot went away for a while. Then he came back alone. The whole town was afraid of him. The sheriff came to our house and talked with my father. He said we were up north at a logging camp. It got Baggot to leave town. But he burned down the church before he left.

Mother and father let me come here to warn you and give you the list."

"Where are you keeping it?"

"A pocket inside my dress."

"I didn't recognize any of the names," said Julie, "Mother and father never talked about those people. I think they didn't want us to know."

"Mother thought Baggot would kill someone if he didn't find the list. He didn't believe we didn't know about it, because you and Newt had run off."

"We're stuck here for the winter. We don't have anywhere else to go."

"You should be okay for a while," said Newt. "He doesn't know what logging camp. There are lots of 'em all the way into Canada. We can't go anywhere until spring thaw," said Newt. "At the end of the river drive, we'll decide what to do."

"But what if this Baggot finds us here?" asked Aaron.

"We'll do what we have to," said Newt. "We have friends to help us."

They looked at each other in glum silence and sipped their tea.

After two weeks had gone by, Julie noticed that Beth was giving her curious looks, which she took as a sign they needed to talk. Such an opportunity did not present itself, since Julie lived, worked, and ate when others crowded around her. Beth's schedule in the cookery fully occupied her with preparing and serving meals and gave them no time for pleasantries. Julie trekked into the bush with the crew before dawn and returned after dark. The hours were filled with work and did not allow for deviation from their routines.

One hasty moment occurred because of a delay at the barn so Roy Ludgate could treat a leg wound on one of the horses who had overstepped and caught a front heel with the protruding caulk of a back shoe. The cut had festered overnight and Roy was applying a poultice of his own special medicines.

Beth come out of the cookery carrying a metal pot of slops for the swine pen and Julie hurried over a snow path to join her. "I'll help you with that."

"Thank you, but I have to ask you a serious question, Julie."

"Don't ever call me that," she coughed harshly under her breath and checked quickly to see if anyone was within hearing distance. "Don't even think of me as who I was."

"It isn't just your name. You're acting strange with everybody, not only me."

"They think I'm dull, that something happened to me in my head. So I pretend to be slow."

"I guess that explains it."

"At least you don't have to pretend. You don't have to remember a different name. And the men know to give you privacy at the toilet. I can only go there at odd times when no one else is around."

"Well, we have some time now. You may not have noticed, but Myles Bennett is sweet on me."

"Everybody has noticed. He doesn't try to hide the fact, singing songs to you all the time."

"Did you know he used to sing in operas in big cities like New York and Chicago?"

"No, but I figured he didn't get that voice calling hogs."

"He said with my natural voice and professional training, I could go on the stage."

"Who knows but you have to get through the winter here first."

"Myles would have to take me to the city and help me along in my career. He says he knows people who have influence."

"Right now, your influence is in this slop bucket and those pigs are a hungry audience."

They lifted the heavy pot up and over the top log of the low fence and the garbage it contained sluiced into the wooden trough to the delighted squeals and grunts of the swine.

"You don't have to be unfriendly," pouted Beth.

"Sorry, didn't mean to tip your apple cart."

"Are you mocking me? And after all I've done for you."

"I'm not. I hate to admit this, but I envy you. You can just be yourself, be who you are and it's acceptable."

"Well, there are some who object to my being in the camp."

"Do you know what would happen if they found out I'm a girl?"

"I know. I'll go along with it."

Julie hurried away on one path to the stable and Beth retraced her steps to the cookery.

Chapter 14

The Drive

The slow steady drip of melting icicles hanging like jagged stalagtites from the edge of cabin roofs signaled the beginning of the spring thaw. A warm afternoon sun tempered the chill in the air and the bubbling ripple of running water preceded its appearance along the shores of the dormant river. Julie, Newt, and Aaron saw three enormous flocks of Canadian geese spread across the blue-gray sky in winged formation migrating from the south to their breeding grounds in Ontario. Their navigational honks to each other establishing their position confirmed that the change of season was upon the land.

Within a few days, the river came out of hibernation. The ice shattered with staccato cracks and explosions and jagged upheavals as the water churned southward in the opposite direction of the geese.

Jack Moulton, the foreman, read these signs as a time to prepare for the river drive, the fifty mile journey of the logs down the Frazier River to the McClatchie lumber mill on Lake Wannatchee.

"Timing is important," Charlie explained to Newt and Aaron and Julie. "We have to move the logs off the dumps and out of the side creeks and ponds onto the river at the height of the flood. If we're too slow, the water 'ill run off and leave the logs behind."

During the summer months before the three friends had arrived at the logging camp, some of the crew had constructed log saving dams across creeks and streams that would back up the water during the spring thaw. The dams would be opened to use the powerful thrust of the contained volume to start the logs down a chute and float them to the main river channel.

All around them, the rivermen were taking their pike poles, iron tipped peavies, and boom chains to the blacksmith to be overhauled and repaired.

Aaron, Newt, and Julie were not river drivers. Since his fall through the ice, Aaron did not want to get close to the water, let alone travel on its surging rapids. Newt, on the other hand, decided to give it a try under the tutelage of Helmut Hass and Bill Shelly, both expert rivermen with years of experience. In watching Newt's early lessons before the drive began, Julie could see the work was fraught with danger and death.

Aaron would be driving a team pulling the cookery wagon, containing a stove and pots and pans and stocks of food that would be needed to feed the men. Julie was assigned to assist with any tasks where she might be needed on the banks as they trekked along the logging road that paralleled the river. Beth would travel with the cookery wagon and help with the preparation and serving of two hearty meals each day for the drivers. Most of the clean up was relegated to her, as well, although Myles Bennett never failed to assist her.

Julie was watching from the bank at the top of the first saving dam that spanned a side creek a mile upstream from the camp. The water had backed up to form a small narrow lake extending along the banks denuded of trees that had become the logs now floating in a solid island formation contained by boom logs chained together around the perimeter. Wearing caulked boots, six drivers walked about on them, pushing at one or another log to better position them before the sluice was opened at the center of the dam.

What Julie witnessed was Newt's initiation into the brotherhood of rivermen. Bill Shelly and Helmut Hass first demonstrated, then gave him directions on how to move about on the logs using his pike pole as a balancing device.

Knife sharp caulks protruded from the soles of a new pair of driving boots purchased at Walter's general store near the train stop. Having been a driver himself, Walter knew how to cobble boots with caulks that did not bend as the wearer clambered over logs and rocks in the river. Newt had selected knee high leather that laced up the side like those worn by Helmut and Bill. That style kept their lower legs and feet dry except when they had to wade in to a jam and dislodge a tangle of logs that had stacked up against the shore or on exposed rocks at midstream.

Newt also wore wide tan suspenders, a long sleeve wool shirt, and a brimmed hat to shade his face like the other drivers.

Bill Shelly told Julie that Newt demonstrated a natural skill riding the logs. He had shown Newt how to remount if he fell off, by using his pike pole to lever himself aboard. Getting and often staying wet in the frigid water was an expected part of the job.

A few days earlier, the drivers had to dislodge the logs piled forty and fifty feet high at the dry dumps at various locations along the bank. It required that they locate the key log that was holding the stack in position and dislodge it so the high dense wall would collapse and roll downhill to the stream in a thunderous avalanche. Whoever loosened the key log risked being crushed by tons of massive timber if he didn't escape to the side. Newt was told to be extra careful around the logs and that some drivers had been killed in such a manner.

The flotilla of logs were contained by a boom of additional logs linked by heavy chains around the perimeter. The boom controlled the logs in a compacted space much as a herd of cattle tightly fenced to prevent them from independently drifting aside. Drivers at both sides of the spillway positioned the individual logs to be pulled onto the sluice by the powerful suction of the sudden current. The logs catapulted through the opening as though shot from a large cannon. Other drivers waited at the base of the dam to thrust the freed logs on their way out onto the river where they bobbed and careened crashing into thousands of others at the beginning of their long torturous journey south.

As the final logs passed through the spillway, Newt followed Bill and Helmut down to the main channel. Julie watched them each leap aboard a passing timber as though catching a ride on a whale. Standing tall, they rode the huge logs like toboggans on the swift current that, within moments, swept them downstream and out of sight.

Six other loggers and the foreman, Jack Moulton, clambered into two canoes and a square-bowed punt to bring up the rear of the drive.

Aaron and Julie returned to the main camp. They joined Myles Bennett and Beth at the cookery where they and Thomas LePier, the bull cook, were loading food and supplies onto the wagon that would follow the rivermen on their drive and provide hot meals over the next two weeks at sites along the way.

Myles and Thomas sat up on the front seat with Aaron, who was driving the team. Julie and Beth sat in the back of the tarpaulin covered wagon bed where they watched the rutted logging road, a glistening ribbon of mud from the melt, slowly recede behind as it curved and wended its way through the forest.

The road paralleled the river so they were never far from the rushing rattle and hum and splash of rapids.

From time to time, they stopped at a high promontory lookout that gave them a view of the ten drivers traversing back and forth across the span of rapidly moving logs that snaked along like a long dark train whose beginning and end could not be seen. She waved at Newt, but he did not see her. She did not expect him to divert his attention from concentrating on the moving carpet of wet wood and bark on which he rode.

She recalled him the week before taking her aside and warning her that her hair was growing too long. "You need to have it cut off," he said. "You're starting to really look like a girl."

"Get some scissors from the cookery," she harped at him, "and you cut it for me. I can't do it myself."

"What about asking Beth?"

"No, that would draw too much attention to me. The men would make jokes. Mitchum Hardee is the chore boy. He's the one who cuts hair in the camp."

"Maybe you should ask him."

"I will."

"If you want to blend in."

"I already blend in. I just don't want to blend out. Beth forgets and calls me Julie sometimes."

That night after dinner, Mitchum Hardie trimmed Julie's hair short again so she conformed to the preference of all the loggers.

Patches of snow blanketed the ground and the temperature at night dropped below freezing. Myles selected clearings along the way that were open to the sun whenever he could and always had a high fire burning for the drivers as they came wet and freezing off the river. The drivers ate four meals a day, starting before dawn, which meant Julie, now assigned to be a cookie, Beth, and

Myles had to be up and preparing breakfast by lantern and firelight, two meal breaks at mid-morning and mid-afternoon, and dinner after dark.

Beth and Julie engaged in aimless conversation covered by the churning squeak of the wagon wheels and sucking chop of the horses' hooves in the mud.

"Do you know, a girl could be attracted to a boy like you."

"Stop it, Beth."

"You're taking this all too seriously. We won't be living in a logging camp forever."

Julie's head swiveled toward her with a sharp glance. "What is that supposed to mean? For now, we can only go down this river."

They wrapped large bandanas across their faces as protection from the swarms of black flies and mosquitoes that rose in threatening dark clouds from the swamps as they passed and the insects detected the proximity of flesh and blood. The girls had the appearance of desperadoes.

At each night camp, Myles used pine pitch to create smudge pots in buckets which he placed in the tents to ward off the vicious insect attacks. Some of the drivers who slept out on the ground, cocooned themselves fully clothed inside layers of blankets as a shield against the penetrating insects. Within a few days, everybody in the camp exhibited raised lumps and red welts on areas of their bodies that had been exposed, even temporarily when they made a personal foray into the bush.

Instant adoration and fame had been ascribed to Beth for her ability to bake sugar cookies and nut and raisin pies. When the drivers came in off the river for meals, they were never disappointed at her midday snacks and desserts that followed the standard fare of fried pork, potatoes and beans, and large chunks of warm bread. Breakfasts were much the same, but with the addition of hot porridge covered with black strap molasses and cheese. The men following in the punt and canoes would catch pickerel and pike along the way, a welcome variation to the general larder.

Julie was tasked with gathering firewood for the cooking stove and transporting buckets of fresh water from the river for washing and drinking, as well as gutting and cleaning hundreds of fish on flat rocks at the river's edge.

Thomas LaPier made a heavy use of lard, which a few drivers would eat in its congealed state like a pudding with the captured flavor of pork and onions.

The aroma of their preparations swirled in the wood smoke from the stove and campfires filling the forest air and occasionally attracting the curiosity of bears. A warning blast above their heads from Thomas LaPier's shotgun sent them running. The fires and human noise in the camp kept most wildlife away, with the exception of chipmunks and squirrels, of which several ended up in Thomas's stewpot.

When the drivers didn't come in at mid-afternoon, Julie knew that something had gone wrong upriver. Conyer Rapids was the most dangerous stretch, called the widow-maker by the men who had made this run many times over the years and survived. An hour later, a lone driver appeared, maneuvering toward the shore using his pike pole as a rudder to push off the bottom until he was in the shallows and could leap onto the bank.

"What is it?" asked Myles. "What has happened?"

"There's a jam about three hundred yards back. Pile up on rocks at the center of the water. Someone's gonna die goin' out there to break it."

Without a word, Julie set off running along the trail in the direction of the rapids. Wild birds screeched and screamed in the branches of the encroaching trees and weighed on her mind as a foreboding message. *Don't go out there. Don't go out there.* The words pounded in her head in cadence to her boots thudding the ground. She was breathing heavily as she topped a rise overlooking Conyer Rapids.

A latticework of giant logs jutted askew into the air at the center of the river stopped by a blockade of large boulders. Although some logs broke free at either side of the jam along the nearly vertical cliffs and swirled away downstream, the majority had backed up in a swath of timbers from one side of the river to the other. In most sections, the force of the water erupted up between the crevices and washed over them making the footing extremely dangerous.

To Julie's relief, she saw Newt standing in a cluster of other drivers far upstream on the stalled floor of logs. Immediately below, Helmut Haas and Bill Shelly were making their precarious way to the center of the jam. They carried dynamite charges with which they intended to blow up and dislodge the jam.

She watched them place the explosives in locations sheltered from the spume. Then, together, they uncoiled the fuse as they worked their way back toward the group on the gravel bank to get as safe and as far as possible from the impending blast. Helmut knelt over to shield the match he struck with his thumbnail and touched to the end of the fuse that whipped and snapped like a snake across the surface of the logs until it disappeared into the jamb setting off a roaring conflagration of smoke and flames that reverberated from the cliff walls. The concussion threw Julie off her feet and flattened the men watching from the shore.

She crawled forward and looked over the edge. The entire mass of logs surged like a dark soup poured from a giant cauldron with small two-legged figures leaping and running back and forth jabbing and thrusting with their pikes to keep their difficult charges aligned.

It took the drivers two more days to complete the run to Lake Wanatchee. There they established another boom around the thousands of logs now adrift over the lake. A small barge called an alligator driven by a side paddlewheel hooked up at the head of the boom and dragged the logs slowly and inevitably toward the mill where they would be transformed into lumber. The drivers had an easy time of it just riding the logs across the lake.

Aaron had to drive the horses and wagon around the perimeter of the lake to reach the saw mill and hotel on the far side. For Julie, the two wooden buildings represented a return to civilization after ten months of living at a logging camp and working in the bush.

The hotel tower rose like a beckoning Victorian obelisk to the men with a craving thirst and the need to divest themselves of the stress of their dangerous work and long arduous journey on the slippery backs of moving logs in fast water.

As they plodded along the trail around the lake, Myles reminded them that they would all stop to receive their wages from Mr. McClatchie before they continued to the hotel where a hot bath, clean bed, and strong whisky awaited them. He did go on to explain that they should not expect too much in the way of amenities.

The hotel was really more of a halfway house for drunken loggers who had squandered their earnings in the saloon on the first floor. The rough rooms slept fifty or sixty men who, barely sober, staggered over to the mill after a week of drinking and fighting. Since he owned the hotel, McClatchie knew that the money he paid out in wages to the loggers would eventually find its way back to him. Therefore, he did not shy from paying his men well.

Aaron pulled the team to a halt at the entrance to the mill. "Let's go get our due," said Myles. They followed him up the weatherworn steps and into the mill office.

Gowan McClatchie's face reminded Julie of a giant barn owl wearing a black three piece suit. The breath emitted from his nostrils caused his long gray and white whiskers blanketing his chest to undulate like the soft down of a feather's underwings.

"There was a man here inquiring about the four of you," his Scottish brogue rolled over them.

"Did he give his name?" asked Newt.

"He's a Pinkerton agent".

"Did he give his name?"

"Not at first. And I didn't give out that I employed you, which was a true response, because I didn't know until Jack Moulton told me this morning that you had joined his camp last September."

"Does that mean you're not going to pay us?" asked Aaron.

"I always pay my crews, to the man. Moulton advised me as to your wages. You've earned 'em."

"But what about this man?" Newt pressed for information. "What did he look like?"

"Dressed in a black suit. Rode a big black stallion. I asked him what it was you'd done, what he wanted with you. He said he was on a search commissioned by your mother and father to find you."

"He's lying," Julie blurted out. "He's just outright lying. He killed our mother and father. I know he did."

"Didn't mention nothing about a killing," said McClatchie.

"Where is he now?" asked Newt.

"Over at the hotel. Been here since yesterday."

"We have to go," said Newt, turning away toward the door. Julie, Beth, and Aaron followed instinctively.

"You in such a hurry to leave you don't want your money?" McClatchie lifted a stack of bills from his desktop. "I'd be glad to keep it, but it goes against my nature."

They stumbled back to his desk. "We want to get paid," said Newt. "We worked hard for it."

"I'm sure you did or Jack Moulton wouldn't have come in here to vouch for you." He handed the wad of money to Newt. "That's for you."

They each stepped forward by name and received their wages.

Earning money for the first time in her life was a bizarre experience for Julie. To be paid for doing work had never really preoccupied her thoughts until that moment. The four of them had traveled north for the sole reason to escape the pursuit of Luther Baggot. To their chagrin, as they left the mill office, he was the first person they saw.

He rode toward them astride his black stallion from the direction of the hotel. He saw them clambering down the wooden steps of the mill entrance and knew instantly who they were. He spurred his horse into a gallop across the half mile of open ground along the lake shore that separated the hotel from the mill.

"Run!" Newt shouted. "Run! It's him!"

They leaped down the remaining steps to the hard ground and around to the other side of the mill. Momentarily hidden from his sight, they cast wildly about without any idea how to escape him.

"What are we going to do?" Beth gasped. "How can we get away?"

"He has us trapped, if we stay here," said Aaron.

"The canoes," Julie said, noticing the two that had followed the drive downriver. They had been beached a short distance from where the logs entered the flume to be cut into lumber by the spinning circular saw inside the mill.

They pushed off from the bank as they scrambled into the canoes, Aaron and Beth in one, and Newt and Julie in the other. Within moments, they were adrift and thrust their paddles with deep desperate pulls against the dark water. Their only thought was to escape. They had no direction and no plan as to where they were going and what they would do next.

Julie's quick glance over her shoulder caught sight of Luther Baggot and his horse racing along the lake shore. Guiding from the stern, Newt and Aaron cut the canoes away at a sharp angle toward the river that would lead them south over one hundred miles to Saint Paul.

Chapter 15

Providence

The slide of the canoe and the repetitious dip and pull of the paddles lulled Julie's thoughts to drift in a dreamlike submersion with clouds and sparkling sunlight reflected in the clear water as the trees and banks of the upper Mississippi River slipped past.

A family of settlers along the way had given the travelers enough food for six days, blankets, matches, an axe, fish hooks and line and a few cooking tools. Aaron and Newt supplemented their main diet of biscuits, beans, and wild berries with bass and catfish.

Not knowing where Luther Baggot might be pursuing them overland, they did not linger at any one campsite, kept their fires small, and committed their energy to reaching the nearest city, St. Cloud, a growing frontier settlement fifty miles upriver from St. Paul. Newt and Julie knew of St. Cloud because of the trips their father had made from the farm when he was alive. It was also the source of the many books and pamphlets stored in the large trunk where she and Beth had discovered the list of names.

Flatboats with masts and sails, packets, keelboats, and a stern wheeler shooting black smoke from its tall stacks congested the approach to the narrow wedge of waterfront docks that had not yet been constructed to keep pace with commerce coming from the west and south.

They angled sharply out of the main current far enough upstream to avoid the river traffic and put in to the bank where they could pull the two canoes ashore and hide them in the brush.

Leaving the smell of decaying fish, rotting vegetation and river mud behind, they discovered a path that brought them to a dirt road leading into town.

As they traversed the boardwalk, they peered into storefront windows at common goods and wares that had not been seen in Brainerd. They could not even identify or name some of the modern objects on display.

A few horse-drawn carriages and freight wagons hauling baled and barreled goods from the docks passed them coming and going. A train whistle sounded from the depot just beyond the congregation of businesses at the small urban center of two and three story wooden and brick buildings that lined a short section of boardwalk. At the crack of a whip, a fast trotter kicking up clots of dirt breezed by pulling its cigar smoking owner on a sulky. A businessman posting on his high-stepping Saddlebred tipped his hat to two well-coiffed ladies wearing pink and green *la belle epoque* dresses with leg of mutton sleeves, sweeping flower decorated hats, and carrying parasols.

"Look at those dresses," commented Beth. "That's what I want."

"What are we going to find here?" asked Newt. "It's at least two more days on the river to St. Paul."

"I want one night in a hotel, a hot bath, good food, and to sleep in clean linens," said Beth.

"That could cost some," quipped Aaron.

"We've earned enough," said Beth. "The price of a room in St. Cloud can't be nearly what we will find in St. Paul, which is an advanced city."

"What do you mean by that?" asked Aaron.

"From what I've read, St. Paul is a center of commerce and people have private telephones and phonographs and drive electric motor cars. The article I read said that cities in America are benefiting from advancements in science."

"What about the people in the country?" Aaron bristled. "Why doesn't science do something for us? What is science? I never heard of it before."

"I can't explain exactly, since I really don't know what makes science."

Aaron shrugged. "What good is it to us then?"

"Some good will come of it for people in the country."

"The wheat threshers have motors," said Newt. "Maybe that's because of science."

Beth nodded. "I can't explain the connection." She suddenly stopped and stared at a brown brick two story building across the street from where we stood. "Wait. Wait. Look over there! Look!"

"What are we looking at?" Julie asked. "It's just another building."

"No, no it isn't. Look at the name in the window."

They stared at the dull red letters on a wooden sign over the entrance.

"I see it," said Julie.

"It's a German name – Bauman, Ent."

"What is Ent?" asked Aaron.

"It stands for Enterprises," said Beth. "Bauman Enterprises. It's the name of a company."

"What difference does it make to us?" asked Newt.

"Bauman is one of the names in the list. I remember it. Bauman. Bauman."

"So what are we going to do?"

"Find out who that is," said Beth.

"Are we just going to walk in there and ask?" Julie acceded to Beth's pretense at worldly experience. At the time, she knew nothing of science and advanced cities and *la belle epoch* attire. She was a rustic. A woman of the woods, she thought of herself as a riverman. Even though she didn't drive the logs down the river, she believed in her brother and the other men who actually did that work and loved and respected them for their ethics and honor, daring, and strength of character.

"No, we can't do that," said Beth. "Just look at us. We are a sight."

Their grimey besmirched faces, stringy, oily, filthy hair, and sagging dirty clothes ripe with the odor of their unwashed bodies suddenly became a concern. Anybody they encountered in the Bauman Enterprises Company would think they were mendicants. They would cast them out.

"We all need to bath and clean clothes before we go calling on Mister Bauman," Beth pointed a preemptory finger at a brown brick hotel three stories tall a short distance further down the dirt street. "There."

Shaking his shaggy dark head like a diminutive bear, Aaron fell in step with Newt and they followed their inspirational leader to the hotel.

Julie dozed off while soaking in the large brass bathing tub in the room that she and Beth shared. As she slipped under the steaming water and frothing bubbles, Beth pulled her up choking and coughing to the surface.

"I need to sleep more than I need to be clean," Julie sputtered.

"Not in there. After all the lakes and rivers on which you've traveled, to drown in a tub would be an insufferable irony."

Blinking drops from her eyes, she stared up at Beth. "Where did you learn words like that? Did you make them up? Do you know what they mean?"

"I'm a few years older than you and I've read more books."

"You sound like my mother."

"She had a great influence on me. I'm grateful to her."

Julie nearly broke into tears at Beth's praise of her mother.

"We need to take our opportunities where we find them," said Beth gently.

Julie nodded and accepted the towel extended to her.

"How did you happen to find me?"

Matias Bauman was graced with brown hair that fell in soft waves down his neck and gently touched the tops of his shoulders snug in a doeskin gray suit. Stroking his mustache, he brought his exquisitely shaped face close to the group, intimately inspecting them as though they were strange forest creatures. He nodded his head as he studied them and kept repeating "hm – hm" seeming to agree with himself about some silent inner argument.

He had soft brown eyes that occasionally glowered with emotion when a topic provoked him. At such moments, his thick dark brows twitched in a comic manner that caused Julie to want to smile. She liked him instantly.

From Beth's moon-eyed expression, Julie was certain she had immediately fallen in love with this tall slender gentleman.

"Your mother and father were two of my dearest friends. Did they ever mention my name?" Matias spoke with a slight German accent.

"No," Julie said. "Beth recognized your name from a list."

"A list? What is the nature of this list?"

"It was among the documents and records they had," Beth explained. "Julie and I found it in a storage trunk."

"Did you bring the list with you?"

"We didn't carry it with us," Julie interjected before Beth could speak. She gave Julie a quick curious glance, but did not contradict her statement. She didn't understand the reason for the lie, but she would find out.

"When I learned they had been killed, I tried to find you. The settlers at the neighboring farm, your parents, Beth and Aaron, were suspicious of me and would not tell me where you'd gone. They claimed not to know. I think they suspected me of being an agent for the Government."

"A Pinkerton?" Julie asked.

"A Pinkerton, perhaps. They are predominantly hired by the Government and by companies to protect their financial interests."

"Why our mother and father?" asked Newt. "What did they have to do with anything that the Government or a company would want them dead?"

"We know they were killed by a Pinkerton man," said Julie. "He's been following us."

"A Pinkerton agent is following you?"

"He wants the list," said Beth. "Even after Julie and Newt and Aaron were gone, he came back to our farm with other men in search of it."

"I don't know anything about your list, but later we can discuss it. I don't know why a Pinkerton detective would be involved." Matias leaned back in his chair and remained silent and thoughtful before he spoke. "Do you know what free thinkers are? Did your mother and father ever use those words?"

"Yes, "said Newt. "They raised us to be independent and not be slaves to anybody."

"That's a good way to describe it. What your mother and father were involved in is very complex, which is why I went in search of you. It is important that we become well acquainted for me to explain and you to understand what this is about. I want all four of you to come and live with me at my home in Chicago. I'll introduce you as my nieces and nephews from the prairies."

"Don't you live here in St. Cloud?" Julie asked.

"I have businesses in a number of cities. Your lives are going to be quite different from this time forward, starting with buying you new clothes. I imagine you're wanting something new. I am vastly interested in hearing about your working in a logging camp."

"We apologize for the odor and our appearance," said Beth.

"No need for an apology. I'm delighted that you have shown up at my door. I've wondered how I might ever find you and, at last, here you are. Shall we call it providence?" He grinned broadly showing rows of even white teeth.

"So," said Matias rising from his desk, "the order of the day is to get all of you properly attired."

Beth skittered about his office like an unsuspecting butterfly alighting on a hot stove. "Does this mean I can have a *le belle epoche* dress?"

"You can have as many as may suit your fancy." Matias gallantly reached for her extended hand and planted a light kiss on her delicate fingers.

"If I am living in a dream, please don't wake me," she chirruped.

Julie turned away with an expression of disgust shared by Aaron and Newt at Beth's affected manner.

"It's a dream, all right," said Aaron. "Time to wake up."

"Do you mock me?" Beth stared at him in a posture she must have thought was an insulted coquette. "Matias," she placed a hand lightly but firmly on his arm, "I do believe my brother is mocking me."

Matias winked at Aaron. "Propriet – best not to mock your sister."

Aaron's brow furrowed. He had not the slightest idea as to Matias's inference, nor did the rest of them.

For the remainder of the day, they were occupied with being sized and fitted at a tailor's shop and waited endlessly for the garments to be sewn so that they could step out onto the boardwalk. Julie was astonished to see the transition of Newt and Aaron from ruffians to presentable young gentlemen wearing vested three piece suits, polished shoes, and sporting derby hats.

They were equally overwhelmed by the appearance of Beth and Julie in floor length *la belle epoche* dresses that swept the ground and grand wide-brimmed hats sprouting an arrangement of flowers. Julie had a difficult time wearing laced up heeled boots and trying not to stagger and stumble, but Beth took to such fashion like a duck to water.

For Julie it was a sense of relief that she could allow her hair to grow again and to walk and talk like a girl.

They dined well that evening at Matias' home, modest by his standards, including a cook, maid, and servant, he maintained when he traveled to St. Cloud from Chicago. They had never witnessed such modern conveniences as a water closet and a telephone that could be used to call anywhere else where there was a reciprocal device in the country. They knew only of the telegraph office in Brainerd.

Once again, Beth and Julie shared a canopied bed, as did Newt and Aaron, but in such a luxurious setting. It was not nearly the luxury they would experience during the next few years. Matias had a purpose that would take them on a journey into an America they never knew existed.

Chapter 16

Gateway

Their journey began with the long ride from St. Cloud to St. Paul in Matias Bauman's oak and leather coach pulled by a magnificent team of four black horses whose rich coats and polished harness glistened in the sun. Now that the four travelers had come under the care and tutelage of this mysterious man, Julie felt that they had entered a fantasy world, much like mother had read to them when they were children, populated with barons, fiefdoms, princes and princesses, ogres, and a host of peasantry across the land.

As the coach swayed and rolled forward on its iron clad wheels, Julie listened through a slightly opened window to the rapid hammer beat of the trotting horses at the front and recognized the scent of emerging lilacs on the incipient breeze as they passed budding woodlands and green fields.

She noticed that Matias Bauman tried to avoid appearing obtrusive in glancing at them from time to time, but he was genuinely drawn to them and seemed to enjoy their innocence.

By Aaron's very nature, Matias found him the easiest to engage in humor and poking fun. Julie believed he saw potentially his equal in Newt's heroic and admirable demeanor. He unabashedly flirted with Beth whose quick blush signaled that she relished his attention.

Julie could detect that he was uncertain about her. She was reticent and withdrawn, unwilling to reveal much of her emotions on the chance she might expose some weakness or sensitivity that could be exploited. In addition, her thoughts frequently wandered from the reality at hand and her mind would drift off into some other world of her own imagining.

It was some time later in their relationship that she realized he recognized this characteristic of her behavior, which determined her usefulness to his, as yet, unspoken mission.

Beth's comment had been right that St. Paul was an advanced city. As they passed along the streets, she observed more buildings and congregations of people going about their business of commerce on a larger scale than they had previously known in Brainerd and witnessed in St. Cloud.

When they reached St. Paul, they merged with a hub of commerce, the confluence of the railroad and the port on the Mississippi River where numerous steam ships nosed up to its docks. Matias provided them his observations of the sights and sounds and their significance to a growing industrial economy.

As they prepared for departure at the station, the white-jacketed Negro porter, called George, had carried their baggage on ahead of them to their private berths at the middle of the car. Both a sofa and an upper berth converted to beds with spring mattresses at night. Julie was surprised to discover she had a private toilet, although a shower was farther down the hall. The berth also had a porter call, a reading lamp and a fold down writing desk. Julie felt like they were riding in a hotel on wheels.

The sweating monstrous black steel engine that towed them released explosive clouds of billowing steam that swept up and over the station platform at their departure, erasing the final frantic gestures of waving well-wishers to their recently boarded kin with a long blast of its hoarse bellowing whistle.

They settled back into the upholstered comfort of the seats in the lounge. The journey would be two days by train with various stops in cities and towns along the way. Beth proclaimed in her exulting fashion, "I could grow accustomed to this manner of travel."

They had complete freedom of movement and their choice of seating on sofas and chairs reminiscent of a gilded home in the city. Deep plush carpeting covered the floor. Highly polished brass light fixtures cast their illumination over mahogany tables and fine panel woodwork. Along the aisle in the neighboring dining car were two rows of tables where gourmet meals were served by Negro waiters.

Only people who had a great deal of money rode in the Pullman. Julie felt somewhat out of her element at the apparent vestige of wealth of the other passengers. The men and women were elegantly dressed and did not invite social interaction. Although he made a few restless trips to the lounge for cocktails and meals, Matias seemed to shun and not engage other passengers in conversation. Julie and her brother and the Peets rode silently together and enjoyed the view of the passing woodlands and fields through their own spacious window.

Julie observed Beth sitting across from her. Her disparaging remark that they were leaving "the wilds of Minnesota", as Beth described the origin of their lives in the soil and wheat fields and rural culture, to move to the "advanced metropolis of Chicago" bothered Julie. She valued her origin. Beth was fixated on the idea that all large cities were somehow advanced. Julie grew increasingly agitated and aggravated by her comments.

She did notice how Beth frequently glanced at her reflection in windows and surreptitiously practiced what she considered mannered facial expressions to what purpose Julie did not comprehend. She seemed intent on appearing to belong to the moneyed class without possessing any money.

Julie was not impressed by the manifestations of wealth and privilege into which they had been plunged and she struggled against the perception that the train they traveled was taking them deeper into the urban unknown.

In retrospect, her thoughts were in disarray at what was happening to them. Matias, as he encouraged the children to call him, had not revealed any details regarding his intentions, but Julie sensed they were being drawn into a world of events for which they were not prepared to cope. Despite his claim to support them and to encourage them to champion his cause, of which they were not clear, since he had not yet explained it, a sense of raw discomfort gnawed at Julie's innards as though a tiny parasitic creature had hatched and was feeding on her. Looking at her brother and their two friends, she felt they had been duped in some way, whereas she, in her clear-headed fashion, had not. Although the youngest and most suspicious, Julie assumed the role of guardian.

After Matias inquired a second time about the list, her suspicions of him deepened.

"If you have no further use for it, why don't I hold it in safe keeping? When we arrive in Chicago, I'll make an inquiry about the man who has been pursuing you, Luther Baggot."

"As I already told you, we did not bring the list with us."

A flicker of amusement passed across his eyes. "I understand your wariness, and I'll just have to convince you that I am the person you can most trust in this world."

He gave Beth a significant glance and Julie knew at once that she had told him. That she had not consulted her about the matter and ignored her, making a dangerous decision infuriated Julie. She silently vowed to never trust her best friend again.

"I felt we needed to tell him," Beth said quietly, unable to look directly at Julie, but rather out the window at a flowering spring meadow.

"Which is why I have not pressed the matter," Matias offered diplomatically, "not without your mutual consent."

"Then she did not give you the list."

"No, Beth exercised discretion in the matter, because she respects you and your brother."

For a moment, Julie felt instantly ashamed at her former thought of Beth, but cast the emotion aside at Matias's next comment. "However, she offered the list for safekeeping out of concern for your protection. Luther Baggot is still trying to find you. I advised Beth we must include you both in the matter."

Julie understood at once Beth's motive in offering the list was to curry favor with Matias, because she was so enamored of him.

"How did you come to know our mother and father?" Julie asked.

"It is an unusual and intriguing story," he said. "Our beginnings are similar. Although we were born in Germany, my brother, Kurt, and I had to flee the country to avoid arrest and execution by the Chancellor, Otto Von Bismarck. Even though he was in Prussia's privileged class, our father was active in and supported the socialist movement. He had a profound influence on me and my brother. We joined the social democratic party. My father was arrested. Bismarck's secret police tortured him and he died in prison.

The memories of his escape were as sharp as though they had happened yesterday. In coming to America, he had changed his name from Heinrich Wohlman to Matias Bauman to conceal his identity.

Heinrich wondered who the man was who seemed to be a priest, but perhaps wasn't. "Don't let my collar mislead you," the French accented words hung in Heinrich's mind. Jean Guenoc he said his name was and he knew Gustav and obviously his brother, Kurt, and he knew of their father in prison. Jean's strange sudden appearance and rendering orders had catalyzed Heinrich into an action for which he did not feel prepared. But the urgency of his situation was unmistakable. Their lives had been sabotaged by Bismarck and his secret police. He and his brother must escape.

He turned down Olinstrasse, a narrow side street barely illuminated by dim lantern and candlelight cast out through dirt encrusted windows onto the cobblestones. There were no numbers. The shops and apartments were known only by the names of the residents within. He stopped at one of them and knocked on the door. It was answered by a middle-aged Yiddish woman wearing a headscarf and peasant dress. Heinrich murmured a quick greeting and asked for admittance to speak with his friend.

As she left the Ringstrasse, Sophie Rose was surprised and alarmed to be met by Heinrich's friend, David Jettel, a young musician who played the clarinet at Yiddish weddings and had ambitions to one day play in an orchestra.

"What is it? What has happened to him?"

"Nothing, Sophie. Don't be alarmed. He sent me to meet you and bring you to him. It's merely a change of plans. He can tell you."

David took her arm and led her through the dim back streets of Vienna to where he lived with his parents.

As they came through the front door of the little shop on Olinstrasse, Sophie ignored the squalor and went directly into Heinrich's open arms. " Don't say anything else. Just explain."

"Thank you, David," Heinrich first acknowledged the young man for his help. "You are a true friend." Then, in a voice filled with tension, he spoke to Sophie. "I'm going to meet my brother, Kurt, he just arrived from Berlin. He has been traveling to escape Bismarck's secret police. They arrested my father and now they're after Kurt and me. I could not meet you at the Ringstrasse tonight, because I had to evade the police. I received a telegraph from home. My father has been arrested and put in prison. He is too old to endure torture and will likely die. In his letter, Gustav said the baton has been passed to my brother and me. We will travel on the Danube south, then overland to the Adriatic."

"I'll go with you," said Sophie without a moment's hesitation.

"I'm not asking you to come with me, dear Sophie, not like this. My brother and I are going to America."

"Are you saying goodbye then? We'll never see each other again?" She reflected on their brief romance.

"Unless you want to join me at a later time."

"I have nothing to keep me in Vienna. How would I ever find you?"

"Through my friends, I have people who can get a message to you."

"No, I'll go with you now."

"You're a famous person. You'll be recognized. I don't want to endanger you."

"I'll not hold you back and I am going with you. I don't have to remain hidden, which will be to your advantage. Where will I meet you and your brother?"

"On the waterfront at the main dock at sunrise. There's a steamship."

"Where will you stay tonight?"

"Near the river."

"At sunrise then." She kissed him fully on the lips, then turned with a rush of her skirts.

"David will go with you." Kurt gestured to his friend. *"Make sure she gets home safely."*

David nodded with a sad smile. Heinrich had always felt somewhat sorry for the young man with his dark sprung curls and mild expression. He was not in the least aggressive or assertive, qualities he needed to advance himself in the music world of Vienna. "I'm sad to see you go. Maybe someday, I can come to America."

"Maybe someday."

"My mother and two sisters escaped to Switzerland," said Matias.

"Despite my efforts to locate them, I have never seen nor heard from them again. I don't know now if they are alive or dead and I have not been able to learn what became of them. That was seven years ago. If they survived, my sisters would perhaps be wives and mothers with beautiful children, since they were beautiful, and decent husbands who treated them well. That is how I imagine they are. Imagination is my constant companion. So I use it to envision a new order of life in this country.

"With the assistance of the Morgan Bank here in America, it took my father ten years to secretly move his money out of

Germany. It is my brother's and my inheritance of his wealth that has allowed us to establish and grow our business here in this country.

"My father was discovered or, more precisely, revealed to the *Reichstag* by a trusted assistant who had ambitions to be recognized and favored by Bismarck. Such a fool. But fools do find their place in this world. Because of his position in the business of German enterprise, he became an informer working for the Director of the Secret Police, Rudolf Palm. Palm took ownership of our company until Bismarck was removed by Kaiser Wilhelm II. I'm going to find Rudolf Palm and take back our company.

"Does he know you're trying to find him?"

"I hope not, but I'm sure he suspects. I want him to be unprepared and surprised when I do. It's possible he might have changed his name."

"If he's still in Germany and you live here, how can you find him?" asked Aaron..

"I have my own network of spies and informers, members of the party. They know that Palm no longer lives in Germany."

"Are your spies a part of your enterprises?" asked Newt.

"My enterprises are legitimate businesses. I don't engage in the practice of political intrigue with one exception – to further the cause of the oppressed. I'm following in the footsteps of my father. At the time of his prosperity, the majority of his appointees in the *Bundesrat* allowed him to block changes to the constitution and defeat any amendment he wanted. He did his best to work with the Government. The *Reichstag*, the second house of the legislative branch, were members elected by popular vote. The *Bundesrat* and the king held power over the *Reichstag*, so it would not be able to pass any liberal democratic laws. The only thing that kept the *Bundesrat* and Prussia from having complete control was the fear that if they were forced to constantly use their veto, the people of the working class would revolt and overthrow the monarchy. Bismarck did not want to risk a revolution.

"He ruled Germany with an iron hand. He appointed conservatives to the bureaucracy, the army, and put them in control of the education system to ensure that free thinking was eliminated. Those educators were, in fact, bureaucratic censors. The German Constitutional order after 1871 was not directed by the will of the people. Bismarck made sure he could take back anything that he had allowed. He put unified Germany under Prussian control. Bismarck hated Socialism. He banned the printing of Socialist ideas and Socialist meetings.

"Fortunately, but too late for my father, the next king, William II of Prussia, removed Bismarck as chancellor and shifted more power over to the Socialists. I believe that was when Rudolf Palm embezzled millions from our company and left Germany.

"But how did you come to know our father?"

"Your father and mother were leaders of the social democrats in Sweden. I met Olaf and Ingrid when we were organizing the *sozialdemokrat*. We shared common interests and beliefs and became good friends. When I came to America, your father and mother and I maintained our correspondence. We met in St. Cloud to support the party among immigrants working in the mines of the Mesabi Range in Minnesota. We shared a plan that, if something happened to them, you and your brother would come to live with me. Think of me as your Godfather. When we arrive in Chicago, I'll look in to the identity of the man who is hunting you, Luther Baggot."

III

The Revolutionist

Chapter 17

Pygmalion

They turned onto a street lined with huge mansions, domestic fortresses of families Julie came to term The Royals. Not only did they exist in Chicago, but in exclusive sections of other major cities.

All the rooms of the Bauman mansion were paneled in highly varnished mahogany and hung with *auborgine* dyed damask drapes. Oil portraits of well-known German political figures, and a few Julie assumed to be his relations adorned the long echoing hallways illuminated by electric lamps rather than flickering candles or gas globes.

She saw there was nothing humble about the dwellings of wealthy tycoons, not only from without, but from within. Matias owned paintings purchased through dealers in New York and Paris and amassed collections of recognizable great art as a sign they were successful entrepreneurs who wanted to demonstrate their "cultural refinement." The display of European sculptures and paintings was a public symbol of wealth and high culture.

Like Romanesque fortresses, several stone mansions were built on a promontory overlooking Lake Michigan. They boasted a half-thousand square feet of interior living space and 40 to 50 rooms, 15 bathrooms, and numerous fireplaces.

Upon entering the Bauman mansion, Julie left the group and roamed through the largest rooms on the first floor which housed a collection of enormous landscapes and sculptures. She passed through open French doors into a reception, music, drawing, and dining room.

She climbed the sweeping wooden stairs with their ornate hand-carved railings and roamed the farthest reaches of her new abode hoping to learn more about their host. She had a difficult time accepting that her brother and Aaron and Beth and she were the beneficiaries of some invisible fate. But the more she traversed the empty rooms and halls, she began to realize that other than Matias and his staff of two servants, including a European chef and a *sous chef*, and a Negro maid, no one else appeared to reside in this gray stone edifice he called his home.

Her brother and the Peets caught up with her on the second floor. They were astonished by mechanical systems that employed the new technology. The modern bathrooms had hot and cold running water, bathtubs and showers with multiple shower heads, and flush toilets. Both gas and electric lights were available at the pull of a cable switch. Telephone service linked the home owners to the outside world, and a system of bells and speaking tubes allowed for communication from room to room.

They traversed to the third floor, which housed the guest bedrooms, a schoolroom, a sewing room, and servants' quarters. The kitchen, pantry, storerooms, and laundry, as well as sitting and dining rooms for servants were in the basement.

Entering her private room, Julie unbuttoned her shoes and tried out the high canopied bed. Lying on the blue floral quilt, she stared up at the roof overhanging the thick hand-carved head posts and foot posts and repressed the sensation to enjoy this luxury.

One of the servants who Julie had not seen had removed her newly purchased clothes from the travel trunk and hung them neatly in the wardrobe standing slightly ajar.

Her door suddenly opened and she sat up abruptly at the entry of the Negro maid.

"Good afternoon, Miss," she said. "I'm just checking to see if you need anything and to inquire if the room is to your satisfaction."

"Oh, yes - yes it is. I've never been in a room like this before." Julie slid off the high bed. Her stocking feet thumped on the floor.

"My name is Ophelia Robinson," she said.

"I'm pleased to meet you, ma'am. I'm Julie Josephson." Julie extended her hand, which engendered a strange look from the maid's oval brown eyes. Her dark skin stretched in two symmetrical smooth curves over high cheek bones and descended to a mouth that erupted with thick lips under a wide nose. She was a head taller than Julie and several years older. Her slender body fit snugly into a maid's white uniform.

When Julie noticed she was not going to take her hand, she quickly dropped it to her side to avoid embarrassing her. "Do you live here in the mansion?" Julie asked.

"I have a room, but I live with my mother in the city. Can I get you anything?"

"No, I don't need anything. This is all new to me. You know I grew up on a farm. I fed chickens and milked the cows. I helped my mother with the household chores."

"I'm pleased that you find your arrangements here satisfactory, miss."

"You can call me, Julie. I'm just a farm girl. Our farm was in Minnesota. Have you ever seen Minnesota?"

"No, miss, well, Julie. I haven't traveled much except coming north."

"Where did you live before?"

"Louisiana. We came north when I was still a small girl. My father was employed by the Pullman Company."

"We came here in a Pullman car from Minneapolis. They are very nice. What does your father do?"

"He's a Pullman porter."

"I lost my parents. They were killed. That's why my brother and I are here. They were friends of Mr. Bauman."

"I'm sorry for your loss, Miss Julie. You have my sympathy. Mr. Bauman is an unusual man. If you have no further need of me, I must get back downstairs."

"Thank you for coming to my room, Ophelia. I'm glad to meet you."

"I'm glad to meet you, Miss Julie."

"You can just call me Julie."

"I think you deserve to be called Miss." Her concerned expression blossomed into a broad warm smile as she stepped back and closed the door behind her.

A few days later when Julie asked Gustav, the chief butler about her, he told her she lived part of the time in an area of Southside Chicago known as the Black Belt.

Julie soon discovered the library where she could sink into one of several heavy gilt armchairs before a fireplace that never seemed to be in want of logs ensconced in mesmerizing flames. She decided to spend most of her waking hours reading from his vast selection of leather-bound books. Many of them were written in German, which she did not understand, and by authors she had heard mentioned by her parents when they were alive, Karl Marx and Frederick Engles, Kant, Hegel, Voltaire and Rouseau. There were also more written in English than she would be able to read over several years, novels by Edith Wharton, Charles Dickens, Thackery, Sir Walter Scott, and Mark Twain.

They were unprepared for Sophie Rose. They were overwhelmed by Sophie Rose. Unlike other fashionable women they had observed walking with small mincing steps, she burst into the room from the cavernous entry. Polished black riding boots flashed in her firm commanding stride that matched the dramatic sweep of her plum royal cape and leather skirt with a forest green bodice.

The second difference that distinguished her from other women was the long waves of thick shining chestnut hair that cascaded about her shoulders. Her wide-spaced dark oval eyes set in eloquent chiseled features projected such exuberant energy that Julie, Newt, Beth, and Aaron felt awkward in her presence, unable to move other than to do her bidding.

"Ladies and gentlemen," Matias announced with a sweeping bow that matched his wide grin, "I present Sophie Augusta Rose at your pleasure."

"Thank you, Matias. It is indeed a pleasure to finally meet your prairie urchins. You have dressed them well, I see; but, of course, we will expand on their wardrobe." A soft German inflection crept through her words like an elusive cat.

Transferring her riding crop from her right to her left hand, she graciously extended her free hand as Matias introduced the prairie urchins. Without prompting, the boys each in turn gently took her hand and bowed slightly. Julie did not follow the example of Beth's polite curtsy, but grasped her hand and looked fully and confidently into her eyes.

Sophie's rich operatic laughter enveloped them and floated up into the high ceiling arches. "How delightful. She is just as you described, independent to the core. I look forward to becoming fully acquainted with all of you, but, first, Matias and I are going out for a ride."

Julie noticed that Matias also wore breeches and polished boots. Sophie's comment gave evidence that he had described the four of them to her. Because of her presence and the twinkle of humor in her eyes, Julie did not take offense at being referred to as a prairie urchin. She was proud of her origin.

Matias and Sophie shared an amiable relationship, but appeared not to be married. Matias did not introduce her as his wife, yet their loving affection for each other was transparent.

When they had first arrived in Chicago, Matias granted his new charges a few days to acquaint themselves with his home before the appearance of this enthusiastic woman who would change their lives.

After Matias and Sophie returned from their ride, Julie and the others joined them for lunch in the atrium overlooking manicured gardens spread across the back acreage of the property. Sophie's face was flushed from her exertion, hair windblown, and eyes sparkling with energy, as she entered the room on Matias's arm.

Upon being summoned by Gustav, Matias's butler, they had dutifully followed him to the drawing room where the group scattered to various chairs and ottomans as though staking out individual territories to encompass the vast empty space of the room. They stared at each other not knowing what to say in such a formal place.

"What you suppose they're serving for lunch?" asked Aaron. Gustav had momentarily left them to check on last minute preparations with the maid and cook.

"Whatever it is, I'm sure it will be delicious," said Beth.

"I don't think they eat anything here that isn't," Newt offered.

"Be sure to close your mouth when you chew your food," Beth cautioned them. "People of high breeding do that."

"Where did you learn that?" Julie asked. "Are we low breeding?"

"There was a little book on my night table about etiquette."

"What's etiquette?" asked Aaron.

"Proper manners with others in society."

"Who are the others?" Aaron swung his leg back and forth impatiently.

"I imagine we shall meet them eventually. It isn't polite to swing your leg like that. It is distracting to the other guests."

"There aren't any other guests. There's only us."

"We need to practice proper manners with each other to prepare for when we meet the others in society."

"Who told you we're going to meet anybody. We're just going to eat lunch."

"It is certain that now living as we are, we will soon meet others in society. Obviously Sophie and Matias are counted among them and eventually will include us. But according to the handbook of etiquette, we are clearly not ready. We don't know how to act or even what to say."

"Won't your little book tell us?" Julie sneered in a derogatory tone.

"It just says what is acceptable and what is not. It doesn't tell us how or the content of our speech."

"Then what good is it?"

"It's a starting point. It will guide us in appropriate ways."

"Then why don't you read it to us sometime," said Aaron.

"I would not be interested," Julie protested.

"And why not, pray tell?" Beth cocked her head and looked at her askance in a manner Julie had quickly grown to dislike.

"I don't like being preached at," Julie said. "The rest of the world has never seen or heard of your little book. And if they did, they wouldn't care."

"But you should care. You're not out there in the rest of the world anymore. You're here now. We're all here now, in society. We have to do things differently. We don't want to be an embarrassment to Matias and Sophie. In fact, I will take it upon myself to ask Sophie to teach you and me, Julie, how to be ladies. Matias will guide you, Newt and Aaron, in learning the ways of gentlemen. We have escaped harm and fallen into good fortune. I am confident that a grand future awaits us. We must wholeheartedly embrace it."

"What makes you think you know what the future is?" Julie asked. "None of us knows. You don't know until it happens."

"The future is what we make of it. Think of what Matias has told us. Think of the names of the people who are on that list. They must want a future and others are trying to prevent them. That's why Luther Baggot came after us. That is what has brought us here. I foresee that we are being prepared to forge that future that has perhaps otherwise been lost."

"We don't have any way to do that. We don't know what it is and we're not even grown up yet."

"Within a few years, we all will be. I believe Matias considers us as the promise for that future."

"You always were a dreamer, Beth," Julie said.

"Without dreams, we would have nothing to hope for."

"I thought being here like this was your dream."

"It's only a part of it. I need to be here to become the person I wish to become."

"You can't become someone different," Aaron interrupted in an accusatory tone. "You can only act like someone different."

"And maybe that's what I shall do."

"What?"

"Act like someone different."

"That should be easy enough for you," I said.

"Where?" asked Aaron.

"On the stage. I can become a singer and an actress playing in comedies and dramas."

"How are you going to do that?"

"I'll ask Sophie to help me."

"What can she do?"

"I don't know, but she's that kind of person. She's different. I want to become like her."

"You're not as pretty as she is," said Aaron.

For a moment, Julie thought Beth was going to leap out of her chair and attack her brother. "You don't know anything."

At that point, Gustav appeared and summoned them into the atrium for lunch. They were immediately followed by the laughter of Sophie and Matias, who had been eavesdropping on their conversation from an adjoining room.

"Hello, children," Sophie sang out as she swooped to the table. Matias pulled out a chair for her, then seated himself at the opposite end while Aaron, Beth, Newt, and Julie took seats in between.

A servant placed a small bowl of creamy soup before each of them. Beth and Julie watched Sophie to see which of several utensils she selected. She delicately picked up a round silver carved spoon, dipped outward from the edge of the bowl, and brought the spoon to her lips without a slurp.

Aaron and Newt, on the other hand, shoveled their soup to their mouths with lip-smacking noises until they grew distinctly aware that the rest of the diners were staring at them.

"What kind of soup is this?" Aaron asked, wiping his mouth with the back of a hand.

"It's a shrimp bisque made with fresh cream, minced potato, and sherry," Matias explained with a grin of appreciation at their innocence. They had never heard of shrimp or bisque or sherry.

"What's shrimp?"

"It's a small sea creature encased in a shell, much like crawfish. Did you ever see or catch crawfish out of a river in Minnesota?"

"Yes," said Newt. "We know what crawfish are. We caught them, but we didn't know we could eat them. We just threw them back in the water."

"What about sherry?" asked Beth. "I know that sherry is wine."

"It flavors the soup," said Matias. "Here, would you care to try a glass?" He reached for a decanter on a nearby serving cart and poured them each a small amount in a wine glass set next to their water glasses. They took a sip of the golden colored nectar and marveled at its sweetness.

"As for you young men," Sophie beamed her sparkling smile at Newt and Aaron, "and both of you young ladies, we are going to begin your lessons in proper social etiquette."

Julie glanced at Beth's suddenly precocious expression, as Beth rolled her eyes in her direction. "I was just reading a book of etiquette I discovered in my room," she said.

"Do you have any books about science?" Aaron interrupted. "What is it?"

"Actually, I do have just the book for you," said Matias. "It's in the library. We'll get it after lunch."

"What's it called?"

"The Boy's Book of Inventions. It contains stories of the wonders of modern science. And further, I have a friend who's an inventor. I'll introduce you."

"You mean today?"

"Ah, no, but Sophie and I are planning a *soiree* in three days at which you will all have the opportunity to meet a number of our friends."

"What's a sorr-ee?" asked Newt.

"*Soiree* – A party that takes place during the evening. Actually, it will be a dinner party, but there will also be musicians, dancing, and other entertainment."

"And of course we will have to demonstrate proper etiquette. Isn't that right," said Beth.

Sophie raised her glass of sherry. "Our friends are often informal when we get together, but generally they are proper."

"So you can't slurp your soup," Beth's critical tone aimed at Newt and her brother.

"We will cover some of the basic manners so that others will hold you in high social regard. Eventually, you will also become acquainted with young people your age from families of great wealth who, shall we say, worship class distinction. And we will introduce you to others who live in poverty."

"When you say worship, do you mean like in church?" asked Newt.

"Not like in church, but it is what they believe in."

"Why do we have to meet them?" Julie asked. "It sounds like they think they're better than other people."

"They do believe that their wealth grants them privileges not available to the less fortunate."

"You have wealth," Julie said, looking around to indicate the mansion in which they were seated.

"Yes, but it's for a different purpose than what it might appear to be," said Matias.

"We know many people who are impoverished," said Sophie, "and we do what we can to help them."

"What do you do?" Julie asked.

"We donate large sums of money in support of social programs for the poor," said Matias.

"I mean what do you do? What kind of work."

"Sophie Rose is a renowned opera diva and actress," said Matias. "Among my businesses, we own a theater here in Chicago and a New York opera house. Sophie has charge of them since her name often appears on the marquee."

"You're an actress?" Beth's voice went up and her eyebrows raised with interest.

"Yes, dear. We produce a range from classics to Shakespeare and light modern plays."

"I have always dreamed of acting on the stage," breathed Beth.

"She can sing too," said her brother.

"That is most interesting," said Sophie. "After lunch, perhaps you will show us your voice."

"I can sing for you."

"That's exactly what I mean, dear."

"Oh, show you my voice."

Sophie nodded. "It's just another way of saying give us a demonstration."

"I can do that. I can surely do that," Beth nearly wriggled out of her chair.

After lunch was over, including a light chocolate tort dessert, which Julie thought was the best part, they "retired" (a new word to Julie that Sophie used meaning they walked from one room into another) to the music conservatory. The boys and Julie scattered to the furthest corners of the room where comfortable couches were available and watched Sophie seated at an elaborately carved concert grand piano. Beth stood beside her as Sophie's fingers struck a chord and ran nimbly up and down the keys a few times to prepare. Matias sat in a burgundy and green brocade upholstered Italian chair.

(Julie learned later that it was an Italian style, because Sophie insisted that Julie and the others recognize kinds of furniture as part of their training to enter society. As far as Julie was concerned, a chair was a chair and she didn't bother herself with where it was made as long as someone could sit on it.)

"Let's start with the key of C," said Sophie. "Sing the scale as I play it."

Beth followed the rising tones easily and her lilting soprano voice continued into the next octave and returned with a steady downward spiral back to middle 'C'.

"You hold the tones clearly and your voice is strong. I did not detect any wavering," said Sophie. "Now sing a song that you know – any song."

An energetic tune that Beth had learned at the lumber camp burst from her lips and echoed from the conservatory walls. She smiled and bobbed and swayed, enjoying her performance.

Having never heard the song before, Sophie surprisingly accompanied her on the piano after only one verse had been sung. When the brief song came to its conclusion, both Matias and Sophie applauded.

"Very good, dear, very good," Sophie's praise for Beth grated on Julie's sensibilities. Beth already thought much too highly of herself, as far as Julie was concerned, even if she was her best friend. She didn't need encouragement. When she primped and curtsied, Julie could feel the chocolate tort she had just eaten churn in her stomach. She belched and did not bother to cover her mouth. According to Beth's etiquette book, women were not supposed to burp or pass gas in polite company.

"I will arrange for you to have lessons in vocal technique for singing and speaking," said Sophie. "That and also dance and movement training are essential, if you want to perform on the stage. You can join a class of other young women."

"How wonderful. Oh, thank you, Sophie Rose. Thank you so very much. When can I begin?"

"I will speak with a voice teacher tomorrow, Joerg Goetschel, a friend of mine for years. He provides lessons to many aspiring singers, but he will take on only those he feels have promise. You obviously have some natural talent, but it needs to be nurtured and cultivated."

"I can hardly wait to meet Mr. Goetschel."

"He will not be easy on you, I warn you."

"I am willing to work hard, very hard."

"There will be hours of practice."

"I can think of nothing better I'd rather do with my hours."

"Good," Julie thought. *"That will keep her occupied and out of my business."* But Julie had no idea yet what her business was. What was she even doing there except that Matias had known her mother and father? Newt and Aaron were wondering what was in store for them as well, now that Miss Songbird was feathering her nest. Aaron was at least going to learn what science was. Newt appeared bored, but Matias had indicated he held out some promise for them.

"Okay, my charges," Sophie pivoted on the piano bench and brought her riding boots to rest lightly on the polished wooden floor. "You are all going to learn etiquette every step of the way as part of your transformation. Did you ever read or did your parents ever tell you about Pygmalion?"

"We had pigs," said Aaron. "We know about pigs."

"This has nothing to do with swine and the word is spelled differently, with a 'Y' instead of an 'I'. The tale is about the creation of something perfect that you want, an ideal."

"What do manners have to do with that?" Julie asked.

"Etiquette and manners don't make anyone perfect," she explained. "They do set a standard for accepted behavior among certain people that you will be asked to meet."

"What's a Pygmalion?" Julie asked.

"Pygmalion was a sculptor in ancient Greek mythology who did not care for the local women in his town. They were not serious enough for him and much too playful. One day, he discovered a large piece of ivory and decided to carve his idea of a beautiful woman from it. He fell in love with this image of his ideal woman and clothed her and adorned her in jewels. He gave the statue the name Galatea, which means sleeping love. He was so obsessed with his ideal woman, he went to the temple of Aphrodite, the goddess of fertility and love and beauty, and begged her to give him a wife who would be as perfect as his statue.

"When Aphrodite went secretly to the sculpture's studio, she saw that Galatea was the image of herself and brought the statue to life. When Pygmalion returned, he discovered that his statue had come alive. Pygmalion and Galatea were married, and Pygmalion always thanked Aphrodite for the gift she had given him. Throughout their lives, they were blessed with happiness and love."

"I still don't understand what that story has to do with learning manners and etiquette," Julie insisted. "We aren't statues."

"Of course not, but you will grow and become different than you are now, more knowledgeable, perhaps even powerful. It's the same for all of us."

As for Julie, she didn't see any point in trying to become someone different than who she was. She would not rest until Luther Baggot was being devoured by worms and maggots in his grave.

Chapter 18

The Introduction

The stench of poverty rose in their nostrils as the horse-drawn cab, the hack, they had ridden in drove away with a sharp sucking sound of hooves released from the stew of horse droppings and mud that served as a street. They bowed their heads against the light rain and cutting wind that leapt off the Lake Michigan waterfront, lifted the essence of the stockyards, and caromed at will along the main thoroughfares and infested the labyrinth of ghettoes with the foul odor of animal death and decay.

Although she carried a flimsy parasol at the behest of Sophie, Julie did not immediately raise it to protect her head against the gale until Sophie's sharp glance prompted her to follow her example as they accompanied Matias along the boardwalk to a drab unassuming brownstone office building that housed the Pinkertons National Detective Agency. Julie paused a moment to gaze at the sign above the door of a human eye positioned over the caption 'We never sleep.'

Matias held the heavy door open for them to enter the dark wood interior. A man wearing a badge on his brown suit coat rose from behind a large oak desk to greet them, introducing himself as Clarence Rittenauer.

"I'm Matias Bauman of Bauman Enterprises."

"It is a pleasure to meet you, sir. How can I be of service?" The agent barely glanced at Julie, but she could discern his eye momentarily caught by Sophie's beauty. He must have recognized her from her stage appearances.

"There is a particular gentleman of interest to my company who may be employed by the Pinkertons and I'm here to make an inquiry," Matias explained.

"Of course, I will be glad to help you. And the gentleman's name?"

"A Mr. Luther Baggot."

"His name is not immediately recognizable to me, since we employ several thousand agents, but if you are willing to wait, I can look into our files."

"At your leisure, sir."

"Please have a seat, ladies," Rittenauer gestured to an Ottoman and three additional wooden back chairs along the opposite wall.

"Thank you," Matias escorted Sophie and Julie to the Ottoman where they perched on the edge of the brown fabric cushions. Matias remained standing with his hands clasped behind him.

"If you will excuse me," said Rittenauer.

"Of course, sir," Matias nodded.

Rittenauer turned away and strode quickly down a narrow hall to another room hidden from their view. They patiently waited.

While they were in the hack enroute from his mansion into the city, Matias had explained a little of the background about the detective agency.

"The Pinkertons are the guardians of the wealthy class that employs them," he said. "So they hire an army of agents to search out anyone who opposes the tycoons and prevent their influence by any means. Their spies infiltrate groups that show any resistance to the dictates of the capitalists. They call those who are against them, or even believe differently, anarchists."

"Were my mother and father anarchists?"

"Not in the sense they tried to overthrow a company or the Government. They were progressive in their values and wanting to promote change through the redistribution of wealth to benefit the masses of people who have nothing."

"Why would someone want them killed because of that?"

"I don't have an answer as to who was behind their murder, but the people with money become reactionary when their fortunes are threatened. They will do anything to protect their wealth and possessions and care nothing for those who have nothing."

"And I care nothing for them," said Julie. "I hate and despise them with all my heart and will do anything to go against them. What did you call people like me, like my mother and father?"

"Anarchists."

"I am one of them. I am an anarchist."

"That's where your sentiments lie, but you're not one of them."

"Why not?"

"There's a difference. Partly it's one of age. You'll understand when you meet them."

"And when will that be? It can't be too soon for me." Her blood boiled. It was all she could do to contain herself and stay seated on the Ottoman.

"Soon, you'll meet them soon, and not all at the same time."

At that point, Rittenauer returned empty-handed. His long narrow face accentuated by a reddish goatee puckered as his brow wrinkled, letting them know he had not succeeded in identifying their man.

"I am very sorry," he said. "We maintain alphabetical files on all our agents. We don't employ anyone by the name of Luther Baggot."

Julie jumped off the couch. "But he was wearing a badge just like yours."

"I beg your pardon. And may I have the privilege of your acquaintance?"

"She's my niece, now living with me. We have reason to believe her mother and father were killed by this man."

Rittenauer visibly stiffened. "With all due respect, Mr. Bauman, Pinkerton agents do not murder innocent people."

"I am not casting aspersions on your company, Mr. Rittenauer. She is just responding to what she saw."

"You saw this Baggot person kill your mother and father?" Rittenauer stared hard at Julie.

"He came to our house after he killed them. He wanted something."

"And what was that something?"

Matias quickly intervened. "This is all traumatic and quite personal for my niece. I appreciate your effort in researching Luther Baggot's identity. If his name should come up again, please don't hesitate to contact me. Here's my card." Matias handed him a business card. "Good day, sir." He turned back to Sophie and Julie. "Ladies, let us be on our way." He offered Sophie his arm and gently grabbed Julie's as a caution to not say anything more, and they departed.

Once outside and moving along the boardwalk, he spoke without looking at Julie. "You must be careful who you address about the murder of your mother and father."

"Didn't you trust him?"

"I'm not certain. He could have been lying to us, but then, Luther Baggot could be a rogue agent or working for someone else under the guise of being a Pinkerton."

"How will we ever find that out?"

"I suspect we will have to draw him to us in some manner. That was the only reason we paid a visit to the Pinkertons today. I will double our guards and we will see what we will see. If he comes calling, then we'll know if he's working for the Pinkertons. If not, then we'll pursue other avenues."

"What guards? I don't see any."

"They're watching us. They follow us all the time when we go out. You can feel well protected. However, I don't want you roaming about the city alone."

"Do I have a guard?"

"You do."

"Can I meet him? Can I know his name?"

"You will soon."

She looked back over her shoulder, but no one appeared to be following them, although throngs of men and women and horse-drawn wagons, cabs, and carriages surged past.

After their visit to the Pinkertons office, Julie thought they would return to the mansion, but she was mistaken. Pinkertons was only the first stop on what became her quest for revenge and that soon was inextricably entwined with Matias's plans to undermine the power of the capitalists.

"There are others I would like you to meet," he said.

"Are we walking?"

"Yes, where we are going is not far."

Sophie and Julie matched his quick stride and they left the main street for dank ghetto side streets and alleyways. Without Matias and Sophie at her side, Julie would have been completely disoriented and lost. They appeared to be familiar with the narrow passage through a nightmare of rough, threatening neighborhoods punctuated by the curses of bearded, besotted men and raised voices of haggard women against a backdrop of shrill screams and the cries of children.

They finally slowed deep within the slum of encroaching dilapidated wooden apartments odorous with mold and the stench of charcoal fires and burning garbage. Tattered clothing hung from open windows between neighboring tenements on shared lines strung across the abyss of squalor below. Matias stopped before a closed wooden door and wrapped sharply three times with the back of his gloved right hand, paused, then wrapped again. A few moments passed, then a narrow slit the height of a man slid open from inside and a single eye, black and luminous as a drop of oil, peered out, darting back and forth and up and down assessing who stood on the threshold.

After another moment, they heard the squeak and grind of a heavy metal bolt thrown back and the door was pulled open. Julie's unasked question as to why only one eye had looked at them through the slit was answered. The man's eye patch and curly hair gave him the aspect of a pirate.

The powerful cooking aroma of garlic, onions, and paprika wafted from within, its source a large metal pot of Hungarian stew on the kitchen stove several feet behind the man.

"*Guten tag, mein herr*," the greeter's rugged face broke into a grin. "To what do I owe the honor of your visit, *unt mit fraulein*?" He bowed slightly in Julie's direction, more like a courtier than her initial impression of him as a derelict.

" '*Tag*, Horst."

"*Komen sie, komen sie*," Horst gestured them inside, then quickly closed the door and slammed the bolt shut with a thud. With a final glance through the slit, he blocked that view with its wooden shutter, then turned to his visitors. "You arrived in time for a mid-day meal. I hope you will join us."

Julie wondered who the "us" was, since no one else was in the front room and no other person appeared.

"Thank you for your kind invitation, but our visit will be brief. I wanted to introduce you to our new young charge," Matias angled his body to direct the man's attention to her. "She is the daughter of Olaf and Ingrid Josephson."

Horst's good eye scanned Julie like a burning coal. "You have my sympathies, child. I am sorry for their death. My name is Horst Holzman."

Julie was shocked and curious as to how this man knew of her parents.

"Her brother and two friends also came with her. Through various circumstances, I met them in Minnesota and brought them home with me."

"I am honored and delighted to meet you, my dear." He brought his eye patch so close to Julie's face, she felt she was about to be consumed by a Cyclops. Sensing her discomfort, he chuckled and said. "There's no need to fear the patch, unless you are an enemy. Our enemies know me as The 'Patch' or sometimes call me 'One Eye.' Any who see me this close have not long to live."

She did not step back, but looked him straight in his good eye, which glittered with a kind of dark mischief.

"Don't let him fool you," a rich boyish voice transitioning to manhood announced just behind her. "He's really harmless as a pussy cat. All that bluff is for show. Gives him a reputation he don't deserve."

Julie turned to discover the voice's owner, an overwhelmingly brash and breath-takingly handsome young man only a year or two her brother's senior. An unabashed smile played across his taut chisled face framed with a mop of wavy light red hair.

Although slender, his movement as he paced the room with a cat-like springy stride suggested reservoirs of speed and strength that could outdo an older man bulky with weight and muscle. He bore a small scar near the top of his right cheek, which Julie later learned was the result of one of the many bare knuckle fights in which he engaged for money.

"That is my one and only scar," he told Julie. "I promised myself there would never be another. I let no one get me in the face, but I dropped my guard. Taught me, that one. Won't never happen again." His gray-green eyes glistened like sunlight over a shimmering lake with the promise of something greater in his life than the shabby brown clothes that hung on his bony frame and the rough dark boots that housed his large feet. Even stretching upward, she came only to his chest. "You ever need a fighter, you call on me."

"Conrad is right, you know. He's cool and deadly in a fight, like a cobra. He needs only one strike," said Horst.

Julie's head jerked around at a sudden high-pitched scream from the back room. A moment later, a tall girl about her age with long unruly red hair came through the door. Her large dirty bare feet slapped the wooden floor as she crossed directly to her. Without a word, she tugged at the sleeves of Julie's dress and brushed a foot back and forth within the folds of her skirt. Her thin chapped laps twisted in a sneer of distaste directed at the dress, but meant for Julie. The expression of challenge in her gray-green eyes led Julie to believe she was her brother's twin.

"Just 'cause you're dressed like a lady don't mean you're better 'n me."

"Liesel, is that a nice thing to say the first time you meet someone?" said Sophie.

"It's true. She ain't no better 'n me."

"I'll buy you a dress so you can look like her."

"When?" She continued the irritating tugs at Julie's right sleeve. "I'm tired of wearin' these rags," she referred to her shabby, mended blue dress.

"Where would you wear such a dress?" said her father with a lop-sided grin. "Surely not in this neighborhood. You'd be taken for one of the Everleigh sister's whores."

Julie thought her burning look would disintegrate her father.

"With her hair washed and done and a little make-up, she would look like an empress," said Sophie with a smile of confidence.

"Did you hear that, *Fater*, an empress."

"Just reminding you of who we are."

"I don't like who we are. I would like to be an empress."

"Then you need to marry an emperor."

"Ain't gonna find one in this privy. That's for sure."

"That's for damn sure."

"Where's the rest of the family, Horst?"

"Out earning a living instead of dreaming about it."

"I have a right to my dreams," insisted the fiery girl.

"That you do, Liesel," said Sophie. "And I'm certain you will share them with Julie, since you will become friends."

"Does she have to stay with us? I was hopin' to come live with you in your fancy house."

"Our work is here," said Horst. "You and Conrad will teach her what we're about."

"She can't be lookin' like no empress then, if she's gonna be one of us. She needs to look like me."

"And so she will."

"What am I going to do?" Julie asked.

Horst looked at Matias. "You told her anything yet?"

Matias shook his head. "Too soon. I wanted her to meet you first."

"Are you on my mother's and father's list?"

"She has the list then"

"Yes."

"Do you have it now for safe keeping? If it falls into the wrong hands, we're all dead."

"You must mean Luther Baggot," said Julie

"Don't know the name."

"He came after my brother and me for the list."

"Must be a bounty hunter."

"He is," said Matias. "Disguised as a Pinkerton, but he's not one of them. We checked."

"That could be a risk. Pinkertons're on the other side."

"Our strategy may have to change, Horst. They are too well hidden. We have to draw them out to get them, especially to learn who their leader is."

"It doesn't sit well with me to use the young ones as bait."

"They are less likely to arouse suspicion and our spies will be watching out for them."

Julie turned to Matias. "What spies? You've kept me from knowing something about my mother and father long enough."

Horst's good eye motioned to Matias and they walked off into a corner where they conferred in low voices with their backs to the others.

"Don't worry, dearie," said Liesel. "We'll have good times together. With me to show you around, you're gonna see things the like you never seen before."

After a few moments, Matias and Horst returned. "When we get home, I will explain what we will be asking you to do. Horst and his family are among many operatives you will come to know.

This is not the time and place to divulge secrets. You need to first understand the purpose and scope of what we're doing."

"Are my brother and Aaron going to be part of all this?"

"Yes, but in a different way than you."

"And Beth?"

"Perhaps," said Sophie, "but only in a small way."

"I'm sure she'll be happy to hear that. She already thinks she's an empress."

"You and Newt and Aaron are going to know things she will not."

Julie shrugged as though that distinction were not important to her.

A woman she assumed to be Horst's wife suddenly emerged from the back room. Julie wondered how many more remained there and would make a dramatic appearance.

"This is my wife, Inez." Horst touched her arm and ushered her forward to meet them.

She stood taller than her husband by several inches and Julie could immediately detect where her children had inherited their large feet. Her broad, flat feet had not known the confinement of shoes. Black grit had taken up permanent residence under her toenails. Her solid ankles expanded upwards into thick, stocky legs partially exposed by a shabby, faded-green cotton dress covered by a full-length white apron spotted with food stains from raw meat, flour, and tomatoes. Julie's gaze traveled upward past her large protruding breasts and centered on her robust glowing Polish features, accented with a kind blue-eyed gaze that, during her younger days, men would have found alluring, now supplanted by a motherly expression. She reached out and gently touched the side of Julie's face with her reddened left hand.

"*Schone, Schone Kinder*, how nice of you to join us." She glanced at her husband. "If she is moving back and forth between the two houses, then Conrad must escort for her safety."

Conrad smiled and nodded.

"But she is welcome to stay with us any time."

"Then I should be as welcome to stay at Herr Bauman's palace any time," spoke up Liesel.

"You are always welcome at my humble abode," said Matias. "It is certainly not a palace."

"'Tis compared to this pigsty," Liesel flailed her arm to take in the room and surrounding slum environment.

"Are you my bodyguard?" Julie asked Conrad.

"Ya, I will guard your body." He laughed.

"Will I be able to see you?"

"Most of the time."

"This will prove an interesting arrangement," said Horst. He looked at Sophie. "You educating her on the finer points of etiquette so she can join a Nietzsche club?"

This was the second time Julie had heard the reference, but did not have an explanation.

"I'll take her to one," said Sophie.

Julie asked, "What's a Neetshe club?"

"It's one of the ways we infiltrate the ruling class," said Horst with a grin.

"I will tell you about it later," said Sophie.

"It's how rich women deal with their guilt," said Horst, "through philosophical discourse."

Julie looked at Sophie for clarification.

"It's about the class struggle, the disparity between the very rich and very poor."

"Don't know why they need to have a club," said Liesel disparagingly. "All they have to do is walk through the slums. Course they don't want to get their pretty little shoes and shitty stockings dirty, begging your pardon, Queen Sophie Rose. Yer stockings ain't shitty. I'd love to have a pair. I'd wear 'em everyday up and down the street."

"They see us from their hacks as they drive by," said Horst. "We remind them how lucky they are to not have to live like us. But Matias, you and Sophie are different. You're with us and trying to change things to better our condition."

There was a sudden clamor at the door and Conrad checked through the peek window before opening it. Dutton Koontz, a dark-haired young man about Conrad's age flung himself into the room. Conrad slammed and locked the door shut. "You bein' chased?"

"Ya, by the Chinaman," he said heaving to catch his breath. "I was with Orin Brown handin' out pamphlets. We'd split up to take different corners. The Chinaman come out of nowhere and grabbed me and says he wants his money."

"Then you better give it to 'im. How did you get away?"

"He let me go. Said he'd give me one more day. Then he's comin' after me for good."

"Dutton, you know better than to fool around with the Chinaman, especially if it's his money," said Horst.

"How much do you owe him?" asked Matias.

"Fifty dollars."

Matias handed him a wad of bills. "Here, don't wait until tomorrow. Pay him back today, with interest. And don't play mah jong with him anymore."

"I won't. He cheats all the time. I know he cheats."

"Have Conrad come by for Julie early tomorrow morning," said Matias.

"Be sure you ain't wearin' that fancy dress," Liesel smirked. "Where we're goin' it'll get dirty – real dirty."

"She'll be dressed to look like you," said Sophie, "but she will be wearing shoes."

"Not them fancy ones."

"No, like yours."

"Imagine me teachin' the likes of you," Liesel chuckled.

"You come from the same stock," said Sophie firmly, "only Julie grew up on a farm. You can teach her about the city."

"I do know the city. I do know that."

"Good then, we'll be on our way," said Matias.

Inez suddenly grabbed Julie with her warm heavy arms and crushed her in a great hug. "We're good people, Julie. We'll take care of you."

The salty smell of her skin and cooking odors that permeated her house rubbed off and clung to Julie all the way back to the mansion.

Chapter 19

Discovery

That evening at dinner, Julie shared her Holtzman family introduction with Newt, Aaron, and Beth. Matias and Sophie had gone into the city to dine at one of the finer restaurants and attend a play. The foursome were left alone to enjoy stuffed Cornish hens with blackberry sauce served with truffled mashed potatoes and broccoli, followed by a Viennese lemon tort and coffee for dessert. Gustav served them an elegant red Bordeaux that nicely complimented the sauce.

Julie began to realize that Sophie and Matias wanted them to experience this kind of cuisine, luxury, and opulence so that they could intimately know and contrast the differences in the lives of the rich and those who lived in poverty. After where Julie had been that day, she felt weighed down with guilt that she was actually enjoying the fine food and her surroundings. But it would not be long before she learned how the other half lived.

Newt, Aaron, and Beth had their stories to tell her, as well.

Jean Guenoc had appeared at the mansion shortly after breakfast and informed the boys he would be their tutor in a number of academic subjects and physical skills. In his French overbearing businesslike manner, he did not elaborate, but ordered them to accompany him to a waiting horse-drawn cab at the front door. The hack lurched forward, then smoothed as the horse thrust against its polished harness and settled into a steady trot at the swish and crack of the driver's long whip over its broad, black back in the misty morning air.

For several minutes, the boys listened to the muffled steady clop of hoofs and cast brief surreptitious glances at the stern, clean-shaven countenance of this sudden stranger whose unyielding gaze assessed them in the close quarters of the cab.

Aaron repressed an urge to squirm in discomfort, fearing that he would incur some scathing comment of disapproval from Jean Guenoc. He felt like a dog, cowering before a forceful master and decided he would not speak unless spoken to.

With some hesitancy, but in a clear voice, Newt finally asked, "Excuse me, sir, but where are you taking us?"

To the boys' relief, Guenoc grinned ever so slightly, revealing a row of strong white teeth that, along with intense blue eyes and lean thrusting jaw, reminded Newt of a predatory animal. Although the man was not tall in stature, his body within a snug-fitting dark suit was clearly powerful.

"You will find out soon enough." His slight French accent sounded domineering to the boys. "But it's good that you are curious. Are you also not curious?" he spoke directly to Aaron.

"Sir?"

"I believe you heard the question, but I'll repeat it. Are you also not curious?"

"About what, sir?"

"About anything."

"I am curious about some things."

"For example."

"I was reading a book given to me by Mr. Bauman."

"What was in the book?"

"Scientific experiments."

"I see. So then you're curious about science."

"Yes, sir, I am."

"Well then, I will endeavor to satisfy your curiosity."

"Are we going to do an experiment?"

"Everything we do will be an experiment of sorts. Even the two of you are an experiment, or at least you will be taking part in an experiment."

"I'm happy to hear that, sir."

"It's good to be happy. It's better than being sad. Don't you agree?"

"Yes, sir. Yes, sir."

The boys endured another several minutes of silence. Then Aaron hiccupped.

"What was that you said?" asked Jean, again with his intimidating grin.

"I have the hiccups, sir." Two successive burps escaped Aaron's lips and he quickly covered his mouth. "I'm sorry, sir. They won't stop."

"There is never a need to be sorry about a normal bodily function. Do you know what causes your hiccups?"

"No, sir."

"Well then, consider this your first science lesson."

"Yes, sir."

"Right here," he reached over and poked Aaron just above his stomach, "Is an anatomical structure called the diaphragm. Hiccups are caused by the sudden contraction of your diaphragm that pushes air up into your esophagus, which is the pathway by which food and liquid travel from your mouth to your stomach. You may have swallowed some air or perhaps you are feeling some anxiety with me or you may have eaten some hot spice or seasoning with your breakfast this morning. Anatomy is among the subjects I will be teaching you."

"What else will we be learning?" asked Newt.

"Literature, law, and finance. You will learn how to cook."

"Cook?"

"*Oui*, cook, oh, and you will learn how to speak French and German."

"Are you taking us to France and Germany?"

"There may be an occasion or a necessity. We shall see."

"My mother and father taught Julie and me Swedish."

"That is good that you are acquainted with a second language. It makes it much easier to learn another."

"Where will we learn these things?"

"Herr Bauman has a large library. That will be your place of study, with one exception."

The boys watched him expectantly.

"It is important that you build strong bodies. I will show you how to lift weights to increase the size and strength of your muscles. You will also learn how to shoot and how to defend yourself."

"Guns?" asked Aaron. "We hunted game in Minnesota."

"That's good. It should come easy for you."

 "Why do we need to know that?" asked Newt.

"Herr Bauman wants to prepare you academically for a university, Harvard or Yale. It is his intention that you have every advantage of the young men you will meet and associate with. They have shooting clubs."

"When will we be going there?" asked Newt.

Jean stared at him a moment. "Not for at least two years. We have much to cover, including the study of Greek and Latin. There will be outdoor activities, as well. The first is where we are going today and later you will learn team rowing. It is a popular sport of the male students at the eastern schools."

"Why is Herr Bauman doing this?"

"He has his reasons. Most importantly, he is a humanist and he feels responsible for what happened to your mother and father. They were close friends."

The keening of gulls drifted through the cab window as it neared the Lake Michigan waterfront. The cab stopped and the boys followed Jean along the boardwalk planking fronting a long row of warehouses receiving goods, being unloaded from freighters by shouting burly stevedores operating cranes and pulleys and pushing heavily laden carts. The wind off the lake smote Jean and the boys with the stench of raw and dead fish and oil leaking from a line of ships nosed up to the wharf like suckling young.

Jean and his charges maneuvered through the shifting churning mass of husbandry to a harbor that was home to smaller sailing craft and fishing boats. Newt's and Aaron's expressions beamed their surprise and pleasure as Jean lead them along a private slip to step aboard a sleek thirty foot long schooner with a varnished grain wood hull and sails covered with gray canvas.

A sun-browned shirtless man, ropey muscled chest bristling with curly black hair that thinned down over his navel, came up from the cabin below and greeted Jean with a wave. *"Bonjour,* Jean, are we going out?"

"Not at first. These are my students, Newt and Aaron."

The intense dark eyes of the unshaven sailor studied them as he finished knotting a red bandana around his thick neck. *"Bonjour,* welcome aboard."

"We'll spend a little time dockside to acquaint them with Adeline, then take them out for a turn. I want them to be useful, not on a lark. Boys, meet Etienne Arceneau, a fine sailor and fisherman. He is captain of this yacht. While you are on board, you take orders from him."

"So we begin," said Etienne with a broad, flashing grin. "Meet Adeline, the name of our vessel. She is one-hundred twenty meters from bow to stern, eighteen meters at her beam from side to side," his arm moved in a wide gesture to indicate the sweep across the deck, "and her draft is twelve meters at the hull. That is the bottom of her. Now, follow me as I point out her other fine features."

The boys stumbled awkwardly after him, as Etienne leaped and capered nimbly about the deck explaining the rigging and the function of each feature in the construction and operation of the schooner. An hour later, the structures and terminology began to blur until Etienne insisted they repeat the names and what and how they contributed to the overall craft. The taller mainmast and short mizzen, spars, shrouds, winch, spars and the jib and mainsail as Etienne and Jean pulled on the sheet lines and the white canvas climbed up the masts and filled with the billowing wind once the boat was beyond the jetty.

"Everything about this craft is based on science," Jean shouted from the wheel over the rush and slap of white tipped waves. "It is designed to capture the wind, which is the rapid movement of air, and propel Adeline's sleek body through the water. She is buoyant because of her shape, the length of her keel, which balances her, and the depth of her hull and the height of her masts to the size and cut of her sails."

The schooner rose and fell with a steady rhythm thrusting across the surface of the lake. Within a few minutes, they were miles from the shore. Newt and Aaron looked back to see the diminishing skyline of Chicago shrouded in the black and gray smoke of its factories. Out on the lake, they took in great lungfuls of the crisp air. The clear sky and the bright sun played and sparkled over the surging shifting blue water.

"Your voice is untrained, but natural," said Joerg Goetschel. "Where did you learn to sing?"

Beth gazed downward with a smile of embarrassment. "We lived on a farm in Minnesota. When I was a small girl, every time our rooster crowed, I would crow back."

"Are you saying a rooster taught you how to sing?"

"He helped me discover my voice."

"Well, there is no question you are a soprano and you project your voice well, much like a rooster I suppose." Joerg chuckled, and Beth raised her head. "Meaning no offense, but Sophie told me you were unusual."

"I also sang in a logging camp."

"A logging camp?"

"Yes, my friends and I worked there for one year before Herr Bauman brought us to Chicago. The cook and I sang songs together. We entertained the rivermen after dinner."

"Those are the men who worked in the logging camp."

"Yes, they loved our singing and often they would join in."

"So you had a chorus."

"We did. Yes, we did." Enthusiasm brightened Beth's face. She told Julie she had been apprehensive before her meeting with Joerg, who was an Austrian professor of music. He had been Augusta's mentor in Europe where she had emerged from singing in dance halls and burlesque theatricals to become an opera sensation.

"So that gave you a taste for the stage, your singing with the cook."

"I like to sing for people. I sang in our church choir and at home for my mother and father and brothers. Sometimes my mother would sing with me, but her voice was different, lower than mine."

"A contralto."

"I don't know what that means."

"It is the lowest singing voice for a woman."

"I guess there is a lot about music I don't know."

"That is why Sophie has brought us together. She asked me to assess your potential. If you show promise, we move forward. But it requires hard work from you, study and hours of practice. You will learn music theory and how to play the piano, as well as vocal performance. For now, I will play a note and I would like to hear you match it with your voice."

The slender fingers of his right hand gently descended to the keyboard of his Bechstein grand piano. A high 'G' echoed throughout the studio. Beth's clear vibrato response overshadowed the sound as though the note had floated from her throat.

"*Das ist gut*, now follow me. We are moving slowly *lentement* up the scale." Beth followed with ease as he sequentially played the remaining seven notes of the scale.

"We are going to push a little. The moment you feel any strain in your voice, even the slightest tension, you are to stop immediately. Do you know why?"

Beth shook her head. "Because you can damage your vocal chords and never be able to sing again. Training will help you to strengthen your voice and increase your range, but I am also teaching you techniques for proper breathing, resonance, volume and phrasing, warm ups, and how to move your body. Even Sophie Augusta Rose, who is a diva, continues to train. Live performance alone is not enough to maintain your voice. It is your instrument, just like a violin or a piano. You will need to maintain it properly. Stay out of places where men are smoking. And remember, screaming is not singing. It could cause ruinous damage. You only sing the highest notes. You do not scream. Okay, let us push a little more."

He stopped and returned his hand from the keyboard to his lap. "Okay, now I am going to tell you about voices. They express themselves in what are called registers. A vocal register is a grouping of notes of the same quality, much like here on the keyboard and are produced by the same combination of your vocal chords."

He played a chord, then suddenly sang a few melodic phrases in that same octave. Beth found his singing impressive. "What you have just heard is called the chest voice. It is the register that produces the lowest notes. The male speaking voice usually comes from this register. The Chest Voice has a limited range and is only suitable for certain notes. When you sing in this register, you should feel vibrations in your chest."

Joerg went on to explain the characteristics of the head voice which

caused vibrations to be felt in the head. "This register produces high notes and is the most commonly used in music. A well trained head voice can almost come close to the sound and power of the chest register. There is also a mix of the two, which can produce a strong sound. The highest register, which I cannot sing at all, makes sounds like a whistle. The best coloratura sopranos can use this voice. I take it you have heard Sophie Rose sing?"

"No," said Beth.

"We will arrange for you to observe her with me in a session. Studying the voice and style of great singers will help you to become one yourself."

"He said I could become a great singer," Beth told Julie later. "He also told me I must drink a great amount of water every day for my throat and body. But I find I must constantly run to the toilet."

"I imagine that's the price you pay to become great," Julie goaded her, irked that Beth was taking herself so seriously. "But if you don't become great, you can stop drinking so much water."

"Oh, I will drink water. I will drink lots and lots of water," she retorted angrily. "Perhaps you are envious, Julie, because you do not have such a gift as mine."

"Don't push me, Beth. I will discover my gift."

"If you don't know it by now, then it is not likely to be there."

"Did not your precious teacher, Joerg, warn you not to scream?"

"Indeed he did."

"If you do not get out of my sight at once, I will make you scream."

"Since we came here to Chicago, you have grown to be an intolerable child, Julie Josephson – intolerable."

"Believe me, my friend of long ago, I am not a child and you would do well not to think so highly of yourself."

"I'm sure that Newt and Aaron will be glad to hear of my training."

"Then by all means go and tell them and leave me alone."

With a great exhalation of disgust, Beth turned on her heel and stormed out of what Julie now claimed as her personal room in Matias Bauman's mansion, his library. It was here that Julie would one day make her own self discovery.

Each morning as they boarded the trolley, Newt and Aaron had the sense of joining a massive herd of young and middle-aged men all wearing the same styles of gray or dark suits amid a cluster of round bowler hats shifting about like bubbles on the surface of a pond.

Throughout the city, crowded trolleys jammed with white-collar, middle-class workers commuted from the growing suburbs to midtown office buildings. The close confines of the creaking, swaying cars buzzed with talk of companies and making deals and the rush of municipal and Federal government reform. The energy and forces of change had become a reality. People would no longer accept being exploited and weren't willing to suffer living in poverty in order to support a corrupt elite class enjoying extravagant wealth.

In spite of their youth, lack of political and business acumen and experience, Newt and Aaron were still able to discern the unusual double life they were leading. They had come from living in rural frontier poverty to residing in the mansion of a wealthy urban businessman and working in his company. Yet Matias and his brother were among an increasing number of wealthy entrepreneurs investing and engaged in reform groups promoting the rising middle class.

Kurt had discovered Aaron's natural gift for mathematics and placed him in training as a bookkeeper. Each morning, Aaron poured over the financial section of the *Chicago Tribune* and discussed economics with his mentor.

The world of finance held little interest for Newt, who preferred to be out where the physical work of the company was performed in the massive warehouses on the waterfront docks, interacting with stevedores and fellow employees in the shipping operations where he learned to generate and maintain manifest and inventory records and arrange for land transport by teamsters and by the railroad.

Having lived all his young life among the sparse population of a small prairie town, Newt discovered a profound interest in the seething humanity of the city. The energy and diversity of livelihood had first overwhelmed and amazed him. As time progressed and he assimilated into his occupation, he perceived structure and social order in what appeared to be urban chaos.

It's in the repetition of things, he thought, *people are doing the same things each day over and over again in established patterns until something changes and they have to change and go along with it.*

His observations had begun a year ago, when Kurt Bauman first brought him and Aaron to the downtown offices of Bauman Enterprises. Newt looked every inch like a young businessman among the thousands who populated the office buildings of Chicago, but felt uncomfortable and out-of-place wearing a suit and bowler hat similar to all the rest. The lack of physical activity while sitting at a desk agitated him.

The other riders on the trolley and the men and few women in the offices spoke a language he didn't understand. It was English, but they used business words that were foreign to him and they related to each other with a frenetic formal behavior he had yet to learn. They often rushed about with a great sense of urgency in pursuit of something elusive and invisible, a purpose he did not understand as they made repeated trips to the row of new crank style telephones mounted along one wall.

He noticed that Aaron did not share his sense of awkwardness, as though his friend had discovered a crowd of long lost cousins and blended right in with the enfolding rituals of the group. Within a few days, Aaron, too, worked hard sitting at his desk and, from time to time, rushed about with an intensity of gaze and purpose.

Newt wanted to stop him and question what he was doing, but withheld his curiosity and remained an observer while trying to understand how what he did related to what other employees were doing amid the noise and confusion swirling around him.

Kurt had escorted them past the long rows of desks occupied by an army of clerks and introduced them to several anxious, harried men called supervisors, in charge of departments, and a few others called managers. Each of the managers oversaw the operations of different segments or divisions of the business. Aaron seemed to grasp what Kurt was explaining, but Newt only nodded with a grim smile and shook the hands of the men whose names he instantly forgot.

Kurt was experienced in railroad leasing and shipping transportation. He had been a foreman in his father's company in Berlin, Germany with a routing network throughout neighboring European countries. Now, in Chicago, he favored and managed that part of the company himself and left the operation of the machine equipment and consumer appliance and household products manufacturing to other carefully selected managers with college degrees in business and finance from Harvard and the Universities of Vienna and Berlin. The latter were Jewish classmates Kurt had known during his college days.

Newt and Aaron spent their first month working side by side with mentors, as Kurt called them. Lars Svenson, a ruddy-faced, red-headed Swede who often lapsed into his home language with Newt, and Otto Kepinsky, a heavyset Polish immigrant with a loud bellicose laugh. Both were seasoned clerks who had been with the company for five years. They familiarized their two young trainees taking them step by step through the sequence of the business from negotiating customer contracts, working with material suppliers, the manufacturing process, and scheduling the shipment of products.

Among his observations, Newt noticed that the managers and supervisors never yelled at anybody. Once in a while they shouted to be heard over the general hubbub of voices in the cavernous office and clerical workers often shouted information to each other, but he never witnessed expressed anger, even at tense moments regarding scheduling or when problems arose.

Lars explained that mutual courtesy was a management philosophy of Kurt and his brother, and problems and issues were solved by examining the overall business process for causes, not screaming at and blaming individuals who were just trying to do their best. "It's a manager's responsibility to make sure employees have what they need to do their jobs. That's what they believe and that's what they do."

Newt learned that such a practice was unheard of in other companies. Kurt and Matias had the reputation of being equitable, paying their employees a fair wage and taking care of them should they or a member of their family fall ill. They did not restrict anyone who wanted to join a union. About half the workforce became members. The other half did not feel there was any benefit in doing so.

The Revolutionist

Sitting on an overturned crate in the open doorway of the waterfront warehouse, Newt had been waiting for over an hour for the steamship to heave into view far out on the horizon of Lake Michigan.

The raucous screams of gulls filled the air as the large gray and white birds raised and lowered like elevated puppets on the sharp wind gusting off the lake. The keening water fowl hovered in a swirling cloud over a garbage scow hauling refuse to be dumped several miles from shore. Newt watched them execute daring acrobatic swept wing dives for fish guts and offal tossed overboard from three local trawlers displaying their nets draped on tall masts that rocked back and forth keeping metronomic time with the steady white capped chop.

The sights and smells brought back memories of his childhood near Stockholm, Sweden where he and his then baby sister, Julie, and their mother and father lived in a small stone cottage in a fishing village at the end of a fiord banked by massive blue granite cliffs.

With all that had happened since they made the crossing to America and since the death of his parents, that peaceful early life hung somewhere in the back of his memory only as a dream. Their existence on the wheat farm on the Minnesota prairie had quickly drawn him into the world of adult responsibility and pushed aside his sense of youth and play, but ignited his intelligence and curiosity about people and life. He had inherited his father's sensitivity and steadiness and a small piece of his mother's strong will. *Julie got the lion's share of that*, he thought. *When I want to remember mother, all I have to do is watch and listen to my sister.*

"So, what you thinkin' about, little boss? You gonna make that boat come on any faster?"

Newt grinned slightly at the good-natured comment, but he hated it when any of the men called him little boss. He wasn't physically smaller than most of the stevedores, with a few exceptions of remarkably tall, strong men like the Finn, Magnus Jarvinen, and he wasn't their boss. Newt supposed they treated him in deference to his relationship to Mr. Bauman. Everyone he worked with thought he was a family nephew, a perception that raised some challenges and expectations regarding his job performance, but also created a few advantages.

He had earned the respect of his fellow workers by showing he wasn't a slacker. He worked as hard and as long as any of them and did not seek any favors.

"She's two hours late."

"Means we have to make up for lost time unloadin' her," said Magnus.

"She's in port for only one day."

"Them rails are damn heavy. Need an extra man on the crane and five more on the dock."

"You know where to find 'em."

"Half dead drunk they are. Not worth a lick when it comes to hard work," Magnus spat aside. "Live half their life in the saloons." He was referring to a street near the docks lined with saloons, boarding houses, and brothels.

"How are your wife and children?"

"They miss their friends in Minnesota. We had a nicer house than we can afford here in Chicago. But Bauman is a good employer and he's on the side of the union. I can't complain like some do." Magnus paused. "I knew your mother and father."

"You knew them?"

Magnus nodded. "I was sad to hear what happened. Even coming to America we ain't escaped the tyranny."

"How?"

"When they first came to Minnesota, they lived in the Swedish settlement in Eveleth next to us. You were too young to remember, but I once met you and your sister when your mother brought you to a socialist democrat meeting. The workers came together once a month to talk about changes. The Finns and Swedes get along better over here than back in the homeland, but we Finns got the short end of things working in the mines. We weren't treated as humans by the owners. We worked only as long as our bodies could hold out. The conditions were bad. If one of us died in an accident, the owners did nothing for the wife and children. We weren't nothing more than meat.

"When I first come over, they sent me a thousand feet down the shaft to work as a trammer. Wore rubber boots and heavy clothes, helmet with a light that warn't worth a damn. Worked with a crew that broke the ore and loaded it into cars, 'bout twenty tons worth. Pushed it to the shaft, 'bout ten times a day. Got paid two and a half dollars. Men died down there every day. Had cave-ins and explosions. Floods drowned some."

He recounted his days living and working on the Mesabi Range, a group of iron-ore-bearing hills covering four hundred square miles, extending from Grand Rapids on the Mississippi River to Birch Lake, west of Duluth. Kurt and Matias had quickly discovered the force and power of their competitor, the U.S. Steel Company, owned by the magnate, John D. Rockefeller. Although Kurt and Matias did not produce iron and steel, they did transport it as a small independent company, but they were clearly at a disadvantage in the shadow of John D. Rockefeller and J. P. Morgan, who could swallow them up at any time, which accounted for the Bauman brothers planned strategic move to Kuhn, Loeb, the rival investment bank of the House of Morgan.

Kurt and Matias knew their company was being watched by Elbert Gary, a Chicago attorney selected by J. P. Morgan to arrange consolidations of steel companies under Morgan's corporate mandate.

Through their subsidiaries, U.S. Steel owned and controlled over half the mines that supplied the steel industry. They were also in direct competition with James J. Hill's Lake Superior Company and its leases on many of the Mesabi Range mines. Owning sixty-five mines, five railroads, and one-hundred twelve ore boats, U.S. Steel's transportation capacity far exceeded that of Bauman Enterprises.

The need for workers in the mines, the docks of Duluth, and the machine shops supplying equipment and repairs to the railroads, mines, and boats attracted men like Magnus, who had been contracted by one of the many recruiters of immigrant labor.

"After a year, I moved the family to Duluth and worked on the ore docks for two years before we come to Chicago," said Magnus. "Matias knew me from the Social Democrats in Minnesota. The mine owners tried to stop us from organizing. All they cared about was the money we were makin' 'em. Didn't give a damn about us. Now I go to meetings here in Chicago. Matias and his brother are good men. We need more like 'em."

An hour later, accompanied by two tugboats, the freighter loomed overhead, crowding into the dock. Men materialized out of the dark side streets as though summoned by the deep basso horns of the tugs. Heavy guy-lines were tossed to secure the vessel. The gangway was let down as a massive steel crane swung a conveyer into position over the deck. Members of the crew guided its descent into the hold. The rattling and crashing went on into the night as the refined ore was loaded into waiting railcars where trackmen signaled the engineer with lanterns to adjust the position of the train.

The next day, stevedores loaded the ship's empty cargo hold with tons of rolled steel coils and steel tracks that had been staged, waiting inside the warehouse. The vessel began the long return journey to Duluth, Minnesota where it would be transferred to Northern Pacific Railroad freight cars, then hauled to Seattle, Washington.

Chapter 20

Newsie

Julie waded through bodies that were not dead. Given the unwashed stench that rose from them, crowded and clustered lying huddled in the streets and alleys, they could have been. Her mind and senses reeled with scenes of their forging driven, rotting lives trapped in the sinking despair of ghetto survival. Gray and black-drab dressed men and women from a host of foreign countries and babbling in as many languages rushed streaming out of narrow alleyways and up and down nearly impassable dirt streets congested with carts and wagons bearing half-rotted fruits and vegetables. Rag pickers hauled heaps of diseased remnants salvaged from the scraps of cloth tossed out of the sweat shops, the abode of families sewing twelve hours a day for a few cents per garment for a clothes-maker who lived in a mansion on Chicago's north side.

Yet here and there among the shouts and curses and screams of anguish for which there was no relief in this hell, the energy of life was overwhelming. For a moment, she heard laughter somewhere on the street. But in the swirl of downtrodden harsh humanity, she could not find its origin. It may have been her imagination or the staccato squeaking of cranking wheels mingled with the cacophony of voices that hid the source in the distortion of sound or it may have been her desire to escape from the chaos to some pocket of solace and relief.

After a while, she just focused on Liesel's sturdy, confident back and followed her swinging stride that easily and knowingly navigated through the shifting crowds. From time to time, she paused and looked around to make sure Julie was still with her, then plunged on ahead.

Deep in an alley, Liesel suddenly lurched to the right and pushed open a door. Conrad quickly herded Julie in behind her. They stood in a dark, dank, narrow hall that smelled of wood rot and decaying excrement and garbage. Liesel opened a second door and pulled a string to turn on an overhead light bulb that cast a yellow glow barely penetrating the corner shadows of the room they had entered. Julie noticed stacks of paper, socialist pamphlets written in several different languages, and unsold issues of a newspaper called *The Liberator* on a table. Against the far wall, a small dust-coated hand printing press and racks of composite type and disorderly containers of ink waited for the next futile onslaught of angry, passionate words.

It was Julie's first day working with Liesel Holtzman. Her brother, Conrad, and Dutton Koontz were operating the press that printed the pamphlets. Conrad and Dutton also acted as sentinels and bodyguards. They had taken to carrying handguns under their coats and strapping knives to their belts and legs.

Handing out their seditious pamphlets in the tenements and hawking them on street corners in the business section of the city was to become Julie's daily task. The latter location was risky. She could not remain more than a few minutes on a street corner and had to keep moving for fear of being arrested, or worse, being beaten by rival newsies protecting their territory.

Although the pamphlets were printed in several different languages, they conveyed the same message that corruption is not a matter of individual cases, but is something rooted in society. Corruption exists because people let it exist by creating a society that encouraged people to get rich at the expense of others, and held them up to the highest esteem for doing it.

"The solution to the problem of poverty and repression lies with the people. They must change the system and bring back ethics, morality, and balance into everyday life."

With the large German immigrant population, the underground press was secretly funded by Matias Bauman. The Holtzman's published advice on how to organize socialist branches and they made announcements and wrote about socialist events. Although Horst Holtzman created most of the articles and was the chief editor, the information and stories were brought to him through a network of socialists and anarchists spread throughout the city. As Julie came to know them, she recognized several of them from the names on the list that Luther Baggot had tried to get from her. Unlike the specific foreign language newspapers in the ethnic settlements, the Holtzman's appealed to the broader need for political, economic, and social change.

To Julie, seeing the reality of the world she lived in, at first, the pamphlets were just meaningless words and wasted thoughts. Even if people read them as she handed them out in different sectors of the city, the likelihood of their understanding the concepts, let alone knowing how to change social and economic conditions, was remote. They had no method, no resources, and no one to help them. There was no possibility, nor influence, nor power. So she became a member of a seditious movement to change that.

Horst Holtzman explained to her, "If you can get working class people to read in their own language and reading becomes a habit, thinking will follow. Getting people to think is the foundation for motivating them to organize."

The existence of other presses and newspapers in the settlements provided their inhabitants with a way to relate to their communities, their churches, the exploitation and living conditions of others, the right to become citizens, and to receive news from their homeland, to where many hoped to return.

As she moved from one week to another among the immigrant settlements, Julie saw what was different about them and also the poverty the people had in common regardless of their country of origin. It was through being a pamphleteer, that she became acquainted with the city.

In crossing from one sector into another, she noted the differences in how the people lived, as though they had transplanted scenes from their European towns and villages. On the near west side, she associated the Italians with colorful scarves, red and yellow turbans worn by the women, young and old, who stood behind ash barrel counters hawking stale loaves of round bread, and fish, fruit and vegetables that lost their freshness as the temperature rose in the heat of the day.

They called themselves *paesani*. Many of the men had come from Italy to work on the railroads or in the railroad factories. She noticed that many did not work, but lounged on trucks and in open doorways of tobacco shops and saloons where they smoked clay pipes, talked with animated gestures and roamed the streets. She passed women balancing enormous loads of firewood on their heads with one hand while holding greens and tomatoes scooped into their aprons with the other.

Here and there, young girls nursed their babies and wandered in and out among the stalls formed by hucksters and peddler carts on both sides of the street and haggled with hand-weaving crones over remnants of cloth.

Bloodied in visceral gore up to his elbows, a butcher skinned and hung goat carcasses encrusted with swarming flies among lumpy strings of dark sausages suspended from makeshift wooden racks in the windowless shop behind which the mustachioed knife-wielding proprietor lived with his haggard wife and wailing children.

A health officer scattered disinfectant and swept up dung and waste that flowed from side alleys and passageways where rag pickers lived.

Walking past a section of steamship offices displaying signs that they were also banks and employment agencies, she watched a helmeted policeman leave his call box and dart into the crowd to intercept a gang of young boys who had snatched melons from a vendor stand, and run dodging between rolling carts and knots of pecple gathered in small groups. The boys instantly separated as if on command and fled up different side alleys leaving the blue-uniformed policeman standing confused, holding his baton motionless with no one to strike and his whistle dribbling to silence.

Each section of the city had its own separate areas in which they lived.

As she crossed into the Polish settlement along the North Branch of the Chicago River, an area called Polonia, she entered into the Roman Catholic parish, St. Stanislaus Kostka, a few blocks north of the German parish. The parishes had been established among the Catholic immigrant populations as a haven against Protestants in other sectors.

They were not welcome to stand on street corners and distribute pamphlets in Polonia. Business owners chased them off and policemen threatened them with arrest if they did not move on.

Conrad said they would have a better reception in the Jewish neighborhoods recognized by their synagogues. Peddlers, merchants, gold and jewelry artisans, and factory laborers in the garment industry did not ignore them or toss their pamphlets aside. They were told by many men and women they had already joined and were members of unions, but they would read what the pamphleteers had to say.

The people were markedly different than neighborhoods that exploited poverty and vice. Along with the department stores of Goldblatt Brothers, Polk Brothers, and Meyer Brothers lining the busy streets, there were many offices of doctors and lawyers.

Conrad steered them clear of Chinatown. "Lot of opium dens," he said. "And they don't read English anyway."

The other area he warned them to avoid was the Black Belt. "They ain't like us," said Conrad. "It's as bad as the Levee. And they have their own paper, *The Chicago Defender*. It's just for them."

Teeming with life, the city exerted a force of its own, a vast filthy dark presence shrouded in its own smoke and factory dust. Laid over with the stench and pall from the stockyards, it ingested hordes of hungry ragged immigrants who disappeared into the labyrinthine bowels of sprawling tenements and sordid existence.

The first time, she set out alone to hawk pamphlets in an Irish-dominated area of the city, a strange scruffy granite-eyed boy confronted her, riveting her with anger and accusation.

"You a newsie?"

"What's a newsie?" she asked stepping back. She had the distinct feeling he was about to punch her in the face.

"You sellin' them papers here?"

"No, just givin' them to people."

"This is my corner, ya know. I'm sellin' these papers. You got no right to be here."

Julie looked around. "This is just a street corner," she said. "You don't own it. It don't have your name on it unless it's Donovan."

"That's my name all right, pussy. You don't git yer ass movin', yer gonna be sorry what's gonna happen to you, pussy."

"And what's that?"

"Ya heard of the Levee?"

"No, I just came to Chicago."

"That's where pussies like you git turned into whores."

"Don't know anything about whores."

"You don't want to know, you better move off this corner. All I got to do is snap my fingers and point at yer pukin' body and yer goin' to the Levee."

She stared at this challenging competitor with his torn kneepants and scuffed shoes through which a portion of his right front toe protruded to belie his stature, but not his bravado. "Don't know about the Leevee, but I was standin' here first."

"Yer askin' for it, you little pussy bitch." The stringy brown-haired boy placed a finger at each corner of his mouth and emitted a piercing whistle.

For several minutes, nothing changed on the street. He just stood there grinning at her with his mouthful of crooked dirty teeth. She felt sorry for him and considered moving to some other corner, since this one seemed to be so important to him, but on the other hand, she did not and never had responded well to being threatened and coerced. She stood her ground.

"Wait and see, pussy," he said. "You wait and see."

The only thing she saw and heard was the passing vendor carts piled with rags or rotting fruit and vegetables, until suddenly an arm grabbed her shoulder from behind and threw her to the sidewalk and someone else snatched the pamphlets from her grasp and heaved them out into the traffic of passersby. The incessant wind scattered them and they were ground into the dust and manure of the street by the clopping hooves of horses.

She screamed and kicked out, as she was dragged toward a dark reeking alley by her abductors who growled at her, "Shut yer feckin' mouth, cunt. Ain't no cops here and no one gives a shit about you."

She sensed a sudden flurry and was dropped amid shouts and curses. She heard the impact of flesh upon flesh and blood sprayed over her dress. She looked up, then scrambled to her feet at the sight of Conrad pummeling the two dandy's wearing suits and bowler hats who had attempted to drag her away to some apparently horrible place called the Levee.

"Who were they?" she asked, brushing the dirt from her dress.

"They're from the Levee. They hunt for young girls."

"He said that name. What's the Levee?"

"A place you don't ever want to be."

Once, standing on a street corner near a line of vendor stalls taking in the rising smells of fruits and vegetables displayed in the open air, she had the illusion of seeing her mother and father walking arm in arm along the teeming street. She ran after them, calling their names, "Mother! Father!" chasing their ethereal images only to lose them in the shifting chaos of the crowd. She followed them into a tenement dwelling and up two flights of creaking stairs where she was certain they had entered only to discover she had intruded upon a den of boarders lying about on scattered rags and heaps of befouled straw like animals in a stable. She thrust her arm across her mouth and nose to block the suffocating smell of mold and decay that mingled with the cooking odors of cabbage, onions, frying pork and fish.

"No room!" they shouted at her. "Go away! No room!"

She cast about hoping to see her mother and father, but they did not appear, even as ghosts. When she turned away and went back out into the alley, Conrad was waiting for her.

"What happened?" he asked. "What were you doing?"

"Nothing," she said. "I thought I saw someone I knew."

"Who?"

"My mother and father."

"Aren't they dead. Matias said they were killed."

"Yes, but we never really knew who was in the coffins. We couldn't open them."

"You think they might be alive someplace?"

"Maybe they had to escape and left us so we would not be harmed."

"It's a nice wish." He touched her shoulder and drew her to him in a gentle crushing hug that caused an unexpected surge of comfort. She rested her head against his chest and would have liked to stay in that position for a long time. Moments later, his steel strong arms slipped away from around her back and shoulders and he guided her out of the alley to the street.

Like an apparition, Luther Baggot passed so close to her one day she could have reached out and touched his black horse. He had not noticed her and, if so, would not have recognized her. She looked like most other ragged immigrant girls her age.

Luther's stallion was moving along at a brisk trot. Julie pushed her way around a throng of businessmen surging up the platform steps to the L train and ran after the horse and rider. She didn't know what she would say or do if she caught up to him, but she didn't want to lose sight of him. She was blocked by the jostling crowd of pedestrians and the distance widened between them. She eventually broke through and ran to the corner as he turned down another street.

He was nearly two blocks away, but she could still see him because of the height of his tall mount. Minutes later, she heard running footsteps behind her.

"Julie!" Conrad shouted. "Wait! Where you going?" He easily caught up to her, since a full skirt hampered her stride.

"It's him," she spat out in a nearly breathless gasp. "Luther Baggot - he rode right by me. I want to see where he goes. I want to find out where he lives."

At that point, Luther made another turn.

"That's Dearborn," said Conrad.

"It's just another street. Hurry, or we're going to lose him."

They rounded the corner onto South Dearborn just in time to see Luther dismount in front of a saloon. A man sitting in a wooden chair tilted back against the door jamb stood quickly and came to take the animal by the reins and lead him around the side to the back as Luther entered the saloon. Julie and Conrad slowed to a walk. Numerous men watched them with predatory eyes, particularly Julie.

"It's not just another street," said Conrad. "It's the Levee." His wide gesture took in the several blocks of similar looking three-story buildings, some with elaborate architectural cornices framing their exterior walls. "These are all brothels," he explained. "Even that mansion, the Everleigh Club. It's a high class place. Only rich politicians and millionaires go in there. Some of the girls work on the Levee because they want to and don't have no other way to make a living. But most of 'em are white slaves, prisoners used in the trade. You don't ever want to come here alone. Never. You'll disappear and no one will ever be able to find you."

"What are white slaves?"

"Girls like yourself. The panders dope 'em and lock 'em in behind those walls. They make 'em whores and they don't ever get out. And even if they do, it's too late for 'em. They're ruined. Can't get work. Nobody wants 'em. Some kill theirself or die from the heroine or lose their minds from Chinese opium. A lot of 'em die from the syphilis or go blind."

Julie knew what prostitutes were, but she had never seen one up close. They stopped near the saloon and gambling den where ragtime piano music spilled out through the open door.

"We can't wait for him to come out," said Conrad. "We need to move on."

"I can wait. I want to follow him to where he lives."

"We can never keep up with his horse. For all we know, he could stay in there all day and all night."

"There must be some way."

"This ain't it. Let's go."

"Give me your gun. I'll go in there and kill 'im."

"You'd never make it through the door 'afore someone grabs you. You got to keep your head on straight here, Julie. And I won't give you my gun. Let's go."

Seething with anger, she responded to the pressure of his grip against her arm.

Toward evening, the harsh wind off Lake Michigan whipped along the cavernous streets as they walked through the downtown

Loop, Chicago's business center populated with banks and department stores dominated by the edifice of Marshall Fields where young women lured to the city with the promise of jobs aspired to work as sales clerks and learn the retail trade.

The high-priced restaurants along the main streets were beginning to fill up with businessmen and politicians and their cronies who dined on the finest cuts of beef fresh from the stockyards and swilled imported whiskey, gin and expensive French wines.

Lights began to appear on all floors of the office buildings where young men would return from dining and toil over their business reports and ledgers long into the night. It was generally believed that the harder and longer one worked, the sooner he would achieve wealth and success. The rushing force to make money and improve one's lot and rise up in society pervaded everywhere Julie looked. Men and women hurried along the street with the intensity and expressions of such urgency, they appeared to be chasing down a hunted prey.

As Julie and Conrad left the Loop and continued the long trek back to their tenement, Liesel joined them. "Where you two been?"

"The Levee," said Conrad. "She saw Luther Baggot and followed him."

"Jesus, you don't never want to go there. You told her, didn't you?"

"I told her."

Coming along through the Bohemian district, they saw a small boy of two or three years old wearing a dirty, blood-stained shift in rags tottering about the dung encrusted street. Horse drawn carts and a beer wagon rolled by narrowly missing his small body which would have been crushed under the heavy spoked wheels, since the drivers either did not notice him nor care to stop or veer to avoid him. Conrad dashed into the melee of vehicles and snatched up the sniffling child. Clutching him tightly, he negotiated the traffic to rejoin the girls at the curb.

"Do you see his mother anywhere? Or someone looking for him?"

They cast about, moving quickly up and down the nearest entries of the tenement buildings overflowing with other older children chattering in a diminished version of Polish and Czech spoken by their elders. Julie was surprised to hear Conrad address them in two languages asking, "Do you know who this child is? Do you now where his mother is?"

The crowd of boys and girls clamored like a flock of quacking ducks.

"They don't know," he said. "They're lucky to know where their own mothers are." He stopped an older woman wearing a *babushka* over her head and a dark common blouse and long skirt that extended to the ground over her high-button shoes.

"Do you know where this child lives," he asked, positioning the boy so she could see him. She shook her head and quickly moved on.

"What will we do with him?" Julie asked.

Centered in his wide Slavic face, the boy's nose drooled freely into his rescuer's shirt, but Conrad took no notice. "There's an orphanage at the settlement over on Halstead Street, Hull House. We can take him there."

They made a sharp detour and walked quickly through noisy congested side streets and alleyways reeking of boiled cabbage and onions and charcoal fires.

A short time later, they emerged from Polk Street within sight of the old three-story gray house centered by a gabled attic on a fourth level. A *piazza* surrounded the first floor on three sides with three Corinthian arches at the main entrance.

As they stepped into the cool recess of a main hallway, they heard women's voices in animated discussion about working conditions coming from an adjoining room where the door had been left ajar. Conrad walked to the opening and stood where he could be easily noticed. The discussion dwindled and subsided. Julie heard the scrape of a chair and footsteps approaching across the wooden floor. Although she and Liesel stood several feet behind Conrad, they could detect the gray Victorian coiff of a woman at about the height of his shoulder.

"And who have we here?" her soothing mellifluous voice floated out to them. They could sense her smile, although they could not yet see her face.

"We found this boy wandering on the street in the Bohemian sector. He was almost run down. No one could tell us who he is or about his mother and no one claimed him or came looking for him. Can we leave him with you?"

"He has blood on his shift."

"Don't know if it's his or someone elses."

"We will take the little lad and clean him up." She lifted the child to her bosom and stepped past Conrad into the hall. "We only maintain a day nursery, but we can care for him until we find his mother." She paused to look at Liesel and Julie. "How do you do, young ladies. Are you with this fine gentleman?"

"Yes, ma'am," said Liesel.

"What do you do here?" Julie asked, though it may have sounded rude.

Her patient matronly expression did not waver. "This is Hull House, dear. I'm Jane Addams, one of the owners. We're a settlement house. We help immigrants who are enduring hard times.

"I'm in the middle of a discussion with a group who are organizing a union. But perhaps you would like to come back and visit. There are many things we do here and we are always seeking volunteers. Do you live in one of the tenements?"

"The German sector," Conrad spoke as he came forward.

"And what are your names, my good friends?"

"I'm Julie Josephson."

"Liesel Holtzman."

"Conrad Holtzman. Liesel is my sister."

"I'm pleased and honored to meet you, Julie, Liesel, and Conrad. Now, if you will excuse me, I will turn our nameless child over to one of my helpers in the nursery. Good day to all of you."

"Thank you, ma'am," said Conrad. "Good day to you too."

They watched her receding figure move away quickly down the hall.

"Come on," said Conrad. "We've done what we can. Let's go."

As they walked outside, Julie asked, "Can we come back here sometime. I didn't know there was a place like this."

"There are a few others in different parts of the city, but Hull House is the best known. We also take needy people to Sister Pavalek at her convent in the German sector. All kinds of immigrants come here when they need help, but mostly women whose husbands beat them or left them or went to prison. Most don't know what they got into coming to this country. She helps them learn. She also has social clubs, some for men, and some for women. I never went to any. Just heard about 'em. They talk about business and unions and politics. Our father comes from time to time. Gets ideas to write about. He said they even have music from their countries and give plays. They have a theater in there."

"I'd like to come back."

"We'll come back."

It suddenly occurred to Julie that they hadn't seen Dutton Koontz all day since hitting the streets. "Where's Dutton? I thought he was with you, Liesel."

"He disappears once in a while," said Conrad. "Takes care of some Chinese business on the side. He's had to support his mother and four sisters since he was twelve. She lost most of her fingers on a cutting machine in a garment factory."

"Chinese business?"

"He gambles, but he also does deliveries."

"Deliveries of what?"

"Whatever the Chinaman gives him to deliver."

"Oh, what about his father?"

"He was a drunkard. Gambled away all their money and left 'em. Last time Dutton seen him, the bastard was jumpin' a freight headed west. The girls took up millinery work. When Dutton turned sixteen, he got hired in the stockyards. But after he saw a man fall into the pit and come out as canned meat, he quit. Matter of fact, he won't eat meat anymore, only fish, fruit and vegetables."

"What else does he do?"

"We don't talk about it. He won't take charity and he has to live. Because he goes where we can't, he has his ear on what's happening in the wards. Keeps Matias and my dad informed."

"Is he a spy?"

"Not intended to be. Just happened that way. He does what he has to do. We all do what we have to do much like it was in

Germany and Austria until Matias and his brother were forced to escape."

"Escape from what?"

"There are some things about the family I can't tell you. They were persecuted and had to leave."

It was with these memories of the day and after a basic meal of schnitzel and potato soup that Julie retired to a cramped bed in the crowded room she shared with Liesel. She fell asleep wondering why Matias and Kurt Bauman were so secretive about their past.

IV

Reformation

Chapter 21

Ophelia

Twice a week, Julie would return to the mansion and have access to her beloved books in Matias Bauman's library. During those periods, the maid, Ophelia Robinson would find some excuse to join her and pretend to clean and dust and straighten up the room.

"Next to my mother, you're the only other person I know I can talk to and confide in," she said. "I hope we can become friends."

"I'm glad to be your friend. But there is someone else you can talk to. Have you met Sophie Augusta Rose?"

"I've occasionally waited on her when she and Herr Bauman have dined together. And she's one of three women I've seen who attend his special meetings. She's not a woman I feel I can talk to as a friend."

"She is overwhelming, I know."

"You don't mind my coming in here when you're reading?"

"No, we can talk all you would like."

"Thank you. You are a most kind and gracious young woman."

In reality, Julie felt like a girl compared to Ophelia who was at least ten years older.

Each evening on her route home, with great apprehension, Ophelia quickly walked the gauntlet of brothels, speakeasies and saloons along Dearborn Avenue. She had been warned what happened to young women who had been drugged and enslaved in the rooms behind the saloons and hotel edifices.

She had heard of the victims seeking the promise of employment in the city. Young white women barely sixteen seeking escape from their rural existence in small Mid-western towns and on failing farms.

The pimps and panders loitering about the station platform could spot a victim instantly as she stepped off the train, clutching a carpetbag containing her meager belongings and standing bewildered amidst the shouts and noise and swirling confusion of rushing passengers rudely pushing her out of the way.

Spewing choking black smoke back over the passenger cars, the chugging train had snaked through the outskirts of the city past acres of shacks and hovels surrounding the stockyards from which rose the shrieks and bellows of cattle and hogs and the blinding stench of slaughter and decay. As the train moved on, sections of small residential houses gave way to rows of mansions and the distant rise of tall office buildings whipped by billowing smoke from industrial stacks that ratcheted along the canyons of the cobbled city streets surging with indigent people and horses and carriages and wagons.

Her anticipation would sink into despair at her overwhelming disorientation, not knowing where to go or to whom she might turn for help.

The pander eyed the small purse slung from a cloth belt and thought of the drinks he would buy with the coins they contained. Pretending to be a successful businessman, he would approach the distraught female whose bewildered expression was suddenly snared by his kind condescending smile.

"Excuse me, miss, but I couldn't help but notice you need some assistance. New to the city perhaps. If it's your first time, a friend to show you the way around can be helpful." He would extend his hand and gently touch the sleeve of her blouse as he introduced himself with a false name. "Allow me to assist with your bag. I know of a good rooming house not far from here that I'm sure you will find suitable for a fine young lady of your charms. The proprietess is my maiden aunt Hilda and she has helped many a young person as yourself get settled and find employment."

"Thank you, sir, for coming to my rescue. I was about to go to the station master."

"He has knowledge only of trains and schedules. Chicago has myriad possibilities, but they are not to be found on this platform. Allow me, miss." As he relieved her of her carpet bag, he would offer his arm and escort her away along unknown streets while dominating their sudden unfamiliar physical closeness with lofty eloquence about the features of the city and the promising future she should expect to discover.

"I imagine you're famished from your journey," he would say. "Was it a long one? Where is the place you called home?"

"A small town in Iowa."

"Ah, so you hail from The Great Plains, but as with so many others, it's time to get ahead in life. People come here to make their fortune, you know. Before long, a pretty woman like yourself could even marry one."

"Oh, I have no thoughts of marriage. I want a job. I want to be someone. Back in our town, there is no future for someone like me other than to marry, keep the house, and raise children to work the farm. I have ambition."

"How refreshing to hear that coming from a young woman. These are times to make that a reality. Women are demanding to be heard, especially the reformers who are petitioning for the right to vote and for laws in the workplace. I admire you for your ambition. I truly do."

"And what about you, sir. What is it that you do?"

"I am pleased that you ask. I'm an independent businessman. I provide special services to other enterprises and advise certain members of the city council."

"You work in the Government?"

"Precisely."

"How wonderful that must be."

"Oh, it's wonderful, all right. I consider myself extremely fortunate to be affiliated with the powerful men who care for and run the city."

"Then I also consider myself fortunate to meet you out of all the people on that station platform."

"I'm successful because I seize opportunity when and where I find it."

"That's a lesson I'll remember."

"I'm sure you will. There's a fine restaurant over there. Shall we?"

"I don't have money to eat in such a place."

"I'm offering you the opportunity to have a good meal at no expense to you. It will give me great pleasure to have you as my guest."

"Well, then, I'll seize the opportunity."

He laughed. "That's my girl."

And she blushed because he has suddenly and unexpectedly called her his girl.

After a heavy lunch of beef with mashed potatoes and biscuits and gravy and the unaccustomed effect of the many glasses of wine he has refilled, she is nodding and working hard to keep her eyelids from closing on the image of his lascivious paternal grin interrupted by the poke of a large black cigar.

"You appear to be getting tired, my dear. The reward at the end of a long journey is a nice comfortable bed."

"If you will take me to the rooming house, I look forward to the bed. I am feeling tired." A sudden shadow of alarm clouds her luminous trusting eyes. "It won't be expensive, will it? I have only a little money to get started. But I can explain that I will be finding a job straight away."

"You have nothing to worry about. I will take care of your expenses until you are settled."

"But, sir, I don't want to take advantage of your kindness."

"Just consider it a loan from a friend. I have more than enough money. We can discuss some means of payment at a later time, only if you wish."

"You are a good and decent man. I don't know why I'm having such trouble staying awake."

"Good wine relaxes a person." He took her small right hand in the two of his and gently massaged her wrist and fingers. She never noticed the few grains of white powder he had sprinkled into her fifth glass of Bordeaux.

She began to collapse against his shoulder. Leaving several large bills on the table, he helped her to her feet, grasped her carpet bag, and lead her stumbling out of the restaurant and only a single block down the street to the brothel.

"Bit out of it, ain't she," said the madame, Imogene Restivo, as they enter the front hall ensconced with dense red draperies forming a backdrop to floral deep-cushioned chairs and divans.

"Just enough. Not too much."

"You gonna give her a turn before I take her."

"Of course, need you ask?"

"Of course," she smiled, showing tobacco-stained teeth as she tamps out her cigarette. "You get 'em while they're virgins. You can have the first room on the right down the hall."

"Clean sheets?"

"For you, dearie, them sheets is always clean."

When the young woman awoke, she discovered her male benefactor was no longer with her. Her clothes and purse and carpet bag had been taken. She noticed a raw soreness between her legs where the man had deeply penetrated her. She was dizzy and her head ached. As she sat up on the edge of the bed, she glanced down and noticed a dented, rusted slop bucket rimed with green scum.

Trying to maintain a sense of focus, she stooped over the bucket and voided her bowels and bladder. She selected a fistful of dirty rags from a nearby pile and wiped herself. She rose and stagged to the door and tried the handle. The door did not give. It was locked. She knocked three times. "Hello, is anyone there. Please, someone help me."

She heard footsteps shuffle along the hall, but no one answered. She pounded on the door. "Hello, please, someone let me out."

No one answered.

Her name was Frieda Olson.

An occasional whistle and catcalls from loitering drunks and plaid – suited drummers hounded Ophelia and sped her along until she crossed an invisible urban demarcation from throngs of smartly dressed white men and women into crowds of Negroes wearing common working clothes much as when they had labored in the cotton and tobacco fields in the South. Here and there, a dark-suited Black businessman stared at her, owning her lithe supple body with his eyes, as she passed deeper along the narrow streets and on to the community called Morgan, to the home she shared with her mother and mostly absentee father.

As Julie came to know her better, Ophelia confided she did not understand the origin of her impatience. She refused to accept and was intolerant of everything she saw around her that her people were willing to endure, beginning with her father, a Pullman porter.

From the time she had been a little girl, she remembered the briefest of days when he was home between long absences, sometimes one, sometimes two months. His absences angered her and she would throw temper tantrums and mope around the house when he departed on his trips.

"Your father's a travelin' man. We can live here because he's a travelin' man." Her mother's explanation that they were able to live in a house in Morgan because of his occupation did not mollify her. She did not understand how the work he did took him away from his family. She did not understand that his serving wealthy white passengers in palatial railroad cars gave them all a living slightly above the squalid conditions of the Black Belt slums. They had clean rooms, a kitchen with running water and an ice box, and a bathroom with a flush toilet. There was a small yard in which she could play and her mother could plant flowers nestled against the porch. She didn't know there was such a place nearby in the city called the Black Belt.

Despite her whining and protest, he would never take her with him on the train. As she lay in her bed at night, she listened to the sounding whistle and labored chug of distant trains passing rapidly in the night and wondered if her father might be on one of them. She paused in her play at the sound of trains, which became a fixture in her imagination that conveyed her father to some mysterious existence in some other life that she could not see.

Joseph Robinson could not dispel the image of his daughter's face contorted with tears of rage when he departed and her ecstatic expression when he returned, sometimes two or three months later, and walked through the front door. He lived for her adoration, a different kind of love than the relationship with his wife and three sons. What he did for her, for all of them, made his work meaningful and its low wages and social degradation endurable. Like the other porters, he called himself a *travelin' man* as a means of giving his line of work some prestige.

For most of his waking and very few sleeping hours, the green plush and polished oak interior of the Pullman car was his life and world, his home and place of work combined.

His fastidious habits and eye for detail had done well by him for the past ten years. He was among the early porters hired because of the deep dark hue of his black skin. Others who had applied for jobs at the time with him had not been hired to work the sleepers, because they were not dark enough to satisfy the need for separation as a servant and inferior being to their white passengers. Those with lighter skin became waiters.

The train had departed from Chicago on its eastern run to New York and Baltimore at mid-afternoon. Long shadows crept over the landscape as Joseph glanced out the window of the swaying Pullman. He checked his pocket watch and noted the time was approaching to begin making up beds for his passengers before they started drifting back from the tin can, the dining car. With one or two exceptions, he didn't expect anyone to retire early. He would more likely be serving the men bourbon and cigars, unless their wives objected, in which event the men would make their way to the lounge car where they could drink and smoke and vociferously carry on without interference. Joseph's task then would be to escort them to a sleeping berth without an unfortunate incident. Most inebriated passengers managed to stagger back unassisted to their seats, adjusting to the swaying motion of the luxury palace cars plummeting through the night.

As he was checking his inventory of sheets and brown blankets used only for berthed passengers and towels in the storage closet, his good friend, Lionel Davis, crossed the vestibule from the neighboring car and leaned in through the half-opened door. "Hey, pillow puncher, got a bid whist game goin' tonight in car nine."

"I'll make it if I can. Depends who's troublesome here. Had me a liquor head last night puked in his berth and shit his underwear. Pulled me out of a snooze and kept punchin' his bell even after I was standin' there. Took him to the toilet and cleaned 'im up. Washed down his ass and limp dick and had to make down his bed all over again. Got puke on my jacket and smelled like a still. Turned out he was a fish. When I got him back to his berth, he was all grateful. Opened his wallet and shelled out a big tip. Made my night."

"See you later then, maybe."

"Maybe."

Joseph bobbed his head around the heap of bedding stacked on his arms and moved toward the interior as the door suctioned closed behind him.

He placed the bedding on the first lower berth and started making down the upper with rapid expert tucks and creases with the pillows placed to position the passenger in the direction of the moving train. He covered the brown blanket with a third sheet to protect the passenger's face from the rougher wool fabric.

Boasting a high school education, Joseph was among the limited number of porters who could read and had studied every regulation in the small brown rulebook he had received during his training. He had never knowingly violated a rule. A simple oversight of putting out soiled linen could mean a report by the conductor and the end of his job. Joseph understood the rulebook ensured a high standard of service consistent on every train. A salute touching the visor of his cap conveyed his pride in the uniform, a dark blue tailored jacket, dark trousers, and black shoes shined to a gloss.

He knew his job barely distinguished him in society, but by association with the Pullman Palace Car opulence, it gave him the distinction of working as a qualified servant once removed from slavery.

His clean police record, dark black skin, five foot ten inch height, and slender physique to maneuver the narrow corridors of the train had been factors in his acceptance for employment. The rulebook ensured his status of being treated as racially inferior.

At nine, passengers began to wander back from the dining and passenger cars to the sleepers. Wearing an elegant dress and flashing an expensive string of pearls, four rings inlaid with rare gems, and a diamond bracelet, Adele Phillips half supported her husband, muttering at the unevenness of the floor and weaving drunkenly along the aisle.

"Careful, Henry, careful. You're an embarrassment." She wrinkled her haughty patrician nose.   Next time, don't drink so much. Porter, Porter," she called to Joseph who turned from tucking sheets in the last upper berth of his car, upper seven.

"Yes, ma'am." He smiled, but didn't grin like an Uncle Tom. He wasn't a company porter and refused to demean himself. Smiles often generated tips. "Just makin' down beds, gettin' ready for the night." He quickly came forward. "Let me help Mr. Henry." He supported the leaning bulk of the man who was breathing heavily in the oppressive heat of the car as he pulled his tie loose, releasing the constraint against his wobbling double chin.

"George, George," he wheezed. Passengers often called the porters George, after George Pullman who had created the Pullman cars. "Need you to help me up into my berth. Good of you. Need to go to the head first."

"Suh, I made up a special bed for you tonight so you don't have to climb the ladder. You can just slide right in."

"You're a good man, George, a damn good man. Thank you for lookin' after me. Don't go far. I might need you a few times during the night. Piss out a few gallons of liquor, if you get what I mean."

Joseph laughed in appreciation. "One of the effects of good scotch, suh."

"They do serve fine scotch on this train."

"Henry does love his scotch," said his wife, "perhaps a little too well."

"You enjoy a nip or two, my dear."

"Don't listen to him, Porter. I take only a glass of sherry."

"Sherry is a fine aperitif for an elegant lady, ma'am. Will you be wanting an upper berth this evening?" asked Joseph.

"That would be best, especially if Henry forgets himself and tries to be amorous. Considering his condition, that is not likely to happen. Being amorous in one's own bedroom is one thing, but it's unthinkable on a train, all this swaying back and forth. A compartment does not provide adequate privacy, don't you think? But I imagine you have seen some who exhibit untoward behavior."

"I do my best not to take notice, ma'am. What people do in private is none 'a my business."

"I expect you will be at our beck and call should we need you during the night."

"Always, ma'am. Just press that button right there to ring for me."

"I've noticed how efficient you porters are, better than our servants at home. They could take a lesson from you."

"Why thank you, ma'am. That is a nice compliment. The Pullman Company trains us well. We spend most of our life on trains."

"How clever. You even have a sense of humor for a colored."

"We do have a sense of humor, ma'am. Learn it from intelligent white folks like yourself."

"How sweet. And by the way, you may call me Mrs. Phillips. Henry works for Pierpont. We're close friends of the Morgans. You do know of whom I'm speaking, J. P. Morgan. Henry was on a business trip in Chicago."

Henry had met with Kurt and Matias Bauman for most of the day on the details of their investment account he managed at the Morgan Bank in New York City.

"To my regret, I'm afraid not, Mrs. Phillips. Although I did once see your photograph in the society section of the New York Times." Joseph knew very well who Adele Randolph Phillips and her husband were. The conductor made sure the porters knew the names and social and political importance of all the prominent passengers on his train.

"Do you read the New York Times?"

"Occasionally, I find one left on a seat by one of the passengers."

"So what I hear is true. You coloreds are trying to improve yourselves."

"Thanks to the beneficence of high class white folks like yourself, we do our best."

"Amazing, simply amazing. Your vocabulary is most unusual. None of our servants use words like that."

"Owe it to a fine college education, Mrs. Phillips."

"You went to college?"

"Tuskegee Institute, ma'am."

"Oh, of course, the school for coloreds."

"That's the one, ma'am. That's where most coloreds go. Some others go to Harvard."

"Harvard? They let you in at Harvard?"

"And Yale and Princeton, if you got the brains."

"Fascinating. I thought they admitted only young white men from the best society families. But with a college education, why are you working as a Pullman Porter?"

"Job security, ma'am. Mr. Pullman gives us coloreds a lifetime job."

"Actually, I do recall that Henry has stock invested in the Pullman Company."

"She's right, George," Henry revived somewhat at the mention of money and his wife's reference to Pierpont Morgan and Wall Street. "Pullman created a goldmine. Nothing in the world like these damn cars. Better than most hotels."

"On behalf of Mister Pullman, I appreciate your fine compliment of his company."

"As a matter of fact, when we get back to New York, I'll call Pullman and tell him myself and I'll mention your name. By the way, what is your name?"

"Oh, Henry, you just need to go to bed," Adele admonished him. It's the liquor talking. Just give him a nice tip and he'll be happy."

"No, I'm serious."

"You've been calling him George ever since you boarded the train."

"Is that your name?" Henry squinted up at him.

Joseph smiled. "Just mention George and Mr. Pullman will know who you mean."

Joseph averted his eyes from Adele's thin-lipped smirk and busied himself with assisting her husband out of his coat, which he hung on a wall hook after removing a bulging wallet from the inside pocket and handing it to Adele. The gesture was noticed by Henry, who nodded affirmatively. Later that night, Joseph would press the man's suit and shine his shoes.

Henry sat heavily on the edge of the lower berth. Joseph immediately dropped to one knee and quickly unlaced and removed the man's shoes, catching his breath along with the sour stench released from his socks. Henry could remove his own socks or sleep with them on for all Joseph cared. He wanted to escape from the compartment and this facile man and his bigoted, condescending wife. Other passengers were waiting. But he had to play out his subservient role. As long as Henry was happy, Joseph could look forward to a sizeable tip. All the porters worked for tips to supplement the insulting, meager wage paid them by the magnanimous George Pullman.

Henry fumbled with his belt and managed to open the front of his pants. "Okay, George, now the trousers."

Joseph tugged at the cuffs, and with some wriggling and squirming by Henry's fat rear on the berth mattress, managed to work the fabric over his white briefs and down the man's hairy legs. He quickly rose and hung the trousers on a second hook next to the coat, then turned to Adele.

"Ma'am, will you be needing any assistance to the upper berth?"

"I'm an equestrian and quite capable of mounting horses as well as climbing a ladder. As for the rest..." her lips separated into a sly grin.

"Of course, ma'am."

"Were you imagining things about me, George?"

"Not at all, ma'am. I only think about serving my passengers and I know others are waiting for help. First time on a sleeping car for some."

"Do you find us amusing, George? I somehow get the impression that a colored man with your education finds us amusing."

"No, ma'am. Doing what we do, we find ourselves amusing."

"You have a subtle sense of innuendo, George. I find that admirable, but disconcerting in a colored."

"I don't quite follow you, ma'am, but I have only your interest in mind."

"As it should be."

As Adele's snoring husband collapsed to the side onto his berth, Joseph scooped up the man's legs and rolled him into a sleeping position.

Adele watched approvingly. "You're a good man, George. You do a fine job."

"Thank you kindly, ma'am."

With Henry's shoes clutched in one hand and his suit coat and trousers draped over the other arm, Joseph politely bowed himself out of the compartment and away from Adele's bemused expression.

In the aisle, he was immediately besieged with the call of "Porter, Porter, we need your help here."

He flattened himself against the wall to allow the passage of a large breasted women maneuvering down the car. Despite the close quarters, he had never once rubbed in contact with a white woman or touched them with his hands, even in assisting them to an upper berth. He had learned the technique of using his elbows to push and shove the many overfed and overweight pounds of flesh for support.

One of George Pullman's cardinal directives of the many listed in the small brown rule book that Joseph carried in his hip pocket was that a Negro porter must never physically place his hands on a white woman. An observation by the white conductor or a complaint from the passenger would instantly get him fired.

Or even murdered.

"Porter. Porter. We would like your assistance, please."

The "please" always caught Joseph's attention. He responded instantly by tossing Henry Phillips' suit coat and trousers behind the curtain of lower 7 and maneuvered along the aisle with a wave to the pleasantly coiffed young businessman standing at the opposite end of the swaying car holding his compartment door slightly ajar. He had removed his coat but a gray silk cravat remained snug at his throat.

As he approached the compartment, Joseph heard the squeals and high pitched excited laughter of two children and mentally prepared himself for the impending encounter. He had seen the ten and twelve year old boy and girl come aboard when the attendant decorated the platform back in Cincinnati. They had been giggling and carrying on playing tag instead of sitting quietly with their mother and father. Joseph looked in at the blonde-headed brother and sister whose expressions suddenly switched to a cherubic serenity, but the mischievous energy playing like electricity about their identical blue eyes did not abate.

I'm in for it now, thought Joseph, but he had handled every kind of white child who rode on his trains from frightened and depressed to the liveliest. By and large he found them much easier to relate to than his adult passengers. With a few ugly exceptions, they hadn't yet integrated the racism and pretentious values of their parents. Sometimes they were just plain fun and brought forward memories of his own three sons and daughter.

"Yes suh, Mr. Haggerty, I see you got yourself two bundles of joy here, a real handful." From his slight bend at the waist, he smiled up at the mock strained features of the benign father.

"Oh, Daddy loves us so much, he let us have ice cream for dessert in the dining car."

"Ice cream!" Joseph raised his pitch in admiration. "You young 'uns must be real special. What's your favorite flavor?"

"I like chocolate," said the girl. My name is Stephanie. What's yours?"

"Joseph, at your service, miss."

"What's a young 'un?" asked the boy.

"Charley, that's not polite, even if he is a Negro."

"Not at all, suh, not at all. Curiosity is the first step to learning something new. Excuse me, Charley. I forgot myself. When my children were about your age, I called them young 'uns. But they were still children all the same." Joseph breathed a deep chuckle. So what's your favorite flavor?"

"Strawberry. I don't know how Stephanie can eat chocolate. It doesn't taste right. It's not sweet."

"It is so sweet. It's sweet to me."

"Isn't it wonderful we all have different taste buds," said Joseph. "Makes life interesting."

"It certainly does," said Mr. Haggerty. "I'd like you to look after Charley and Stephanie while I join my wife in the parlor car for a few hours, if you would be so kind, Joseph. Here's a little something for your trouble." He extended a small wad of bills.

"Why thank you, suh, thank you. Your beautiful children are in good hands, no trouble at all. No trouble at all. We'll have a good time." Joseph quickly slipped the money into his pocket.

"Don't let them talk you into staying up late. My wife and I would like to discover them asleep when we return. This is their first overnight train ride and they're a little excited by the experience."

"Rightly so, rightly so, Mr. Haggerty. Riding a sleeper is a great adventure for children. You go and enjoy the evening with your lovely wife. Please give her my regards. I had the pleasure of meeting her and the children when they first came aboard."

"We heard the conductor shout *all aboard*," said Charley. "I shouted it too. Everybody heard me."

"I'm sure your shout helped 'em scoot right on board too."

"They did move faster," said Stephanie. "But I don't think he should try to be the conductor."

"I can't be a porter," said Charley. "I'm not a Negro. But I can be a conductor, because he's white."

"Good observation there, son. Good observation. We all have our position to work. You can be a conductor."

"See," Charley sneered at his older sister. "I told you. If you want to know anything, ask Joseph."

"To avoid further embarrassment," said their father, "I'll take my leave. Good luck, Joseph."

"Thank you, suh, but luck isn't what this is about."

"Enough said. Now you mind Joseph." He gave each of the children a pat on the head. "He has my permission to do whatever is necessary to keep you in line."

"Oh, nothing to worry about there, suh, especially after I tell them about the train dragon."

"You have a dragon on this train?" Charley erupted form his seat. "Can we see it?"

"You don't want to see the train dragon and you don't want him to see you."

"I'm on my way," Mr. Haggerty left the car with a final wave.

Joseph lifted his hand while continuing to watch the apprehension and intrigue creep into the children's faces.

"Can you get us ice cream?" Charley asked in a quiet voice to mask his concern by being polite.

"I believe that can be arranged. And your favorite flavors. A big dish of ice cream. I happen to know the waiter."

"Oh, how wonderful," Stephanie exhaled. "And some cookies too." Her disarming smile melted Joseph's heart.

If only they didn't have to grow up, he thought. "And cookies too."

The children looked at each other with wide-eyed grins at their good fortune.

"First, I have to take care of a few porter things," said Joseph. "So you just wait right here and when I return, I'll have your ice cream and cookies."

"We won't go anywhere," said Stephanie.

"But don't take a long time," said Charley. "We don't like to wait."

Joseph smiled and touched the brim of his porter's hat. He stepped back, closed the sliding door of the compartment and moved on to confront whoever next needed his services.

The sleeping car was a broad ever-changing convergence of personalities from one trip to the next. The shared common belief by them all was the novelty of the experience and its temporary nature. Passengers would disembark from the train at their destination and never see the porter again.

Joseph understood how riding the train, especially in the sleeping car, unleashed inclinations and desires that would otherwise be repressed in accordance with accepted social rules and propriety. During his ten years, he had witnessed and narrowly avoided involvement in a variety of someone's unusual personal needs and fantasies stimulated by the enclosed world of the moving train and the perception that he was not an actual person, only a character, a servant who would respond to and perform their wishes and commands with no consequences to themselves.

Joseph knew that a large part of their expectations was influenced by how the Pullman Company advertised and promoted riding trains as an affordable adventure for those who were not among the rich. The passenger mix had expanded to people from all walks of life from farmers to factory workers who could pay $2.50 a night for a berth.

Not surprised by any behavior the human condition had to offer, he was, nevertheless, unprepared for an attractive woman traveling alone who beckoned him to enter her compartment. "Porter, Porter, I need your assistance here, please." Her urgent undertone put him receptively on guard.

She did not look distressed, but Joseph could smell liquor on her breath. Her gray-tinted green eyes were dilated and intense.

He had made down her bed an hour ago. "Is everything okay with your berth, ma'am?"

"Oh, the berth is fine, porter, just fine. There is one little thing you can do for me though. Please come in."

Seeing she wore only a night dress, he hesitated. "Would you like something from the kitchen or dining car, ma'am? Or perhaps a nightcap?"

"I never traveled on a sleeper before and I don't quite know how to get into a berth. Would you show me?"

Entering the compartment, he avoided any direct looks at the luxuriant mane of red hair she had let down.

"You get in on your knees," he explained, "and just roll over onto your side."

"You mean like this?" She followed his direction, but as she rolled, pretending to lose her balance, with a soft cry, she grabbed his arm. He saw that she had opened her sleeping gown and now tried to embrace him. She pulled him down with her. "Make love to me, porter. I need you to make love to me. I've heard stories about you colored men. I want to find out for myself. No one will ever know we did this."

"Ma'am. Ma'am, please. Don't do this. With all respect, ma'am. I can't touch you. It's against the rules. It's against the law."

As her unbuttoned nightgown fell completely open revealing firm breasts and luscious rosebud nipples, the rush of an erection and her lavender scented skin nearly overpowered him. Her flailing arm knocked off his hat. Grasping him around the neck, she pulled his face down to hers. Her tongue slid deep into his mouth and darted about the back of his throat. He gasped and pushed himself up from the birth. She grabbed the lapels of his coat and pulled him down again.

"I'll pay you," she moaned into his ear. "I'll pay you one hundred dollars."

"Ma'am, please, I'm not that kind of man."

"Oh, yes you are. I can tell you are. I've been watching you ever since I boarded the train. I've been watching how you move. Now get your pants off and get beside me. We both want this. I can tell. I know." She grabbed his hand and forced it down between her legs pressing it against her hair and vagina. He snatched it away from the warm sticky wetness and rolled off the berth onto the floor, scooped up his fallen hat and leapt to his feet.

"Ma'am, I apologize, but I have to leave you now." His last glimpse was of her pleasuring herself, as he sped out of her compartment and slammed the door. The woman's lingering scent clung to him as he rushed back to his station at the opposite end of the car. Fearing she might chase after him, he locked himself in the commode. He washed his trembling hand and sponged the sweat from his face with a towel.

He had come dangerously close to violating a social and moral code. Even when he was traveling, he didn't fraternize with the all too available Negro prostitutes in far away cities like some of the men. He considered his marriage sacred and he never forgot how a young woman who had become his wife had restored him to health after he had been savagely beaten and left lying in the dirt on the main street of her town.

Chapter 22

Protectors

As Ophelia had related the story to Julie…..

"My mother insisted we develop habits of health and cleanliness. My brothers and I had to brush our teeth twice a day and take a weekly bath even if we didn't have a tub or a local river, which we did when we were still living on a farm in Missouri. She did not tolerate odors of sweat and grime. And if you passed gas, Lord help you.

"Are you a dog?' she would say in a voice that froze your blood. She was and still is a strong woman, a woman of principle who refused to accept her Blackness as being inferior. She pounded that belief into our heads, my brothers and me. We could not look her in the eye when she was displeased with any one or all of us, but she made us. Her frown curled down around her chin like the snarl of a panther and the culprit would be called out and banished with considerable embarrassment to the outhouse. Of course, it was mainly my three brothers who suffered that fate. I was then and have always been a quick learner. Our mother taught us at home. She graduated from the Hampton Institute in Virginia under the tutelage of Booker T. Washington and made sure I attended his next institution of higher learning for Black people, Tuskegee Institute. Did you ever hear of it?"

Julie shook her head. "I'm sorry. I don't know about it."

"Most white people don't. Hampton Institute was the first college for Negroes. My mother had no money and only one set of clothes. But members of her church donated enough for her to buy her books. She had to work for her board and clothes. Her life has been hard and she is a devoted and demanding woman. After she graduated, she returned to her home town to become a teacher of poor children. At the end of the work day, men and women came to her classes in the church, as well.

"She met my father when he was a young Pullman car porter. His train had made a stop at her town and he had stepped off to buy chewing tobacco for one of the passengers. The general store was in a white section of town and he made the mistake of trying to walk in. A group of white men on the porch were not impressed by his uniform. They dragged him out into the street and beat him bloody. His uniform was torn and covered with dirt. My mother saw what those men did to him. She helped him to his feet and supported him until two other Negro men helped her. He could barely talk and kept saying he had to get back to his train. They could hear the whistle, as the train pulled out of the station and left him behind. He said he would be fired from his job.

"Mother took him to her parents' home where she lived at the time. They cared for his injuries. When the train came through again two weeks later, the white conductor wouldn't let him on board, because my father's face was recovering from cuts and bruises and his right eye was still swollen half shut. The conductor told him if he looked better the next time the train came through, he would let him back on, but headquarters might still fire him for leaving the train.

"Well, mother not only felt sorry for him, as she got to know him, she fell in love. He was well mannered, educated, and he pitched right in helping my folks with work on their farm. He could even cook and he made up beds better than any of them.

"His face healed and the conductor let him back on the train. Mother didn't see him again for a year. She thought he had been fired. But one day, she received a letter asking her to marry him. He had been transferred to a northern route. He asked her to join him in Chicago. Mother didn't have money for train fare. She had a sister in Decatur. Her father took her there on his farm wagon. She said it was a long hot dusty journey. Sometimes they had to sleep near a stream at the side of the road. Other times, when they stopped to inquire at a church, people were kind enough to give them a meal and a place to sleep, even if it was in a barn. Then her sister's husband took her the rest of the way on his wagon to Chicago.

"My father had instructed her to go to the Pullman Club where he planned to meet her. He wasn't there when she arrived, but a fellow porter, Lionel, who was a friend of father, said he would return in three days and offered the hospitality of his home and family. Mother was forever grateful to him. After mother and father were married, they bought a house next door to Lionel."

As Joseph walked the aisle of the sleeper and listened for snores and the occasional moan of someone dreaming, satisfied that everyone was sleeping in their berths, he emptied and washed out the spittoons containing acrid half-smoked cigars and stringy reddish stained saliva of chewing tobacco jettisoned from the jowls of wealthy businessmen during the day's journey. He refilled soap dispensers, cleaned toilets, and arranged fresh towels. A small tin of polish and a soft rag he carried brought out the shine of the brass lamp fixtures, cushion buttons, and hand rails. Encapsulated in luxury that he could never enjoy, he was responsible for providing and maintaining the comfort of the white passengers. His legs and feet and lithe body reflexively balanced and enjoined him as one with the thrusting momentum of the train.

Occasionally, he heard someone call out, "Porter, Porter, I'm too hot. Can you do something about it?"

He adjusted the temperature of the car by a slight turning of a valve on the steam pipes at the storage end of the car.

Another common summons from small children, "I have to go potty." He helped a child with curly brown hair and heavy eyelids flitting down from an upper berth. The parents slept on, oblivious to their son's urgent need. Joseph held his hand and directed his small penis as the boy's head lolled sleepily against him. He picked up the slumbering boy and carried his limp body sideways along the aisle and gently placed him back in his berth, tucking the sheet and blanket under the small dimpled chin.

"Our mother taught my brother and me, too," Julie shared. "We lived on a wheat farm way out on the prairie in Minnesota. We had a wonderful life until the day they were killed by an assassin. He later came after my brother and me in search of a list. He wanted the names so he could find and kill them all I think. I didn't know why then. I didn't know mother and father were members of a secret society."

"A secret society? What kind of society?"

"They were free thinkers."

"You mean revolutionists."

"I don't know what that means."

"A revolutionist fights for freedom from tyranny.

"They were farmers. They weren't fighting for anything."

"I know what tyranny is. Every African person knows. Perhaps in the past, where your mother and father came from there was tyranny."

"When Newt and I were small children, they brought us from Sweden."

"You said they were murdered."

"Newt and I never let him have the list. We escaped to a lumber camp in the north. The killer tried to track us down. I've seen him here in Chicago. But I don't think he knows we are here."

"Do you still have the list?"

"We gave it to Mr. Bauman."

"That explains it."

"Explains what?"

"The people who come and go from the mansion. They hold secret meetings. I think they're revolutionists. Gustav has me serve coffee and cakes. He warned me not to enter the library without knocking and waiting to be admitted. I can hear their voices, but they stop as soon as I knock. When I roll in the food cart, they pretend to be reading or a few of them talk about their wives and children. I once heard them mention the homeland and the old country, something about the Kaiser. Sometimes they stay for dinner. I have also served them then. When they've been drinking wine, they don't seem to care what they say and they become loud and boisterous. Sometimes when they notice I'm listening, they speak German.

"I know that Mr. Bauman helps people. He gives them money. He has me work with other people to deliver a newspaper and pamphlets on the streets. "

"What are they about?"

"The newspaper is called *The Liberator*. The pamphlets are written in different languages, but they talk about human rights and how to join the socialist party."

"Could I see them? Do you have any here?

"No, I don't bring them here."

"Would you sometime? I'd like to read them."

"I'll bring some of them. But you might also see me out in the city. I'm a newsie."

"I avoid the white sections of the city."

"I could come to where you live."

"You will not want to do that. White people don't come into the Black Belt. It isn't safe for you."

"There are other places that aren't safe either."

"You must be speaking of the Levee."

Julie nodded. "I went there once. I saw Luther Baggot on his horse and followed him. My protector made me come away."

"You have a protector?"

"His name is Conrad."

"How did you come to have this protector?"

"He and his father work for Mr. Bauman. They publish the pamphlets and the newspaper and I suppose they do other things."

"So you're one of them, the group."

"I don't know anything about the meetings. I haven't seen those men."

"Sometimes, there are women who join them too. One of them is the wife of a city alderman. Her name's Maureen Keeley. She wants to get the law changed so women can vote. She always brings a preacher with her, Reverend Thrasher. He organizes and leads marches against brothels and vice dens in the Levee district and he campaigns against corrupt politicians. Maureen Keeley's husband is one of them. Mrs. Keeley and the Reverend don't stay for dinner. Probably because the other men get drunk."

Ophelia hung her maid's uniform neatly among the dozen domestic uniforms in the closet of the servant quarters. She quickly donned her street clothes, a dark shirt-waist blouse and long straight skirt for the cross-town journey to her home in Chicago's south side, the Black Belt.

She stared at her image momentarily in the mirror. She was twenty-six, a beautiful, vibrant Negro woman with prospects of marriage to an eligible man who was acceptable to her mother, but Ophelia had hesitated. She had resisted his offers for nearly a year. She sensed the frustration, and recent anger, of her suitor and did not blame him, but he would just have to live with her refusal.

"I am not who you think I am," she told him. "I am not like other women."

"You're a woman to me in every way I could ever want," Alphonse Munch had groveled at her feet. "I will do anything you ask. I am your servant."

It was the word servant that had triggered her response to reject him.

"I work as a servant," she said. "I don't want to be married to one."

"You don't understand. When I say servant, it is a profession of my love for you. If you will marry me, I will dedicate my life to you."

"I don't want dedication, Alphonse, as nice as you make that sound. I want independence. I'm not here just to carry your babies around in my belly."

"If we get married, why don't you want to have babies? That's what being married is all about. Didn't your mama teach you that?"

"My mama taught me that I have a brain, a good brain and that I should use it to do something meaningful."

"I have a brain, Ophelia. I have a brain too, but I also have a body. I have a body with needs just like you have a body. And I know your body has needs like mine."

"You're a man, Alphonse. Your needs are not like mine. You can take care of your needs in the Levee, if you're so inclined."

"No, no, why you makin' this so hard on me, Ophelia. I never been to the Levee and don't never want to go. I want us to be man and wife and raise a family of wonderful children, boys and girls. We gonna raise 'em to go to church and praise the Lord. We ain't gonna be no drinkin' family. We gonna be what the Lord wanted us to be, good Christians. Good Christians. I have work. I have a clean job. Don't gamble like your brother does. I ain't goin' to leave you."

"We don't use the word ain't in our family. We say aren't."

"I am sorry on my hands and knees for not knowing the right words to say. I am tryin' the best I know how to tell you how much I love you. I'm hopin' a word here and there you don't cotton to don't get in the way. If you will teach me, I will glady learn anything you want me to - anything."

"What is it about me that makes you want to marry me? I'm not beautiful, so don't start with that or I will toss you out into the street. I look like a Negro woman right off the farm."

"To me you are the most beautiful woman I have ever known."

Ophelia rose from her chair in a fury.

"No, no," Alphonse raised his arms to avoid being struck by the thunderbolts of a goddess. "I didn't mean that. You're beautiful in a way I can't explain. It comes from somewhere inside you and I see it lookin' at me. And you are a smart woman. Your mind works."

"No one knows what goes on inside of me."

Alphonse paused and looked up at her with puppy dog eyes. "Ophelia, why you makin' me do this? I just love you. That's all. Why ain't it enough?"

"Because ain't isn't enough. I don't want to be married to a man who is not educated. We do not tolerate ignorance in our family."

"I can't help it where I come from. We all come from somewhere down there or our momma and papa did. We ain't that long ago from bein' slaves. I come to Chicago to better myself. Why won't you give me a chance?"

"For one thing, I'm not ready to marry anybody. There are certain things I want to do and marriage and children will only get in the way. You don't want to be married to a woman who will resent you, maybe hate you, and her children."

"You got ambition, Ophelia. That's what you got, ambition. I got ambition too. We don't got to have kids right away. Kids can come later after we're settled in our ways and taken care of the things we need to do."

"I'm not going to stand here and argue about this. My answer is final. It's no."

"I am heartbroke, Ophelia. I am truly heartbroke."

"There are lots of women out there who would make you a good wife."

"No one can hold a candle to you."

"I am asking that you respect me. I don't want you to call on me again."

"I can wait. Maybe another time."

"There will be no other time."

Nodding and bobbing with pain and rejection in his eyes, Alphonse backed out of the door she held open for him. "I won't forget you, Ophelia. I promise I won't."

He stumbled away down the front porch steps of the home Ophelia shared with her mother. Awash with self pity and emotional anguish, he wandered to the Levee district and went into a saloon for the first time since he had come north from Missouri.

A professor in a far corner pounded out a rousing ragtime tune that washed over the smokey haze undulating above the heads of huddled Negro men swilling beer and whiskey and shouting to be heard. Slightly disoriented, Alphonse scuffled through the sawdust on the floor to an open spot at the bar.

The sting of the first whiskey slithered down his throat, causing a sharp gasp. He ordered a mug of frothy beer to chase the second. After the third, his mind slipped into a pleasant euphoria. He turned and leaned back with his elbows supporting him on the bar and looked out over the crowded room. He felt strangely relaxed and comfortable as though he had arrived at a place where he belonged, but had never known it before. The sins of drink and the flesh had been the subject of countless lectures and sermons he had received since he was a small boy sitting on a wooden bench in his father's church in their small Missouri town.

But he was a man now with a man's desires that needed to be fulfilled. Since he saw no possibility of that happening with Ophelia in a marriage blessed by his father, Alphonse felt no further obligation to comply with religious dogma, especially now that he lived in the proximity of the Levee.

Several women circulated among the men congregated in small groups at tables where the rattle of skillfully shuffled cards and the ring of coins vied with the garrulous voices of the gamblers.

Alphonse had money, but he didn't know how to gamble and didn't want to risk being cheated out of it in a game of chance. But he would not object to spending it lavishly to explore one of the beautiful black bodies in a private room. He watched and waited until one that caught his eye approached him with her thrusting breasts, a toothsome smile and inviting lips. He nodded as she slipped her arm through his and led him away to his fantasy.

There was another man who attracted Ophelia's interest. She had seen him give a speech at a church-sponsored political gathering. She had missed his introduction other than hearing he was a lawyer, but from his presentation, thought he might be running for public office. He had once worked as a Pullman car porter to earn a living, since most Negro lawyers were not given cases to represent in court and Negro folk could not afford to pay lawyer fees. Ophelia liked what he said and that he credited his comments to his sociology professor from Atlanta University, William Du Bois.

Since there were thousands of Pullman car porters traveling back and forth across the country, her father, Joseph, did not personally know him. When Ophelia expressed an interest in meeting the man, Joseph said he would make an inquiry at the Pullman club. He had heard the name of Bernard Hutchins spoken in various circles of the Pullman porters, but she was eventually able to learn more about him from an assistant preacher of the Negro Church, which functioned as a local government for citizens of the Black Belt. Laws and politicians barred Negroes unless it was to prosecute them for crimes against white citizens. These were the cases that Bernard sought, Black defendants in the dangerous territory of white courts.

Although he rarely won a case, because of the racist jurists and all white members of the jury, he detected he had the respect of at least one of the Chicago city judges, even though they were all on the dole of Bathhouse John Coughlin and Hinky Dink McKenna, who maintained their own form of moral crookedness.

As he attempted to carve out a law practice, Bernard made it a point, to associate with educated Negroes like himself who had matriculated from slavery and the dirt floor hovels of Negro schools throughout the South taught by graduates from the normal schools and Negro colleges, Fisk University, Spelman Seminary, Tuskegee Institute, and Tyler University, to become businessmen, doctors, clergymen, lawyers, and teachers. The majority of these fellow achievers came together within the society of the church.

He fervently believed in the truth and necessity of Dubois's philosophy for Black men and women to organize and advance themselves according to their ability and worth in pursuit of the highest ideals. He had dedicated his career and his life toward that goal. But in attempting to shed the weight of a former slave economy created by white capitalists, he had encountered the implacable wall of economic oppression and racist hate.

In his most recent case, Bernard had defended Edward Thomas for burglary. The young man had been caught late at night stealing goods from the textile warehouse where he worked during the day. He claimed the owner had not paid him his wages for the past two months and Edward had a wife and child to feed and support.

The warehouse foreman painted a picture of Edward as a malingerer who had repeatedly not shown up for work, and when he did, he had been drinking, accusations that Edward denied. When on the witness stand in open court, Bill O'Riley, a tall florid Irishman with hoary gray muttonchops, pointed his stubby tobacco-stained finger at Edward sitting next to Bernard at the defense counsel table and said, "What I'm tellin' ya is God's truth. He's no different than all the rest of the Nigger bucks. They ain't to be trusted."

Ignoring the statement, Bernard continued his line of questioning. "Mr. O'Riley, how long did Edward Thomas work for you?"

"Cain't remember exactly, maybe a year."

"In fact, Edward Thomas worked at your warehouse for over two years."

"You callin' me a liar?"

"No, Mr. O'Riley, I'm saying that in the throes of labor and running a business, it's easy to lose track of how long a valued employee may have worked for you."

"If he was a good worker, I'd remember."

"But you just told the court you can't remember exactly, in your words."

The prosecuting attorney rose from his table. "Objection, Your Honor, defense counsel is badgering the witness."

The keen blue-eyed glare of Judge Kettering focused on Bernard. Even though it was his courtroom and the attorney's question was legitimate, he could not allow it to go into the record.

"The defense counsel will stay on the circumstances of the incident and not engage in speculation of the memory of the witness. Objection sustained. Proceed."

Bernard swallowed his humiliation at this unbalanced treatment. He gave not a flicker of expression, because he knew his case would worsen if he challenged the objection, even by a casual nonverbal gesture. A Negro lawyer in a white man's court was in a subservient position. His line of questioning had to be indirect so as not to appear he was drawing answers from the witness by using common logic. Despite his disadvantage, Bernard determined he would do the best he could for his young defendant. He hoped to at least reduce the jail-time sentence. The foreman's refusal to pay his employee would go unremarked. The jury would accept his lies.

"I'll rephrase the question, Your Honor. Mr. O'Riley, how many Negro employees do you have working for you?"

"I don't keep track of 'em. They come and go as I need 'em. Don't recognize half of 'em. All Niggers look the same to me."

"Up until this incident when Edward Thomas was arrested for stealing from the warehouse, you paid him for the work he performed?"

O'Riley bristled. "I said I did. He got paid fair and square."

"For the last three months before the incident, did you ask him to continue to work for you?"

"I told him I had work."

"Did he come and do the work?"

"I saw 'im from time to time. But I got better things to do than stand around watchin' Niggers work."

"Was the work done to your satisfaction?"

"What the hell do you mean by that?"

"Answer the question," Judge Kettering barked before the corpulent prosecuting attorney could raise an objection.

"Did you like the way Edward Thomas did the work you asked him to do?"

O'Riley shrugged. "Good enough."

"Edward Thomas claims you did not pay him for the work he performed during that time of three months and it forced him to commit a desperate act to support his family."

"You callin' me a liar, you black piece of shit?"

The gavel cracked like an explosion throughout the courtroom.

"Mr. O'Riley, this is a court of law. It is my court and all rules of legal decorum will be observed. If you make another outburst like that, I will have you arrested and fined for contempt and you, not the defendant, will spend time in jail. Do I make myself clear?"

O'Riley's rheumy eyes lowered to his white-knuckled fists grasping the top edge of the witness stand. "Nigger lover," he muttered.

Bernard heard him, but the judge did not. "If you have something to say, say it to the court. Don't mumble in your beard."

O'Riley shook his head. His slowly raised eyes came back into contact with Bernard. He was surprised by the clear intelligence and power he saw in the attorney's expression. O'Riley blinked. Bernard did not.

"Your Honor," said O'Riley. "I'm truly sorry. And to you," he pointed at Bernard, "I apologize. I forgot myself. The judge is right. This is a court of law. I spoke out of turn. It won't happen again."

"Your apology is duly noted in the record. Now, please answer the question."

"Would you mind repeatin' it? I forgot myself."

"Counsel, repeat the question."

"Did you like the way Edward Thomas did the work you asked him to do?"

"He did fine."

"Did you perhaps just forget to pay him?" Bernard was giving him the opportunity to redeem himself.

"Like I said, sometimes I don't remember every detail and I could maybe forget. But now that it's come to all this, I'll give 'im the back pay and be done with it."

The prosecuting attorney leaped up from his chair in a state of red-faced bloating apoplexy. This admission would not be a precedent he agreed to. "Your Honor, a crime was commited here. My client is not on trial. What are you going to do about the criminal?"

"The witness may step down. Would counsel for both sides approach the bench?"

Amidst a low rumble of opinions, O'Riley returned to the audience and Bernard and the prosecutor, Reginald Groggins, met at the bench.

"We have two issues here to resolve," said Judge Kettering quietly. "One is clear. The young man will be paid for his work. The second is not. He broke the law. He will have to answer for that. Do I make myself understood, gentlemen?"

"Yes, Your Honor."

"Mr. Thomas will have to do time, but under the circumstances, I am inclined to be lenient. He was looking at three years in prison."

"For petty theft?" asked Bernard.

"Stay with me here, Mr. Hutchins. I am reducing his sentence from three years to one year and he may be paroled early for good behavior."

"Thank you, Your Honor."

"And Mr. Groggins, I had better not see your client in my courtroom again. His behavior is unacceptable. Next time, I will not be so lenient. Do I make myself clear?"

"Yes, your honor. Thank you, sir. I appreciate your leniency."

"Let's get on with the summaries. It's almost time for lunch."

As the bailiff marched the shackled prisoner, Edward Thomas, out of the courtroom to a holding cell, Bernard went immediately to console Winnie Thomas and her young daughter. He offered his handkerchief. "I'll walk you home."

"It ain't fair, Mr. Hutchins. That evil man told what he did to my husband."

"I wish I could have had the sentence removed, but the situation was against him. I asked the judge to let me bring the money to you. He said it would be three days."

"I don't care about the money. I just want my Edward."

During the pretrial visit with Edward in preparing his case, the young man had reminded Bernard of his own brother, a handsome quiet boy just out of his teens. The fear and uncertainty in his eyes caused Bernard to hold Edward's thin trembling body in an embrace.

"You will get through this," he assured him. "I can't promise you there won't be a sentence. I know people who will help your wife and girls. I'll do everything I can for you."

"Thank you, suh. I am grateful."

Bernard's own words echoed in his memory three days later when he returned to the court to receive Edward's back payment from the clerk. He counted it carefully, surprised to discover the full amount. O'Riley clearly didn't want any further problems with the judge. Intending to see Edward at the jail, Bernard was told by the desk sergeant that, "we shipped him yesterday to Joliet Prison."

The news worried Bernard. Joliet was known for the brutality of its white prison guards and the sordid living conditions for inmates. Edward was not a fighter. He was a gentle soul and he was a Negro.

The despair of the Negro lives around him closed in on Bernard as he walked along the narrow dirt streets of the Black Belt slums to the apartment Winnie Thomas shared with two other families. One of the wives worked as a maid in a cheap south side hotel. Winnie did piecework in a sweatshop. The third wife stayed with the small children.

Winnie clutched his arm in gratitude when Bernard handed her the money. He could not avoid noticing how thin and sinewy her body was under her faded dress.

"Did you see Edward? Did you see my Edward? Are they treating him well?"

Bernard explained where Edward had been taken.

"Can I see him?" Her dark eyes bulged from the whites of her bloodshot eyes.

Bernard looked away toward her little girl in the cluster of children. Tight black curls sprung from Tonia's head. Three pigtails sprouted like burnt tufts of wheat pulled back from the brow of her little friend, Anna, holding her hand. Bernard was moved in a paternal way by their innocence and natural pure beauty. The absence of their father would be difficult for them.

"I can ask, but I don't have much hope."

"Oh… Oh."

"I'll come to see you from time to time. I'll try to get information on how Edward is doing."

Winnie nodded and wiped at her sudden rush of tears with the back of her hand.

Chapter 23

The Nietzsche Club

"Hurry, Julie. *Schnell! Schnell!* You're eating too slow," Liesel coaxed from across the table.

"I just sat down, Liesel. I can't help it if you ate before anyone else."

"If we're late, Sophie won't take us and it will be your fault."

"Sophie is not even at the house. She goes riding early in the morning." Julie stuffed a large spoonful of hot oatmeal mixed with dried fruit into her mouth.

"Where did she learn to ride?" Julie asked. "I saw her once. She jumps her horse over fences."

"Her uncle was a cavalry officer in the palace guard of the Emperor Franz Joseph in Vienna. He taught her how to ride. I need your help at the shop today," Horst nodded at Conrad, who was shoveling in his breakfast as though someone would try to take it from him. "There's a finishing job on a table. Dutton sanded the wood yesterday. You have a fight tonight?"

Conrad nodded, "Reinekees." He slurped coffee from a large crockery cup that his mother placed before him.

Julie swallowed and said, "I thought he would be going with us. Who will guard us?"

"Not to buy a dress," said Conrad. "Just don't hand out any pamphlets along the way. I noticed you have some in your bag."

"Those are for one of the housekeepers, Ophelia Robinson. She likes to read and asked me to bring them."

"She a Negro?" asked Horst.

"Yes, she went to college though. Her mother's a teacher."

"There should be some other kind of work for her," said Frau Holtzman.

"Things will change. *Schwarzer* are kept down here. They do the *schieze* jobs." Horst held out his coffee mug for a refill.

"Can we come and see you fight?" asked Liesel. "I'll wear my new dress."

"Reinekee don't let nice girls into his saloon.   But it don't matter. It'll be out back of his place. He lights it all up. People can buy drinks and bring 'em out. He don't want us breakin' up his place."

"Who are you fighting?" Julie asked.

"Whoever wants to take the challenge," said Horst. "Havin' a fight brings in customers and that means sellin' more beer and whiskey."

"Have you ever lost?"

Conrad looked deep into Julie's eyes and smiled. "Never."

"He has a secret punch,"said Liesel. "I seen him use it on a man the size of an ox. Put him out like a sleepin' babe."

"Reineke gives me a cut from the drinks sold, as long as I win. So I always win," said Conrad.

"And I handle the bets so no cheatin' goes on," said Horst, "unless I'm the one doin' it." He laughed.

"I want to see you fight," said Julie.

"You do, do you?   You worried I'm not good enough to protect you on the streets?"

"No, you already saved me once. But what if Luther Baggot is there?"

"I'm not goin' to be handin' out pamphlets and he doesn't know who I am."

"If Baggot shows up, I'll be watchin' him," said Horst. "We know who he is and who he works for. Rudolph Palm was a senior officer with Otto von Bismarck's secret police. Through his spies, Palm followed us when we left Deutschland. He knew we helped Matias escape from Vienna."

"That isn't his real name?"

"No, it's Heinrich Wohlman. Only some of us know that. Be sure you keep it to yourself. "

"All those names on the list--he said he knew my mother and father."

"They worked for us in Sweden."

"What did they do? What did you do?"

"What we do here in America. Only, in Deutschland, Germany, it was different. We were not just *buergertum, bourgeoisie*. We were socialists, just as we are here. The aristocrats, the *Reich*, tried to control us. Our lives were always in danger. We were hunted by Bismarck's secret police. Some of our people were tortured. That's how I got this." He pointed to the black leather patch covering his right eye. "Palm's mission was to discover who we are and destroy all of the organizers, even in other countries. He ran a vast network of spies. Some infiltrated our organization. When Bismarck was no longer chancellor, we think Palm found another use for Luther Baggot's skills and he followed us here to America. But since we changed our names, he has not been able to find us. We don't know where Palm is or who he works for, but we believe Luther Baggot is connected to him. Baggot is a hired assassin. He sometimes works as a strike breaker. He also hires himself out as a bounty hunter. Ask Sophie Rose to tell you what happened in Vienna. She was with Matias and helped him escape. She can tell you more."

Liesel growled, "Will you stop talking to her and let her finish."

"I'm done," Julie said and stood up from the table. *"Danke, frau Holzman."*

"Wilkommen." She took the bowl and spoon and empty mug of coffee Julie handed her.

She was now anxious to get moving. She wanted to hear what had happened in Germany and Austria and how her parents had been involved. With cries of *"wiedersehen,"* Liesel and Julie raced out the door into the noise and stench and misery of the crowded street.

There were no cabs in their neighborhood because of the poverty, few could afford to ride in them. They dodged along narrow dirt streets and side alleys until they came out at the loop on LaSalle Avenue.

At first they couldn't get the attention of a driver until Liesel stepped in front of a horse and held her money up for the man to see. Dressed as they were and coming from the tenements, they didn't look like paying customers. He leaned down and took her money. As they opened the door to step inside, Julie shouted the Erie Street address amid the din of clopping hoofs and passing carriages and wagons. The driver gave them a doubtful glance, as if they would have no business at the north side location unless it was something illegal.

As the hansom lurched forward then settled into a gentle swaying motion at the horse's steady trot, the girls watched the city sights, tall buildings, women mincing along wearing *la belle epoque* dresses and wide-brimmed hats with lavish plumage of tropical birds. Businessmen wearing dark suits and cloaks, white spats winking from their shoes at each step, touched the brim of bowler hats in ritual acknowledgement of others entitled like themselves. Many of them smoked cigars and thrust slender fashionable canes in a dapper way as they paraded along the sidewalk.

A short time later, they left the churning urban mass behind and passed along quiet shaded streets lined with a procession of elegant, expensive homes and mansions proclaiming the wealth of their inhabitants.

Liesel's body twitched with anticipation. The hansom finally turned in at the curving driveway of Matias Bauman's modest mansion, by comparison to others that looked like massive stone temples transplanted from European estates. Before the cab even stopped, she kicked open the door, leaped to the ground, and fled up the granite front porch steps.

Julie still could not reconcile in her own mind why Matias Bauman owned such wealth and was a socialist who had changed his name. She wondered why he and his brother, Kurt, were so mysterious. At the first opportunity, she would ask Sophie Rose to tell her what happened in Vienna.

She followed in a mildly sedate and calm manner, while Liesel rattled the polished brash knocker against its plate. The door slowly opened. She let out a whoop and rushed past a surprised Gustav. The butler scowled at Julie, then smiled. "Who gave you permission to bring that wild animal home with you?"

"Sophie Rose is taking us to buy dresses today."

"Had I known, I would have ordered a cage. How have you been the past month, my dear? I've missed seeing you reading a book in the library."

"I'm in need of a bath," Julie replied walking past him into the entry hall.

"Indeed you are," he sniffed and closed the door with a cheery wave to the cab driver turning his horse about. The whip popped inches above the animal's back snapping him into a brisk, high-tailed trot.

"Is Sophie here?" she asked Gustav.

"She hasn't returned from her ride. But she left instructions for me to tell you that Ophelia is drawing you and your loud friend a bath. Yours is in your room and Liesel's is in the room across the hall."

"You know Liesel?"

"For many years, since she was a child. She is still *eine kind*."

"Were you with them in Germany?"

"I served in the household of Herr Bauman's father."

She stared at him. "Where is he? What happened to him?"

"Another time my curious cat. Your bath is waiting." He strode ahead of Julie in pursuit of Liesel. "Liesel! Liesel! *Komst du fur ein bad, du shrecklish kind*!"

Julie bounded up the stairs to the second floor and walked quickly down the hall to her room. The door stood ajar, as well as to the room directly across from hers. She entered and saw Ophelia bending over the white porcelain tub with curved cast iron legs. A cloud of steam swirled up around her as she tested the hot water gushing from the tap. She waited a moment for her to turn.

"Oh, you're here. Gustav said you would be arriving shortly. Your bath is nearly ready." She grinned as Julie held out a stack of pamphlets. "How good of you to remember."

"Hi, Ophelia."

"Good morning to you, Julie. Thank you." She flipped the pages of the top pamphlet. "You are so gracious."

"There's more where those came from."

"I'll accept all you can get for me. After I read them, I'll give them to my father. He takes them on the train and gives them to our people at stops along the way. You would be amazed how much they learn from reading the white man's newspapers and pamphlets like these. They give them hope. They give all of us hope."

"Liesel is not far behind me. Gustav is scolding her."

"He always does. He's her godfather."

"Her godfather? There's so much I don't know about the people who live here."

"I have to check on her bath. I started the water running a few minutes ago."

Liesel suddenly burst into my room. "Gustav is such a terrible man. He still treats me like I am five years old."

"Your bath is ready across the hall, Miss Liesel."

"Ophelia is the only older person I know who treats me like a lady."

"If I treat you with respect, then you will be respectful."

"Tell that to Gustav. He's becoming a grumpy *grandfader*."

"That's his way of showing he loves you."

"Then I would not want to have him hate me. I can't wait to get into that bath. Did you scent the water?"

"Will you listen to her, Julie? She is a princess in disguise, *princesse en charade*. Your water is scented, *mon cherie*."

"Do you think I'm French?"

"You act French enough. That is a compliment."

Leisel lifted the sides of her skirt and executed a clumsy curtsy while sticking out her tongue at Ophelia, who cast a sidewise glance at Julie and shook her head. "Respectful." She preceded Liesel across the hall.

Julie closed her door, quickly shed her clothes into a soiled pile and eased her naked body into the hot, inviting water. Ophelia had scented her bath too, with rose water. The aroma caused her to wonder if Rose was Sophie's real surname or if she too was a *princesse en charade.*

The water was so soothing that she settled down, lay her head back and closed her eyes. She slipped into a doze and the next thing she remembered, Liesel was shaking her by her shoulders and splashing water in her face.

"*Dumkoff, dis ist* not time sleep. *Schlaft du nicht*! Sophie has returned. She is preparing to take us for dresses."

"Go away," Julie sputtered. I can get ready sooner if you stop shaking me." She noticed Liesel was wearing a clean skirt and shirtwaist blouse. "Where did you get those?"

"Ophelia provides us. Yours is on de bed. Dis is how I want to live from now on. *Nein shrecklich.* I never want to go back to that pigsty in the tenements. "

"You know we both have to go back. It's our job. Hand me that towel and give me privacy."

Liesel took a thick wooly towel from a wall hook and thrust it at Julie. "You don't have to be ashamed. You have nothing I don't have, except *meine brusts* are bigger." She hefted her breasts. "We are the same."

"Your mouth is bigger too. And you have bigger feet. They might not even have shoes that fit you. And my waist is smaller, much smaller."

"You are envy of my mouth."

"I am not envious of your mouth. The word is envious."

"You read more books than I do."

"I also speak more English than you do."

"But you do not know much *Deutsch.*"

"*Touche'.*"

"See. *Das ist Franzosisch.*"

Julie rose up with a splash deliberately trying to get water on Liesel's skirt, but she leapt back. *"Acht du liebe!"*

Quickly wrapping herself in the towel, Julie pointed imperiously to the bedroom door and saw Beth wander in. "Well, sisters, I see you've decided to come up in the world. I hear Sophie Rose is taking you to buy some suitable clothes. How's life treating you down in the gutter?" she smirked at Julie.

"Who invited you to come in here?" Julie snarled at her. "Nobody, that's who."

"Now, now, don't be apoplectic."

"You didn't learn that word back on the farm."

"I have learned a great deal more than you can imagine since coming to live here in these pleasant and suitable surroundings. Do you know that I'm going for a vocal audition for a musical? Sophie and my voice teacher arranged it. They said I'm ready for the stage."

"Since this is the first I've heard of your audition, I'm sure you're going to tell me more."

"So glad you inquired, Julie dear."

"I'm not your dear. So stop putting on airs. And you're not going to tell me until I'm ready to listen, which is not at this moment. Both of you leave the room so I can dress."

"She is ashamed because her brusts are not as big as mine," said Liesel.

"Get out!" Julie shouted at them. "Get out!"

Laughing at her frustration with them, they left the bedroom but did not close the door. Julie shambled across the thick carpeted room with her towel and slammed and locked the door.

Julie was amazed that Sophie Rose could come in sweating and stinking of horse, then be ready to go into town on a shopping trip looking clean and elegant, not a hair out of place, and smelling as fresh and jubilant as the broad gleaming smile that was her trademark. When Julie asked how she transformed herself so quickly, she explained that she had years of practice executing quick costume changes during opera performances. She also gave Ophelia credit for assisting her.

Augusta would rush into her bedroom, sit on a bench and raise her legs so Ophelia could pull off her boots, step out of one set of clothes, douse herself with a scented sponge bath, run a towel over her body, pull on an undergarment, then step into her dress in all of fifteen minutes. She said she never wore a corset, but she didn't need one. Riding horses kept her figure trim and slender, as did the physical and emotional energy of rehearsing and singing the lead in opera productions.

Matias had taken Newt, Aaron, Beth and Julie once to see her in a production of the Italian opera *Cavalleria Rusticana* at the Chicago Theater. She described it as among the first of the *verismo* or natural librettos that people who were not rich could relate to. She said that the constant stream of musicals and operettas that came through town originated with the *verismo* operas. That she could speak and sing in five different languages amazed Julie. As a diva in Vienna, she had sung and performed in many of the great operas by Mozart, Verdi, Puccini, Rossini, Strauss, and others.

She joined them in the foyer and raised her hand to silence their chatter. "Just a little cautionary advice – Marshall Field is a fashionable store. Genteel women and, occasionally, but rarely, gentlemen will accompany their wives shopping in the women's dress department. You will not whoop and holler and carry on.

Your voices will be respectful and sedate. That means calm and mannerly. Follow my example and you'll be just fine. They do not tolerate unacceptable behavior. Guards will escort undesirable customers from the store. Now, let's be on our way. *Danke*, Gustav."

He held the massive front door open for the three women to walk out to a waiting carriage pulled by a team of black horses. Their well-groomed hides glistened in the sun.

Prodding Julie and Liesel ahead of her, Sophie Rose waited patiently while the driver assisted them on board. They took the opposite facing seat to her own. Moments later, the driver switched his long whip over the animals' strong backs and their muscled shoulders leaned into the polished leather harness.

Their ride into the city gave Julie a different perspective than she had experienced leaving behind the labyrinthine maze of the tenements and ghettoes that sprawled for miles beyond the tall buildings of central Chicago.

A short time later, they merged with the horse and cartage and carriage traffic streaming into and out of town. The noise and human bedlam of the streets displaced the clear-aired silence of the stately mansions on the north side.

The driver maneuvered their carriage to avoid the clanging approach of a trolley throwing fierce sparks from the overhead cables as they turned onto State Street at Washington Street and stopped before the nine story edifice of the Marshall Field department store.

Recognized as a prominent and favored customer, Sophie Rose was greeted by a male floorwalker as though her arrival were always expected. "Good morning, Madame Rose, you appear absolutely stunning. Welcome to Marshall Field. How can I be of service to you?"

"*Guten tag*, Lars. We are here to buy dresses for my nieces, Leisel and Julie."

"Charming ladies, we look forward to showing you our finest."

Julie blushed. No one had ever called her a lady before and Leisel didn't look anything like a lady, even with a clean white Gibson Girl shirtwaist and skirt and her blonde hair washed and brushed out. She looked more like a German *frau* than a *fraulein*. She was not in the least delicate in Julie's opinion.

Trailing behind Sophie Rose like her entourage, Julie noticed straining heads turn to stare at her beauty and regal bearing. Flecks of light from store lamps graced her coiffed red-chestnut hair as she swept along the central aisle past solid mahogany hand-carved counters trimmed with bronze fittings. They moved deep into the interior of the nine acres of retail space, then entered one of thirteen high-pressure hydraulic elevators that carried them swiftly upward to the seventh floor. They exited into a forest of women's dresses, garments and an explosion of boots, shoes, purses, belts and othr accessories advantageously displayed to catch the notice of shoppers while perusing the aisles of merchandise.

Lars escorted them to a sitting area where Liesel and Julie settled onto a comfortable divan and waited as Sophie glanced at several nearby racks of dresses while casting an occasional assessing eye in their direction and consulting with Lars and the department manager, Miss Flynn, a severe looking woman with gray hair pulled back into a tight bun. She wore a plain white high-button blouse and a dark skirt that plunged directly to her polished boot tops. She obviously had no intention of competing with her customers.

Lars spoke to her in a low confiding voice. She disappeared into a fitting room. A few minutes later, she emerged pushing a rack of dresses of various patterns, but all of the popular *belle epoch* style.

The gored skirts created an elongated trumpet bell shape. As Liesel and Julie alternately moved in and out of the rooms trying various colors and sizes, Julie discovered she preferred the modified versions that didn't billow over the hips and simply flowed to more width at the hemline. This style suited Liesel, as well, since she was already a tall, strong woman and slightly broad in the rear.

To complete their small wardrobe, Sophie had them measured for a tailor-made outfit. "These will be suitable in case you are invited to a wedding," she informed them.

The bodice was heavily boned like a mini corset itself worn over a foundation S-bend corset. The top bodice was mounted onto a lightly boned under bodice lining which fastened up with hooks and eyes.

"This stay garment gives stability, contour and shape beneath the delicate top fabric," Miss Flynn explained. She added dress fasteners, deep high lace fabric collars that tucked under the chin and elongated the neck. Julie didn't like the way they felt, since they were kept in place with wire covered in silk that was twisted into a series of hooks and eyes from one piece of wire.

"The high necks fashion is for the daytime," said Miss Flynn. "For night, at dinner and parties and balls, the low *décolleté* neckline is to display fine jewelry and a peek at your breasts."

Miss Flynn had a difficult time suppressing Liesel's large bust into what she called a monobosom. Julie, on the other hand, did not have such a probem.

Sophie selected from an array of finely embroidered evening gloves made in suede and silk.

When they got to footwear, Sophie had to shush Liesel, who until then, had behaved in an exemplary manner. Julie could see the frustration mounting in her tense face and narrowing eyes.

"Narrow feet are the fashion for women," said Miss Flynn. "Whether it's true or not, some believe small feet to be a sign of breeding and gentility. We find that both men and women wear shoes that are too small. I have a few customers who had their little toes removed to make their feet narrower."

"That is the stupidest thing I have ever heard," Liesel sputtered. "*Dummheit! Dummheit!* I walk barefoot before I ever cut off my toes. Small feet do not make one person better than another. It is what you do – what you have in your head and your heart."

"I mean't nothing personal," said Miss Flynn. "We don't have a choice how we come into this world, with big feet or small feet."

Julie had no difficulty in selecting and fitting button-up boots with beaded straps for the day and two pairs of court shoes for evening wear with what Miss Flynn termed a Louis heel. White metallic thread and glass beads decorated the toes.

Julie exercised restraint in not calling attention to her "breeding and gentility." Liesel would have given her no rest if she did.

While staying her first two months at the mansion, Julie had read the phrase 'The New Woman' in advertising and seen pictures drawn by Charles Dana Gibson of the hourglass, monobosomed, tiny-waisted and small-footed gentile lady. At first she didn't understand he intended her to be a cartoon character, because the drawing reminded Julie of Sophie Rose.

The New Woman' was beautiful, competitive, an athletic sport and emancipated. Her clothes set the fashion for the narrow, gored skirt worn with an embroidered blouse or shirtwaist. Looking in the full length mirror at Marshall Field, Julie fancied she herself had the perfect Gibson look wearing a shirt collar and a tie. In retrospect, she was perhaps more opinionated than emancipated, but she could hold her own in any woman's sport. Although croquet and lawn tennis held no interest for her, she wanted to learn to jump horses over barriers like Sophie Rose.

Her brother told her he had watched Sophie practice fencing with Jean Guenoc and seen her shoot a dueling pistol and a rifle. Newt had taught Julie how to shoot a rifle when she was a much younger girl. Fighting with a *sabre* or *epee* and shooting a pistol sounded to Julie like good skills for a woman to have, especially for herself, since one day, she fully intended to seek her revenge against Luther Baggot.

That evening at the meeting of the Nietzsche club, Julie discovered the source of her rage and that she was not alone in her unrest.

"Tonight," Sophie told them before the meeting, "there will be both men and women in attendance. Your brother and Aaron may appear, since Jean Guenoc often participates with a blistering rebuttal to anyone supporting the status quo. For an ex-priest, he is truly a devil's advocate." She laughed. "I think the unmarried *jeune dame aux societe* come to the meetings more because of him than the philosophical *tete a tete*. They cluster around him afterwards seeking his favor and attention as though he were a star actor of the stage. In addition to his intelligence and prowess as a speaker, he is a rather dashing figure. The fact that he is a former priest is of great interest to certain young ladies, because he appears to have wealth. Money combined with a kindly disposition is always an attraction for an unmarried woman searching for an eligible bachelor."

To avoid drawing attention to his sponsored purpose of the meeting, Matias and Sophie referred to their "social gathering" as a "salon," in emulation, explained Sophie, of the salons in Vienna.

"We are Jews," she said, "Fletcher, Gustav, Jean Guenoc. I myself am not a Jew by birth, but I identify with them. There were many of us in Vienna. That city attracted their people like no other. They became the writers of books and plays, the composers and performers of symphonies and operas, the architects of the city, of buildings, the merchants and bankers. They were Jews who were no longer Jews. They were everything that the Hapsburg monarcy and the elitist *Reich* were not. Ironically, they denied who they were. They had no place in society except for the culture they created. They did not have aristocratic pedigrees. They did not have an identity. Their mothers and fathers pushed them toward education and the arts. If you did not have an education, you were nothing. The Hapsburg court did not place any value on intellectual pursuits. But the Jews were the artisans. Without them, the monarchy of Franz Joseph would have collapsed. Some of us were sons and daughters of businessmen who propped up the monarchy. Others were anarchists who met in coffee houses and salons, because they had no other social world. But within that world, they brought dreams to life."

"What kind of dreams?" Julie asked in all innocence. This was the first time she had ever heard about people who were Jews. And her parents had had some attachment to them.

"The monarchy was not interested in what my father and Matias and Kurt's father did, only that the emperor knew they supported him."

"Herr Holtzman told me Matias had to change his name."

"He was hunted by the German secret police. His father was a wealthy merchant and banker. He was also a Jew. And Von Bismarck's secret service discovered he was giving a great deal of money to the social democrats with the intent to change the government, to peacefully overthrow the monarchy in Germany and Austria. He did not want violent revolution, but the emancipation of the Jews by their domination in commerce and education and music and the arts. Jews were the achievers in Europe. The monarchies were reluctant to admit their economies depended on them. If it were not for the Jews, there never would have been an Enlightenment and now they have brought their culture to America."

"I thought you were one of them."

"No, my family was among the upper class, the elite, the *haute bourgeoisie*. Our name was Rosenberg. We were German Austrians by birth. I changed my name to Rose as a stage affectation. As an artist, I shared the Jewish culture and their lives. I believed in them and supported them."

"What became of Matias and Kurt's father?"

"He was arrested and imprisoned for treason against the Chancellor. Bismarck's agents shut down his businesses and seized his fortune, only to discover he had moved much of it out of the country to London and America. He clearly did not trust the monarchy.

Matias was a student at the university in Vienna and a political activist, a liberal in the beginning, until he saw how liberals were being used. Then he became a socialist. When I first met him, he was a young poet and playwright and cared little for his father's business. He wanted to bring politics into art. I know him as Heinrich Wohlman. He had to change his name and stay in hiding. The police were looking for him and for his brother, as well."

"If what they were doing was peaceful, why would they be arrested?"

"The monarchies did not want to change how they ruled Germany and Austria. They would not give up their power and they prevented the attempts by the people and in their governments to do so. As spies infiltrated our organizations, continuing our work became dangerous for us. I will tell you more at another time. The meeting is about to begin."

With a rustle of women's skirts and low rumbling of men's voices amid the scraping of chairs, the vaulted meeting hall, a ballroom hung with massive chandeliers, quickly filled with some two-hundred people. Liesel, Sophie and Julie joined Matias, Newt and Aaron among the front rows. The boys had been working as apprentices for Jean Guenoc in the Bauman Enterprises shipping and export company.

Beth scurried in late unnoticed and all attention shifted to Jean Guenoc, as he strode to the podium and surveyed the audience with a broad smile.

"Welcome, ladies and gentlemen. It seems our number has grown since the last two meetings. Perhaps it is a sign of something in the wind besides the stock yards."

His comment elicited polite laughter.

He placed his hands behind the tails of his black frock coat, stepped out from the podium and began a measured pacing back and forth across the slightly raised stage large enough for a dance orchestra to play.

"The purpose of our club is to promote social and political thought and discussion of all kinds. When I say something is in the wind, it is change, and change is inevitable in every aspect of our lives. You need only to walk the streets of the city to see it happening before your very eyes. Change is life and what we see is that people have come here traveling thousands of miles from foreign countries in search of a better life.

"Some of you may have studied philosophy and, perhaps, many have not. But we are not here to discuss only abstract thoughts. Some of you may not know who Frederick Nietzsche is and why we take his name. It doesn't mean that we agree with him, but we recognize the reality of the world he describes and seek our place in that world.

"Nietzsche observed that people and even animals want power. So they create groups, societies, rules, armies, religion and laws. The purpose of what we do in life, then, is to promote power.

"Does this mean that we don't desire some form of happiness and contentment?" He let his rhetorical question hover over the audience. "I propose that we want both, but need a position of power, however great or small, to achieve that coveted happiness, even if it is having food to eat, clothes to wear, and a decent house to live in.

"At our last meeting, we talked about Nietzsche's argument that God is dead. As a former priest, I can tell you that the existence of God in some form can neither be logically proved nor disproved.

"The death of God is a way of saying that we humans no longer believe in a cosmic order. This leads to a rejection of values and a belief in moral law. The loss of morality leads to nihilism. Nietzsche looked for a solution to nihilism by exploring the foundations of human values, which is happening in the lives of us all. We believe there are foundations deeper than religious values.

Nietzsche believed there can be possibilities for humans without God. Creative abilities can be developed without acknowledging the supernatural, but believing in the value of this world. By creating our lives, by the conquest of our own nihilism, we enter a new level in human existence, the *Übermensch*. You yourself are the hero. You do not need Promethean gods and goddesses or the abstraction of any other god to look up to."

As he continued, Julie began to understand the answer to her unspoken question as to why someone needed wealth and power over others. She did not accept the answer, but was forced to confront the reality that had caused the murder of her mother and father. It was the same reality that Sophie described about the tyranny of the ruling class and its repression of the Jews and in her escape with Matias from Vienna. They believed in a greater humanity. Jean Guenoc called it the nobility of the mind, the nobility of humanity, that renounced the wealth and power of aristocracy, and transcended religion and was accessible to them all.

Chapter 24

Assassin

"Who is the stranger? Who let him in here?" Horst leaned toward the union leader, Joe McNeil on his right. McNeil looked toward the door and shook his head. "Comrade Janaszewski is with him. He must have brought him. Janaszewski is careful. It should be okay." The blonde, cleancut young man wearing a trim dark blue suit loosely clutched a pamphlet that Julie Josephson had handed to him on the street that morning.

The young man began to read the phamplet immediately, without moving away from her side. His nearness made her uncomfortable. She worried that he might be a plainclothes police officer, maybe a Pinkerton, who might at any moment arrest her.

He did not. Instead, after a few minutes perusing the document, he turned to her and said with a detectable Polish accent, "This is exactly what I'm looking for. Is there a group? Do you hold meetings?"

"Yes, we do."

"Where? When? I would like to come."

Julie stared up at the taut boyish features punctuated by intense faded blue eyes. He trembled with anticipation. "Tell me where. I am one of you. I will be there. I will come."

Julie looked around to see if anyone else was watching them or moving toward her in a menacing way. She prepared herself to run.

"Miss, I've been looking for your people. I am a worker. I have been in the front line striking with my fellow workers. I have been beaten by goons hired by the owners. I want to be part of what you're doing. I want to join you." He noticed her wary expression. "Oh, please don't be frightened. I'm just very passionate about this." He stepped back. "My name is Leon Czolgosz." He held out his right hand. "You will never have a stronger supporter for your cause than me. What is your name, Miss?"

Julie hesitantly took his hand with a light brief shake. "Julie Josephson."

"Julie, may I be invited to your meeting?"

Julie nodded. "I cannot give you the location. But if you will stand here on this corner at eight o'clock tonight, someone will come for you and bring you to the meeting."

"Thank you, young miss. I will be standing here tonight at eight o'clock on this spot. I am grateful, truly grateful."

Julie turned and quickly drifted away into the crowd of pedestrians. Something about the man to whom she had just made a promise bothered her. He was almost too well-mannered compared to the rough immigrants she was accustomed to seeing at the organization meetings, with the exception of the writers, artists, intellectuals and several businessmen who shared progressive values with the Bauman brothers, whose identity Julie now knew as Heinrich and Kurt Wohlman.

Horst Holtzman was not at the tenement when she arrived. Frau Holtzman said Julie would not see him until the meeting that night. Julie explained her dilemma.

"Maybe Conrad could go."

"He is with his father."

"What about Janaszewski?" said Leisel, who was helping her mother prepare dinner. "Nobody would make trouble with him."

Janaszewski worked as a conductor on the North Chicago Elevated Railway and was a member of the American Federation of Labor local union. He and Horst had met at an organization meeting three years ago. Their friendship had grown during their collaboration on spreading the union doctrine to workers throughout the city and he was a frequent visitor to the Holtzman tenement.

"Go and tell Latislav about the man and let him decide."

"Come on, Julie." Liesel pulled her by the arm. "He will be coming off duty and going home for dinner."

Czolgosz sensed that the broad-shouldered dark-haired man approaching out of the night shadows cast by the gaslight lamps was coming to meet him. He waited with a smile. The man's dour, jowly expression did not change.

"You Czolgosz?" he spoke in Polish.

"Yes, yes I am." Czolgosz was delighted to speak in his parents' native language.

"I'm Latislav Janaszewski." He extended his thick calloused hand, the hand of a working man.

"I am grateful to meet you, Latislav. Please call me Leon. I see you are a conductor," Czolgosz referred to his cap and uniform.

Latislav pulled at his long nose. "On the elevated railway. You say you want to come to our meeting."

"Yes, I want to join you. I have been in strikes before. I am one of you."

Latislav hesitated. "Who said anything about a strike? We are not planning to strike."

"No one told me. I assumed there is to be a strike about something. If not, there should be. We must fight back. Just like you say in the pamphlet," he held up the publication given to him by Julie that morning, "We can no longer live under the heel of the barons of wealth and their fiefdoms."

As they set off walking through the tenement streets, Latislav questioned him in a curt, but friendly way. "Where do you work?"

"I just arrived from Cleveland. I am looking for a job."

"What kind of job?"

"I worked in a steel mill and later in a glass factory. There were strikes. Many of us were beaten. Then we lost our jobs."

"Go to where you see the smoke stacks."

"The smoke stacks, it is always the smoke stacks."

"What do you mean?"

"I was born and raised on a farm in Ohio. I had good food to eat and clean air to breathe. I lived outdoors in the sun and the weather. But because of the railroad and their control of the shipping rates, we did not prosper. When I was ten, I had to go to the city with my two brothers and work in a steel and wire factory. It was hard, brutal work for long days and little rest and we were treated like scum by the supervisor. We joined a strike for better pay and working conditions and were fired for our troubles. With nothing but the clothes on our backs, we went back home to the farm."

"Why didn't you and your brother stay on the farm?"

"Our stepmother was a tyrant. I could not understand why my father married her. There wasn't work to sustain all of us. After our parents sold the farm and moved to Detroit, my brothers and I had to leave again and work in factories. By then, I was sixteen. Everywhere, the workers would go on strike. I was beaten by thugs and guards and told never to come back. I could not tolerate living with my father and stepmother. They were Roman Catholic. I am not. I do not believe in such ritual superstition as they do. I am an atheist. The church is a monarchy ruling people's lives. I have read the works of the great philosophers Frederich Engels and Karl Marx and I once heard Emma Goldman speak. I greatly admire her. She is the most independent and free person I have ever seen."

"Well, you talk like a socialist."

"I am more than that. After reading your pamphlet, I know I can help your people."

Horst stood up from the table at the front and raised his arms to silence the throng of two-hundred immigrant workers tightly packed shoulder to shoulder, seated on wooden benches and standing to the side against the walls. Julie, Liesel, Conrad, and Dutton were among the onlookers at the back of the room so as to leave seats available for other attendees.

"Ladies and gentlemen, welcome to our meeting, your meeting, because what we have to say here tonight is about you, the work you do and the way you live. There is great unrest, not only here in Chicago, but everywhere in America. Citizens like yourselves will no longer tolerate the corrupt officials and politicians and the captains of industry who steal the wealth of this country, profit from our labor, and control our lives."

The crowd erupted with cheers and applause.

"There is ample evidence that the people who do the work show their discontent. The Municipal Voters League has made great progress in driving out ward politicians who have no interest in reform, but instead put their efforts to winning votes through bribery and patronage. For many years, the boss system and the wards transplanted from Irish towns and villages have ruled people's lives here in the city. Many of you here tonight are Irish. So I take that as a sign you also are not content."

His remark caused a ripple of laughter.

"Progressives, and we are all progressives, are changing the way politics is done so that we citizens have a voice and that our votes count for what we believe in, what is important in our lives, our families, our health, and our places of work. You will soon hear and learn about something called the initiative and the referendum. We are promoting direct primary voting, and home rule for our cities. And of greatest importance is to end the exploitation of our lives and the economy by giant corporations. We, the workers, the people, are the engines of the economy. We are taking control of our lives."

There was another burst of applause.

"Much of what happens is because workers, especially newly arrived immigrants, are not informed and do not understand what is being done to them. Our purpose is to make sure they do understand. We must continue to spread the word about human rights. It is through education that we can bring about change. Tonight, we have a special guest speaker who will share with you what you can do. It is my privilege to introduce Mister Joseph McNeil, an Irishman," more laughter, "from the local Federation of Labor." Horst beckoned him, "Joe."

McNeil looked up from speaking with Hillar Kuznetsov, a Russian émigré who worked in the same textile factory with him. He rose from the front bench, stepped forward, and turned to a greeting round of applause.

"Thank you, ladies and gentlemen. It is an honor and a privilege to be here tonight and have this opportunity to speak to you." He paused. His eyes brimming with enthusiasm swept the audience.

"Ladies and gentlemen, as of tonight, membership in labor unions here in Chicago alone is at one hundred thousand workers. Think of that--one hundred thousand. Not more than a few years ago, union members could only join an open shop wherever they worked. Why? Because these were not unions at all. They were company unions run by the owners. We have the right to bargain to challenge employers from firing a good experienced worker and replacing him or her with someone not as skilled, not as good, at lower pay."

He waited for the rumble of assent to pass.

"Still we do not receive the pay and working conditions we deserve. There are far too many accidents that maim and kill workers in our factories and cause sickness and health problems for which there is no compensation, only the loss of a job and poverty for the rest of their lives and, in many cases, death. Since the courts do not stand behind us, we have only one other recourse, that is to strike. When production stops, the money stops, and only then will the company owners listen."

"Or they can fire you or lock you out," Czolgosz shouted from the back of the room. "That happened to me on every strike. So what you say is not enough. It's not good enough. We have to be stronger. We have to go in with guns and plant bombs in the factories. If guards and goons shoot at us, we have to shoot and kill them."

Horst jumped to his feet. "That is not how we go about this. We do not want to use violence. It will gain us nothing. We only stand to lose more. Employers are already against unions. Violence will only increase their resistance. We have to educate them as well or they will never listen. They have to know that what we offer can benefit them.”

“You will never get them to listen to you.” He shook his raised fist. “They are the enemy of the proletariat! They must be brought down! A strike is not a strong enough statement! Bombing and assassination are!”

“Who are you? What is your name?”

“Leon Czolgosz. I know how to do these things. I can help you.”

“We do not seek your help. If you wish to work with us, it must be according to our rules. Will you do that? If not, you are not welcome here.”

Flushed with anger, Czolgosz, turned and pushed through a few bystanders at the door, then paused and turned to look at the crowd now staring at him. “I will do it for you! I will be the one!” He went out into the night.

“Ladies, gentlemen, please,” Horst raised his arms attempting to calm the sudden uproar. “Please, let us continue. Let us continue. That man is a radical, an anarchist. We are not anarchists here. We are not anarchists.”

“How you gonna tell those bastards?” a voice bellowed from the center of the crowd. “He’s right, you know! They don’t listen! They don’t want to listen!”

“We have to meet with them face to face. We have to talk to each other.”

Joe McNeil shouted over the hubub. “For now, just listen to what we have to say! Listen to what we have to say!”

The noise subsided. “Okay, thank you. Thank you.”

“We’re listening. But we don’t think you can do anything about this.”

"Alone, none of us can do anything, but together we can. Know this, if we have to go on strike, we will strike."

"A strike is only one event," said Horst. "It might not bring them to the table. It might not change anything. Our goal is to involve the Government, not just the city, but Washington. Our human rights have to be upheld by the law, the force of law."

"How you think you're gonna do that?"

"Just like the Muncipal Voters League, through the power of the vote. We also have the teamsters union and the teachers union working with us and the Citizens Association. They are businessmen who want the Government to run like a business, not by graft and corruption. Do you understand what I'm saying? Do you see the direction we are headed?"

Heads began to nod.

"What do you want us to do?" A woman called out.

"Give out the pamphlets we provide you and spread the word in your neighborhoods so people know what is being done to help them."

"I can do that."

"Me too." "So can I." "Show us." Others chorused.

Smiling, Julie, Liesel, Conrad, and Dutton began distributing pamphlets from where they were stacked on a table against one wall.

"Ladies and Gentlemen, we thank you and you should thank yourselves. What you are doing will soon change your lives for the better."

"If we don't get killed first!" shouted a naysayer near the back.

"Who's going to kill you? You have rights. Nobody's going to kill you."

"We don't have the same rights as those rich bastards and we all know it."

"We are going to change that, sir. We are going to change that."

"I'll believe it when I see it!"

"It might happen faster if you don't watch from the sidelines."

"I didn't say I wouldn't help," the thin man wearing wrinkled clothes and a slouch hat muttered. "I just said I'll believe it when I see it."

"There are plenty of pamphlets, so take all you want," said Horst. "Thank you and have a good evening."

As the men and women gravitated to the door, Horst and Joe McNeil, with Hillar at his side, commented to one another on what had transpired that evening.

"When all is said and done, are you working toward a strike?" asked Horst.

"Damn right we are. We don't have a time yet, but we sure as hell don't need any more provocation. The workers in this city are on the edge. They've had enough. We've all had enough."

"Well, when you're ready, my newsies and I will help you get the word out."

"And I thank you for that." Joe turned to the young woman. "Well, Hillar, can you make it home okay, or do you need company?"

"I can make it home just fine."

"You sure?" asked Horst. "I have a young man or two can see you safely home."

"I will be all right, Herr Holtzman. I don't fear the streets."

"It's what's on 'em that can be a problem."

"As you like, Fraulein. As you like. Thank you for coming tonight."

"And I thank you, sir."

After handshakes, Joe and Hillar departed.

As Conrad and Dutton crowded after Julie and Liesel to the door, Horst called to Conrad to wait. "I want you to follow that young woman to see that no harm comes to her as she walks home. I offered you to escort her, but she's very independent and refused. Don't let her see you're following. Just keep an eye on her."

"Who is she?"

"Hillar Kuznetsov. She works with McNeil at the O'Riley factory."

"Yah, on my way."

"Don't look so jealous," said Liesel at Julie's expression. "There is more than one Fraulein who needs protection."

"I don't know what you're talking about," said Julie, miffed.

"Of course not." Liesel stepped out into the street with Julie at her heels.

From a hidden position in the recessed entrance of a nearby building, Luther Baggot watched the people leaving in small groups so as not to arouse suspicion that there had been a gathering. He had followed Hillar Kuznetsov from her tenement. While waiting for her to appear, he saw Julie, Liesel, and Dutton hurry away in the opposite direction. He did not see the other young man, the bare knuckle fighter circle back. They were shortly followed by Horst Holtzman. Then Joe McNeil and Hillar Kuznetsov came out and exchanged a few words at the door before going their separate ways.

Staying a half block behind, Baggot followed Hillar until they were clear of the area. The sudden increase of his footsteps bearing down frightened her and she whirled with a small knife in hand to confront her attacker who stopped a few feet away upon seeing the knife.

"How did you know I was there?

"I simply followed you."

"I don't like this. You're spying on me. You work for O'Riley."

The interview for the job had proven embarrassing, because the agency man had kept staring at his face in what seemed to be an insulting manner. Luther considered any staring as a personal insult.

Upon learning of Luther's background as a special agent in the Secret Service of the Prussian Emperor Otto von Bismarck, Clarence Rittenauer remembered when the president of Bauman Enterprises had come into the office about six months ago with a young woman seeking information whether a Luther Baggot worked for Pinkertons. There had been no such name on the payroll list. Clarence thought it odd and a rare coincidence that Luther Baggot was now sitting before him seeking to become a Pinkerton's detective. Baggot's sudden appearance was also timely in another way.

Bill O'Riley, one of the largest textile and mercantile manufacturers in Chicago had come into the agency office just two days ago wanting to hire a security manager for all his operations. He had recently lost a legal case involving one his employees, a young Black man by the name of Edward Thomas, who had been caught stealing merchandise. Although Thomas was serving one year at Joliet State Prison, the judge had not held back in castigating O'Riley for his failure to pay regular wages to the employee. O'Riley wanted to ensure that no pilfering would ever occur in his company again whether he paid an employee or not. Rittenauer had promised he would find the right man and the right man had just walked in.

Clarence pushed back his chair and smiled. Baggot controlled his internal surge of anger, but his dark eyes bore an unmistakable threat until Clarence, realizing he was somehow causing Baggot discomfort, ceased smiling and leaned forward with a serious demeanor.

"I'm smiling, Mr. Baggot, because you are just the man I've been looking for. We have a very special job with a very special client. You may have heard of him. He's a big name here in Chicago. Bill O'Riley, the president of O'Riley Textile and Mercantile Company.

"I'm still new in the city," said Baggot in his guttural German accent. "I don't know the names of companies. What is the job?"

Clarence explained the scope of the position and asked if he would like to interview with Mr. O'Riley. A few minutes later, they were riding in a horse-drawn cab to O'Riley's office in the warehouse district.

"And you are working for me." Luther handed Hillar a roll of green bills. "Here, take this. I don't expect you to give me information without paying you."

"I – I don't want your money."

"Of course, you do. You need it. Just take it."

"I can't."

"You can and you will. If O'Riley should suddenly decide to fire you, I can make sure you keep your job. Do you understand what I'm saying?"

Bitterness rose in her throat. She nodded.

"Good, now take the money. This is only between you and me. No one else will ever know."

She took the money and stuffed it into her purse.

"Now," said Luther, "I'll escort you home and discourage any ruffians and we can pleasantly talk."

"I have nothing pleasant to say."

"I recognized a few faces. Tell me what was said at the meeting."

Conrad had instantly recognized Luther, but he did not rush out from his hiding place in an alleyway and confront him. He and the woman were talking as though they knew each other. Nevertheless, he continued to trail them as they walked on.

"They talked about educating people," said Hillar.

"Educating?"

"Yes, helping workers understand they have rights."

"That is interesting. What kind of rights?"

"A fair wage and better working conditions."

"And if their demands are not met, was there talk of a strike?"

"No, the leaders do not want a strike. They don't want violence."

"If they do strike, that is all they will get."

"They want to talk with the owners, to negotiate."

A smile shivered across Luther's lips. "That is not likely to happen. What else did they talk about?"

"Change – changing the way things are for the workers. We are not slaves and servants of masters."

"No, you are paid for your work."

Hillar remained silent.

"Anything else?"

"No, nothing, that's all that was talked about."

"You did well, Hillar Kuznetsov. Perhaps next time you will have more information, more details of what they will do. I know they are planning something. Meetings like that are not held for information alone."

"I am sorry, Herr Baggot. I have told you all I know."

"And I have expressed my gratitude in kind."

"You do not have to walk me to my door. In fact, it is best that we are not seen together."

"My thought, as well. I will leave you then and see you in the factory, but I will not take notice."

"Nor I. Goodnight, sir."

"Goodnight, Fraulein." Luther moved purposefully, yet casually away from her departing figure, then quickly back-tracked down a parallel side street. He had glimpsed a movement not far behind them and determined to surprise whoever was following them.

When the tall dark-cloaked figure stepped out of the shadows and lunged for him, Conrad knew he had been spotted and cursed himself for not being more careful. He looked for the flash of a knife, but there was none, only a strong arm with a steel grip around his throat.

"So, it's the fighter," Baggot's voice rasped into his ear. "What interest do you have in the Fraulein? You will tell me. I will know." He tightened his hold.

Conrad tucked his chin, grabbed and pulled down Luther's wrist while simultaneously pushing up his elbow and continued the defensive move of twisting the arm into a painful position that threw the attacker off balance. Conrad countered with a direct open-handed blow to the exposed side of Luther's neck and downed him with a kick to the knee. As Luther collapsed, Conrad turned and sprinted away down the alley.

Muttering to himself, Luther staggered to his feet. "Next time will be different, you with your fancy fighting."

As Conrad let himself in through the front door, he saw that everyone was asleep. The house was dark except for a burning lantern on the kitchen table. He decided his information could wait. At breakfast, he revealed that he had seen Luther Baggot talking with Hillar Kuznetsov on her way home after the meeting. He did not mention the assault.

"That is not good. Baggot is getting too close," said Horst. He must not discover who we are and our collaboration with the Wohlman brothers. We have to tell Joe McNeil about Hillar. I'll go to him today."

"Hillar."

She jumped at the sudden closeness of Joe McNeil's voice. She had not detected him, but he had maneuvered through the crowd and was within a few feet of her when she boarded the trolley.

"You startled me."

"Sorry, Ma'am. We got something important to talk about."

"A trolley car is not the best place for a private conversation."

"Where you gettin' off?"

"Two more stops."

"Okay, we'll talk then."

When the swaying trolley sparking from the overhead cables careened to the designated stop, Joe and Hillar descended the steel steps to the street. Moving away from the teeming crowd, they continued walking along the main street.

"What is going on?" insisted Joe. "Why is that bastard even talking to you?"

"He singled me out at work. He even followed me to where I live. I'm deathly afraid of him."

"What did he ask you?"

"What happened at the meeting? What was said?"

"And what did you tell him?"

"I told him that we talked about spreading the word, educating people."

"You didn't say nothin' about a strike."

"Just because I'm a woman doesn't mean I don't have a brain, McNeil."

"I never meant any different."

"I told him there wasn't any talk about a strike."

"Good, good, this gives me an idea."

"He paid me to tell him."

"He paid you?"

"Yes, more money than I make in a month."

"He's payin you to spy for 'im."

"I'm not spying. I'm not a spy."

"I know you're not. That's what makes this even better."

"How do you mean?"

"You can feed him information all right, the wrong information. Then he can tell it to that bastard, O'Riley. When we make our move, he won't know what hit 'im."

"But I don't want to talk to him anymore."

"Oh, yes you do, lassie, yes you do. You are gonna take his money and you are gonna tell him everything he wants to know, only it will all be lies. You get me? Give him the wrong information. He won't be ready. He won't know what to do when we go on strike."

"I suppose I can do that."

"You suppose? You can do that. You will do that. He's playin' right into our hands. This is an opportunity."

"What happens if he finds out I lied to him?"

"Nothin', absolutely nothin'. You tell him this is what you were told. This is all you know. Let 'im feel like a fool, the bastard."

"I will try my best."

"That's all I ask. Try your best."

"President McKinley is dead."

"Dead? How?"

"He was assassinated."

Matias leapt out of his chair and came around to the front of his desk in the grand library. "By whom?"

"It's here." Horst held up a copy of the Chicago Tribune. "In the morning paper."

Matias snatched it and scanned the front page headlines.

President McKinley Assassinated By Anarchist

On September 6, 1901, while attending the Pan-American Exposition in Buffalo, New York, President McKinley was killed by Leon Czolgosz, a Polish immigrant. The President was greeting men, women, and children inside the Temple of Music. When Czolgosz stepped forward at the head of the line, he fired two shots point blank from an automatic revolver concealed by a handkerchief. The President collapsed into the supporting arms of his staff. The nearest members of the crowd wrestled the assassin to the floor. National Guard soldiers and police beat him into submission.

Czolgosz To Be Executed

"I met Czolgosz," said Horst. "He came to one of our meetings. He told us we should plant bombs and attack with guns."

Theodore Roosevelt Sworn In As President

"This could be a turning point," said Matias.

"What do you know about Roosevelt? Will he support us?"

"We have to wait and see."

"Morgan and his chronies will do everything they can to buy Roosevelt. We need someone there," said Horst.

"It's time to bring out our plan."

Chapter 25

Opium

Frieda Olson took a pencil and piece of note paper from the frock coat of the man who had come to her room. As she searched his pockets for a wallet, she listened carefully for any change in the pattern of his snores. She tucked the few dollars she discovered under a corner of her mattress.

The man had fallen asleep sprawled on top of her and she had managed to extricate herself from under his sweating, fleshy bulk. Wringing out a wet rag from a crockery water bowl on her nightstand, she scrubbed savagely at the sticky semen coating her legs where he had ejaculated trying to unsuccessfully enter her.

She pulled on her smock over her head and tugged the garment down over her body, thin except for a slight bulge pushing out her abdomen. The madam had not yet noticed, but when she did, Frieda knew she would be taken to an abortionist and the barely formed fetus destroyed.

Two other girls had told her of their experience. One had died a few days after her return to the brothel. Frieda had no feeling for the life inside her. She thought of it as a growing demon, a diseased creature of which she wanted desperately to rid herself and escape the sordid degradation that had become her life.

A sour, odorous gas erupted from the man's anus. Gagging for fresh air, Frieda moved to her steel-barred window which she could open only several inches. She inhaled gulps of the tepid atmosphere laced with smoke snaking along the city streets from the factories.

Because of the drugs that contaminated her mind and body, she had not fully realized what had happened to her until three days after her abduction by the drummer. She had staggered up out of her soiled bed to discover her door was locked from the outside and that the slit opening at eye level was controlled by whomever peered in at her. That person was usually the madam, but also the elderly housekeeper, Lucy Campbell, who came to clean the rooms once a week, sometimes more often if customers vomited or defecated on the bed.

She had tried once to escape by running from the room when the door was left ajar, but had been caught by the guard at the entrance. At the madam's orders, he had tied her by her wrists and ankles to the bed for two days, while paying customers raped her.

Once a week, Frieda received a clean smock in exchange for her soiled one, and two towels after being escorted by the madam to a large porcelain tub in the basement where she stood watch over each of the whores while they bathed.

Unappetizing food, usually a potato stew or bean casserole was brought to her room twice daily, served on tin plates. Fresh drinking water in a crockery pitcher stood available on her night table. She was taken to a shared toilet twice a day at the end of the hall and a slop bucket resided under her bed for emergencies.

Although an annual coat of paint was applied to the walls, it did little to eradicate the reek of mold that pervaded the building and caused an incessant bronchial irritation in Frieda's lungs. Sometimes her hacking cough warded off men that the madam brought to her room. Most were married and had families and did not want to carry some illness like pneumonia home to their wives and children.

Frieda's condition angered Imogene Restivo, because the girl was not making her money. Frieda hoped that might be her key to escape being a white slave, but her door remained closed and locked.

She was given few diversions, old worn magazines to read. The madam did offer her drugs, mostly opium to lull her into a permanent state of lethargy. Most of the other girls were addicted, but Frieda resisted succumbing to hallucinations. She deposited the drugs in her slop bucket and avoided being beaten for such waste by pretending to dwell in a state of euphoria.

Silent crying and memories of her family farm gave her a way to cope with the abuse and long, lonely hours. The waddle of ducks along the banks of a green algae-covered pond, the frenzied rush and flurry of clucking chickens, the glottal grunts and shrill squeal of pigs, the lowing and heavy swaying bodies of cows ambling out to pasture took her out of her squalid room.

There had been too many brothers and sisters, seven of them. But they had eaten hearty food, meat and corn, beans, squash, tomatoes and baked fruit pies from freshly picked berries and apples. They had been treated well by their mother and father, who had exacted long arduous work hours in the fields from them. They had labored under clear blue skies flooded with the warmth of sunshine on their arms and faces, and sometimes in cold pelting rain. They had read books and told stories and played outdoor and indoor games together. She missed the togetherness and looked back with fondness and bitter regret that she had left them in search of something better.

She sat on the single chair in the room and looked at the sleeping man with his trousers still about his legs. His nose and dark mustache twitched and his snores suddenly became uneven as though the imagery in his dreams had taken a disjointed turn.

Frieda expected to hear the madam's knock at any moment and her inquiry, "Are you finished?"

Hoping to catch sight of the boy, Dutton Koontz, who made a weekly delivery of opium and cocaine from Chinatown to brothels along the Levee, she moved to the window. He usually came at the same time on Thursday afternoon in preparation for the weekend users.

Through her opened barred window on the second floor, she heard a man call his name and enact a transaction at the entrance to the brothel. If she could get a message to him, she believed he could be her connection to the outside world. He appeared to be about her age and had a friendly face.

He made regular deliveries of opium to Imogene Restivo, who smoked it in her clay pipe while the girls took their weekly bath.

Dutton Koontz hated being viewed with suspicion each time he walked through the streets of Chinatown to Song's laundry. He was the only Caucasian face in a surging crowd of Chinese conical hats, waist length pigtails, queues, and long gowns worn by many of the men. The tinny singsong Mandarin language assaulted his ears like a swarm of droning insects and grated on his nerves. He did not know quite how to relate to Song, who deliberately spoke only a few words of Pidgin English, but clearly understood far more.

Dutton had originally sought work as a stockroom and delivery boy in an apothecary on Monroe Street. The druggist and proprietor, Clarence Burke, praised his diligence and trustworthiness, and after one month, had him making deliveries to homes in Chicago's north side, to doctors' offices, settlement houses, the Augustana Hospital, Provident Hospital for Negroes, and to Dutton's surprise, to brothels in the Levee district.

Burke's framed two-year degree in pharmacognosy from the University of Wisconsin and membership in The American Pharmacists Association hung prominently displayed on a side wall near the shop entrance and established his credentials as a professional. The pharmacist's clipped rapid-fire pattern of speaking reminded Dutton of a carnival barker sporting a waxed black handlebar mustache and matching glowering brows that hooded studious, faded blue eyes and a long narrow nose. Stylish suspenders held up his pin-striped trousers. When he was creating a prescription, he removed his dark frock coat and hung it on a hand-carved wooden rack with ceremonial aplomb.

Dutton had no knowledge of the prescriptions and what the vials, bottles and packages contained that lined the shelves of the apothecary cabinets in the storefront and stockroom. Many of these used as sources for preparation and compounding were not labeled. With great interest, he watched Clarence adjust counter balance scales and weights and measures mixing precise ingredients to create special drugs requested by doctors for their patients.

Dutton began to recognize the names, camphor, quinine, laudanum, morphine, cannabis, sulfate, and penicillin and a few patent medicines displayed in the shop window next to a show globe, Lydia Pinkham's Vegetable Compound, Snake Oil Liniment, Lily's Herb Chest, Sanbourne's Kidney Remedy, Paine's Celery Compound, Burdock's Blood Bitters, and Colden's Liquid Beef Tonic.

He did wonder about the Chinese stampings on the tins that Clarence showed him how to carefully wrap, and stressed that they be concealed from prying eyes. Dutton contained his curiosity until the day Clarence introduced him to the Chinaman, Mr. Song, who was waiting in the back room of the apothecary.

"Dutton, this gentleman is Mr. Yan Wu Song, one of my main suppliers of pharmacy products. I have told him about you and what a good worker you are and most important of all, that you can be trusted. Mr. Song and I have worked together for many years. Recently, he lost his delivery assistant and has come to me asking for help to find a replacement. I believe you are the right man for the job. I told Mr. Song you have the interest and potential to become a pharmacist yourself someday. And, of course, you would continue to work for me."

At first Dutton was confused that the Chinese man did not take his extended hand by way of introduction, but briefly bowed his head in greeting while maintaining steady eye contact, which was disconcerting, since the man's dark pupils could barely be discerned behind the slitted folds of his eyelids.

In deference to Song's custom, Dutton bowed in return. He stood a head taller than the man, but somehow felt awkward and inferior. He did not want to appear rude staring at the taut Asian features and slight body. Song did not wear a queue like other Chinese men Dutton had seen. His dark suit, straight cut black hair, and a bowler hat conveyed he was a businessman.

Dutton thought Mr. Song might have a question to ask him, but, other than the polite bow, offered no further sign of communication.

"Mr. Song would like you to accompany him to his place of business. It's a laundry in Chinatown. You will go there every Tuesday at noon and he will provide you with medicinal products that you will bring here for inventory and repackaging. He speaks only a little English, so if you have any questions, now is the time to ask."

"Will I be handling any money?"

"I will give you money to pay Mr. Song. The transactions from your deliveries will continue to be as before. Everything comes through me."

"I don't have any more questions."

"I've explained to Mr. Song that you're an honest lad. So honesty is what he will expect from you, just as I do."

"I'm glad for the work. I'm not a thief."

"You must be discreet about your deliveries and transactions. It is nobody's business but yours and mine about your pick-ups from Mr. Song and your deliveries. You could be noticed by the police, so be cautious where you enter and leave Chinatown. It's a good idea to vary your route once you know the location of the laundry."

Dutton didn't know that Mr. Song's primary business was the distribution of opium. Using the laundry operation as a front, he received contraband shipments of the drug from Vancouver, British Columbia. Upon migrating from Canton, China, Yang Wu Song had worked in an opium factory for six years, becoming an expert in the conversion of crude opium imported from Patna and Malwa, British India, in coconut shells. He controlled the manufacturing process by boiling the crude into powdered opium and preparing it for smoking.

The refined opium was packaged in cans, each holding a half pound. As a wholesaler, Mr. Song sold his product at a price of six dollars and eighty cents per tin. As a distributor, he retailed to his customers at a markup of two dollars and twenty-five cents per tin.

After Mr. Song and his family moved to Chicago, he maintained his ties with the smugglers who used to buy the refined opium from him and bring it across the Canadian border by bribing customs officials and using clandestine means of shipping the concealed product in crates labeled as freight. Traveling by train from San Francisco, Portland, and Seattle, other trusted carriers or mules would show up at the laundry from time to time with baggage containing tins of opium.

Dutton shuffled his feet with impatience while he waited for Mr. Song to finish packaging his deliveries, small tins of opium concealed within a large bag of freshly cleaned laundry. He feared and respected the Chinese man, but constantly worried about the dilemma in their relationship. Except for the money Dutton made as a drug courier, the threat of being caught by the police and arrested on the one hand or having his throat slit by Song on the other if he suspected cheating left him nervous and wary and ready to cut and run at the slightest provocation.

Dutton sniffed at the acrid sweet aroma of Pearline laundry soap and yeasty starch from steel tubs of boiling water in the back room. The hiss of steam irons taming the wrinkles out of cloth, and the ever present odor of cooking fish and rice and the sweet floral perfume of burning jasmine incense gave rise to Dutton imagining a Chinese dragon dwelt in the recesses of Yang Wu Song's tenement. He had never been invited to look or step behind the front counter and the curtain that concealed the sights and smells and Yang Wu Song's illegal secret activity. He knew other Chinese people were back there, probably lived there. He occasionally heard children's voices and a woman's voice that sounded like she was scolding them.

Dutton didn't even see the first pick-up. Mr. Song had buried several tins of prepared opium deep in the folds of bedding and clothing contained within a canvas sack that Dutton slung over his shoulder as he walked back through Chinatown. To avoid possible surveillance by a policeman at the street level, he then took the elevated train into the loop, the business center of the city.

Clarence insisted Dutton use the back door rather than the front entrance to the pharmacy so as not to draw attention to the arrival of his laundry. Once the delivery was safely inside, Clarence quickly transferred the tins of opium into a locked windowless cabinet, which he only opened long after dark when the streets were mostly deserted and few, if any, policemen were about.

When the crumpled wad of paper bounced lightly off his shoulder, Dutton barely glanced down at it on the sidewalk. He continued on his way until the young woman's frantic voice calling his name from the second story window of Madame Restivo's brothel stopped him.

"Dutton! Dutton! Please pick up the paper! Please pick it up! Please read it!"

He returned to a spot just below where she peered out at him. "How do you know my name?"

"I know who you are. Please read the note and please help me."

Dutton then heard Madame Resitvo's voice behind the girl. "Who are you talking to? Get away from that window, you bitch!" The girl disappeared with a scream. Dutton heard the sound of a slap and the window was slammed shut.

He stooped and snatched up the ball of paper. He unraveled and smoothed it against his leg and read the hastily scrawled note.

'My name is Frieda Olson. I am a prisoner. Please help me escape.'

Dutton carefully folded the note, stuffed it into his coat pocket and walked on to make his next delivery.

The momentary sight of the young woman's attractive face coupled with her frantic appeal and the written message awoke an unexpected stirring of sympathy that Dutton had buried long ago in the face of the poverty and despair he encountered daily. The image of the girl trapped in the brothel reminded him of how his six-year-old sister, Eugenia, might have looked had she lived. She had died of consumption.

His father had lost his hand in a factory accident and his mother earned only a few dollars a day working as a sweat. From the time he was eight, Dutton had joined the thousands of thin, sickly under-aged boys and girls who worked as child labor in mills and factories and tenement sweats under dangerous and sordid conditions for pennies a day.

The past five years, his friendship with Conrad had brought him a few additional dollars working his corner on the fights and from distributing pamphlets for the socialists decrying the exploitation of labor and the lower classes by the rich. Not until he began working for Clarence Burke did the wage slowly increase. Before the apothecary, he had never thought of the future, just getting by day to day. Now, that he envisioned a potential occupation as a pharmacist, he felt a kind of hopeful glow, like Clarence Burke's show globe in the apothecary front display window. Somehow, it carried over to the possibility of rescuing the young woman from Madame Restivo's brothel.

Later that night after a supper of black bread and potato and cabbage soup, he took out the note and read it over and over again until her voice became a chant in his mind: "My name is Frieda Olson. I am a prisoner. Please help me escape."

The Revolutionist

All his efforts to overcome the squalor he abhorred came to nothing. He realized he contributed to the problem as a drug messenger boy, but he reasoned he did it so he and his family could survive. Now, here was a chance to help someone in a way that would actually make a difference, even if just for one person. The question was – how?

Madame Restivo had recently hired an armed guard, Hugo Bocelli, who spent most of his time dozing in the lobby and making occasional rounds up and down the halls of the two story building. He had twice forcefully removed customers for beating up the girls they'd hired. Dutton knew it would be foolhardy to rush in and try to overcome the florid-faced man. He was large and heavyset, but deceivingly fast on his feet. In addition, he wore a holstered revolver prominently displayed on his right hip and kept a police baton close at hand.

Imogene Restivo was short and bulky, with the thick arms of a wrestler softening to a flabby red mottled discoloration as she reached her middle years, but she never lacked body strength when any of the girls disobeyed or tested her.

Frieda once saw her slam one of the whores twice her size against the wall and punch and kick her into a screaming puking puddle onto the floor. Face purple with rage, Restivo lunged at her like some heinous goblin crowned with electrified black hair that refused to be tamed by any amount of brushing. The lack of control she had over her hair often infuriated her and fueled her intolerance and temper. A cruel tyrant, she managed her girls by a combination of mothering protectiveness and fear, except for one, a milky-eyed submissive little blonde, Lavinia, whom she favored like a daughter, treated like her darling child, and forced her to sleep with her.

Restivo confused the other girls who were constantly on guard as to which personality would confront them. They were rarely allowed to congregate and socialize, only occasionally three or four together during their weekly bath or when Madame Restivo "entertained" in her studio where she and the girls smoked opium. Those who chose to not smoke were not invited. Madame Restivo believed that they were the most likely to commit acts of conspiracy.

She knew the girls hated and despised her for treating them like prisoners and ruling their young lives. But they all realized that being prostitutes, there was no opportunity for them to rejoin acceptable society. They would not be able to find regular employment and marriage was no longer an option now that they were soiled.

Restivo knew some women who voluntarily worked at the high end brothels. They catered to wealthy and well-heeled clientele, and prospered economically with considerably more freedom than married women whom they viewed as their husband's chattel without any legal rights.

Imogene Restivo sold her girls to a different market. Any man who could pay the price was allowed in to her place. Her rules for decorum were not as demanding as the upscale houses. She did not maintain the overhead of luxurious rooms, gourmet food and liquor, and a piano playing professor. She felt no emotional attachment to any of her stable, not even her pet. She ran a business, and that was all, a business.

Years before becoming a madam, Imogene had been married to a worker in the steel mills. She ran a boarding house then. After her husband died from an accident, crushed by a falling one ton beam to be used in the construction of a skyscraper, she saw how much money men wasted in the Levee, and determined to profit from their desires.

Converting her boarding house to a brothel was easy enough. The building was already located on South Dearborn Street near pubs and saloons frequented by working class men and with access to neighboring brothels. Rather than being a competitive location, the vice district offered a full range of options to customers choosing where to spend their money seeking drunken and libidinous pleasures.

Dutton thought carefully how he would have to distract the guard by creating a situation to draw him away from the lobby into another area of the building. A fire would be easy to start and could not be ignored. If it were not brought under control and spread rapidly, all the girls would have to be evacuated. In the ensuing pandemonium, he could slip away with Frieda. He had no idea where he would take her or what he would do with her after that.

The metallic clank of her door being unlocked and pushed open woke Frieda from a mild doze. Restivo waited a moment for Frieda's eyes to open and see her, then stepped out into the hall.

"Get up, Olson. Your turn for a bath."

Frieda slowly rolled over to a sitting position. Her hesitation and lethargic movements caught Restivo's attention. "Somethin' wrong with you?" Detecting a sour acrid odor, she sniffed the air. "You sick? Got the clap?"

Frieda shook her head. She had vomited twice into her chamber pot that morning.

"Can't bring a man in here with that smell." She walked to the top of the stairs and shouted down to the lobby. "Tell Lucy there's a pot to clean in Olson's room!" She returned to Frieda. "Let's go. Bath time."

The wooden floor squeaked with age, as Frieda shuffled after her to the bathing room. Two other girls were already soaking in sudsy water. Hot steam rose and swirled about the room condensing on a large fogged mirror as a third discolored greenish brass metal tub slowly filled.

Keeping her back to Madame Restivo, who was busy tamping opium into a clay pipe and preparing to light the powder, Frieda pulled her sleeping gown up over her head and dropped it on the pile with the others. As she eased her legs and feet over the edge of the tub into the almost unbearably scalding water, she winced and turned sideways exposing her profile to Restivo's sharp eyes.

"Wait a minute, Olson." Restivo placed her pipe on the counter and stepped over to the tub. "What's this?" She rubbed her hand over Frieda's protruding belly. "I know. You got bread in the oven. That explains the puke in your pot. Go ahead and finish your bath. Then we're gonna pay a visit to Buskey."

"No, not her, please not her. Please, don't take me there. Hayden Hagerty died after you took her there."

"It wasn't the abortion. She had other problems, other complications. And don't you give me any back talk, Olson. There's nothin' to be afraid of. Buskey knows what she's doin'. She's the best midwife in Chicago and she's in demand. She even works with doctors. You sure as hell don't want that little bastard inside you. Next time you get fucked, douche yourself out better."

"Madam Restivo, please, you have to let me go." Tears streamed down her face. "I can't do this anymore."

"I own you, dearie. You can and you will do this until I kick your ass out or they carry you out."

"I feel like I'm gonna die."

"That's when they carry you out. Your problem is you don't smoke opium. If you smoked opium, life would be so much better for you. My girls who smoke the stuff don't complain and they don't have to stay in their rooms all the time. You want to get out of your room once in a while, come down and smoke with us. You don't take any of the drugs I give you, that's your problem. That's your own fault. Now sit your ass down in that tub and clean yourself up. You don't have no choice in this."

Frieda's body slipped further into the water until it rose to the level of her chin. She thought of drowning herself, but Restivo would drag her out and beat her. She lathered soap on an over-sized sponge and gently rubbed her shoulders and arms, squeezed it across her breasts and pushed it down and pressed it between her legs. Leaning back, she submerged her head and face to dampen and wash her oily misshapen hair.

I have no hope, she thought. *I have no hope. I'm going to die, but maybe that is best. I have no way to get out of here, no way to escape. That boy Dutton won't do anything for me. What could he do anyway? He sells drugs to Restivo. He's one of them. He's one of them. He probably didn't read my note. He probably just threw it away.* Her eyes closed, she drifted into sleep, her mouth opened letting the warm water surge down her esophagus and windpipe into her lungs. She choked and thrashed about.

Madam Restivo's hand grabbed her by the hair and violently jerked her head up out of the water. "You tryin' to drown yourself, you little bitch! You ain't gettin' away like that." Gasping for air, Frieda choked and heaved expectorating what she had swallowed. Resivo leaned down nose to nose with her. "No, you ain't gettin' away." She dragged Frieda out of the tub and propped her into a standing position. "There's a nice clean dress over there. Now dry yourself and put it on. Your shoes 'll be downstairs." Frieda hugged the towel thrust against her stomach.

Shoulder to shoulder, Restivo marched her young ward through the derelicts and pedestrians. The broad brim of her feathered Edwardian hat bent against the side of Frieda's face as she extended her stride, thrust along by the determined momentum of the shorter woman's rapid steps. She could not pull away or hold back. Restivo's right arm interlocked with Frieda's and the left hand clamped her wrist in a vice-like grip.

A small sign propped in the window of a brownstone boarding house identified the services of Beulah Besky, Midwife. No mention was made of abortion.

With Frieda in tow, Restivo pushed open the door, passed through the front parlor, took a sharp right turn at the end of the hall just before the kitchen, opened a second door, and went directly down a flight of steps into the basement.

Frieda panicked and pulled back at the sight of three other women in various stages of being relieved of their unwanted, premature babies. Lying on their backs, their spread legs and feet were held elevated by stirrups. Two of the women whimpered in agony as they waited for the bloody mass of unformed tissue to exit their bodies through gaping vaginas stretched and held open with a metal speculum.

A middle-aged woman with gray hair tied back in a bun was inserting a catheter deep into the cervix of the third woman to agitate the uterus and induce labor. Blood spots and smears stained her full white nurse's apron.

"Beulah," Restivo shouted over the moaning of the other two women. "Brought you another customer. She's at an early stage."

Without looking up from concentrating on her task, Beaulah said, "Sit her on the bench. I'll get to her shortly."

"Over there," Restivo pointed. "Sit down and wait. Won't be long."

Frieda obediently scuttled over to the bench against the wall. Her eyes widened as one of the women on the table began to hemorrhage. Frieda looked at the stairs, now blocked by Restivo's broad hat and sturdy body. There was no escape. She watched the midwife pack towels against the flow of blood leaking from the woman.

"It'll be over soon," said Beulah. "It'll be over soon."

And Frieda suddenly realized Beulah was not only talking about the unborn child, but the woman's life herself. Frieda screamed and leaped up from the bench.

"Sit down, bitch!" Restivo roared at her. "Sit down and shut up! You're disturbin' these women!"

Frieda collapsed onto the bench. Sobbing, she buried her face in her hands.

When he entered the front lobby and stepped to the counter, Dutton was greeted by one of Restivo's trusted prostitutes, Elke Eberhardt, a tall freckled sanguine-looking young woman of about thirty wearing her long red hair swept back in a French twist.

"Restivo ain't here, dear boy. You makin' a delivery?"

"Not today."

"You want to buy some time? I happen to be available."

"There's another one I heard about, Frieda Olson."

"I can take care of you better than that fresh young brat. How'd you hear about her anyway? She hang a sign out her window?"

"From someone I know."

"Well, too late. Restivo discovered she's pregnant. She's gone for an abortion."

"Do you know where?"

"Buskey's, the same place Restivo takes all the girls when they need one."

"Can you tell me where it is?"

"Sure, go two blocks and turn right. You can't miss it. There's a sign out front."

Dutton turned and ran out the door.

The girl called after him. "What the hell you want with her? She your cousin or somethin'?" She laughed.

Dutton plunged past men and women who blocked his way on the sidewalk.

He hadn't thought to ask how long ago Frieda and Restivo had gone to the abortionist. Because he was not sure of the location, he worried he would be too late. Not quite knowing where he was going, he turned the corner at the end of the second block and scanned the building fronts as he ran. He did not see any sign that advertised abortions and nearly passed a small shingle that read 'Midwife'.

The door led into the entry of what he recognized as a boarding house with several other doors along the length of the hall. All were closed. The creeping fumes of alcohol and iodine pulled him to the last door next to the kitchen. He went down the steps into the basement and paused in amazement at the prostrate women in various stages of bloody excruscence.

He saw Restivo and Frieda leap up from the bench, but Restivo was faster on her feet and came at him when she realized something was going on between him and Frieda. She pushed Frieda back onto the bench and confronted Dutton.

"What the hell you think you're doing here?"

Buelah Buskey looked across the room from where she was about to administer a procedure with a catheter. "Who is he? What's he doing here?"

"That's what I want to know."

"It's none of your damn business." Dutton violently pushed her aside and she staggered and fell between two of the operating tables.

Frieda flew off the bench and ran to him. Chased by Restivo's screaming threat, "I'll get you for this! You're a dead man!" he grabbed Frieda's outstretched hand and they clattered up the steps.

They burst out of the boarding house into the street. Dodging through traffic, they ran on until, gasping for air, Frieda pulled Dutton to a stop and collapsed against him.

He held her thin heaving body. The sensation of her bulging abdomen pressing into him raised an unexpected protective sensation and the realization that now he was responsible for her and didn't know what he should do next.

After a few minutes, Frieda's trembling subsided, but she continued to cling to her rescuer out of fear that to lose his touch would cast her adrift in the crowd of immigrants surging about them.

"You okay?" he asked. "We have to keep moving. Restivo will try to find us."

Frieda nodded and hooked her arm in his.

They continued walking quickly through neighborhoods that were strange to her in the way the Europeans dressed and amid the confusion of shouts and cries from street vendors and the smells of food in the air.

When they arrived at the Holtzman tenement, only Frau Holtzman, Liesel, and Julie were there.

A wide-eyed Frau Holtzman immediately relieved Dutton of supporting the pregnant young woman and guided her to a kitchen chair while waving at Liesel to "Get tea. Bring soup." Then to Frieda, "There you go meine Liebe." Then back over her shoulder to Dutton, "You were keeping her a secret?"

"No," said Dutton, "I rescued her from a brothel. She was a prisoner."

"Ah, Ich Verstehe, I see. Poor child. Ach du liebe."

"I brought her here because I don't know what to do now."

"Since you are not the father, that is a problem."

"Restivo took her for an abortion."

"Who is Restivo?"

"A madam."

"Abortion is dangerous."

"Is there someplace she can stay, someone who can take care of her?"

"There is a settlement house near here," said Liesel. "I know Sister Pavalek. She is from Austria."

"What is your name, child?" asked Frau Holtzman.

"Frieda Olson."

"What about your mother and father?" asked Julie. "Where are they?"

"On a farm in Iowa. I could never go back. They could not take care of me. There are eight children. I had to leave. I came to Chicago to find work."

"Sister Pavalek can help you," said Liesel, setting a steaming mug of tea and a loaf of bread before Frieda. "I know."

"Thank you. I am grateful." Frieda sipped at her tea, then broke off a crust of bread, thrust it into her mouth and chewed slowly.

"I will get soup," said Frau Holtzman, walking over to the stove.

After Frieda had eaten enough and pushed back from the table, she profusely thanked her benefactors. Liesel, Julie and Dutton escorted her through the tenements to a convent in the German sector.

"When I was a young girl growing up in Austria, my mother and father and my friends called me Pavi." Sister Pavalek pulled Frieda to her in a gentle embrace. "Welcome, my child. We will take care of you. You are safe here."

She looked directly at Liesel, Julie, and Dutton. "And you young people who brought Frieda to me. You must promise you will not forget her. You cannot just leave her here and go off into the world. My sisters and I will provide her with food and clothing and a home. We will bestow our love and spiritual guidance. Your responsibility does not end because you brought her through my door. It is a beginning. I expect you to come and visit Frieda, to include her as your friend. Do I have your promise?"

Three heads bobbed in assent.

Chapter 26

Graft

Conrad landed the first blow to the other fighter's chest and leaned back just out of reach as the clumsy return roundhouse swing intended for his head found only air and the man lurched off balance. Conrad read the flicker of anger and frustration in his opponent's bloodshot eyes. From his flushed jowly cheeks, facial ticks, and jerky hyperkinetic movements, Conrad knew the man had taken drugs, probably cocaine so readily available in the Levee district. That meant he would be able to endure more pain than usual before going down, so Conrad would have to finish him quickly.

As he circled looking for the next opening, Conrad estimated the man was about ten to fifteen years older than himself, judging from the slight softening of flesh around his neck and waist. His precise age would be hard to determine, since he had shaved his head to a sweat-glistened shine. The shadow of a dark beard delineated his jaw which Conrad planned to break.

He stood a few inches taller than Conrad, who topped six feet and was blessed with long arms that put him within striking distance without exposing much of his own bare torso as an easy target. Other than an occasional reddish bruise, his quick head dodges kept his handsome young face unmarred.

Both men wore black tights and laced knee high fighter's boots with flexible flat soles to maintain contact and balance with the hard packed earth in a circular pit surrounded by a vociferous crowd of men and a few prostitutes calling out drunken advice to the combatant on whom they had placed their bets.

Jean Guenoc stood near Conrad's father at the edge of the small ring, some fifty feet in diameter, enclosed by the slightly elevated audience of spectators. Jean had coached Conrad to concentrate on his opponent's eyes, giving only peripheral attention to his fists and legs and feet. When aggressive moves were made, they tended to happen at lightning speed, but the eyes communicated the moment of intent.

Julie, Liesel, Newt and Aaron had arrived by horse and carriage with Jean just prior to the beginning of the match and now stood among the shouting arm-waving crowd just behind Horst and Jean. Liesel had seen him fight before, but their attendance was a new experience for Aaron and the Josephsons. Beth had expressed that she considered fighting uncouth and Matias and Sophie preferred the theater to watching bare knuckle battlers pummel each other.

As always, Dutton Koontz stood in his corner ready with a dipper in a bucket of water and towels to swab his friend's sweat-drenched face between rounds.

The no-holds-barred match was fought without a referee. The only rule observed by the combatants was to back away when one of them went down or called it quits. Conrad used a combination of kicks and punches in a martial arts pattern taught him by Jean. None of Conrad's opponents could figure out his style or ever beat him. In the world of bare knuckle fighting, he had become a legend in the Levee.

Standing on the risers in the tightly packed mob reeking of unwashed bodies, whiskey and beer, and undulating smoke from a multitude of brandished cigars and bellowing pink mouths, Julie did not cheer and shout Conrad's name. Nervous tension and concern wrapped around her beating heart that her man might be seriously injured.

She had never articulated to herself or expressed to anyone that she considered Conrad her man, other than he was her protector on the streets. But his attraction for her was an undeniable reality.

The opponent suddenly rushed Conrad and grappled him with a hard thrust against the wooden wall of the ring scraping open a ragged wound across his back. The older fighter hoped to overcome him by crushing his ribs, but Conrad deftly slipped his head and shoulders downward out of the man's sweat-slicked grasp, enduring the slimy garlic and onion stench of his armpits, then pivoted away while delivering an open handed cut to the side of his neck. The fighter hesitated and staggered at the sudden interruption of blood flow to his brain. Conrad grabbed his shoulder and spun him around to connect with a hard right that shattered the fighter's nose, followed by a swift uppercut dislocating his jaw with a resounding crack. Spewing blood, he clawed the air as he fell with a splat of flesh to the ground. He rolled over once to protect his face, but did not rise to his knees.

The pit manager counted out loud to ten, then held up Conrad's right arm as the undisputed winner amid a cacophony of boos and cheers. Conrad smiled up at his supporters and waved specifically at Julie, who blushed and turned her head aside.

Liesel poked her shoulder and leaned in close to her ear. "Why don't you shout for Conrad?"

Julie shrugged and clapped her hands. Liesel scowled at her and screamed loudly enough for both of them.

Horst huddled with an assistant to the pit manager to take possession of Conrad's winnings. Conrad quickly toweled off, pulled on a shirt and he and Dutton joined Horst, who was grinning broadly while rolling up the wad of dollar bills and stuffing them into a money belt under his coat.

They walked past the downed fighter who was being helped to his feet by his second and holding a blood-soaked towel to his face.

"That was good, son, said Horst," clapping Conrad on the shoulder. "The poor bastard never knew what hit him. How's your back?"

"Raw."

"*Mutter* will fix it."

Jean herded Newt, Aaron and the girls ahead of him scuffing through the shavings of the barroom floor as noisy patrons flooded in from the fighting pit out in the back. At the entrance, Horst handed Dutton a fistful of cash for his assistance in the ring and, with a brief wave, Dutton jogged off down the street lit by columns of flickering gaslights. Conrad assisted the girls into their waiting carriage, then he, his father, Newt, Aaron and Jean climbed aboard.

"So what did you think?" Horst asked Newt with a grin.

"It's not like I expected. He outweighed Conrad by at least fifty pounds."

"Speed and accuracy compensate for size," said Jean. "Conrad's opponent was slow and had no focus."

They sat squeezed together for the short ride uptown to a corner where Horst and Conrad jumped off and headed into their tenement neighborhood.

Back at the saloon, Luther Baggot remained sitting alone on the risers staring at the empty pit. He could not believe his stroke of luck at recognizing both the Josephson children and their friend, as well as the Frenchman that had forced him to leap from the moving train in Germany. He could bide his time. Knowing that they were somehow connected and living there in Chicago was enough. He surmised that the Frenchman would lead him to Heinrich Wohlman. He would find them again and take his revenge at his leisure. But before then, he would send a letter to Rudolf Palm in Italy.

Lately, he had not heard from his patron. That his stipend had not arrived in the mail for two consecutive months aroused Luther's curiosity and anger. He had been forced to seek employment with far less remuneration as a Pinkerton's agent working under a restraint against his specialty, murder and assassination.

He wondered why Palm had suddenly lost interest in his search for the list and annihilation of social democrats. Something must have happened to interfere with Palm's purpose. Luther had faith he would eventually hear from him, but he decided to no longer concern himself with the list. Now, his objective was a personal vendetta against the Wohlman brothers and their guardian, Jean Guenoc.

Convoys of large wagons pulled by four and often up to six draft horses, Percherons, Clydesdales, driven by shouting, cigar chewing, whip cracking teamsters came empty to long lines of loading docks and left filled with barrels and crates and boxes of merchandise. The congested streets steaming with mud and manure left barely room to pass in and out of the district. Forced to stop and wait for the second time, Rittenauer and Luther finally left the cab and dodged and maneuvered on foot through the creaking groaning traffic punctuated by wet mucous-flecked equine snorts and trumpeting neighs.

They entered O'Riley's office amidst a furor of angry shouting between an explosive flushed O'Riley and one of his supervisors who had the gall to contradict his boss. O'Riley paused and glanced at them. "What the hell do you want?"

"I found your man," said Rittenauer.

A malicious grin replaced O'Riley's snarl. "Good, then I can fire this one. Get your ass out of here, McNeil. You're done. Go work in Packing Town. That's all you're good for, butchering cows and pigs, you bum."

The equally fire-eyed supervisor looked Luther up and down with contempt. "You'll be sorry, O'Riley. He don't know what I know."

"You don't know shit, McNeil! You're fired! I don't want to see your face around here again!"

The livid lean-faced man in his rumpled workmen's clothing and slouch hat raised his fist in defiance as he backed out the door. "You ain't seen the last of me, O'Riley! The union'll bring you down."

"Feck you and yer union! You call a strike and I've got men waitin' to take yer place."

"You try to bring in any feckin' niggers and there'll be a war. There ain't no work here for scabs, 'specially nigger scabs! We'll burn this feckin' place to the ground!"

"I've heard enough of your scum! Get the hell out!"

Cursing under his breath, McNeil clattered out the door and down the wooden platform steps to the street.

"Can you beat that?" O'Riley looked over from behind his desk. "That asshole came in here and told me all the workers in my place and every warehouse here are in the union and they want to make demands. I told him to go feck hisself." His bloodshot eyes flickered up and down making a quick assessment of

Luther's powerful body topped by his fearfully ugly face. "So, this is your man," he spoke to Rittenauer. "I know you wouldn't waste my time if you didn't have what I asked for. He looks like he could stop a train."

"Careful what you say, O'Riley. You don't want to get on his bad side either."

"Mmph, what's his name."

"Why don't you ask him yourself? You gotta talk to him if he's gonna work for you."

"I don't talk to my workers. I give orders. Other than that, I don't want to hear anything back from 'em."

"My name is Luther Baggot," Luther's deep basso voice and guttural German brought O'Riley up short.

"You're a kraut." O'Riley decided then and there to address him in as polite a manner as he was able to invent, since being polite to anybody was not his nature. But he wanted this overseer to support him and only him, to be on his side.

"He used to work for Bismarck in Germany as a special agent in the secret service," said Rittenauer.

O'Riley looked at Luther with a sudden new level of respect, stood and came around from behind his desk and extended his right hand, which nearly disappeared in Luther's crunching grip. With the safe return of his hand, O'Riley stepped back and gestured to a second door opening onto the warehouse.

"I am interested to hear more about your work in Germany. Let's talk as I show you the factory."

Luther and Rittenauer followed him out onto the factory floor. The deafening thrum and roar of two hundred steam powered looms and ten thirty foot long finishing reels at the process end of wide dye vats through which the woven fabric was passed crowded the massive fifty thousand square foot warehouse.

Dense, toxic chemical odors permeated the air, attacked the eyes and lungs and made breathing difficult. Most of the workers 'masked their faces with scarves or bandanas and stuffed cotton or pieces of cloth into their ears. A few braved the daily intake of fumes and swirling cotton fabric dust that would eventually erode their lungs and brains and kill them.

As they walked along the main aisle, O'Riley attempted to shout over the din despite that Luther and Rittenauer could not hear a word. His description of the operation added little to what could be seen. The noise of the looms receded behind them, as they approached the cutting and shearing tables and progressed into the packing and shipping area. Large doors opened onto the loading docks where a crew of ten men hefted the heavy rolls of carpet and fabric onto horse-drawn wagons.

Luther mentally noted the ease with which finished product could be stolen by transfer to an unauthorized wagon and how small boxes of yarn and cut materials could be picked up and carried off amid the flurry of activity on the crowded dock. Four shipping clerks dashed back and forth verifying the product being loaded against their packing forms and bills of lading and demanded that the teamsters sign for their loads.

"How many people work here?" asked Luther.

"About three-hundred. I run two twelve hour shifts with four supervisors. They get two ten minute breaks and a half hour for lunch. I stagger 'em by two sections so everyone has a chance at the commodes. Shows I'm considerate for their well-being. Anyone not at their station when the alarm bell rings gets their pay docked."

"Speaking of pay," said Luther, "what is mine?"

"O'Riley pays Pinkertons the fee and I pay you," said Rittenauer.

"Don't want it that way. O'Riley, you pay me my share and Pinkerton's separate."

"That's not how we operate, Baggot. We have a separate contract with O'Riley and with you."

Luther's glare caused Rittenauer to look away. He had neither the strength nor confidence to argue with this man. "We can change the contract. Okay with you, O'Riley?" Rittenauer made the feeble offer to save face.

"Good for me."

"First payment in advance and cash once a week," said Luther.

"You start today?"

"I start today."

"Good." O'Riley individually shook hands with the two men and lead them back through the rumbling factory to his office.

After Rittenauer departed, O'Riley invited Luther to have a seat in his office. He grinned and struck a pose of confiding in his new hire. "So, Mr. Baggot, Luther, may I call you Luther?"

"That's my name. I answer to it."

"You have experience I can use not only here, but outside the plant. And that will involve additional special compensation for you that is between the two of us. Rittenauer and the Pinkertons don't need to know about it."

"What is it you are asking and how much will you pay?"

"I'll get to that in a moment. First, I want you to establish a surveillance system in the factory. You used to work in Bismarck's secret service, so you know about spies. I want you to set up a spy system. After you've had a chance to observe the workers, select one in each of the production areas. Tell them they will get extra pay for informing on any worker they see trying to cheat me. Of course, they have to keep their mouths shut or they will lose their jobs. Anyone finds out, they'll likely end up with their throat cut in a back alley."

O'Riley offered Luther a cigar from a handcrafted wooden box and conducted the ceremony of lighting it and his own. When both cigars were going and filling the air over their heads with wavering smoke, O'Riley continued.

"There are seven other textile factories like this one in Chicago. Even though we're in competition, the owners talk to each other. We don't want any more plants and we pay to keep it that way. We have friends and supporters on the city council, if you get my drift. It's how business gets done here in Chicago. Hell, it's done that way in every feckin' city everywhere." He paused to inhale and then exhale a ragged cloud of smoke.

"The garment workers union contract will run out this year. I had to run a closed shop for the last five years and grant concessions that cut into my profit. As soon as I heard about the contract, I kicked McNeil's ass out when you and Rittenauer got here. McNeil is a union man. He ever shows his face in the plant again, take care of 'im. You don't have to do it yourself unless you want. You can hire someone."

"What's the second thing you want me to do?"

"I have another little business I plan to run on the side. I'd like you to take care of it for me. I'll have you meet my contact, but not right away. I want you to set up here first and be sure we understand each other."

Luther nodded slightly in acknowledgement. O'Riley was unscrupulous, but then so was everybody in Chicago, or so it seemed. The whole point of running a business was to make money and not let anything get in the way.

"I'm going to spend some time out in the factory. I have to watch the people before I decide who to ask."

"Take all the time you need. And by the by," O'Riley opened a ledger on his desk and dashed off a check for one thousand dollars.

Luther looked at it and nodded with a slight rise of his eyebrows.

"Later, I'll double that. This is to get you started. Where do you live?"

"Not far."

"Good. When you visit the second shift, you can sleep here in the office. I have a cot. Do you want me to introduce you to the supervisors?"

"No, just point them out to me. I will introduce myself."

"Here are their names." O'Riley quickly jotted the names of the supervisors on a notepad and handed it to Luther. "The last two come on at six o'clock. I'll show them to you before I leave."

"You leave the workers alone here all night. They could steal you blind."

"I have a Pinkerton's security guard who's here at night. He patrols the factory and he's armed."

"Then I'll meet him. Who runs the production during the day?"

"I schedule all the work for both shifts and buy the raw material. I also have two maintenance men, one for each shift. We run all the looms and I can't afford to have any go down for long. I pay them well, more than the operators."

Luther started for the door. O'Riley jerked open a desk drawer and pulled out a blue bandana with a white paisley border design. "You might want to wear this around the looms and here's cotton for your ears. You spend much time out there, those machines 'll make you go deaf and the fumes can kill you."

Luther took the bandana and pocketed the ragged chunk of cotton. Carrying the bandana, he walked slowly along the aisles between the looms. He wanted the operators and assistants to clearly see his face for a while. He would wear the mask another day.

He paused to watch workers direct raw cotton through rollers aligned in a series in the head of the drawing frames that straightened the strands of yarn which were then spun and twisted on bobbins to tighten and compress the fibers. The spinners, mostly women, moved up and down the row of frames to detect and repair breaks and snags along with spoolers. Winders received the yarn coming off the frames and spoolers operated machines that combined single threads from ten to twenty bobbins onto one.

The speed and attention to detail the spinners demonstrated impressed Luther. They efficiently moved the product in sequence to various forming devices, balls of yarn, tubs for the weavers and cones, tubes, and reels that were moved to other sections of the plant for further operations.

As he walked slowly along in the weaving sector, Luther noticed the eyes of a particular woman followed him with unmistakable curiosity over the top of the bandana that covered her nose and bottom half of her face. Her eyes were dark and her hair brown, so Luther took her to be from a northern European country, but she could have emigrated from any region in Europe. She wore the standard long skirt and shirtwaist blouse seen on most women in the mills and factories. He decided he would confront and talk to her later in O'Riley's office. For now, they were mired in the clashing sound of machinery.

Hillar Kuznetsov concentrated on positioning a loom beam, then began the rapid passing of a shuttle containing the weft back and forth across the warp threads rhythmically raised and lowered by a harness to create the weave pattern of a wide sheet of cloth. The yarn had been cooked dry on steam-heated drums in the adjacent preparatory process. The smell of a hot starch and oil mixture and odor of the yarn that had been passed through it rose to the warehouse rafters.

Having worked on looms for the past five years, Hillar was a skilled weaver. Since emigrating from Estonia with Finnish relatives, she had found employment in O'Riley's textile plant starting as a filler in the weaving room. She advanced quickly and within one year learned the tasks of a creeler and beam warper and took over the position of one of the many weavers, a woman who had lost the four fingers of her right hand when it became caught and crushed in a moving loom beam.

She wondered who this tall man dressed in black with a partially disfigured face could be wandering around watching people at work in the factory. He did not talk to anyone, but intently observed specific individuals in different areas of the operation, then moved on. It concerned her that he might be singling out co-workers who would soon lose their jobs. There was no mistaking that he had looked steadily at her. She was one of them.

Hillar rarely made a mistake. She would be more likely to catch someone else's error in the loading of the creel or not tying off a break in the yarn coming off the spools. Watching every functional task was impossible, since she was constantly moving among the five looms she was assigned to operate.

The weaving room supervisor, McNeil, held her in high regard and, despite the constant pressure to meet the production schedule, he treated her and the other women in a kindly, gruff manner. He wasn't above shouting. Everybody had to shout to be heard in that chaos. But then something had happened. Not more than an hour ago, McNeil had gone into the owner's office and had not returned. Instead, this stranger and another man had come out onto the factory floor with O'Riley. She suspected O'Riley had fired McNeil, who was a union steward and acted as a buffer between the tyrannical O'Riley and the mill employees who had to suffer his abusive tirades.

During the mid-shift break, Hillar and her co-workers conjectured and gossiped as to who the stranger might be.

"What do you suppose happened to his face?"

"I don't know, but I sure wouldn't ask. He's frightening."

"McNeil never came back."

"Can you find out what happened to him?"

"He was gone after that man arrived."

"More of us are gonna go. I can feel it in my bones."

"O'Riley has it good with us. We work hard. We get the work out on time."

"And some of us don't steal from him."

"I bet that's it. Because of the theft."

"Must be a Pinkerton."

"That's it. That's gotta be it. He's a Pinkerton."

"Had a brother down south in the Virden coal mining strike in '98. He was killed by a mine guard. They're mean sons-a-bitches. Shot through the head. Left his wife and children with no way to live."

The imagery of violence against working class people made Hillar feel vulnerable and unprotected. Those with money and power could take her life if she stood against them in the cause of better pay and working conditions.

McNeil had secretly talked to her and others about an impending strike being planned by the union. The fear of violent acts and the loss of her job unsettled her. Her work contributed to the support of her cousins and aunt and uncle. Their collective income paid for the tenement they shared and the food that sustained them.

A few days after McNeil's departure, a man with less experience than Hillar was promoted to the position of supervisor over her section. She and her co-workers quickly learned that they had to compensate for what he didn't know. Other than to check that the operation stayed on schedule, he gave few directions, and made repeated trips back and forth to O'Riley's office.

Luther made his rounds of the factory several times a day and often appeared unexpectedly on the second shift. His lurking presence and his silence left the workers nervous and on edge.

O'Riley gave him access to the payroll roster so he could learn the names of certain individuals in whom he might be interested. He came across Hillar Kuznetsov, weaver, who was paid five dollars and forty cents an hour. He now recognized her face when her bandana was removed during a work break. He had watched her enough that she knew he was observing her for some reason.

In coming to and going from the factory, she made a point of always joining a group or having someone with her, usually a female co-worker. But one morning he surprised her by waiting at the end of the street on which she lived. She grew terrified. She realized he intended that she see him. It was too late to turn back or detour down a side alley. Trying desperately to control the sudden pounding of her heart, she walked on toward him, determined to conceal her apprehension.

"You're a Pinkerton, aren't you?" she stated

"Why do you think that?"

"I know you're going to ask me to spy on the people who work with me. You aren't one of us."

"I was just hired. It takes time."

"Everybody already knows."

"How do they know?"

"By watching you. We see you watching us."

"Are they afraid of me?"

"They fear what you might do to them."

"I hold nothing against them. I was hired to do a job."

"It is who hired you and why that they fear, that we all fear, we who do the work that makes them rich."

"And do you fear me?"

Hillar stopped walking and turned to face him. She decided she would not let him intimidate her. "No, I am not afraid of you."

Luther's slow smile caught her off guard. "That's good. You have nothing to fear from me. Most people are put off by my face. I was a soldier in a war in France. These are scars from a gunshot wound. I am not what I appear to be. I am not a monster."

"Your wound must have been painful."

"Yes, at the time. There are deeper wounds. I am reserved and not at ease with people because of my appearance. I'm grateful that you're willing to talk to me."

Hillar's uncertain smile indicated that her willingness was not all that forthcoming. "I didn't expect to see you here in my neighborhood. I don't countenance being followed."

They continued walking.

"If I approached you in the factory, becoming acquainted would be more difficult. You would suspect my position and others would not be kind. They would talk about me and I would not become acquainted with you."

"We are from different worlds. Why do you wish to be acquainted with me?"

"I know your homeland. You are Estonian, yah?"

"Yah," she broke into German explaining she had come to America with her relatives from Finland.

They conversed in German for the duration of their walk. Luther described how he had served as an infantryman in Bismarck's army until he was wounded. Then he had worked as a detective in Berlin for several years. When she asked what had brought him to America, he made up a story. "I came seeking a new life. Germany is changing and I was told that America had great opportunities for enterprising people. I thought I would be a detective here in Chicago for only a while until I discovered another path to follow."

As they drew near the vicinity of the textile mills, he explained it would be better for her if they were not seen together. "I will not speak to you at work and I will watch you less," he smiled.

This time her return smile was relaxed and conveyed his acceptance.

"Would it be an inconvenience or embarrassing to you if we met near where you live from time to time. It is a pleasure to talk to you, nothing more."

"I think it will be all right. Let's wait and see. My cousins and aunt and uncle are very protective of me."

"They must be good people."

"They are good people."

Luther watched her disappear into the chaos of morning horse and wagon and carriages and foot traffic of pedestrians sidestepping fresh piles of steaming manure. An immense flock of crows passed low overhead. Their raucous hawking cries blended with the bawling of tightly penned cattle and shrill grunts and squeals of swine awaiting slaughter. The crows made an unerring descent on the stock yards a mile to the west to feed on offal and carrion. Luther altered his route to approach the factory from a different direction.

Gold spangled hoop earrings drooped and brushed heavy beaded necklaces with a metallic rattle each time the Gypsy woman nodded. She turned her head wrapped in a red silk scarf that matched her floor length dress partially covered by a blue and red green embroidered coat. The piercing jeweled glitter of her dark clairvoyant eyes staring at him from the wrinkled folds of her nut brown face held Luther in a trance.

He called her Die Ziguener. Whenever the darkness spread and clouded his mind, he sought her soothing words and comforting advice. The deep hoarseness of her voice bespoke and echoed ancient wisdom describing and explaining his astrological signs while she gazed into her crystal ball. Only one time did she reach out and gently touch his scarred face with her gnarled long-nailed fingers.

His obsession with the extrasensory world had become an addiction that began after his near death on the battlefield in France. For two weeks, he had wavered on the fine line of slipping into the oblivion of endless sleep, but the void that would come and go in his mind never detached itself. He struggled to find a source of support and to substantiate his sense of who he was and his purpose as a living creature. He saw oppression all around him in the mire of suffering and death and destruction through the centuries. Turning his back on the church and Catholic religion by which he had been raised, he sought the mysticism of Gypsy fortune tellers.

Die Ziguener fed his illusions and, in time, became his confidant and confessor. He believed she communed with the diseased souls and spirits of the dark world. She told him he himself had come from that world and that he was an emissary of darkness.

When he had been commissioned by Rudolf Palm in the secret police, Palm had instructed him, "Everything we do is justified to keep the elite in power, even if it is not in Germany. Socialists everywhere are the enemy and we must do our utmost to destroy them. We must crush those who survive and believe they are entitled to something greater and grander and do not accept their lower station. We are tools of our masters, the monarchy and others who possess wealth and wield the instruments of power. That is your mission. That is our mission."

Believing in astrological and spiritual forces himself, Palm channeled Luther's assignments and controlled and held sway over the man. With no way to subdue his malaise, Luther accepted and reveled in his identity as a ruthless envoy of evil.

O'Riley slurped at his mug of beer, then carefully wiped the froth off his mustache in two different directions. Through lidded eyes, he surreptitiously glanced across the table at Luther who concentrated on driving the wedge of a sharp knife through a thick rare steak dripping with bloody juices of which some dribbled over the edge of his plate and stained the white linen tablecloth.

O'Riley noted that Luther had turned down his offer of beer and hard liquor, the best scotch, and ordered a bottle of French Bordeaux. *"Off course,"* conjectured O'Riley. *"Everybody in Europe drinks wine. They raise their children on it instead of milk."*

He wondered if Luther had any children back in the old country either in or out of wedlock. It was a bit of information O'Riley thought would be good to know.

O'Riley believed he had earned the right to his success. Not more than twelve years ago, he had come off the boat from Ireland. Upon landing in New York, he had been processed with thousands of other immigrants through Ellis Island. He had traveled by train to Chicago and lived for a short time with relatives in the St. Patrick's neighborhood parish. Having the advantage of already speaking English, he was able to find work immediately by scoring high marks on the competitive exam to become a postal worker. He used his knowledge of mail routes and access to Irish Democratic social and political networks that enjoined the city's ethnic centers of population and its dominant industries of meat packing, steel production, and the processing of grain and flour products. Then he recognized an opportunity and pursued it.

As a child, he had learned the rudiments of textile production from his mother and father, who had both worked in linen mills in Belfast. He himself had been employed from the age of ten. Garment workers in Chicago depended on cloth produced by mills in Massachusetts and Connecticut and Southern states. O'Riley determined he could eliminate the distance from those suppliers and the high cost of rail transportation by distributing the cloth there in Chicago. Once his system was established, he would move looms into the operation and compete directly on a small scale with his suppliers in the East.

He met Moira McGinley, a comely parish school teacher, at a church social, courted and wed her in one month. Respectfully married and, being a devout Catholic, he had fathered seven children in the past twelve years. He contributed publicly announced donations to St. Patrick's church to be granted blessings from the Bishop and ensure his place in the afterlife.

His patronage caught the attention of Francis Keeley, an alderman on the city council alert to possibilities of personal gain. When O'Riley made it known he was offering a competitive bid to purchase the gas utility that served the parish, Keeley asked him to come to his office and discuss the option in exchange for a franchise award. On the day he went to the city hall accompanied by Luther, O'Riley did not anticipate his access being blocked by the vociferous impenetrable mob of the Municipal Voters League.

After one month of overseeing the security of his factory operation, O'Riley decided he could trust Luther to shadow him with a political objective. Associating with him as a law enforcer, however a corrupt one, would be an advantage. Most of the police were on the take one way or another and often benefited from criminal acts by not being available or just looking the other way.

O'Riley did not give the urban social conditions a second thought. He shared those values and practiced them with skill, insinuating himself and his business into the heart of the political machine.

It was the way of life, a viscous elixir of a diverse ethnic stew, a multitude that flailed and ebbed and flowed seeking to survive. Graft and crime were how things got done in the city. Bribes, extortion and blackmail were common practices in business and city government.

An angry crowd had gathered at the front of the city hall's bronze, stone and colonnade edifice at the corner of La Salle and

Clark Streets. The Hansom cab in which O'Riley and Luther were riding could not get any closer than a half block from the steps. Luther noticed that many of the mob shouted demands and epithets that echoed the terse hand-painted signs thrust high and waved over their heads like square antennae of a churning pulsating sea beast.

No Corruption   No More Graft   No More Boodling
Stop Gray Wolves   End to Gray Wolves   Death to Gray Wolves

The citizens of Chicago called corrupt politicians "gray wolves."

The Municipal Voters League published the qualifications of candidates who demonstrated ethics and moral values in contrast to the voting records of aldermen holding current offices in the thirty-four wards. The League promoted candidates who pledged to support the merit system of civil service and end the bribes and kickbacks that diverted funds meant for the city into personal bank accounts. The purpose of the League was to remove the Gray Wolves and end their strangle hold on the city government.

The most prominent case that outraged voters was the award of a franchise to a fictitious Ogden Gas Company. The current franchise holder was forced to purchase the rights of the non-existent company and the conspirators directed the payment into their own pockets.

Luther followed O'Riley circling the outer edge of the mob and maneuvering toward the entrance blocked by a line of grim-faced policemen wielding clubs. Approaching the nearest guard, O'Riley could not make himself heard over the roar of the gathering. A billy club arcing through the air forced him back.

"I'm not one of them! I'm not one of them!" he shouted.

"Nobody gets inside!"

"God damn League!" O'Riley pushed and shoved to escape the crush of bodies and was ejected to the outside again.

"Who are they?" asked Luther

"Municipal Voters League."

"What do they want?"

"They don't like the way city hall works and they want to change it. Come on. I know another way to get in." O'Riley set off at a brisk walk to one corner of the building and led Luther to a rear entrance guarded by only one policeman. He waved a handful of bills in the face of the young officer and said, "I have to get in. I have business with the council."

"You ain't with them out front?"

"Hell no! I got nothin' to do with them bastards!"

The sergeant took the bills and stepped aside. "You know where you're goin' once you're in there?"

"Damn right!"

Luther withered him with a glance as he passed through the open door. The officer immediately pulled it shut after them.

Once they were inside and walking along a spacious office-lined corridor toward the front of the building, O'Riley grabbed Luther by the arm and maneuvered around a swarm of city officials emerging from the council chambers to tend to personal agendas. When he found an isolated quiet corner in the main foyer removed from the echoing rumble of disjointed conversation in the cavernous hall, O'Riley stopped and faced Luther in a slash of anemic illumination from high recessed windows coated with grime and pigeon droppings.

"Here's what's going on. There's a reason I brought you with me. We're meeting with Francis Keeley. He's an alderman from the St. Patrick's ward where I live. We're going to discuss a business opportunity and I want you to be my witness. I'm going to introduce you as my body guard and right-hand man. You've done a fine job at the factory and there will be additional compensation for you in this. You have a fearsome countenance. I want Keeley to see that. You don't have to say anything. I'll do the talking. You get what I'm saying?"

Luther nodded.

"Good, his office is on the next floor. Let's go." He walked away quickly and clattered up a flight of heavy oak stairs. Luther followed close behind.

A short distance down the long hall, they saw the door to Francis Keeley's office standing ajar and heard voices in a loud argument from within. They paused and O'Riley raised his hand slightly. "We'll give 'em a minute."

"I'm not payin' you another dime, Keeley, you goddamn bastard," wailed the complainant. "You're bleedin' me dry. At this rate, I won't have nothin' left to run my business. I can't compete with Brannigan when you're givin' 'im all the advantages."

"That's how it is. Take it or leave it. I can't do anything more for you."

"You can, but that son-of-a-bitch is payin' you not to. I know it. I can smell it and it sure ain't roses."

"Then you know what you're up against."

"Oh, yeah – oh, yeah. I'm thinkin' I'm gonna join that mob out front. I hope they bury your ass in the next election."

"That will never happen. And now you need to get your ass out of my office. I see two gentlemen out in the hall waiting to do business."

"The league will bring you down, Keeley. Mark my words. They'll bring you down."

"I've had enough of your blather." Keeley pointed to the door. "Get out or I'll call the cops."

"Sure, they're on the take right along with you. You ain't seen or heard the last of me."

"Oh, I think I have."

The blustering red-faced man stormed out, causing Luther and O'Riley to step back. "You're wastin' your time with that prick." His heels struck the floor with each resounding step in a staccato of retreat.

Keeley waved in O'Riley and Luther. "Shut the *feckin'* door."

Chapter 27

Rising Up

For the past week, the frequent arrivals and departures following meetings and intense discussions in the mansion library had not gone unnoticed by Newt and Aaron and Julie, who had matched most names of the visitors to the list Matias now kept under lock and key, but allowed Gustav access to share with them.

"Herr Bauman wants you to know who these people are," said Gustav, "since you have risked your lives to preserve the list. Most of them are Jewish friends and businessmen and their families who were forced to escape from Germany and the tyranny of Bismarck just as he and his brother did. Since Wilhelm the Second became Kaiser, the political influence of the social democrats has changed in Germany just as it is changing here in America. We want to seize on the momentum in both our countries and keep it moving forward in support of working class people.

"The Bauman brothers and other exiled members of our group want to return to Germany and take back their companies stolen from them by the Bismarck regime. Most will stay and continue in America. We learned not long ago that a highly ranked officer in Bismarck's secret police has ownership of Kurt and Heinrich's company. Someday he will pay dearly for what he did to the Bauman family.

"Here in America, our organization is hoping to see an end to the excesses and opulence of capitalist wealth and ownership and the exploitation of working people. We look to the new President, Theodore Roosevelt, as a leader."

Jacob Schiff nodded with satisfaction and put aside the financial report that Kurt Bauman had handed to him a half hour ago. "You've done well since you came to America, quite well. I also admire your philanthropic orientation. You may know I do much the same for the settlements, schools and Zionism." He stroked his carefully trimmed white goatee nested above a gray silk cravat that matched the handkerchief neatly tucked into his left lapel pocket. He turned slightly in his chair and favored Sophie Rose with a gracious smile where she had spread her favorite-colored, forest-green skirts to either side of her on the divan.

"I so enjoyed last evening's entertainment, Sophie dear. You have such a beautiful voice, such incredible range. You know, I saw you only once in Vienna. It was a performance of *Die Fledermaus*, on New Year's Eve. Even if Kurt and Matias, who I now know as Heinrich, were not such astute entrepreneurs, my bank would be most happy to provide fiscal management to your company, if only because you are on Herr Bauman's board."

"Thank you, Jacob. Your kind compliment is in keeping with your reputation as a gentleman banker, which is why we would like to do business with you."

"Jacob's benevolent blue eyes surveyed them with a bemused gleam. "And I'm sure that anti-semite, Morgan, has something to do with it. I'm surprised you didn't want to escape the old tyrant's clutches sooner."

"The railroad situation has made it impossible for us to stay with Morgan," said Kurt. He wants to take over and own everything he touches. We have reason to believe our company is on his list."

"Morgan is the boss of the United States. You can't rake much more muck than J. Pierpont Morgan. Although we are enemies on Wall Street, I have to respect him as a financier, if only to be aware of his stock manipulations and strong-arm tactics. You know that he calls me 'that foreigner.' Wall Street is a battleground between the Yankees and the Jews." Jacob flicked a thread of lint from the left arm of his black wool suit. "I assume you followed in the news what happened between us over the Northern Pacific Railroad."

"That is the first reason we asked you to come and see us. We would be at the mercy of J. Pierpont Morgan."

"Who's your fiscal manager at the Morgan Bank?"

"Henry Phillips."

"I know Henry. He's a good man when he isn't drunk. If you will accompany me for the authorizing signatures, I will personally handle the transfer of funds. Henry and Pierpont won't be happy about it, but we are. Pierpont will want to lock us in his black room hoping to starve us into submission to keep your account with him so he can more easily take it away from you. But we'll go in prepared. We'll hide food in our satchels and pockets, enough to last for forty-eight hours. That's the extent of his patience without chasing us around the room with a horse whip. Pierpont enjoys making his victims suffer. On the other hand, he might not even be there. He spends a great deal of time on his yacht giving parties. "

"When would you like to proceed?" asked Kurt.

"In two days. You can travel to New York with me in one of my private rail cars. I have three on every trip you know."

Kurt smiled. "So we've heard."

"That's two more than Pierpont travels with."

"It's good to have extra space," said Kurt, humoring the man's ego, "to accommodate guests."

"You know for many years we have been the banker for the Southern Pacific Railroad," said Jacob, "owned by Edward Harriman. You have to understand that railroads are the arteries of commerce. Whoever owns them can control every other industry. Morgan has always been out to control railroads. At one time, he rescued ten of them, back in 1893, saved them from bankruptcy by having his bank take them over and run them. That's what he does best, reorganize and bring them under his control.

"He convinced James J. Hill to consolidate his Great Northern and Northern Pacific Railroads. They already controlled shipments in the Northwest. After that, Morgan and Hill together made a move to buy the Chicago, Burlington, and Quincy. We immediately saw they were trying to connect into the Chicago system. Then logically, very clever, Morgan's New York Central Railroad would become a link to establishing a transatlantic shipping route and control European markets.

"Harriman and I went to Morgan and Hill and asked them to let us join them in the venture. When they turned us down, we decided to compete with them directly. We secretly bought seventy-eight million dollars in shares of Northern Pacific. As you know from the press, the economy nearly crashed from the speculation that followed on Wall Street. Investors traded up and when the stock went down, so did they. We ended up on the board of a securities company that merged the three railroads. After that, we were going to partner with a steamship line to China and Japan. You see, Harriman envisioned a global transportation network, but Morgan wanted control of the North Atlantic to himself. He won't partner with us on that account. But now that you and your brother are taking back your company from Palm in Berlin, he might sniff something in the wind with that bright red nose of his."

"There's another matter of interest we would like to discuss with you, as well," said Matias.

"Shall I call you Matias or Heinrich?"

"Between us, in private, Heinrich is preferred. In mixed company, I have to maintain my contrived identity as Matias Bauman."

"How mysterious and dramatic. I love the intrigue. It appeals to my sense of subterfuge. Your idea, Sophie, coming from the theater?"

She smiled in turn under his regal benevolent gaze. "It was Kurt's and Matias's idea. I only helped them with the name."

"Excellent, excellent." He turned back to Matias. "Perhaps I should just call you Matias, in case my memory fails me in a public venue."

"Your mind is the sharpest among investment bankers. You wouldn't be the President at Kuhn, Loeb were it not so."

"Oh, that, I just married into the family."

"You are too modest," said Sophie.

"And you know it's not my nature to be modest."

"Then we appreciate your discretion, if not your modesty."

They laughed.

"Altering my identity and the name of the company were essential," said Matias. "Not only were we hounded out of Germany and Austria Hungary, we were followed here."

"Followed?"

"By a paid assassin."

"You're joking."

"No, Jacob, I wish this were just some plot from the stage, but we live with this situation. Potentially being confronted by a killer is a reality for us."

"You should be attended by bodyguards, an army of them posted outside the house."

"That would draw attention. Someone does keep an eye on us, but he remains inconspicuous."

"And are you all targeted for assassination?"

"Kurt and myself."

"Amazing – shocking and amazing. How did this come about?"

"Our father was a supporter of the Social Democratic Party in Germany when Bismarck was in power. He was arrested by the Director of the Secret Service, Rudolf Palm, and died in prison. We know he was tortured. We had to relocate our families and go into exile to avoid arrest."

"Kaiser Wilhelm II came into power in 1890," said Jacob. "My understanding is that he was accepting of Social Democrats."

"But not of Jews."

"That's true. He keeps a token Jew in his court. Interesting that we Jews handle stock shares here in America for German investors. Please continue."

"We exchanged private letters with our friends who had escaped the notice of Bismarck and his police. About three years later, we considered returning to Berlin, or at least joining our enterprise here with the former Wohlman Company in Berlin."

"Former?"

"We learned that Chancellor Bismarck had given ownership and control of our company to Rudolf Palm as a reward for his years of excellent service. We had nothing to return to."

"This becomes more intriguing by the minute. But why would this assassin still be after you? For what reason?"

"We don't have an answer, other than Palm wants to make certain we never return to Germany. We do know the assassin is somewhere here in Chicago. One of our organizers had an encounter with him."

"What happened to the organizer?"

"He fought him off."

"If he's still trying to find you and Palm continues to hire him, then Palm most certainly doesn't want you to return and reclaim your company. Have you considered that possibility of a takeover? It can be arranged."

"No, but it sounds logical. Palm was ruthless before and would stop at nothing. There's no reason to believe he's changed."

"You've been gone fifteen years. Would your chances have been better to return seven or eight years ago?"

"By then we had established Bauman Enterprises here in Chicago and were growing rapidly. We determined there was nothing we could do to regain our company in Germany," Kurt paused, "until now."

"With the assistance of Kuhn, Loeb I imagine," Jacob ran a finger across his silver-tinged handlebar mustache, a gesture that conveyed the cutting of someone's throat.

"With the assistance of Kuhn, Loeb. You are well connected with European investors and, therefore, we would like to propose a plan."

Jacob nodded assertively. "I'm listening."

Julie, Liesel, Conrad, and Dutton traversed the crowded streets of Chicago disseminating new pamphlets and literature every day informing and encouraging the people to become involved in the increasing momentum for political, economic, and social change.

One of the pieces read: *Like a swollen river cresting into flood waters that can not be stopped, the tributaries of unrest have merged and ruptured the weakening dikes of greed and corruption that have become the foundation of capitalism and that hold back the mounting undercurrent of "fierce discontent," described by the new President, Theodore Roosevelt.*

The *Tribune* carried the statement that: *Although the President has praised the "strong and forceful men" who have "done great good" by building up the commerce of the nation, he has also stated that "there are real and grave evils" that need to be corrected. He has proposed that the Federal government "assume power of supervision and regulation over all corporations doing an interstate business."*

Waving signs to use the power of the ballot against corruption in the city government, the girls stood on street corners and in front of the town hall.

They marched with a column of suffragettes demanding the right of franchise for women, the right to vote.

They marched through the levee with Sister Pavalek and a platoon of nuns, wives, and other members of the clergy bearing signs to stamp out prostitution and were met with catcalls, hoots, and guffaws.

When Dutton Koontz reported to work a few days after his rescue of Ingrid Olson, Clarence Burke, the druggist, called him into the back of the store to arrange for the day's deliveries. Dutton noticed that half the packages contained opium.

"I can't deliver those no more," he said.

"What are you talking about?"

"These, he shoved at them on the table. I can't deliver 'em. I won't deliver 'em."

"What's the matter, Dutton? You suddenly get religion?"

"No, nothing like that. It's not good. It's just not something I want to do anymore. I'll take care of the other deliveries."

"What happened to you? Something must have happened. Ain't I paying you enough?"

"No, I don't want to take money for this. I just don't want to do this. It's wrong. It ruins people's lives and it's against the law."

Clarence laughed. "What law? What the hell are you talking about, boy? I know cops who use the stuff. What people do is their own damn business, not those uptight upright nuns and collars been marchin' up and down the street. They should leave well enough alone."

"It don't matter, Mr. Burke. I can't go back to the Levee anyway. Madame Restivo has her man gunnin' for me."

"Madame Restivo? What the hell for?"

"I rescued one of her girls."

"You rescued?" Clarence swiped a hand against his head. "What did you do? Fuck her and now you're gonna marry her?"

"No, sir, I saved her from having an abortion. Madame Restivo took her to an abortionist and that's where I got her away."

"Now I've heard it all. And what did you do with the whore?"

"Please don't call her that. She's not a whore."

"Well, a whore's a whore in my book."

"I took her to a settlement house."

"You amaze me, Dutton. Do you now what happens if you don't deliver these drugs? I make more money selling opium than I do all the rest of it and you make good money too. If you walk out on me, you better watch your back. The Chinaman won't look kindly on this. And have you forgotten your career? I was gonna send you to pharmacy school. You want to throw that away too?"

"Yes, not if I have to do this."

Clarence shook his head. "I'm really disappointed in you, Dutton. I thought you had what it takes to succeed in this business."

"I do thank you for giving me the chance, sir. But it ain't right for me anymore."

"Getting your throat slit in a dark alley ain't right either, boy."

"I'll take my chances. Goodbye, Mr. Burke."

Clarence continued to shake his head and waved for him to leave.

When Frieda Olson gave birth, she decided to keep her illegitimate child rather than give him up to an orphanage. She moved in with Dutton and his parents. Dutton took a job working in a Bauman machine manufacturing plant. Frieda got a job as a "Hello Girl" telephone operator and placed her little boy in child care at Sister Pavalek's settlement house.

Ophelia came home one evening to find a woman and her six-year-old son sitting in the kitchen talking. The little girl was drinking a tall cold glass of milk and eating her way through a plate of chocolate cookies.

"Ophelia, come in, my dear. I would like you to meet Winnie Thomas, and this is her daughter, Tonia. This is my daughter, Ophelia."

"I am pleased to meet you, ma'am."

"I told Mrs. Thomas about you and who you work for. Her husband is serving time at Joliet Prison. Her lawyer tried to arrange a visit, but the warden wouldn't let her see her husband. Her lawyer is one of us. Mrs. Thomas tells me he is looking for someone to help him. I said you might be able to do that."

"Who is this man?"

"His name is Bernard Hutchins. He was my husband's defense lawyer at the trial. If it wasn't for him, my husband would have gone to prison for longer."

The name sounded familiar to Ophelia. "What did your husband do?"

"Edward worked at Mr. O'Riley's garment factory for three years. He was the only Negro. Toward the end, he stole a few things to sell, because the owner, Mr. O'Riley stopped paying him."

"What happened to Mr. O'Riley?"

"Nothing. The judge gave him a reprimand and said he didn't want to see him in his courtroom again."

"Did you receive any compensation?"

"I never got no money. My daughter and me had to move into a settlement house. I do piece work."

"I'll help if I can. What do you want me to do?"

"Could you meet Mr. Hutchins and just talk to him? He'll have to tell you what he wants. He told me he is blocked in the court for getting the money Mr. O'Riley owes my Edward and he could not git me the right to visit. I just told him I'd talk to your mother."

"How did you know my mother?"

"She came to teach children at the settlement house. I watched her in the classes."

"We've become friends," said Ophelia's mother.

"Where do you want me to meet him?"

"At his office."

"Can you take me there?"

"Yes 'm." Winnie rose from her kitchen chair. "Tonia, we have to go now, Honey."

In desperation, the little girl attempted to stuff an entire cookie into her already full mouth.

Ophelia's mother wrapped the remaining three cookies in a napkin and handed them to Tonia. "You can take the rest of them with you, Tonia."

"What do you say," directed Winnie.

"Thank you, Mrs. Robinson. These taste real good."

"You're welcome."

Cookie crumbs dribbling from her chin, Tonia followed her mother and Ophelia out the door.

Ophelia was not impressed by Bernard Hutchins meager office, but she was caught off guard by recognizing the distinctive handsome features and height of the lawyer, whom she had seen speak at the Baptist church over a month ago. Her father had not been able to find out information about him at the Pullman Porters club and she had given up the prospect of meeting him.

After introducing Ophelia, Winnie promptly left with her daughter.

"Mr. Hutchins, I heard you speak once at our church." She did not want him to release the warm grip of both of his large gentle hands wrapped around hers.

"I'm pleased to meet you, Miss Robinson. I hope you don't mistake or misinterpret my request."

Ophelia smiled. "I have yet to hear it, but I doubt I will misinterpret it."

"Since you heard me speak, you might surmise I'm hoping to find a sponsor."

"And you think I could be that person?"

"Not directly, no. But I understand you are employed by a man who could be approached."

"I'm just a house maid, nothing more."

"Be that as it may, I've heard that Mr. Bauman is sympathetic to the Negro cause and is a man of philanthropy."

"Mr. Bauman barely knows who I am, but I could speak with his niece on your behalf. She is an outspoken and delightful young woman. We do have a kind of respect for each other."

"Would it be an imposition to ask if you could arrange an introduction? Of course, I can't openly go up to the north side."

"I could accompany you. You could go with me."

"This would not be disagreeable to you?"

"Mr. Hutchins, anything I can do to help you would not be disagreeable."

"It embarrasses me somewhat to have to ask for such a favor."

"You should never be embarrassed at striving to succeed."

"It isn't my success that concerns me, it is the success of our brothers and sisters."

"I fully understand your position, Mr. Hutchins."

"There is no need for us to be formal with each other. Please, call me Bernard."

A bubble of laughter escaped her. "Only if you call me Ophelia."

"Ophelia it is."

"Well, Bernard, now that we've met, what would you like to talk about?"

Bernard's boyish grin widened into a pleasant smile. "For the moment, I'm at a loss for words, which is quite unlike me. I generally do well in the court room, but my social skills are wanting."

"I think your social skills are elegant."

"Ah, well, now I am embarrassed."

"Please don't be. We are on a first name basis. You are an eloquent speaker, but I saw only a glimpse of what you are advocating. I sense you would like to become a leader."

"Elegant and eloquent and now I'm tongue-tied. Please, let's sit down." He offered a straight-backed chair and carried his own from behind his desk and placed it next to hers so they faced one another, their knees barely, unavoidably touching.

"In your speech, you mentioned DuBois."

"Yes, I support and espouse his social and political philosophy. Negroes can no longer wait for the white establishment to accord us our constitutional rights. We must pursue them and more than insist, we must demand them on our own behalf."

"I agree, but what avenues do we have to make such demands?"

"We have to do so politically, through government and the law."

"Of course that takes money and influence."

"Politics is all about money and influence, but it's also about people and the power of the ballot."

"As a woman, I would cast my vote if I had one to cast."

"Franchise for women will happen. I have no doubt."

"But it is not happening for us, for Negro women. The white suffragists don't want us. They won't let us join them. So we are forming our own league."

"I have noticed that Mr. Bauman supports that movement, as well as others."

"He does and his young niece is an activist."

"What is her name?"

"Julie Josephson."

"I look forward with great anticipation to meeting her."

"She will be equally pleased to meet you."

Bernard reached across her lap and took both her hands in his. Their eyes did not waver.

One month later, with the help of his attorney, Matias Bauman arranged for Winnie Thomas and her daughter to visit her husband, Edward Thomas, at Joliet Prison.

Chapter 28

Scabs

Jonah Delacroix's head nodded in the afternoon heat. He dozed despite the rhythmic squeak of the right rear wheel axle that had needed grease for over a month. The accustomed lurch and sway of the wagon bed barely woke him and he drifted in and out of a restive stupor induced by the clouds of dust rising from the hooves of the plodding mule team.

From time to time, his dark eyes opened and scanned the ten other young and middle-aged Negro men reclining on bedrolls or seated firmly against each other to buffer the jarring shudder of jolts shooting up from ruts and potholes through the creaking frame of the wagon. He did not notice the sameness of his companions, crushed brim slouch hats pulled low over their eyes and compressing tight black or gray curls like sprung wool. With the exception of a few who had acquired short coats and sported bowler hats and chewed on dead cigars, most of the men wore the collarless linen shirts, coveralls, and work boots of field hands. Rarely able to bath unless they were near a stream or a river or an available water pump, a sour odor emanated from their sweat-encrusted skin. In appearance, they were perceived as interchangeable by their common color and their place in the social hierarchy of unskilled labor.

They lived and traveled together like a nomadic herd in search of work and food and shelter wherever they could find it. On that day, a train of one-hundred mule-drawn wagons, half of them loaded with similar male cargo, wended its way out of St. Louis, Missouri and north along a country road toward Chicago.

An announcement by a local recruiter had reached those working on nearby farms and by word of mouth in the alleys and saloons and flop houses in the city that a strike by the garment workers in Chicago was imminent and the factory and mill owners were hiring non-union strike breakers to transport their finished clothing products to department stores. They sought Black laborers accustomed to temporary work, since they could pay them less and fire them when the strike ended, although such information was not shared with the scabs.

With no opportunities to be apprenticed and barred from establishing any business by companies that might hire them, they could not earn a livelihood in a major city like St. Louis or Chicago.

"Negroes are not capable of performing skilled work," the head of the Employers Association proclaimed and was echoed by the white-dominated trade unions. "Because of their race, they do not have the temperament and mentality to do what a white worker can do."

Jonah never heard those words spoken, but the racial barrier prevented him and hundreds of thousands of others like him from making a living. The sting of discrimination had dulled in him years ago through what he was taught by his mother and father and by the colored men and women he observed when he was old enough to go in search of work and discovered he had a few limited options.

With only six months of schooling and unable to read and write, he and his friend, Orville, joined the mass of illiterate brothers and sisters in servitude that had not changed with the changing of the Federal law abolishing slavery, a law about which he knew nothing.

His thoughts turned to the new opportunity promised by the recruiter and the escape from the share cropper's existence of his parents and two brothers and a sister, who was hoping to marry a preacher and move into the next small town ten miles down the dirt road from the farm where Jonah had been born and raised.

Although he had had trouble learning letters and words in the wooden Baptist church that doubled as a schoolhouse for a few hours each day of the week after the children had finished early morning farm chores, his last ten years of plowing fields and harvesting crops had not extinguished his desire to find something better.

"You be slow, but you be steady," his mother had told him. "Your sister can read, but it won't do her no good. No one g'wine give her no job, jist make babies for the preacher, he ever git 'round to askin' her. She fourteen now. Gonna be too old soon. You hear that, Theda? When's Preacher Shippe gonna axe you to marry 'im?"

Theda shook her head. "Don't know, Mama. Don't know. He talk about it and say we gonna be happy, but he got church things to look after first."

"He need to look after you first with that buck from the next county comin' over here sniffin' 'round. You body is round and ripe. Don't you let 'im git you alone."

"I am wantin' the preacher for my husband, not that field hand. Don't want to marry no field hand."

"Careful what you say. Yo' brothers and father be field hands. They keepin' us alive."

"I know, Mama. I know. Don't mean no disrespect. I want to become a teacher anyway just like Miz Hatcher. She said I could make a good teacher. She said I'se smart and I got a good head on my shoulder. She want me to go to Tuskegee."

"How you gonna do that and be married to the preacher and have his babies?"

"I'm thinkin' of goin' to Tuskegee first and then git married. Then I kin be a teacher over in Marquand."

"Then it ain't Preacher Shippe. Yo' the one holdin' up the mule. How long you think he gonna wait fer you?"

"We talked about it."

"He may be a preacher, but he got a fire in his pants like any other man."

"You likely to come back and find someone took your place in his bed."

"Mama, don't talk about him like that. He ain't like that. He do truly love me."

"How long you talkin' 'bout at Tuskegee?"

"Two years to git my diploma."

"Two years! Gawd, Daughter! For someone smart, you sho actin' dumb. No man his young age gonna wait that long. No man. Ain't that so, Jonah?" She turned to her son who was trying to edge out the door.

"No, Mama, not me. I don't git them thoughts."

"Ha! I don't believe you. Yer Papa talk to you? Yer friend, Orville talk to you. I know fer a fac he been wit a girl. His Mama made 'im tell. She knew. She whipped it outta 'im."

"You don't got to whip me." He feared and respected the power and authority of his scrawny mother and her coal burning dark eyes. "I ain't been wit no girl. I ain't even thought 'bout no girl."

"You 'spec me to b'lieve that? You know what goin' on down there in yo pants. Well, dat girl up to no good. She come lookin' fer you boys and spread her legs come git her honey. She a whore. That where she gonna end up, in a whore house in St. Louis."

"Mama, Orville and me gonna go find work in St. Louis. We talk 'bout it. We done workin' in the fields."

"Make no diff'rence to me. You be one less mouth to feed and with Theda gone, that make two. Just don't go to no whore house in St. Louis. Them whores kin give you a disease that make you sick and die. You git work, you find yo'self a proper woman, mebbe a teacher like yo sister gonna be. Then you kin raise smart babies, a lot smarter than you."

"Yes 'm. Don't plan on nothin' like that fer a long while. Orville and me got to find work first. When I git married, I gonna bring my wife back to meet you."

The scene with his mother and sister lingered in his memory. He missed the hard earthen floor of their cabin and the smell of his mother's cooking pork and greens and hot cornbread. How he wished for a fistful of his mother's hot cornbread. When he parted, bawling hot tears, she clung to him. "Now, you take care yo'self. You my boy. You always be my boy. Don't you fergit me and yo papa. We love you. We always done right by you."

"I know, Mama. I know. I be careful. I come back to see you." He embraced his sister who stepped forward from where she stood nearby. "You become a good teacher."

"I will Jonah. You won't recognize me the nex' time you see me, I be so full of knowledge, it spill out all over."

"And look out for that Orville too," said Mama. "He don't got a good head on his shoulder laky yo."

"I take care a' him. He listen to me. I lak his brother."

After walking in the dank heat not more than two hours from home, Jonah suddenly stopped in the middle of the dirt road.

"Why you stoppin'?" asked Orville. "You tired? You got a stone in yo shoe?"

"No, not tired. No stone."

"Then why you stoppin', brother. We got a long way to go."

"That's what I was thinkin', Orville. We got a long way to go and we don't know where it ends. We don't know what's gonna happen to to us and what we gonna do."

"Work is what we gonna do."

"But we gotta find work. Mebbe this ain't right for us to be doin'. We leavin' somethin' good behind."

"It was good, Jonah. It was good. And now we lookin' fo somethin' better and we ain't gonna know what dat is 'til we find it. And it ain't pushin' a plow starin' at a mule's ass."

"I like our mule, Lily. She a good mule, a good steady worker."

"You like her good 'nouf to spend the rest a yo life starin' at her ass."

"She has a nice ass. It a sweet ass fo a mule."

"You a crazy nigger lovin' a mule's ass."

"Didn't say ah loved her ass. Just say she had a sweet ass fo a mule. Next to mah mama and papa, Lily done raised me from a pup. Taught me how to plow a straight line."

"Well, ahm walkin' on. You kin stay here in the middle of the road rememberin' yo mule's ass and I see you in St. Louis."

"Oh, I comin'. I comin'. Just don't like what I don't know."

"Nobody laks what dey don't know 'til dey know it."

"Guess ahm hungry and missin' Mama's cookin'."

"We ain't gonna find food standin' here, but we might find some we keep goin' down dis road."

"Mebbee we kin ketch us a catfish and pick some berries. Go good wit de corn bread Mama fix us."

"Find us a riva fust."

"I look and listen."

"Good. We walkin' agin now."

"We walkin' agin."

The dull yellow glow of lights in the distance led them onward to the city. Stumbling and tired, they discovered a stable near the outskirts and slipped through a side door of the barn in search of a spot to sleep. They were rousted out early the next morning by a skinny Negro stable hand who told them about a man hiring workers down at the riverfront warehouse.

"Where we find it?" asked Jonah brushing away wisps of straw that clung to his clothing.

"Stay on dis street all the way to the river. Dey be a big warehouse der. You see it when you git der."

"We git us some food? We et all we had comin' on the road."

"Dey got food der when you sign fo' work."

"Good," said Orville, relieving himself in the corner of the empty stall in which they had slept. "We real hungry."

After walking several blocks, they found the recruiter, Darius McFey. A lean, mid-sized man. The history of many bare knuckle fights etched his ruddy scarred face. His narrow blue eyes squinted at the two young *Nigras* coming toward him along the street. He registered their size and loose-limbed athletic stride and assumed they were candidates for his work crew. He removed the freshly lit glowing cigar from his mouth and rose from where he was seated on a bale of straw, as they approached the open door of the warehouse.

"Evenin', mister," Jonah took the initiative. "We here lookin' fer work. Man at the stable tol' us you hirin'."

"This is your lucky day, gents. Yes, I am hirin' as long as you're willing to go to Chicago."

"Chickgago?"

"Chicago. You ever hear of Chicago?"

"We know it a big city up north. Ain't never been there. This is our first time here in St. Louis. This our first time most anywhere, 'cept Pinkneville. We take our cotton der to da gin. Orville and me, we good workers. Work all our lives on da farm. Our pa's share croppers."

"Well, if you want to work, Chicago is waitin' to welcome you with open arms."

"What we gotta do?"

"Oh, when you get there, they'll tell you what to do. Right now, I have to hire 'bout ten more *Nigras* afore we leave tomorra mornin'."

"How we gonna git there?"

"By wagon. You'll get food and sleep here in the warehouse tonight with the others. You interested?"

Jonah and Orville looked at each other and grinned. Jonah returned his attention to the recruiter. "We take the job."

"Good, just sign right here." He shoved a tablet at them and handed Jonah a pencil. As Jonah carefully printed his name, the recruiter eyed him shrewdly. "Had you some schoolin', eh? Most *Nigras* only make an X."

"My sister and me went to school and Orville here too. Cain't read much though. Do we gotta read to work in Chicago?"

"No, you don't have to write neither."

"Then, we kin do it, whatever it is." Jonah handed the pencil to Orville, who just as carefully signed his name, then handed the pencil back to the recruiter.

Jonah tipped his hat. "We thank you, suh, fer hirin' us."

The recruiter nodded and puffed his cigar. "Find yerself a place inside."

"Thank you, suh, thank you."

"Get in line for chow. Eat all you want. Shit house is out back. Corn husks, but no paper."

"We used to corn husks."

"Pump and water down at the other end next to the chow line."

"Thank you, suh. We headin' that way."

Jonah and Orville joined a long slow-moving line of young, middle-aged, and older Negro men waiting in anticipation for their turn at the serving benches. Sporadic eruptions of flame from fat drippings sent up the tangy aroma of sizzling barbequed pork on a large open charcoal grill next to rice and baked beans simmering in a huge pots. They salivated with hunger, since they had not eaten a good meal in two days.

Jonah nudged Orville and his eyebrows raised with a twitch to accompany his grin. Orville bobbed his head in acknowledgement and equal anticipation.

"Hope they somethin' lef for us. This line sho is slow."

"See them big pots," said a high yellow, skinny man just ahead of them. "They always full and they's always meat cookin'. I been here two days and would do me jus fine to stay here and eat 'til I bust. No one go hungry here what I see. They take care of us so we be ready for work in Chickgago. Where you gents from?"

"Sharecropper farms over near Pinkneville. Yo?"

"Name's Zacaria Brown."   His bad teeth flashed in a genuine good-hearted smile. "Live right here in St. Louis, but heard work pay better in Chickgago."

"You live here in the city?" queried Orville.

"Born downriver, but grew up most here."

"We don't know no one here."

"You know me."

Jonah's shoulders shook with laughter. "We do dat."

Orville grinned and stomped. "Food comin' up."

They arrived at the long serving table and were handed metal plates, a cup, and utensils. With full plates and coffee, they settled at an empty space along the wall and their jaws joined the chorus of gnawing, chewing and belches of the others.

Upon finishing, they loosened their belts and settled back allowing their stomachs to expand unrestrained from the internal swelling effect of beans and rice.

"Eat jus as good as home," said Orville.

"It's good all right," said Zacaria. "Not as good as mah maman make. She cook for white folks in dey big house."

"You eat in da big house?" asked Jonah.

"We live out back when I a chile. She always bring us food from her kitchen. That why I such a tall handsome *bourgeoisie gentilehomme.*" He flashed a grin.

"You talk French," said Jonah. "Where you learn dat?"

"My maman is Cajun. She talk it all da time. I hear it since I was born."

Orville giggled. "Da girls, dey love me too. I ain't so tall as you, but I big here." He stroked his crotch. "Da girls luv me in dey jelly roll."

Jonah snorted. "You only been in one jelly roll and you luv it."

"I been in jelly roll you don't know 'bout."

"I know everthin' you done since we was chillen. And you ain't had but one jelly roll in yo life. And you catch hell fo' dat."

"You don't know how to count, nigga. You don't know how to count."

"I kin count what I see and it ain't but one jelly roll fo yo."

"All this talk 'bout jelly roll makin' me itch," said Zacaria. "And we got a long ride ahead of us in a wagon."

Suspecting what Zacaria was leading up to, Jonah quickly interjected, "We got to git us some sleep is what we gotta git us afore that long ride in da wagon."

"We kin sleep in da wagon," said Zacaria. "Got no mo to do but sleep."

"Don want to git us in no trouble," said Jonah. "We here to go to work in Chickgago. We not here lookin' fo jelly roll."

"I know a place," said Zacaria. "I know a place."

"Dat ain't no place fo us," said Jonah.

"You speak fo yoself," said Orville. "Zacaria and me got da itch."

"Zacaria jus gonna take you to a cat house and you gonna lose what money you got."

"I gonna make lots money in Chickgago. I make mo money den I spend."

"Money is fo havin' a good time," said Zacaria. "Dat all it good fo."

"When it all gone, you got no ting to eat and no place to sleep. You jus a nigga got nothin'. Don't you want a house and find a good woman fo a wife?"

"I just got away from a home," said Zacaria. "Don't want to have 'nother one right now. Want good times. Dat what I want."

"Yo mama tol' me to look afta yo. Take care my boy, she say."

Zacaria laughed, enjoying the argument. "Maybe she right, Orville."

"What you say?"

"She still think you a boy, not a man."

"I ain a boy. Not no mo. I don hide under her wing. And I don hav ta listen to yo, Jonah. You ain my pappy."

"I am lak yo big brotha. I look out fo yo hide yo don lose it."

Zacaria edged toward the large warehouse door. "Yo come on wit me, Orville. We have us a good time."

"You cain go there, Orville. What money you got gots to buy you food, not hooch. Soons you show you got money, some bad Nigra woman gonna take it from you, sho."

Orville pushed past his friend. "I see you when da sun come up, Jonah, and I gonna tell yo about mah good time." Ignoring Jonah's threatening scowl, he stepped over the legs and feet of men still sitting or reclining on the ground and followed Zacaria, who was already outside.

"You got to listen to me, Orville. You want to make it to Chicago, you got to listen to me. You gonna be a fool, you gonna end up in a fool's grave," Jonah shouted after him, but the words fell on deaf ears.

"Hey, where you boys think you're goin'?" Smoking an after dinner cigar, the recruiter, Darius McFey, was leaning against the warehouse wall just outside the door.

"Uptown," said Zacaria. "Find us a juke joint. Celebrate afore we go on da road."

"Find us some jelly roll," a lascivious chuckle rose from deep in Orville's throat.

"Need some fun 'fore we go to Chickgago."

"Juke joint? Fun? Jelly roll?" McFey spat a piece of tobacco that had separated from the cigar and adhered to the tip of his tongue. "Uh-uh, boys. Uh-uh. You signed on to work for me and I want you to be here in the mornin'."

"Oh, we be here," said Zacaria. "We be here with big smiles on our face. We jus' two *gentilehomme* goin' uptown to enjoy the evenin'."

"*Gentilehomme*, you say." McFey spit again. "You two don't git yer *Nigra* asses back in the warehouse, yer gonna be *gentile merde*. Since you speak French, you know *merde*. You git what I'm sayin'."

Zacaria's expression fell and his shoulders slumped in submission. "I know *merde*. I know what you be sayin'."

"That's good, *monsieur*. That's real good, 'cause you don't stay here, you don't git to go to Chickgago and you don't work and you don't get paid."

"Mebbe in Chickgago we kin git us some jelly roll," said Orville, his voice heavy with disappointment.

"Oh, yeah," said McFey. "Lotsa jelly roll in Chickgago. It's jest waitin' fer you."

"Then we jus' wait for it," said Zacaria. "We jus' wait and think 'bout dat jelly roll waitin' fo us."

"That's right," McFey blew a cloud of smoke. "All good things come to those who wait, even jelly roll."

"We gonna wait," said Orville and started back toward the warehouse where Jonah stood watching and listening at the open door. He grinned as Orville and Zacaria approached.

"What you grinnin' at?" Zacaria pulled a mouth harp from the vest pocket of his coat. "You look like a possum starin at a full moon." He ran the mouth harp past his lips eliciting a short quick blast of atonal notes.

As Zacaria played his mouth harp, a man sitting nearby, a stranger in the crowd, began to hum. His low bass voice moved throughout the gathered mass like spreading water and was picked up by the others and the sound expanded upwards into the warehouse rafters and reverberated with the drone of swarming of bees on a hot summer day.

McFey listened with a kind of fascination. His *Nigras* never ceased to amaze him. Although not a religious man himself, he had once attended a revival and witnessed the chanting and emotional call for the congregation to come to the Lord. He could not conceive their screams and writhing and falling down, since he felt no such intensity except when he was in a fight. But he began to hum quietly to himself and discovered the sensation was soothing and calming with the chorus of Black men behind him.

Chapter 29

Strike

Joe McNeil planted a kiss on each head of his five children sitting at the table scooping porridge and dried fruit into their slurping, chomping mouths. He had arisen earlier and eaten rolls and drunk strong Irish black tea with his wife, Emma.

Ten years ago in 1895, he had met Emma O'Brian coming from Ireland on the same boat. That she had a four-year-old daughter in tow did not deter him from admiring her youth, energy and beauty revisited in their mix of red-headed children, four girls and a boy who was the middle child and of the most concern. Johnny had been breech born and was mentally slow. Without being asked by her mother, his older sister, Erin, dedicated herself to helping him. Despite her limited education, she continued to attend school part-time and brought home books from the library on a regular basis. She would often read to Johnny, who listened intently to her every word, most of which he did not understand. What he did know was she loved him.

The expression of love and mutual respect was the cornerstone of the McNeil family. Joe and his wife never beat their children like so many other parents they knew. They spoke to them in direct nurturing tones that influenced how they related to each other, despite common sibling rivalries.

Being able to provide for his family drove Joe to work long, hard hours. He had risen in position and importance at O'Riley's Textile Company until his recent firing and replacement because of union activism. Having his livelihood threatened angered Joe to the point of moral outrage. Although he had since found another job with the assistance of union friends, he would lash out against any force or influence that came between him and his ability to support his family. Above all else, he treasured his wife and children.

He vowed to go out and confront his former employer and every other employer who undervalued him as a worker and a human being.

The organization meeting he had attended one week ago included members of the teamsters and their leader, Cornelius Shea, who had agreed to collaborate with the garment workers should they decide to strike against the employers' hiring of nonunion subcontractors. Since December, six months ago, Joe had seen clothing cutters bundled in knit caps and heavy dark wool coats against piercing high winds and freezing temperatures, carrying their protest placards parading along the snow-encrusted sidewalk and blocking the entrance to Montgomery Ward. He knew their appearance and a man's amplified voice on a bullhorn proclaiming their grievances over the noise of passing trolleys and horse-drawn carriages and wagons were a precursor of union activity to come.

"Those goddamn Montgomery Ward owners locked 'em out," said Shea, rattling the gold watch chain slung across the tightly buttoned vest over his protruding belly. "Got word the tailors are gonna join 'em." He referred to the National Tailors' Association, a coalition of clothing manufacturers and retailers. "Five thousand of 'em will hit the streets tomorrow." He thoughtfully fingered his rust-colored mustache precisely trimmed across his upper lip. "If they ain't makin' clothes, we got nothin' to haul, comin' or goin'. That puts us out of work. If raw material don't get delivered, Ward and Sears and Roebuck can't make nothin' and we're all at loggerheads. Nothin' gets made, nothin' gets sold, nobody buys, no one gets paid, and everythin' stops. It's a damn lousy kettle 'a fish to be in, 'cause the stink'll get worse as time goes on. But we ain't gonna let that damn Employers Association kick out the unions. We got a right to protect ourselves from those bastards. So here's what we're gonna do." He tugged at his starched collar and black cravat where a diamond stud nested at the center under the swollen fold of his pasty white jowl.

Joe looked about at the standing room only crowd that had stuffed itself shoulder to shoulder into Shea's spacious office. Seated in his leather-quilted, hand-carved mahagony chair, the union president surveyed these men like a corpulent ruler would his subjects, the union's lieutenants, each one an experienced loader and wagon driver or a supervisor of other loaders and drivers. The transfer, trucking, and local express companies were the lifeblood of urban commerce, their thousands of horse-drawn flatbeds, trucks and drays flowed from dawn to dusk along the traffic congested Chicago streets back and forth from warehouses lining the waterfront. They tracked for miles in the garment district to downtown State Street department stores and other wholesalers and retailers located in outlying regions of the city. They carried the raw material for construction, lumber and bricks and steel, and coal to power furnaces. And from the countryside, they transported harvested crops and butchered and canned meats from the stock yards to markets and restaurants throughout the city. A blockade in every mercantile center would paralyze the business of the city.

Joe McNeil knew that two days ago this meeting would not be taking place had he not carried a satchel filled with ten thousand dollars in cash to Shea's office. The bribe from the garment workers union bought Shea's cooperation in leading the teamsters to join the strike. The amount of political effort it took to overcome the inertia of union leaders and confront the employers who would not back down or compromise on their position of the open shop frustrated Joe. Not until money changed hands did anything move forward. The conflict centered on power and profit on the side of the employers and job security, compensation, and working conditions on the side of the unions. The differences in personal interests and demands staggered him. He did not see how both sides could ever come to an agreement, but the attempt had to be made. What the employers were doing to victimize union workers was an outrage, the same outrage that had resulted in Bill O'Riley firing Joe.

Joe thought of himself as a good worker and a decent family man. His skin prickled with degradation the day O'Riley sent him packing. Enroute to his union headqurters, fomenting with agitation, he was nearly run down by a team of Clydesdales hauling a beer wagon and subjected to the curses of the teamster who challenged the legitimacy of his birth. Joe barely acknowledged him and, with shoulders hunched against the encroaching forces of the city, hurried on among the heavy traffic of horses and wagons and carriages and crowds.

For the past month, Joe noticed that the trickle of disgruntled discharged union men lining up at the hall had increased to a flood. The news was circulated that the management of twenty-seven garment and tailor warehouses had announced an open shop policy. Six thousand garment workers surged to the hall jammed with griping swearing men petitioning for the union leaders to take action, to call for a strike or at least have a conference with the employers, since the union contract had three months left before renegotiation.

Joe led his delegation to the first of many meetings with the Employers Association that ended with angry shouts, threatened lawsuits, and accusations of bribery, greed, and corruption. The wealth of the Employers Association subsidized the cooperation of store owners and warehouse wholesalers to hire only non-union employees, including their own teamsters.

The carpeted floor, hand-carved furniture, heavy drapes and elegant chandeliers in the Association conference room reminded Joe of entering a hotel. The building and offices bespoke money and lots of it. He resented the haughty manner of the committee seated across from his small group of five officers representing the garment workers.

"You broke the contract," said Joe. "You sent those men out on the street and brought in non-union to take their place. We have a list of grievances here," Joe pushed at the sheaf of papers before him on the table."

"We have our own grievances," said their spokesman, Stephan Fiore, one of the wholesale tailors who had joined the Employers Association. With dark curls and a vanity that matched his handsome face, Fiore was also an attorney instrumental in the formation of the Employers' Teaming Company. Funded by the capital of the Employers Association, it was preparing to handle enough deliveries to keep the stores in operation should the teamsters join the garment workers in a sympathy strike. Unknown to the teamsters, he was also arranging to have Negro drivers brought up to Chicago from St. Louis.

"We reserve the right to make employment decisions for the betterment and profitability of our companies," said Fiore.

"Since we are still under contract, we should go to arbitration," said Joe. "Will you agree to arbitration?"

"The contract terminates in three months. There isn't enough time for arbitration. We do offer to have a conference for new agreements, however."

"But we can only talk about the current grievances. That's according to the contract."

"What you and your fellows have to do, Mr. McNeil, is come back to us with a new agreement to allow for and support the hiring of non-union employees, an open shop."

"Goddamit, you damn well know we can't and we will not do that."

"Then you leave us no recourse but to discharge all union employees."

"Then you leave us no goddamn recourse but to strike!"

"We are prepared for that possibility, but you cannot and will not win."

"When we strike this time, it'll be nothing like you've ever seen before. We'll shut down the whole goddamn city."

"And you will go to jail, my friend."

"And you can go to hell!" Leaping up, Joe kicked over his chair. "Let's get outta here!" He led his delegation in a rush for the door.

Seeming to float in the dense early morning mist, twenty teamsters drove and maneuvered their wagons from each side of Rush Bridge, a squat double lane structure of steel girders supporting an over-arcing open frame that spanned the Chicago River. But for the chop of hoofs and clatter of metal-rim spoke wheels on the dense tarred wooden floor of the bridge, the progression was strangely silent. The occasional inquisitive neigh of a horse broke the predawn silence like a gathering army positioned to charge at sunrise. The drivers dismounted from their wagons and fastened oat bags to the heads of their draft animals. Although the teamsters and wagons would periodically rotate throughout the day to relieve strikers on the bridge, all mobile and pedestrian traffic was stopped.

Shea instructed the teamsters to block all the main streets and connecting arteries coming into the city with long trains of empty wagons to create impenetrable barriers. Under direct orders from Shea, no teamster could deliver or receive goods of any kind for any business throughout the city. The affect was instantaneous. The managers and store owners of the Employers Association activated their counter strategy and the battle began.

Luther Baggot accompanied Bill O'Riley to the Pinkerton's downtown office and were met at the door by Clarence Rittenauer, the Chief of Detective Services, who had been watching the chaos on State Street through the front window. Armed with clubs, metal pipes, rakes, hoes, axes, knives, rifles and small firearms, teamsters had commandeered the street by creating a barrier of horses and wagons impassable to citizens on foot or in cabs or on the trolleys that had ground to a halt, their overhead connectors casting sparks and hissing like surrounded and cornered Medieval beasts.

He saw an ink bottle hurled from a fifth story office window narrowly miss a striker and shatter on the sidewalk spraying the man's trousers with black viscous liquid. The gesture was a weak attempt at retaliation by regular non-union white collar employees prevented from working because of the strike.

Another teamster was killed, struck squarely in the head by a heavy paperweight from above. A call from the local patrol box brought a horse-drawn patrol wagon that could not get through the crowds and barriers to remove his body. Another striker fired his rifle at the upper windows blowing out the glass. A shard sliced across the face of the man who had thrown the paperweight and he fell back screaming and writhing next to his desk. Shouting curses, his co-workers dragged him to the center of the office and stayed clear of the windows as a second blast sprayed a shower of glass across the room where they crouched on the blood slick floor.

The manager crawled to the nearest wall phone. The call was taken by the desk sergeant, who told the man, "Wait, I'm gittin' the sheriff. You gotta repeat that." He handed over the phone to the sheriff, who listened for a moment, then scrawled frantically on a tablet.

He immediately passed on his written notes to the Chief of Police, who stared at the hasty scrawl of his subordinate in exasperation.

"Barrett, how do you expect me to read this? You have to at least take the time to make it legible."

"There ain't no time, Chief. No time. The city's goin' to explode. Teamsters are blockadin' the streets all over town. Nothin' can git through. There's gonna be some heads knocked sure. Startin' to happen. Already startin' to happen. Teamster killed over on Dearborne. Them strikers are goddman armed. They're shootin' out windows. Our men can't use their signal boxes. Can't even git to 'em. They try to contact us, they git beaten to smithereens. Badge and uniform don't count for shit out there."

The loss of social control and the recognition and respect for law and order deeply disturbed Superintendent of Police, Francis O'Neil. A sincere, straightforward man who swore by his belief in ethics and morality, he had been a champion of reform in the city since his appointment as Chief of Police in 1901. He began making arrests and closing down saloons and brothels in the Levee District and met head on with Michael "Hinky Dink" Kenna, the First Ward Alderman, who had become wealthy on bribes and paybacks from supporting the vice trades and helping the purveyors evade the law.

O'Neil was not a newcomer to graft and violent encounters. Criminals and adversaries were cowed by his imposing hard-muscled physique, handsome heroic features of a prize bare knuckle fighter, and piercing challenging expression that commanded attention and brooked no nonsense. His receding hairline emphasized the slight upward crook of his right eyebrow when he confronted and interrogated suspects. They tended to remember that eyebrow.

No one could buy him to look the other way when crimes were committed and he fought against the system of corrupt politicians and influence peddling of police officers by wealthy friends and relatives to divert them from prosecution of criminals they had arrested.

As a young police sergeant in 1894, along with United States Regular Infantry and Cavalry, he had been in the front line clashs with thousands of striking stockyard workers who set fires to boxcars in the yards and overturned others uncoupled from trains.

Yet again in 1894, he confronted thousands of Pullman Porters striking against their wages being slashed and jobs cut while the salaries of managers and dividends of stockholders were left untouched.

As missiles of various kinds continued to descend on strikers below from buildings throughout the city, news of the attacks reached Edward Dunne, the Mayor of Chicago. He sent his aide to summon the police chief to his office.

O'Neil was already receiving a briefing from two officers who had been stationed at the seventh precinct where they had witnessed the beating of a local storekeeper, a Slav who had shouted at the strikers to "Get off my street, you morons! You're stopping customers from coming here and you're ruining my business!" Two burly teamsters had grabbed him, thrown him to the ground and kicked and beat him with clubs while his wife pulled at the coats of his attackers in an attempt to stop them. They had turned on her, bodily lifted her kicking and screaming off the ground, and heaved her over the fruit and vegetable stands back inside the store where she lay sobbing and retching on the stained wooden floor.

"Barrett, you come with me," O'Neil called out to the sheriff in the next office, as he grabbed his hat and headed for the door. "It's the mayor."

When they arrived, they were blocked by an unruly crowd that jammed the hall and entrance to the Mayor's office. O'Neil held his badge high.

"I'm the Chief of Police. Let me through. I'm the Chief of Police."

Upon seeing O'Neil and Barrett pushing and struggling their way through the room filled with men insistently demanding to be heard by shouting over each other, Mayor Dunne waved his hand. The two police officers continued forward as others parted to let them pass through the noise and bedlam that continued unabated.

O'Neil noticed the hatchet-faced attorney, Clarence Darrow, waving a sheaf of papers in the Mayor's face decrying, "This is an injustice! It's a clear breach of contract by the Employer's Association! The teamsters have a legitimate claim under the law! You cannot ignore their demands! The teamsters and garment workers demand and deserve recognition, sir! This issue must be arbitrated and brought into court! It's the only way to prevent violence and bloodshed in the streets!"

"O'Neil, thank God you're here! You have to do something to stop this! Everybody in the city has gone berserk! I want fliers and every other kind of news publication and public announcements throughout the city. Send your men out there with bullhorns warning pedestrians and everybody who is not part of the strike to go home and stay off the streets! Arm your men with rifles! Tell them if shooting starts, they are to shoot back! Shoot to kill!"

An hour later back at headquarters, Barett briefed two-hundred police officers. "You will be given rifles and ammunition. I'm telling you that if you are attacked, I'm giving you a direct order from the mayor to return fire and shoot to kill."

Captain Melaniphy unlocked the arsenal and distributed rifles and ammunition. Streaming out of the building, the policemen broke up into squads, each led by a lieutenant. Within moments of turning the corner onto State Street, their pell-mell rush was blocked by a seething mob of teamsters and horses and wagons. A fusillade of stones, wood, pipes, and bottles drove them back, pursued by the mob, forcing them to seek refuge in stores and offices where projectiles shattered the display windows in their wake.

Shouting and cursing at the men who had grabbed his plunging, rearing team by their halters, Darius McFey looked frantically around for the police, nowhere to be seen. He could do nothing to prevent two of his Nigras from being dragged from the wagon and brutally stomped and beaten until their screams and writhing bodies were still. McFey leapt from the driver's seat to the ground and ran for his life. Minutes later, the police reinforced by Pinkertons arrived and drove the teamsters away, firing into their midst and killing two. Howling with insurmountable rage, they regrouped and mounted an attack against the lawmen, returning the direct fire and closing with them in hand to hand combat using axes, clubs, and knives. The lawmen could not withstand the onslaught and retreated, leaving half their number dead or wounded.

"Keep the wagons moving," shouted Luther to Pinkerton gunmen on several following wagons. He hefted his rifle into the air and fired off a shot for emphasis. "Don't stop for anything or anyone. If a striker jumps on, kick him off. You see a gun aimed at you or anyone on your wagon, shoot the bastard! Don't think about it! This is a war! You kill and let someone else count the bodies! Just be sure you're not one of 'em!"

The convoy of Negro drivers, urging on their horses, pulling the wagons filled with Pinkerton sharpshooters and riflemen, swept along the open areas of the city streets. When they encountered the teamsters' blockade and hail of stones, bottles and gunfire, at the direction of harried terrified managers from the stores and warehouses, they took unobstructed side streets and alleys that kept them headed in the general direction of wherever clothing products were to be loaded and transported back into the fray.

White men with guns everywhere shouted at him, "Nigger, go home! We'll kill you scabs! You can't come up here and take our jobs!" Chicago was no different than in the South. They would kill him as soon as look at him.

"Orville," he leaned in close where they lay huddled on the bottom of the bouncing, swaying wagon. Rocks and stones and bottles flew by overhead. They heard the crack of a rifle followed by a man's scream. "We got to git outta here. Those white men gwine kill us sho. Fust chance we got to go."

"But where we go? We don't know where we are. We don't know how to go and we can't jump off the wagon."

Jonah glanced up at Luther sighting down on a man in the crowd who was shooting at random and wounding Coloreds in the passing wagons. A single shot passed through the sniper's head and exited into the back of the striker next to him. "We ax him. He keepin' us alive."

"Now ain't no time to be axin'. We got to stay down."

"Wait 'til we git to where we goin'," said Zacaria. "We be safe there and can figger this out."

"That 'cruiter didn't tell us 'bout this."

"He prolly didn't know," said Zacaria.

"They don't have sheets on so we can't see they faces," said Jonah, "but they all the same tryin' to kill us. They callin' us Nigga jus' like back home."

Twelve hours later in the dead of night, less seventy of the original one-hundred wagons, the caravan arrived at McNeal's warehouse in the mercantile district.

Jonah nudged his sleeping friend. "Wake up, Orville. We here now."

They looked over the edge of the wagon in both directions as gas lanterns were lit and the occupants of the other wagons began to stir. The police officers commingled with the Pinkerton guards and shared comments and opinions on the gauntlet of teamsters they had escaped by going to outlying sectors of the city, including the Southside Black Belt, and coming around again to the north.

During the day, as they passed through the Black Belt, Jonah, Orville, and Zacaria exchanged glances of recognition at the distinct ethnic transition from the dominant white areas of the city to where their own kind were subject to live.

"Jus' like home," said Orville, "Only bigger. Didn't know there was so many of us in one place."

"This our way out the city," Zacaria spoke in a low voice so Luther and the other two dozing guards on their wagon wouldn't hear. "We got to come back here."

"How we evah gonna find it?" asked Jonah. "We lost fo sho."

"We find it. We find it," said Zacaria. "We got no choice."

"Where we go?" asked Orville.

"Nothin' for us here," said Zacaria. "We go back home."

Jonah nodded. "I wish we nevah left."

"Ain't gonna git no jelly roll," said Orville.

"How kin yo think of jelly roll at a time like this?"

"Helps me from bein' scared. I thought we gonna die back there. I too young to die."

"We all too young to die," said Zacaria. "We got to go home and start over."

"Right now I got ta pee," said Orville. "Been sittin' in this wagon a long time."

They noticed the occupants climbing down from the other wagons. Within minutes, the splatter of urine against the side of the warehouse building was the only sound heard followed by groans and sighs of relief.

"That take care of one ting," said Orville. "Now ah got me another. Ah'm hongry. Ah'm real hungry."

"We all hongry," said Zacaria. "Hope they got some food waitin' inside."

The line began to move through an open door. "Right this way," they heard a voice call out. "Right this way. Got vittles inside and a place to sleep. Keep the line movin'. Right this way."

The next morning, as they rounded the corner coming out of the mercantile district, Jonah saw the street was blocked by an army of teamsters. Zacaria and Orville stopped their horses and garment-loaded wagons in front of his own and the rest of the caravan shuddered to a halt behind him. The single guard riding with Zacaria jumped to the ground and bolted away down the street along the wagon train back the way they had come. Zacaria and Orville looked in fear at Jonah.

A roar erupted from the crowd and it charged in an onrushing wave. The Colored drivers leaped from their seats and ran, with the howling fiends in hot pursuit. Jonah saw Orville and Zacaria disappear in the crush of attacking men who hacked with axes at their flailing bodies sending founts of blood spurting into the faces and soaking the clothes of those nearest the melee. The sight and smell of blood and screams of fear and agony drove the mob to a greater frenzy. With the exception of Jonah and three other drivers, they caught and overwhelmed the rest, stomping and grinding them into the dust until their faces and bodies were disfigured beyond recognition. Then they climbed onto the wagons and flung armfuls of garments, scattering and trampling them in the dirt and wind of the street.

The screams of dying men and images of their decimated bodies drove Jonah, fleeing through the streets. He did not slow until the mayhem faded behind him displaced by the normal crowds of pedestrians and horse-drawn traffic. Without the recruiter, Cornelius Shea, to tell him where to go and what to do, he reeled and stumbled about in disorientation. The street names and signs on buildings told him nothing he could understand. He searched frantically for another Negro face and saw European men and women who were white and a multitude with various shades of brown and tan skin, but none of his own kind.

After shuffling about trying to gain some sense of where he was, he saw a police officer standing outside his patrol box. With great trepidation, Jonah approached the policeman who glared at him with distaste and suspicion. He had just returned to his post from the carnage several blocks away. Jonah detected his foul mood even before he spoke.

"What you want, Nigger? You with them others?"

"'Scuse me, suh. I ain wit nobody. I jus lost. I jus want to go home."

"You're lost all right. You're in the wrong part of town."

"Don know 'bout no other place."

"Where you from, boy?"

"Mizzura – farm near by Pinkneville."

"You're a long way from home."

"Jus' want to go back."

"Well, I can't help you."

"You know someone?"

"Just keep walkin' down that street and you'll find a place."

"Dat street?"

"Yeah, dat street. When you come to the end, turn left. You'll find a place."

"Thank yo, suh. Thank yo. I find a place."

"Don't thank me. Move on."

Weaving in an out of the bustling crowds, Jonah strode quickly in the direction indicated by the officer. He came to where the street ended and turned left, entering the Levee District. His eyes widened at the recognition of saloons and brothels.

"Poor Orville," he thought. "This is what yo lookin' fo and never got."

He peered through the open door of a saloon where the syncopated rhythm of ragtime piano music tinkled out into the street. An Irish drummer shouted at him from the bar. "What you want here, Nigger? This ain't no place for you!"

Thinking he was being addressed, the piano player, a professor, glanced over his shoulder without missing a beat and saw Jonah standing in the doorway. Jonah raised his hand and waved. The professor did not wave back. He finished his piece with a flourish, rose from the piano bench and crossed the sawdust-covered wooden floor with angry strides.

"Don't stand there. You can't come in here. Move on 'fore you git in trouble."

"I tol to come here. I don know where else to go."

"Who told you to come here?"

"A policemans."

"What you lookin' for? What you want?"

"Ah wants to go home, but ah don know how git there."

"You with those Nigger scabs come up from Missouri?"

"I come from Mizzura. Mah friends got killed. Jus want ta go back home."

The professor pointed. "See way down the street there?"

"Ah see where you pointin'."

"Keep on walkin' and y'all come to the Black Belt. That's where us Chicago Niggers live. Y'all wait there and I'll come 'nd git you in about one hour. I know someone who can help you. What's your name?"

"Jonah Delacroix."

"Delacroix, you wait there for me."

"Ah'll wait. Ah'll wait. What yo name?"

"Johnson, Leroy Johnson."

"Ah thank you, Leroy Johnson."

"Now git the hell outta here."

Bobbing his head in gratitude, Jonah hurried away. He looked back once, but Johnson was no longer standing at the saloon door. He wondered how it was that a Negro piano player could work in a white man's saloon.

An hour later, he saw the handsome young man with the clean-shaven boyish face walking toward him, searching among the congregation of Negroes passing through the area. He raised his hand, motioning Jonah to follow him. Jonah had to quick step to keep up for several blocks into the Black Belt tenements. Leroy finally stopped at the door of a settlement house.

"You go in there and tell 'em what you want. They can help git you home."

"Thank yo, suh. Thank yo." Jonah turned to face him.

Leroy was already rapidly walking away and quickly disappeared among the people moving about the street.

Jonah stepped up to the door and timidly knocked. A few moments passed. He knocked again. It opened and a middle-aged Negro woman with a kind expression gestured for him to come inside.

Over one month had passed since Josiah Delacroix had watched her son and his friend, Orville, walk away from the farm down the road. Now, she saw him climb down from a neighbor's wagon and shuffle slowly toward the house. As though in a state of suspended animation, he came forward. He did not raise his head until the sight of his mother's dusty bare feet appeared in his line of vision. He stopped and looked into her eyes.

"He dead, Mama. Orville dead. They kill 'im. They beat 'im. They stomp 'im dead. I ran, Mama. Ah couldn't help 'im. They grab me and ah fight 'em off and ah ran."

His body shuddered and drooped over the small frame of his mother. She held him in her arms. One hand patted him softly and gently on his long broad back. Her little boy, her son.

V

The Plot

Chapter 30

Morgan

"You've had your account at Morgan for thirteen years," Henry Phillips protested. "Why do you want to leave us?"

"Because of Morgan," said Kurt.

"Morgan? He's the richest most powerful man in America. He and I have helped you to increase your own fortune."

"That's the point, Henry. He's a tyrant. We no longer want to be beholden to him, which is a polite way of saying we no longer want to be ruled as part of the Morgan trust. He controls our company and our lives. We want to end the relationship."

"You believe what you read? Wasn't the Sherman Act and Northern Securities suit enough?" Henry referred to the legislation prohibiting corporate monopolies. Before the legislation had been enacted, trusts had become a tool to increase mergers and eliminate competition. They also gave control of national wealth to a few millionaire families who created dynasties to perpetuate their wealth.

"We do," said Kurt. The trusts must come to an end. Uncontrolled growth and development to the detriment of the rest of society must be brought under control. The time has come to end *laissez-faire* economics."

"You sound like that bastard newsman, Baker."

"We support Baker and we stand behind the President."

"Then you are against business and prosperity."

"No, we are for corporate responsibility to workers and society."

"You don't really believe that speech Roosevelt gave, do you?"

"We do."

"It won't change anything."

"It will change everything." Kurt shoved a copy of the newspaper containing the President's speech across the table. Henry quickly read the concluding statement.

The great corporations which we have grown to speak of rather loosely as trusts are the creatures of the State, and the State not only has the right to control them, but it is in duty bound to control them wherever need of such control is shown. The immediate necessity in dealing with trusts is to place them under the real, not the nominal, control of some sovereign to which, as its creatures, the trusts shall owe allegiance, and in whose courts the sovereign's orders may be enforced. In my opinion, this sovereign must be the National Government.

Henry looked up from the article. "Morgan won't let you go without a fight and in a fight, he always wins."

"There won't be any fight," said Kurt. "We have the legal right to take our money out of your bank and place it in another. If Morgan doesn't cooperate, then he will be breaking the contract, as well as the law, and we will sue him. In addition, he won't want any more press criticizing him than he already has."

"He isn't here today, but I will present your position to him when he returns."

"We have come all the way from Chicago to take our money back with us today, Mr. Phillips. We have armed guards waiting outside with steel trunks and a patrol wagon to take us to Kuhn, Loeb. From there we will go to the train station where our personal Pullman is standing by. We are firm in our decision.

There is no purpose in Morgan trying to follow us. We will not return."

"Morgan is not going to like this."

"He has no choice. Matias, bring in the guards and the trunks and, Mr. Phillips, if you would be so kind as to lead us into your vault."

J. Pierpont Morgan woke with a start and stared up at the polished oak ceiling of his cabin on board the *Corsair*. His thoughts focused on the gentle rolling swells of the Hudson River bumping his 300 foot black-hulled steam yacht at the dock. The seventy-man crew had taken him on an extended three week cruise along the eastern seaboard and come in to the harbor late that night. He did not relish the prospect of having to leave his ship and go into the city, but a growing premonition of trouble at the bank had begun to aggravate him like a spreading rash.

Henry Phillips, one of his partners, had sent him a troublesome message about their client in Chicago, Bauman Enterprises. The stress that Pierpont had repressed by going off on his cruise surged back at the lack of information contained in the telegram, only that there was a serious problem.

Coughing mucous and passing gas, he rose from his oversized bed and down-stuffed *douve*, pulled his nightshirt off over his head and left it in a pile on the floor. Walking naked into the massive Italian marble bathroom, he relieved himself in a porcelain flush toilet, then stepped into the shower. The hot water beating down over his head and shoulders relaxed his muscles, stiffened from sleep. He scrubbed himself with a soaked sponge frothing with suds and rapidly thrust the long ebony handle of a soft-bristled brush like a piston over his back and fleshy torso. The heat of the water dripping around his testicles prompted an erection accompanied by the memory of an attractive young woman with whom he had slept a week ago. He had forgotten her name as soon as she had introduced herself, Lily or Lilac or somesuch.

After eating a hearty breakfast of eggs, fish, sausage, pancakes, fruit and cheese, Pierpont smoked one of his eight inch black Meridiana Kohinoor cigars while sipping Jamaican coffee and reading about the latest industrial mergers in the New York Times financial section. But the food and cigar did little to ease the apprehension gnawing at his innards.

Plagued by depression and contrasting moods he did not understand, he had been taking extensive trips on the *Corsair* and managing the affairs of his bank from a distance by written and telegraphic correspondence. He preferred dining on his yacht to going home to dinner with his estranged wife. The sea gave him solace, an escape from a woman he didn't love and the constraints of Victorian society. He had formed a social club of select businessmen to disguise their drinking binges and parties with women discreetly brought on board.

He argued with himself that his interest in banking was not declining in his waning years, but he took no pleasure in his success. To fend off an increasing loneliness, he spent more and more time away from Wall Street to add to his collection of Italian art and submerged himself in the mystic rituals of religion, increasing his attendance at church, to absorb the spiritual undertones of organ music, and singing gospel hymns at revival meetings for their emotional ecstasy. He hung on every word of an astrologer who read his horoscope. Although he visited the grave of his first wife, he ignored his relationship with his second, who lacked the ability and desire to take part in the necessary social and civic events that supported and expanded his business.

Morgan paused as he walked along Wall Street crowded with pedestrian traffic, and stared at the edifice of the Kuhn, Loeb Merchant Bank located not far from his own House of Morgan at number 23. He contemplated entering and confronting the "Old Jew," Jacob Schiff on his own turf, then thought better of his impulse, which would place himself in a defensive inferior position.

He was beginning to realize that his traditional business strategy of issuing orders and demands had failed him during the past two years. In the press, he had once been called 'The Boss of The United States' and 'The King of Wall Street' and now he felt his crown was slipping.

In contrast to his trademark domineering manner and arrogance of riding roughshod over anyone who challenged or disagreed with him or merely stood in his way, he was also analytical in his approach to making decisions. Because of his success in financial dealings, kings, royalty and foreign governments had sought his advice.

He was the richest man in America, having more personal wealth than the Federal Government. In 1895, he and the House of Rothschild in London had kept the country from converting to a silver standard and economic collapse by restoring and controlling the gold reserves through a purchase of three and a half million ounces of gold from European sources. Acting as a central bank, both Morgan and Rothschild sold bonds at inflated prices that cheated the Government and profited the syndicate by millions.

Since then, he had been the primary force influencing and manipulating the United States economy. In addition, he had also become America's most hated and despised capitalist. This perception grated on him, since he thought of himself as an astute businessman, not a robber baron.

At sixty-three, his rheumatism flared up more often and side-lined him in bed. His bulbous nose, enflamed with rosacea, had made him a cartoon in newspapers. He hated the loss of energy and zeal he had known during his youth. He had formed his own merchant banking company in 1861. Now, in 1904, he had come under the scrutiny of Theodore Roosevelt and the Federal Government. He longed for the old days when his hands weren't tied by unimaginative bureaucrats. He wanted to direct and control change in the world of finance, not be influenced by it. He believed he had a religious and moral responsibility that he and he alone could bring stability to the chaos and confusion of America's out of control economy, plunging onward like a runaway train without an engineer.

One of the barons of wealth and society, his father, Junius Morgan had raised Pierpont to believe "The bankers calling is hereditary and is passed along from father to son. Because we finance foreign trade, we are recognized throughout the world by our name, so we must breed wisely and keep our wealth in the family to preserve the bank's capital."

Pierpont threw his father's conservative maxims to the four winds and engaged in what others called reckless risk taking that quickly caught on as the standard practice of merchant banking, the control of business. Pierpont recognized that his position in the financial world was tied to railroads and the manufacture of heavy industrial products. Without regulation of securities, he manipulated investors' money in any way he saw fit to make a profit for them and for himself. He had flourished in the unstable economy of companies racing to make fortunes. Because they lacked sufficient capital, they had come to him. He had engaged in business and formed partnerships with only those he considered worthy of his elite Wall Street bank. In the beginning, he had confined himself to managing and manipulating railroad securities and shunned manufacturers. Now, the move was to the creation and establishment of industrial trusts through holding companies.

The industrial recession of 1893 had been the catalyst of his rise to power. Fifteen thousand companies and six hundred banks had failed. Every reorganized company became indebted to its rescuing bank. Morgan had generated huge profits. Bringing ten railroads out of bankruptcy, he transferred control to his bank and gained revenues valued at more than half that of the Federal Government. The New York Central, Great Northern, Philadelphia and Reading, Lehigh Valley, The Erie, Chesapeake and Ohio, Jersey Central, Santa Fe, and the Southern had been "Morganized." Millions more accrued from liens he established against land and mineral rights owned by the railroads.

With Pierpont gone most of the time, his staff enjoyed the freedom of working at the bank without his constant authoritarian presence, but they experienced his continued orders and influence from a distance. And when he returned, the tension he created was almost intolerable.

As he continued walking, he began to hatch a plan to crush the Bauman brothers. By the time he reached his bank, the action he would take had crystallized in his mind.

"Henry!" he roared out as he entered the main floor.

At hearing the commanding voice, Henry Phillips burst from one of the glass-enclosed wood-paneled offices and hastened to greet his master. He remained standing, trembling at attention like an office boy before Morgan's desk.

"So, what's the old Jew up to?" Chewing and puffing on an ever present black cigar, John Pierpont Morgan referred to his arch Wall Street merchant banking rival, Jacob Schiff at Kuhn Loeb. "Does he think he can get away with capturing one of my clients? We have contained Bauman Enterprises by keeping them in the fold and allowing them to realize suitable profits without taking them over. They came to this country with nothing and we gave them everything."

"Their father did have investments with us, three million to be exact. We were talking about some manner of collaboration with their trans-Atlantic shipping until Bismarck threw him in prison for being a socialist."

"All socialists should be thrown in prison. So how have the Bauman boys benefited. What are they worth?"

"They're stable with us at eight million. The Bauman's wear two hats. They're business entrepreneurs, but they invest a few million in progressive causes in support of the unions and anti-trust politicians."

"Damn them to hell! Damn them to hell! How long have you known this about them?"

Henry Phillips blushed and tensed his trembling body, fearing Morgan would bludgeon him with his heavy black cane. Even after fifteen years under the financial mogul's iron rule, Henry feared Morgan's rages when the old man didn't get his way. His imperious threatening blue eyes glowering from behind a bulbous red nose veined with acne rosacea and underscored with a handlebar mustache reminded Henry of a bird of prey. Yet he knew there was a little seen gentler side to the flamboyant tycoon who hated social affairs, but engaged in them because his business demanded it. What the general public didn't know was that despite his pompous arrogance and personal flaws, Morgan was devoutly religious and attended church on a regular basis.

"Since yesterday."

"Yesterday? Why didn't you call me in? I would have put them in the black library until they came to their senses." Morgan referred to his conference room where he would, on occasion, lock a difficult or adversarial client who disagreed with him. He had retained three of them for an entire day and night until they begged to sign his version of the contract and release them.

"You were not in the bank, sir. You were on the *Corsair*."

"Why can't I even go for a sail without the world falling apart around me? Dammit, I can never drop my guard in this business, Henry, never. We must know everything about our clients. They are not entitled to privacy when we are handling their financial affairs."

"That is their reason for leaving."

"What? What did they say?"

"In their words, they want to be independent and they don't want to be beholden to you."

"Rot! What rot! Beholden my ass! It's that damn cowboy President who's behind all this, isn't it? I'll bet they support Roosevelt and contributed to his campaign. Thinks he can run the country from the back of a horse. Find out what's really going on here, Phillips. I smell a conspiracy. See if the Bauman brothers are in cahoots with the President. He won't deal with me. Why would he deal with them?"

"They don't talk with the President, maybe senators and congressmen, but I learned they do finance publications critical of business owners and in support of the labor position. I think they're in league with the muckrakers."

"Those sons-of-bitches writing about me, trying to tear me down! I made this country what it is and others with me. The problem with Roosevelt is that he thinks he owns the press. He invites them to special meetings and feeds them drivel that they print as news. And they eat it up. Makes 'em feel important like they have a say in the important matters of politics and business. They're bystanders, all of 'em, standing outside looking in. And none of 'em are worth a damn. But you know? They're not going to get off so easy. No damn Jews can pull out on me just because the weather changes. I will have their ass! I will ruin them and take their damn business away from them!"

"I'm outraged with what has happened with Bauman Enterprises."

"Yes, sir, Mr. Morgan, of course, sir. It was unforeseen."

"But not forgotten."

"Sir."

"Here is what we're going to do. Bring me their balance sheet and portfolio. I want to know the full extent of their holdings and business both here and in Europe."

"Yes, sir, I'll bring them immediately." Henry rushed back to his office and returned with the requested documents.

Morgan's glowering eyes studied the data and information for several minutes. "Here's their weak spot," he finally said. "Right here, Henry. This is our point of entry and penetration."

"You have my full attention, sir."

"As I thought, they're going to try to take back the company they lost in Berlin. That's the reason they went over to Kuhn, Loeb. They have extensive dealings and connections with Berlin and European banks and investors. It's a position I've always wanted, but I'm not a Jew. Rothschild is though and he has influence over there. I want you to get in touch with August

Belmont at Rothschild in London. He worked with us to our mutual advantage on the gold issue. He can help us derail the Bauman brothers."

"As a reminder, Pierpont, sir, the Bauman's are also Jewish."

Morgan glared at him. "Do you think I'm an idiot?"

"No, no, sir. That was not the intent of my comment."

"Just shut up, Henry. Shut up and listen."

"Yes, sir, of course, sir. What would you like me to say to Mr. Belmont?"

"Tell him he has an opportunity to purchase the majority stock in the Wohlman Company along with the Morgan Bank to take them over. We're going to prevent the Bauman boys from ever getting back into the European transportation market."

"A stroke of genius, if I do say so, Pierpont. A stroke of genius."

"I want you to watch this day and night even if you have to sleep on the floor of the stock exchange."

"You have my word."

"This would not have happened, if you had been reading the signs."

"The signs? What signs, sir?"

"You've been working for me for fifteen years, Henry. You should have learned by now to read the financial signs, the indicators of who is doing what to whom. You need to know before it comes out in the *Wall Street Journal*. When was the last time you "looked at the Bauman Enterprises financials?"

"I do it once a year according to our standard policy. I made a trip to Chicago and met with them. There was no indication that they were planning to move their account."

"Obviously, once a year isn't enough. And if they were planning to move their account, they weren't going to tell you about it. You had to find out by other means on the exchange and by word on the street. Where was Bacon in all this? He should have been informed. "

"I can't speak for Mr. Bacon, sir. I will increase the frequency, sir, with all my accounts."

"If we lose this one, then you won't have to be concerned with any accounts."

"Do I understand you, sir, that you would relieve me of my job?"

"You understand correctly, Phillips. The House of Morgan has very high standards for performance."

"As I'm fully aware and have done my best to live up to over the years. This has been my only mistake."

"There is no room for mistakes in this bank."

"Of course, we all try to meet your expectations."

"That's why I always hire the best and the brightest."

"I am grateful that you considered me among them."

"You don't have the latitude of age as an excuse. I'm much older than you are and I'm still at this business."

"You deserve to enjoy the fruits of your labor."

"I've built this institution and become wealthy by not having to labor. We become wealthy by advantageously positioning investors' money to maximize our commissions."

"I'm well familiar with the system, sir."

"Don't let that thought slip away, Henry."

"Most assuredly, sir, it will not."

"Send Belmont a telegram now. I want his answer by the end of the day. On your way out, tell Robert Bacon I need to see him so we can draw up papers."

"Right away, sir. Right away."

Henry blundered out of Morgan's cavernous office and ducked into the office of the banks second in command, Robert Bacon, a recent Harvard graduate. With a Greek god-like physique and masculine beauty that shone from him like an aura, he portrayed star quality among the dour strait-laced members of the Wall Street banking world. He looked up startled at Henry's abrupt entrance.

"Yes, Henry, what is it? You look upset."

"I am upset, but right now that doesn't matter. Pierpont wants to see you on the double. A bit of a warning, he is quite agitated at something that has happened."

"Is he agitated at you or at me?"

"Unfortunately, at me."

"As long as it isn't me, old boy," Bacon rose from his desk with a boyish laugh. "What does he want?"

"He's going to want you to draw up some papers."

"Sounds like an easy enough task."

"Let's hope it goes well."

"We'll give it a touch of gold." Bacon stepped past him out of his office and entered Morgan's without knocking and without any announcement."

"Robert, Robert my boy, we need to move quickly on this." He waved the Bauman Enterprises paper in the air and smacked them down on his desk with a sense of finality.

"And what is it you would like me to do? How can I assist you, sir?"

"Henry is sending a telegram to Belmont in London to look into a takeover shared by Morgan and Rothschild. Rothschild has access to the European markets. We are going to block Bauman Enterprises from taking back their European operations, specifically in Berlin. I'll capture what I have long been wanting, a transportation link across the Atlantic with a rail network throughout Europe. Oh, and Robert, the Bauman boys have overstayed their little corner of the steel business in Chicago. It's time for our U.S. Steel trust to eliminate them. We control the ore mines and have a larger faster fleet of ore boats. From now on, ore taken from our Minnesota mines can be transported only on U.S. Steel boats. Communicate that policy to all of our operations immediately."

Bacon caressed the long, waxed handlebar mustache that extended a few inches to both sides of his lean jaw. He looked more like a fighter than a banker. "I'll take care of it. So you want me to draw up a contract with Rothschild on this."

"Exactly. Have it on my desk by the end of the day."

"Do you want to wait for details from Belmont?"

"Wait? There's nothing to wait for. He's in London. Not due back for another week. We'll give him the details."

"Are we looking at a full partnership?"

"Sixty forty – Morgan will hold majority control."

"Are you allowing for negotiation?"

"There is no negotiation. Belmont is a friend. He'll go along with whatever I say."

"Anything outside of the standard clauses?"

"I'll let you know after I read your draft."

"I'll get right on it." Bacon turned and left the office. After three years with the firm, it galled him that Morgan continued to treat him like a clerk and used him as a showpiece at executive level meetings. His title of partner was meaningless without any authority attached to it.   As be became familiar with Morgan's staff, he noticed that Morgan had selected them because they did not have sufficiently strong personalities to challenge and stand up to him on any issues. They were yes men. They were numbers men. They all worked long hard hours and did Morgan's bidding, just like he himself was doing. Robert's wife had commented that he looked like he was constantly under great stress, an observation with which he agreed.

Morgan could not believe what he read in the return telegram from August Belmont at Rothschild in London.

Results not good from investigation. Unable to penetrate. Company not traded on stock exchange. Strange history. Name changed from Wohlman to Bauman in 1888. 90% majority stock held by single owner, Rudolf Palm. Maintains secret identity. Whereabouts unknown. At a loss. Cannot proceed.

Belmont.

"Cannot proceed!" Morgan leaped up from his desk and lunged about the office looking for someone to attack. "Cannot proceed!"

Henry cowered away against the wall.

"Who is this Palm anyway? Can't someone find out anything about him?"

"Apparently not, sir. The only information available is that he was once the director of Bismarck's secret police."

"Bismarck! That ancient fart! The Kaiser should know who this secret upstart is and where he is. Send a telegram to Wilhelm. Tell him what we need. I cannot believe that the majority stock holder can just disappear. Get moving, Phillips. I'm waiting."

"Yes sir, right on it, sir." Henry scurried out of Morgan's office.

Chapter 31

Reaction

Kurt Bauman 'took the first bullet' as he called the boycott by U.S. Steel in excluding Bauman Enterprises from purchasing and shipping iron ore from the Mesabi Range mines in Northern Minnesota.

"Morgan is putting us out of business," he complained to Jacob Schiff during a panicked phone call to his new banker on Wall Street.

"It's just his way of trying to get back at me for taking away his account," said Jacob. "U.S. Steel has become too big and powerful and has caught the attention of the Federal Government. Just hold steady. With President Roosevelt at the helm, the U.S. Steel monopoly will likely be broken up or at least devalued by the Bureau of Corporations. Rather than waiting for your company to dry up, sell your shipping capital to U.S. Steel for ten or twelve million. Make Morgan pay for his wounded pride and adversarial pettiness. You're going to get five times that in current assets and projected earnings when you take back your European company. You can still maintain your appliance manufacturing and your railroad transportation leasing operations in Chicago."

"Have you heard anything yet from Berlin?"

"As a matter of fact, I have. Come to New York next week prepared to travel. I'll give you the details when you arrive."

Kurt hung up the phone and strode down the hall to his brother's office.

"Matias, we're in trouble. Morgan is using U.S. Steel to cut us out of the market. I just got off the phone with Jacob. He says we should sell out to U.S. Steel and concentrate on taking back our European operation."

"Has he made any progress?"

"Yes, I'm joining him in New York next week. Then we're traveling to Berlin."

"Are you planning to go alone?"

"Yes. Jacob will be with me."

"I think you'd better take Jean Guenoc. Palm is ruthless. I'm sure you haven't forgotten."

"I'll never forget."

"You're not likely to have a civil meeting with Palm across the table. Things could get ugly."

"As I'm well aware. I'll ask Jean to accompany me."

"I'll certainly feel better."

"How to you want to handle the reorganization?"

"Jacob will have one of his people at Kuhn, Loeb set up the transaction with U.S. Steel. You represent the company. I anticipate that I will immediately relocate to Berlin. At the appropriate time, I'll inform you and Gustav can help my wife and children prepare for the move. He's an old man. I'm certain he'll want to stay here with you and Sophie."

"What about our boys, Newt and Aaron? They need a university education. Then they can come back and run the company here."

"Prepare them for Harvard. Newt's strong on law and Aaron has science and technology in his blood."

"It feels strange that we've reached this impasse."

"It will feel less strange once Rudolf Palm is in prison."

"And Jacob has no doubts about finding him and restoring the European division to our family?"

"He has no doubts. We live in different times."

"We should be thankful for that."

"We should."

After printing and distributing pamphlets and newsletters and fliers and witnessing so much of what was happening in her time, Julie believed she had discovered her calling, to capture what she experienced and observed by the written word. Starting with her journal, she intended to expand her skills as a writer and strive to join the esteemed ranks of such activists and muckraking journalists as Ida Tarbell, Lincoln Steffens, Ray Stannard Baker, and Florence Kelly.

Upon reading their publications and witnessing first hand the lives and working conditions of the oppressed, Julie concluded her overriding issue rested with the business world, particularly Wall Street, its financial greed and corruption and exploitation by robber barons, particularly J.P. Morgan.

Matias learned of her endeavors when she interviewed him and Kurt for their insights and information. They confided their plan to move their account from the iron heel of Morgan's bank to Kuhn, Loeb.

"The only thing I have to say about merchant bankers," said Kurt, "is that they guarantee nothing but their own profits and are never to be trusted. What we learned in coming to America is that this economy has always promoted and praised advancement and wealth by the exploitation of others. We, all of us, are the ones who have to change the system. People are suffering because there are no ethics in the business world. The only thing people have to change society is the power of the vote. Our father was called an insurgent and died in prison at the hands of a dictator, because he tried to change conditions for the people. The rights he sought were finally granted, but we have other legal issues to settle in Berlin. We didn't have a vote. The freedom to vote here in America is in the law."

"But not for women or Negroes," said Julie. "Sophie and Ophelia can't vote. I can't vote."

"There is pressure to change the law to allow them the right," said Matias. "The day will come when the ballot will be available to all citizens. Change is always a struggle against those who want to keep things in their favor, keep things the way they are. We are putting our faith and our money in what President Roosevelt is doing to change the Government and the economy in answering to the voices of the rising middle class."

Luther Baggot didn't know what to expect when O'Riley told him that the alderman Francis Keeley wanted to talk to him. "Whatever he wants you to do, it's okay." As part of his arrangement with Keeley for favors in city contracts, O'Riley had proposed that his man, Luther Baggot, could be made available for "special jobs" that required his talents.

Luther had no trouble locating the alderman's office and arrived a few minutes early to find the door closed. He hesitated, then hit the door with three firm knocks of his fist. He heard the scrape of a chair from within and footsteps approach the door. Keeley greeted him with a broad smile and an effusive handshake.

"Right on time, Luther, that's a good sign. Thank you for coming." He gestured him in, closed the door, and offered a stiff backed chair. Luther sat facing him across the desk and watched him pour two glasses of amber whiskey from a half-filled bottle. He held out one to Luther and raised the other glass. "To our friendship." He sipped his drink and Luther followed suit, enjoying the burning warmth of the liquid coursing down his gullet.

"For we are friends, Luther. At least we're going to be. Bill O'Riley tells me you're a good man. You can be trusted to take care of business and keep your mouth shut. Am I right? Are you the man I want?"

"I've done a lot of things in my life and can keep my mouth shut. Depends what you want me to do and how much you pay me."

Francis laughed. "I like you, Baggot. Nothin' is worth doin' if you don't get paid to do it. That's my motto. We're gonna get along just fine." He poured him a second glass of the Irish whiskey. "Comes from the homeland. I have six cases shipped over every Christmas. My da' was born in Dublin, you see. Worked in a brewry. Damn near died there. Still have family ties. I was ten when we came over on the boat. 1870 the year it was. Da' the whole lot of us, seven kids and our *aus wan* near dead with grief that he was drinkin' down his earnings and couldn't feed us. She took in piece work, washing, ironing, cleaned toilets, whatever she had to do to keep a roof over our heads and food on the table. Da' finally said he had enough of her shouting and nagging and told us all one day, "We're goin' to America and that's that." He waved a few wrinkled food-stained pages of a letter. "Got news from me cousin there's work a'plenty for all of us, includin' you brats. Everybody works."

"Includin' you," said my ma.

"Includin' me," says he.

"So we arrive on the boat with not much more than the clothes on our backs and smellin' like fish and garbage. My Uncle Angus sent my da the money to pay our train fare to Chicago and my *aus wan* took it 'fore he could drink it away or a *pavee* thieved it from 'im.

"So we come to Chicago and see how my Uncle Angus is livin' high on the hog as a ward boss. 'We do things here just like we did in Ireland,' he says. 'We keep the *pavees* poor shits happy and the liquor flowin'. So he hires my da to work for him, runnin' numbers and such remindin' people what they owed him. My da was a *feckin'* brute and Uncle Angus could trust 'im, which is why he wanted 'im to come over, to keep things in the family, so to speak. My bein' ten, he put me right to work runnin' jobs and such and put money in my pocket. So I learned how things get done in Chicago and how to climb the ladder and my Uncle Angus groomed me to become a boss when he decided to shitcan the place. The Keeley's been runnin' this ward for fifty years."

He paused to take a drink. "Loosens the tongue, but ain't an Irish mick alive who don't have a loose tongue. What we don't like to hear is the *feckin'* R word. Reform. You know what that is bein' a *kraut*. Your people comin' over here to get shut of the Kaiser. It's the feckin' newsmen and clergymen and proper types who want to change things. The *pavee* immigrants don't. They like things the way they are. Keeps it nice and simple, since they don't speak the King 's English.

"Progressive reforms like the direct primary are dangerous to us. They break apart the voting strength of ethnic blocs and ethnic bosses. The bosses decide the political nominations because they recruit party loyalists. If the boss's lose that control, a direct primary can remove the convention system and destroy their power."

Dubbed a gray wolf like all the other aldermen who plied their political trade of graft and corruption, his flashy attire and accessories were anything but gray. He sported red or black or plum or cream colored cravats with an eye-catching diamond stickpin, wore diamond or gold cuff links, and preferred dark striped suits, which gave him a slick lawerly appearance and, therefore, to his way of thinking, more credibility as a public official who dispensed privileges and favors to patrons in exchange for their votes and a rigged ballot system.

"Which brings me to my purpose for callin' you here." Francis pulled at a corner of his fox-red handlebar mustache. His blue-gray speckled eyes flickered. "There's some feckin' proper types who need to get a loud clear message to back off and the message ain't with words, if you get my drift. I'll tell you who they are and you take care of 'em in your own way to threaten 'em, maybe hurt 'em a little, but don't get too violent about it and don't leave a trail to my door. Once I pay you and you do your job, you and me never talked. I don't know you, never saw you or met you. You get my drift on that?"

Luther didn't know what the word drift meant, but understood the rest of what Francis was telling him, as he was handed a thick wad of bills.

"This is half. You get the rest when the job is done."

"What is the job?"

Francis pushed a scrap of paper with an address scrawled on it across the desk.

Maureen Keeley put aside the faded yellow dime novel she was reading and gazed out the spacious front window of her sprawling home in the most desirable neighborhood on Chicago's north side. All of the custom designed and built Victorian houses were large and set back from the quiet streets on wooded properties separated from each other by a wide swath of trim lawns. Although each had a stable and carriage house at the rear of the property, black Ford model-T automobiles had begun to appear parked in the long curving gravel driveways, affecting a sense of change in her life and the lives of her children. Because of a gnawing discontent exacerbated by the romance novel, she did not include her husband within the bounds of her growing awareness.

The dime novel romances like the one she was reading, *Willful Gaynell*, by Laura Jean Libbey, portrayed the virginity of their heroines being constantly under assault. Although she was no longer a working woman, but had been before her marriage to Francis Keeley, she still identified with their struggle against male chauvinism and the castigation of her sex as chattel. She had engaged in heated discussions with her friends when they played golf at the country club and the subject never failed to come up when they met for tea or to play whist. She knew the perception and the current status of women had grown out of a long tradition that deprived them of any rights and made them the property of men.

Until recently, Maureen had considered herself an attractive upper-class woman, stylish, but upon reading a book entitled *The Theory of The Leisure Class*, now wore that label with a sense of shame and irresponsibility. Along with her peers, she was guilty of conspicuous consumption, being rich enough to spend money in the department stores for items she didn't need. She realized she was a victim of her husband's wealth and only trying to be equal to others like her and to set herself above the poor.

She had once been among them, a dark-haired svelte working girl in a typist pool. Her meager income did not allow her to afford "nice things." She had dressed conservatively in the Gibson Girl fashion of a shirtwaist blouse and long skirt. Unlike some of her co-workers, she did not sacrifice or skimp on meals to buy a frock or an accessory in imitation of more fortunate upper-class women.

She contributed a portion of her earnings to her parents with whom she lived in an ethnic Irish neighborhood. She had met the young Francis Keeley at a celebratory political function in her tenement block where he was campaigning for votes. Standing near the front of the flag-waving crowd, her sparkling blue-eyed beauty had caught his eye and he sought her out following his speech. There had been food and drink and an Irish band playing Celtic tunes and they had joined the lively dances.

He had returned to court her and meet her mother and father, who had emigrated thirty years ago from the County Cork in Ireland. The marriage of Francis and Maureen had produced three children, a freckled red-headed boy, Hogan, who looked like a smaller version of his father, and twin girls, Fiona and Colleen, who inherited their mother's brunette features and a love of books and learning.

Their early years in school coincided with the introduction of a new educational philosophy introduced by John Dewey, a professor at the University of Chicago who had established a child-centered program whose premise was freedom in the classroom and learning by doing. Progressive men and women encouraged and supported his published and experimental theories, because they taught young people the responsibilities of democracy.

Maureen's recent awareness that her husband made frequent visits to the Everleigh Club bordello in the Levee District left her in a powerless rage except for one alternative. Just as the heroines in the romance novels defended their virtue against the belief of middle-class men that working women were promiscuous, Maureen would confront her husband with the threat of divorce.

Without revealing what she knew, her statement to her friends that whether a woman was married or a prostitute, she was still being bought and paid for brought cries of indignation and disapproval. None of them, including herself, considered prostitutes to be their equal. Prostitutes were soiled defiled women not blessed by the sanctity of marriage. Yet Maureen had heard of more than one woman previously married leaving their husbands to become prostitutes so they could have their independence and their own money.

Prostitution was very much on her mind, not to leave her three children and become one, she was a devout mother, but to push for its eradication and the conditions that fostered it. As she read in the newspapers and consulted clergymen and noticed the increasing number of women and men demanding social and political reform, she realized how rampant and entrenched prostitution was in society and its connection to City Hall where her husband held public office and the power to maintain an open city dedicated to vice and corruption. She learned that he was among thousands who drank, took illegal drugs, and gambled and fornicated as their normal way of life.

She chose to cast her lot with domestic, sober, pious, hard-working middle class men and women and joined the campaign for women's suffrage and reform against her husband and the other gray wolves at City Hall.

"How dare you throw this in my face," Francis exploded with irritation and rage that Maureen had somehow found out about his visits to the Everleigh Club. It was one of the damn progressives that spied on him who told her, no doubt, trying another way to bring him down. She had confronted him that night as soon as he walked through the door. He had expected her to be asleep. She was not in her nightgown, but still wore her dress of the day.

"You have wealth and privilege because I am the wage earner. How I make my money and spend it is none of your damn business. Just remember I spend most of it on you and our children."

"Do you want your children to know their father is a profligate, a whoremonger? Because if you keep doing it, I will divorce you and I will tell them why."

"You'll do nothin' of the kind, bitch!"

"I'm not your bitch. Your bitch lives at the Everleigh Club!"

The unexpected back of his hand caught the right side of her face. Her body twisted, following the force of the blow as she went down.

"Now, you listen to me, bitch. I seen you out there marchin' with your pavee friends wavin' your feckin' signs. You're an embarrassment to me."

Holding onto the arm and back of a nearby chair, she staggered to her feet. "No, no sir, you are an embarrassment to me. You're an abomination and I will see to it that you and all the others like you are removed from office."

"In a pig's eye."

"This will happen, Francis. This will happen."

It struck Luther as oddly poetic that he was setting fire to the house of, Reverend Thrasher, a man of the cloth. He thought of himself as the Devil's man paying the preacher a visit. He left his black stallion tied a block away and stalked along the line of trees and shrubs fencing the boundary of the church property and cemetery. Swaying in a fierce wind, the high bare branches of tall elms splintered the rising moon in the wintery sky sending down shards of pale light that enmeshed the church, vestry, and adjoining house in disparate quivering shadows.

To his satisfaction, Luther noted that the buildings were constructed of wood. Had they been stone, he would have sent fire through the windows. He carried two containers of kerosene, one for the house and one for the church. His boots crunched on the gravel drive. He stepped off onto the lawn and paused to listen for a dog's bark. The silence urged him on.

As Luther encircled the house twice pouring kerosene along the foundation, He envisioned the sleeping clergyman and his family. How unsuspecting they were that he was sending them to hell.

The carriage horse nickered a low greeting as he entered the barn. He would spare the horse. He released him from its stall and drove him outside into the yard where it nibbled at the grass. Luther grabbed an armload of straw and returned to spread wisps intermingled with dry leaves over sections of the kerosene. He then prepared the church for immolation in the same manner and considered the barn.

Touching a lighted match to each line of fuel surrounding the two buildings, he waited for a few moments to watch the flames lick upwards into the painted wood soaked in linseed oil which added a catalyst to spread the fire in an explosive climb that simultaneously enveloped both structures.

Walking quickly away back down the street to his horse, Luther did not hear the screams from within.

"They're marching down Dearborne at two o'clock this afternoon," said Francis to Luther, who had taken the call in his office at O'Rielly's factory. "They'll be carrying signs and shouting slogans. You can't miss 'em. Go break 'em up. You got me?"

Luther grunted and hung up the receiver on the wall unit. He would have to go take his horse from the livery stable. That gave him two hours. He could buy a sausage sandwich from a vendor along the way.

The burning of the church and the Reverend Thrasher's family trapped inside the house had made the front page of the Chicago Times trumpeting headlines of arson by an "evildoer." Francis had paid Luther the other half of the money with a wink and a smile.

Luther mounted the stallion and left the livery barn at a brisk trot he maintained through the city streets until he reached Dearborne Avenue. He pulled to a walk, then stopped the animal and patiently watched. He checked his pocket timepiece on its chain. At two minutes to ten, he saw the crowd of women wearing sweeping long dark skirts and wide brimmed hats festooned with tail feathers from exotic birds. They appeared out of a side street and came on quickly like a rushing flock of hens. He remained still until they were within thirty yards of where he waited.

Julie saw him coming. "It's him. It's Baggot. Run." He charged his horse into the women, knocking them aside, sending them rolling on the cobblestones whose impact broke and splintered their signs demanding franchise for women. He chased and lost them in the alleyways of the nearest tenements. The horse reared and pawed the air where vendor wagons blocked the passage. He brought the trembling animal down and continued on his way.

Chapter 32

The Plot

"Palm is very secretive," said Jacob. "Not only secretive, but paranoid. Since he took possession in 1891, he created a network of spies throughout the company. They are well paid to inform on their fellow workers. Palm merely transferred what he did for Bismarck to managing the organization of a commercial enterprise. Of course, he is hated and despised by the employees who worked for your father before he was incarcerated. They believe Palm was responsible for his murder in prison. The element of suppressed discontent in the company is our key to bringing down Palm. My contacts in the Berlin banking community have shared they would relish seeing the demise of that bastard. To say the least, he is not well liked nor highly regarded by either his company or the financial community."

"What manner of involvement can we expect from your Berlin contacts?"

"Other than passing on information to us, very little. You see, Palm has become quite wealthy over the years and subsidizes many of Berlin's key politicians and the chief of police and first level of officers."

"So, he built himself an empire, his own monarchy."

"Except it is founded on a criminal act, an ongoing criminal act."

"How do you mean?"

"According to one of my sources in Berlin, unknown to stock holders and the board, he secretly transferred funds out of the company into private accounts in Switzerland and Italy. He now lives in a villa just outside of Florence and collects Italian art. He loves everything Italian, especially boys."

"Could your source provide a figure?"

Jacob scanned the small group of men with a grim smile. "In the vicinity of twelve million dollars."

Kurt grinned. "That could keep a lot of trains running on time."

"And a lot of stockholders happy, or unhappy if they knew," said Matias.

"Oh, they will come to know," said Jacob. "That is part of the plan."

Jean Guenoc raised his head from where he had been staring at the floor during this briefing. "Given his network of spies, he is bound to know that we are coming after him. He will try to disappear, perhaps change his identity."

"In addition to young boys, he surrounds himself with armed guards. I'm told his villa is like a fortress and he has bodyguards."

"It will be my job to penetrate his walls," said Jean.

"Before you set sail for Europe, we have to lay the groundwork with the assistance of my financial contacts in Berlin."

"What will that involve?" asked Kurt.

"We have to find a way to freeze his financial assets," said Jacob. "That includes informing company stockholders to establish the crime that Palm has committed so he can be arrested, prosecuted, and indicted."

"He will most certainly disappear with that on his tail," said Jean.

"Most certainly. So we must move secretly and carefully. Stalk him, if you will, so that when you pounce, he has no way to escape."

"When and where will I meet your man in Berlin?"

"I have to make some arrangements with him so he does not expose himself to danger. If Palm's spies get wind of what we're doing, our contact will disappear. Palm will have him murdered."

"What is his name?"

"I can't tell you, not yet. And when I do, it will not be his real identity. Suffice it to say he is a prominent highly visible *burger* who would bring down Palm single-handedly if he could. He and Palm were political enemies when Bismarck was in power. Among many other social democrats, he was a friend of your father and worked with him in the underground. He will contact me, then I will contact you with specific directions to find him."

The head servant, Gustav, slowly nodded his head capped with thinning silver hair. He knew about the man Jacob described, but would remain silent until the appropriate time. When Jean went in pursuit of Palm, Gustav wanted to go with him. Of course, Jean would not allow him because of his age, but Gustav wanted to at least make his feelings known.

Jacob finished the ceremony of lighting his cigar. Puffing a cloud of smoke, he concluded the meeting. "Gentlemen, are we in agreement?"

The other four men nodded their assent.

The next day, Jacob began laying the financial groundwork with his associates in Berlin.

Gunter Hagan was a manufacturer of fabricated metal parts for the steam engines that were built and maintained by the

Hessische Ludwigs-Eisenbahn-Gesellschaft, the major railway system in Germany. Matias' and Kurt's father, Alfred Wohlman, and Gunter had met conducting business in 1873, when Alfred expanded his distribution company by consolidating and combining a number of small shipments into single railcars.

Alfred had built the company through the promotion and sale of railway forwarding services linked to a succession of contracts including the Great Eastern Railway in London. After he negotitated a contract with the *Hessische Ludwigs-Eisenbahn-Gesellschaft* and a contract with the *Chemins de fer de Paris à Lyon et à la Méditerranée*, based in Paris, he had risen in prominence as a German entrepreneur.

With the expansion of railroads in Europe, the need for steam engines had created a demand for metal. Gunter's small machine shop in Berlin had grown and expanded into a large factory that employed eight hundred tradesmen and thirty women who worked as secretaries and administrators in processing sales and purchase orders.

That Alfred's and Gunter's paths crossed was inevitable, since they were both active in supporting *sozialdemokrat*, the social democratic party. Through group meetings at secret conclaves, their political affiliation had grown into a social friendship that, from time to time, included their wives and children.

Eluding the surveillance of Rudolf Palm's secret police had almost become a game until Alfred's arrest, incarceration, and what amounted to an unproved murder. By association, Gunter himself had to withdraw from his activities and maintain a low profile to escape arrest and protect his family. He learned from Gustav of Matias and Kurt's flight into exile. Then Gustav left Germany, escorting Kurt's wife and children from Bavaria, and

Alfred's wife, Anna, who had gone to live her remaining years with her daughter in Switzerland.

Gunter remained a target of innuendo and received threats of persecution from Palm and his agents affecting his business. The pressure against him continued to increase with secret service agents breaking into his office and ripping files out of drawers and terrorizing his work force, hauling some off to jail with no other purpose than to intimidate and create an environment of fear. Gone were the close supportive friendly relationships he had cultivated with his employees during the years he had worked to build his company. One incident in particular weighed on his mind like a scar and appeared in his sleep as a recurring nightmare.

From his office window, Gunter saw a phalanx of armed police arrive at his factory and block all the doors. Led by Palm himself, a cadre of plainclothes agents stormed into his office.

"And to what do I owe the pleasure of your visit, *Herr Commandant*?" asked Gunter with a straight face.

"Being derogatory will not help your cause, Hagan. When we come to see you, our purpose is not to give pleasure."

"Duly noted. Then how can I help you?"

"Announce to your employees that they must stop work immediately. Shut down all the machines and form a line at the center of the factory floor."

"Is that really necessary, *Herr* Commandant? We have orders to fill and shipments to make on time. Can we not just discuss whatever business you have with me?"

"My business, *Herr* Hagan, is with whomever I choose to make it. I have given you a direct order and you will follow it or suffer the consequences."

Gunter rose from his desk without another word and, watched by Palm, walked out onto the manufacturing floor to, Heinz Gebhardt, his lead supervisor, who had noticed the entrance of the unwanted visitors. He recognized Palm from a past intrusion during which he had been summoned to the office, interrogated as to his political affiliation and warned to stay clear of the *sozialdemokrat*. Bestowing glaring stares at the machinists and metal benders at their presses, they had then walked briskly up and down the aisles as though in search of someone to arrest. When the agents finally departed, they left the workers in a state of heightened agitation. They wanted to know what or who the police were looking for.

"Nothing," Gunter responded. "There is nothing here for them to find. They are just trying to make trouble. They cannot harm you. If they should return, I will deal with them. Go back to work."

But the intended damage had been done. Employees began to worry about spies or informers in their midst who might falsely accuse a fellow worker of some clandestine or insurrectionist involvement just to divert attention from themselves and better their own position.

From the show of force as *polizei* infiltrated the factory floor, Heinz realized that this time, something was different. Something unpleasant was about to happen.

Gunter told him what needed to be done and the brawny mustached Heinz moved quickly along the rows of machines and ordered the operators to shut them down. Twenty minutes later, the whir of motors and clang of metal against metal was silenced and the leather-aproned workers looked expectantly and fearfully toward Gunter and the huddle of agents enclosing him. Some workers tugged their slouch hats low over their eyes, looked away or down at the floor or at the machine fixtures and templates and, hoping to avoid being noticed and singled out, most sidled away from the main aisle.

Not wanting to desert his boss during the stressful encounter, Heinz fell in beside Gunter as he led the way slowly, but without hesitation, along the aisle. The two men side by side overshadowed the noticeably smaller slender physique of Palm, who strutted to compensate for his lack of height and masculine strength. Himself a heavily bronze, gray-bearded laborer of many years, Gunter was just as imposing a figure as the red-headed Heinz. Shoulder to shoulder the two men nearly filled the width of the aisle, causing Palm to hop-skip along a step behind them with supreme aggravation.

At mid-point in the factory, Palm shouted, "Halten Sie!"

Gunter and Heinz turned to face him.

Palm's baleful gaze roamed over the nearest machinists. "It has come to my attention that there are those among you who are insurrectionists or working with those who would attempt the overthrow of the monarchy of King Wilhelm the First and Chancellor Otto von Bismarck. Until such time as those names are given to me, and the guilty parties removed, this factory will be shut down and its operation stopped. There are some of you who know who those people are and need only come forward and provide their names. In order to avoid reprisal by your fellow workers, you may come to me secretly and undetected. I will imprison and severly punish anyone who takes reprisal against a fellow worker for doing his duty."

With the exception of a sharp release of steam from a pneumatic control valve further back in the factory, only silence greeted his proclamation.

"You will all leave your machines and work benches immediately," Palm called out his order. "Go home and do not return until you have been notified this factory is open again for business. That will happen only when I receive the information I am seeking and the traitors are caught. Keep in mind that you will not receive any form or manner of compensation, secret or otherwise, while you are out of work. All accounting records will be confiscated."

Afraid to move, no one did. Then Gunter raised his hand to indicate that all his employees should pack up and go home. They gathered up personal tools, coats, and other belongings in rapid fits and starts to cover their emotion and exited the building in quiet confusion, pushing past the lines of police outside and running along the streets and around the nearest corners to put themselves out of sight and out of reach.

Gunter shook Heinz's hand and clasped his shoulder in farewell. Moments later, Heinz joined the exodus, but he did not run. He proudly walked.

"You will now hand over the keys to the building," Palm ordered Gunter, "along with the books of accounts and any cash and negotiables you have in the office. In addition, your financial assets in the *Commerzbank* will be frozen until my demands are met."

Gunter nodded and solemnly walked back to his office.

The shutting down of Gunter's factory was not the end of Palm's persecution. Gunter became aware that his nemesis was also spying on his family and advising friends to no longer associate with them.

"Maybe we should leave the country and go to America like the Wohlman brothers before that beast, Palm, commits the ultimate act that will destroy us," said his wife, Friede, later that night after their daughters were in bed asleep. "There is nothing to prevent him putting you in prison like Alfred, and the girls and I could not endure that. We are helpless before him, Gunter. He has the power and authority of Bismarck behind him."

"I can't just walk away from all I've built up over the years." His expression begged for her understanding. They had been married for twenty-eight years and, although their eldest daughter, Corinna, was at a marriageable age, the other three girls, Gertrude, Gisella, and Isabell, ranged downward from fourteen to ten. He loved them all equally and was careful not to bestow any special favor on one to the exclusion of the others. They watched his dispensation of affection like hawks, their assessing eyes and sharp hearing attuned to his every word. One misspoken reference could bring young female wrath down upon him or momentary rejection as a father unfit to be raising such brilliant, beautiful daughters.

Taking their Germanic beauty from their mother, each daughter fashioned herself on Friede's airy, effortless, blonde blue-eyed elegance that did not condescend to anyone. An understanding and appreciation of other people, whether at work or socially, was a common gift they shared. Having come from impoverished backgrounds themselves, the couple were first and foremost humanitarians, a belief that had influenced Gunter to become politically involved with the *sozialdemokrat.*

"Yes, but Palm can just take the company from you and Bismarck can give it to one of his cronies."

"There is no one that I employ who is an informer or would compromise himself and ruin the life of an innocent fellow worker so Palm would allow the factory to reopen. Palm is just trying to start a fire where there is not even any smoke."

"But people can go hungry and go without for only so long before someone capitulates. And consider us, your family. How long can we hold out. You can't even remove money from the bank for us to purchase food and pay our bills."

"My employees will find jobs elsewhere until this is past."

"If you try to find other work, Palm will only follow you and do the same thing again."

Not long after the factory incident, their youngest daughter Isabell, came running home in tears when the mother of her best friend told her at the door that her daughter could no longer associate with her and was not welcome to visit. When Gunter went to inquire, the husband and wife related how they have been threatened by Palm, who came to the house accompanied by two policemen, pushed his way inside, and verbally bullied the entire family, especially his two younger sons and ten year old daughter, Adele. They described how horrible the experience had been with the threatening presence of the hovering policemen and their ugly expressions and laughing red mouths opening wide under their thick mustaches.

The girl's father, Klaus, explained they were pressured to sever their friendship with Gunter's family to protect themselves. His anxious apologetic wife pleaded, "Please, you must understand the situation. Klaus doesn't want to be arrested by the SS on some trumped up charge. What would become of us?"

"I do understand and I am so sorry for what is happening to you. If there were some way I could make all this go away, I would."

Gunter's rage and inner turmoil morphed into thoughts and fantasies of reprisal and revenge. Fifteen years would pass before the opportunity would present itself. A significant change occurred in 1881 with the assumption of power by the new king, Wilhelm II. But Gunter never forgot nor forgave what Rudolf Palm had done to him, his family, and his business.

Jean Guenoc and Kurt Wohlman felt tired and gritty after their exhausting journey from America by steamship to England, across the English Channel to the port of *La Havre*, then by rail to Paris and Berlin.

The city had grown and expanded during the past fifteen years so that Jean and Kurt did not recognize old familiar landmarks with the exception of a few established foundation streets and buildings. The mile long Unter den Linden stretched from the *Brandenburger Tor* to the Royal Palace.

Accompanied by a tall thin man, Gunter Hagan met them at the *Bahnhof*, inquired as to whether they had had a pleasant journey, then introduced Eckerd Keufer, whose pointed ascetic features reminded Jean of a few gaunt Jesuit priests he had known in the past. Jean would not have taken the soft-spoken Eckerd to be a private investigator, but then decided Eckerd's quiet non-threatening manner would serve him well when talking with suspects.

Explaining that he would take them to their hotel after a brief meeting with Gunter's attorney, Gunter escorted the group to a waiting *Landau* carriage that took them along the bustling *Leipziger-Strasse* to the straight streets of *Fredrichstadt* and arrived at *Behren-Strasse*, the center of Berlin's financial district. They entered an imposing building and took the elevator lift up fifteen floors to the office of Jacob Schiff's Berlin attorney, Jurgen

Gunter quickly dispatched the introductions.

"Guten Tag, Herr Wohlman," Jurgen took Kurt's hand in a firm grip. I knew your father when he was alive. He was a fine upstanding citizen. I'm familiar with what Bismarck's secret police did to him. When I received the letter from your American banker, Jacob Schiff, I agreed immediately to take the case which I have presented to the *Bundesgerchtshof*, the highest Federal court. Later, I will explain the research that has been done and our sources and witnesses in building the case. Among the most important is my visit to Switzerland to meet with Hermann La Roche-Burckhardt, chairman of the Swiss National Bank. Arrangements have been made to seize Palm's financial assets illegally gained from the Wohlman family and its company. Once Rudolf Palm is arrested, he will be prosecuted under the *Strafprozessordnung* code of criminal procedure. Thanks to the intervention of Herr Hagan, we have sufficient evidence of Rudolf Palm's crimes to proceed.

Gunter explained. "I have followed Palm's career to the extent of hiring Eckerd Keufer, a private detective, who uses his own network of spies when investigating cases. If Palm can hire spies, then, so can I. This is what we know.

"When Wilhelm II became king in 1891, everything changed for us in Germany, for the *socialdemocratz*, all the workers, company owners, everybody. Palm no longer had a job as head of the secret service. King Wilhelm didn't want him spying on citizens and arresting them for their politics, so he gave him your company.

"For five years, Palm secretly transferred funds to private accounts. Resigned and named his successor, a man of the same unethical persuasion as Palm and equally distrusted and despised by his employees."

The Revolutionist

Thirteen years have passed since Palm imprisoned and tortured your father for being a social democrat. I believe Palm's life has changed so much he has nearly erased the incident from his mind. During his tenure as chief of secret police under Otto von Bismarck, he imprisoned and tortured thousands under his regime. Bismarck gave him ownership of the company in appreciation and payment for his service to the monarchy. In turn, knowing little or nothing about business, Palm hired a highly paid general manager to run the company for him.

Now, he has no regime. He lives a life of unobtrusive opulence and leisure in the Tuscan hills overlooking Florence, Italy. Considering that no one from either Vienna or Berlin has followed and prosecuted him for his illegal acts, Eckerd confirms that Palm has relaxed his vigilance. We need only to draw him into a compromising situation. We are moving toward that event with the inside assistance of his lover, Marco Fagione, a con man whom we have promised a substantial reward."

Rudolf Palm lowered the goblet of champagne from his lips and gazed out across the city of Florence from his villa. With heavy spiritual import, the deep sounding bells from the Renaissance *duomo Cathedral of Santa Maria Dei Fiori* tolled over the stained orange tile roofs and crept up the Arno River on the morning breeze rising to caress his hilltop home with a comforting distant sonority. Each morning, he gazed down at the river and the four bridges that spanned it, focusing on *Ponte Vecchio*, his link to *Galleria Egli Uffizi* and the famous painting it housed by Sandro Botticelli of the Birth of Venus, the goddess Palm considered to be his spiritual mother.

Palm had purchased the thirty-room villa constructed in the *Italianate* style with Renaissance balustrades for its strategic position high on the hill and its appeal to his sense of self importance.

"Breakfast is about to be served, Rudolfo," Marco had just come from the large fully appointed kitchen that was the creative conclave of Aldo Sansone, Palm's personal chef. Aldo had arisen at five that morning to make his daily trip down the hill and across the river to the town market to purchase fresh meat, fruit, and vegetables for the day. As he rode in Palm's fashionable *barouche* pulled by a team of black high-stepping *Ostfriesen* horses, Aldo enjoyed the cool morning air and admired the emerging beauty of the sunrise casting its golden halo behind the *duomo* and sending shafts of light into the mist rising off the water. Other than the usual greeting, *buon giorno*, between them, Aldo appreciated the uniformed driver's silence, which allowed him to mentally plan his menus for the day. He never wrote down his thoughts, but preferred to verbally communicate them to his *sous chef*, Stefano Celli, a young man whom he had brought with him from Rome. They kept up a constant dialogue regarding ingredients and the process of food preparation. Aldo relegated preparation of sauces and the baking, desserts, and pasta making to Stefano and treated him as an equal, a relationship that both enjoyed as friends and professionals. With the same fair blonde features, blue eyes, and slender physiques, they looked like brothers and were often taken as such by visitors.

When he arrived at the open market, Aldo went directly to a butcher in search of choice cuts of veal for the *osso buco* he planned for that night's dinner. Tossing the wrapped meat in his canvas shopping bag, he browsed the stands for fresh greens, *zucchini*, tomatoes, pears, grapes, goat cheese, and *fava* beans, indulging himself with a few crisp juicey green kernels. Beginning the menu with a white *fagiole*, ham and vegetable *zuppa*, he would serve the *osso buco* over a cheddar *risotto*, and end the meal with chocolate coated *profiteroles*, coffee, cognac, and cigars.

"Nice looking produce this morning."

Aldo abruptly turned, startled out of his culinary reverie. He did not recognize the stranger standing next to him and did not remembering noticing him before in the marketplace. *"Ah, buon giorno, si,"* he busied his hands with checking kale leaves. Normally, on Marco's advice, Aldo didn't talk to strangers. He knew that Rudolf Palm valued his privacy and did not appreciate strangers prying into his affairs, particularly about his sexual preference. Aldo and Stefano were not homosexual and just looked the other way.

"Are you not Aldo Sansone, the famous chef?"

Aldo glared at him with intense suspicion. "What is it you want, *signore*?"

"I thought I recognized you. I dined in your restorante in Rome several years ago. It was a meal to remember. I have never forgotten it and you, personally, came from the kitchen to ask if I enjoyed it."

Aldo softened a little. "Ah, I am pleased and honored that you remember after so many years."

"I recently moved to Florence and am delighted to discover that you also are here. What is the name of your *restorante*? I will become a patron at once."

"I am no longer serving the public. I am a personal chef."

"Oh, congratulations. Who is your lucky employer?"

Aldo stiffened. "Please excuse me, senore, but I have a busy morning and must be on my way."

"Of course, of course, *Signore* Sansone. My apologies. Seeing you brought back fond memories of my days in Rome."

"*Buon giorno, Signore, buon giorno. Addio.*"

"*Arrivederci, Signore Sansone.*"

Aldo quickly walked away to the cashier. There would be no next time. When he turned to look back, the stranger had disappeared.

"Signore Sansone is not one to engage in conversation," Eckerd Kuefer joined Jean Guenoc on a narrow cobbled side street walled by five story stone apartments near the market. "It's obvious that employees of Rudolf Palm have been ordered to be careful what they say and to whom they say it."

"He's being cautious," said Jean. "That means somehow he knows he is not safe anymore. Depending on the source of his information, he could decide to run."

"We are prepared to detect any move he makes."

Of his two houseboys, Palm preferred the young man, Marco Fagione, who was 28 and experienced, to the fumbling but energetic enthusiasm of Lucio Lomeli, 14, whom he had taken off the street while traveling in Rome. Lucio's effeminate features and golden curls had caught Palm's attention and caused him to think he was seeing a manifestation of Simonetta Vespucci, Botticelli's model for Venus and many other paintings. Resenting Palm's obsessiveness with the boy, Marco had conveniently controlled Lucio. Enjoying the boy's innocence and naivete, Marco had repressed his own envy of the boy's beauty and nurtured a relationship with him akin to that of a mentor so that he might use him to advantage in gaining access to Palm's wealth.

Marco himself had no emotional feelings for Palm other than as a source of magnanimous income. A seasoned male for hire,

Marco played the role Palm wanted him to play, a handsome sophisticated worldly lover and companion. Marco was a dilletante of the arts, music, food, and wine and a foil for Palm's rough ignorance of such knowledge and experience. Although he had begun as a casual lover encountered in a bar where Palm was vacationing in *Napoli*, he had quickly positioned himself as Palm's tutor and guide to decorative extravagance and finer culinary enjoyments. Lacking in all else but a diabolical talent for political intrigue and brutality, Palm had a great deal of money, of which he allowed Marco limited authority to spend for their benefit and maintaining the life of the opulent villa.

Marco had discovered and hired Aldo Sansone, whose rising reputation in Rome had not yet peaked in a major *restorante*. Although he fully appreciated the salary Marco offered and the freedom to experiment with new and traditional cuisine, he did not find his position challenging, cooking for a small patronage of five men. He requested that Palm and Marco occasionally expand the array and number of guests, if they expected him to stay.

Entertaining and bringing prominent local citizens into his home made Palm nervous, but Marco assured him that full security measures would be observed and the guests hand picked for their discretion. Marco informed Palm that he would have to start attending Sunday mass and give the appearance of being Catholic. Palm vehemently argued against Marco's advice, but his resistance faded when Marco pointed out that his perceived status as a citizen would be enhanced. Earlier, he had been snubbed and excluded from social circles in the community.

"So, you really think things will change just because I go to mass?"

"I am confident they will. I have no doubt."

Palm weighed the advantage of concealment and the robe of righteousness he could outwardly wear to deter suspicion as to the source of his wealth and to his sexual behavior.

To protect his investment, Marco had recruited and hired two rough-hewn Sicilian bodyguards, Maffuci and Ragno, both unmarried former policemen, womanizers, and opportunists well-known by Marco, who had participated with them in various scams to bilk money from the rich. Lately, Maffuci and Ragno had expressed impatience at the slow progress Marco was making in gaining Palm's confidence to manage his finances and to have access to his bank accounts. Marco had no knowledge as to the source of Rudolf Palm's wealth, but since he had been approached by an investigator from Berlin and offered a fortune for his participation in a scheme to capture Palm, he knew the *Deutschmarks* were in the high millions.

Whenever Marco broached the subject, he observed how quiet, tense and withdrawn Palm became. Once, in an outburst of red-faced anger, Palm had smashed a crystal wine glass brimming with clear bubbling *prosecco* and left the room. Palm's response to overtures of financial confidence left Marco no doubt that access to his benefactor's millions would not be forthcoming by any agreeable and open contractual arrangement. He chided Maffuci and Ragno for their impatience while he chaffed at his own.

After the third casual attempt by Marco to engage him in the subject, Palm's suspicion went on alert. He decided he needed to test the integrity and commitment of his companion. The test would be an easy ploy, the creation of a false account that would appear to entrust Marco with complete fiscal responsibility as Palm's financial manager. A scheme by Marco to embezzle him would be soon detected. They would take a trip down to Rome to visit his bank and give the physical appearance of a sanctioned authorization.

Marco expressed his delight, but was quietly amazed and suspicious at Palm's sudden changing of his mind. Marco knew he would have to proceed with caution to not risk losing the golden goose. He knew Palm was not a man to be trifled with.

A spinach and artichoke frittata sprinkled with shaved *pecorino* and *parmesan* cheeses and a side of boar's meat sausage was set before Palm, as he arrived and sat down at the massive hand-carved oak table.

"I've noticed for the past several days that you seem pensive, dear *caro* Rudolfo. You have not been your usual self," said Marco. "Something must weigh on your mind."

What weighed on his mind was not a confidence that Palm was willing to share. A lingering vestige of fear of being discovered had begun to gnaw at him since he had crossed the line from law enforcer to criminal. Thirteen years ago, he had hired Luther Baggot as a bounty hunter to track down and kill the Wohlman brothers, whom he feared would one day return to Berlin and reclaim their company. If they did, they would discover his embezzlement scheme and take legal action against him, if they could find him. Baggot's infrequent letters from America had stated he had not been able to locate the Wohlman's and suspected they had changed their identity.

A recent extension of Palm's fear fed his paranoid suspicion that he might be investigated by authorities through the prompting of the Wohlman family. He had noticed, or at least imagined, that he was being followed, but could never detect who might be watching him. He believed that the exiled Wohlman brothers had changed their surname, resettled in an American city and developed a thriving business enterprise.

Given the silence of the past thirteen years, Palm struggled with the quandary of being free and clear of his crime and not knowing what legal forces or other manner of revenge might be moving against him. He had always been in a position to know what others were thinking and doing. The possibility that he was out of touch and now potentially at the receiving end of a legal surveillance had begun to worry him.

Palm pretended to be jovial and in good spirits on the day's travel by train to Rome. That Palm chose to take his dinner privately in his hotel room concerned Marco, but Palm brushed him aside with the excuse he was tired from the journey.

Marco tried to dispel his anxiety the next morning as they entered the *Banca d'Italia* in Rome where they were greeted and shown into the spacious expensively furnished offices of the General Manager, Giuseppe Marchion, who knew nothing of the scheme about to enfold. After initial greetings, Palm explained the purpose of his visit and the wish to establish an additional account under the financial stewardship of Marco Fagione.

Marchion requested an assistant to bring in Palm's financial statement. While they waited, Marchion's secretary served coffee and light pastries. Marchion engaged Palm in polite conversation until the documents arrived. With no outward sign of alarm, he asked to speak to Palm privately in his inner office. The banker then showed Palm his accounts.

"*Signore*, I am sorry to have to tell you that all your financial assets have been seized by the *Bundesgerchtshof.* As you know, they are the highest Federal court in Germany."

Palm leaped up and raced out of Marchion's office through his front office and onto the main floor of the bank. The manager shouted after him, *"Signore! Signore!* You did not let me explain!"

Marco catapaulted from his chair and rushed to the door. Catching sight of Maffuci and Ragno loitering in the lobby, he pointed and motioned to them to stop Palm, who skittered across the marble floor to avoid them. He thrust open the front doors and was about to race down the steps when he stopped short upon seeing ten armed *carbinieri* and a patrol wagon waiting for him. He also recognized a figure from the past, Jean Guenoc, but not the tall thin man standing next to him.

Looking to the left and to the right, he saw more police officers. He turned and rushed back inside the bank and collided with Marco. Both men went down and Palm struck him in the face again and again and cursed him for being a traitor. As Marco kicked him away and rolled to his feet, Palm pulled out his hidden revolver and fired three shots at Marco's back. Two bank guards closed down on Palm and one stepped on his wrist causing him to drop the weapon. Marco lay in a widening pool of his own blood seeping out over the highly polished marble.

Maffuci and Ragno blended with customers who had crouched and huddled away in fear and were now quickly departing by the front door.

The weight of one guard's knees crushed into Palm's back while the other jerked his arms behind him and cuffed his wrists.

On November 7, 1905, Rudolf Palm was sentenced to life in prison by the Berlin high court for embezzlement and for the murder of Marco Fagione. Kurt Wohlman's company was restored to him and his brother, Matias, who had decided to remain in America.

After a rough sea voyage from England, Jean Guenoc was on the train from New York to Chicago, when the threat he most feared happened.

Chapter 33

Songbird

Luther Baggot loved vaudeville. The entertaining performances of musicians, comedians, acrobats, trained animals, melodramas, minstrel shows, and burlesque provided an escape from the dark side of his existence. As a member of the theater audience, he discovered laughter. His booming howls of amusement turned heads and also fueled the audience response to the barrage of humor from the stage. He read the Chicago Times mainly for announcements of productions coming to The Alhambra and North Clark Street theaters.

He did not know what to expect from a play at the Auditorium Theater bearing the title of *Faust* by Goethe, a German playwright. The story of the aging scholar, Faust, selling his soul to the devil, caught Luther in its spell. His identification with the character of Mephistopheles was so complete that it further manifested his life's purpose as conveyed to him by the Gypsy fortune teller, *Die Ziguener,* whom he believed communed with the diseased souls and spirits of the dark world. She had told him he himself had come from that world and that he was an emissary of darkness, a harbinger of death.

The orgy depicting the last act, Walpurgis Night, held him riveted. He drew the pulsing music and writhing characters into his imagination and possessed them as his own. In his mind, he became Mephistopheles, the all-powerful indestructible harbinger of death and damnation.

A few months later, only by chance did he see and recognize Beth Peet perform a medley of popular novelty songs of a tearful variety depicting the degrading and oppressive lives of young women. In checking the program for her name, he saw that she would appear the next night in the role of an *ingenue* in a musical operetta.

Although much had happened during the past two years in preparing her for a singing and theatrical entertainment career, Beth took her good fortune for granted as her due. Both Sophie Rose and her voice teacher, Ronald Tomlin, had commented on her natural talent and a Chicago Times reviewer had lavished praise on her debut soprano performance in a variety show.

She loved the musty backstage smell of the theater, the stirring of the audience anticipating the performance, and, looking in the green room mirror, seeing the enhancement of her natural beauty emerge from within the make-up she applied. Her large expressive brown eyes, high cheek bones, and perfect nose and chin rendered her a star's image under the bright lights. And her ballet instructor and acting coach had given her the training to move in character with grace and balance.

She was excited above all at being cast in the leading role of a shop girl who falls in love with a young man she believes is a poor factory worker. When he reveals his true identity, she discovers he is the son of a wealthy industrialist who will disinherit him for wanting to marry beneath his class.

The plot was a commonplace story that appealed to the rising middle-class audience tastes as the industrialization of America forged ahead. New found discretionary income sent families out of the home in search of elevated wholesome entertainment, suitable for men, women, and children. Theater entrepreneurs termed their productions *polite vaudeville*.

At the conclusion of the production and two curtain calls, as the applause dwindled and faded, Luther rose from his seat. He always preferred a location at the center rear of the auditorium giving him an overall view of the stage and performers that depicted them contained in a lighted box and separated them in a brief depiction of a different world that mirrored reality.

The more plays and operas he attended reinforced a growing sense in Luther that he also lived in a different reality, that the world in which he existed was just a larger stage on which the events and lives of millions of people from impoverished immigrants to businessmen to politicians and tycoons played out. From what the gypsy fortune teller, *Die Zeiguner*, had told him, he was one of the most important actors on this world stage. He created the counter balance, the antagonist against the forces of good as a force of evil. In his own mind, he was *Mephistopheles*.

As he sidled along the aisle about to leave, he noticed and recognized two people down in the front row moving toward the stage apron steps. They went up onto the stage and slipped off behind the curtain into the wings.

Luther had planned to wait on the side street for the actress, Beth Peet, to leave the theater and follow her home. Now, fortune had presented him with another opportunity.

Sophie and Matias worked their way through the vociferous cast and crew until they found Beth, already surrounded by several young male and female admirers who had rushed backstage at the conclusion of the performance to seek her autograph.

"I think we have to wait our turn," said Matias with a broad grin.

"Rightly so," said Sophie with a quick laugh. "This is her moment."

"One of many and well deserved."

"She's worked hard and it paid off."

"There's no question about her talent. Another producer called at my office the other day inquiring about her availability for a new play he's staging out-of-town. He wants to bring it to Chicago, then to Broadway."

"So we have a young star in the family."

"They have become our family, haven't they, Beth, Julie, Aaron and Newt?"

"Were you surprised when the boys said they wanted to have their own place?"

"Not at all. But in another two years, I expect to enroll them at Harvard University."

"Will they be ready?"

"Jean says they'll be. He said they're both very intelligent in different ways. Aaron has an interest in science and Newt is strong in understanding law."

"Both promising careers."

Matias nodded. "With my brother returning to Europe, the boys will be in line for succession here."

"Have you thought about going back to Germany?"

"Only in passing. Chicago has become my home."

"I'm thinking of making the trip next year to visit friends and family."

"Her fans are giving us a chance to move in," said Matias. They stepped forward with smiles and congratulatory waves.

"Wonderful performance, Beth. Outstanding. The audience loved you."

"Everything worked tonight," said Beth, her face flushed with satisfaction. "Nobody missed a line and we were all on cue."

"A perfect performance," said Sophie.

"Are you returning to the house with us or going out with the cast to celebrate," Matias gave her a brief hug and a kiss on her forehead.

"We're having a cast party after the performance tomorrow night. I'll ride back with you. Have to get this makeup off first."

"We'll be waiting outside."

Beth blew them a kiss and hurried off to her dressing room.

As Sophie and Matias came out into the side alley through the stage door, Luther stepped far back into the shadows beyond the pool of yellow light thrown by an overhead lamp. Arm in arm, the couple strode to the brightly lit front of the theater to where their carriage and driver waited at the entrance.

Not knowing when the young actress, Beth, might appear, Luther did not want to lose his opportunity. He also did not want to risk being seen by the man and woman he intended to follow home. He hurried to the front corner of the theater and cautiously peered out at the street bustling with chattering patrons leaving the building, hailing horse-drawn cabs, boarding waiting carriages, or just walking off into the night. He decided his position would be best somewhat to the rear of the Bauman carriage and would allow him time to hire a cab and wait and see if the actress would come out and join them. Leaving by the stage door, she emerged ten minutes later from the side alley. Matias met her with a gallant bow and assisted her into the carriage. The driver snapped his long whip over the backs of the team and they pulled away down the street.

Luther instructed his driver to follow them at a short distance. "Just don't lose sight of them," he ordered. "We have business together."

The horse's left front shoe slipped on the cobblestones and the cab lurched forward.

Large snow flakes began to fall in the cold November night. Sophie and Beth bundled their fur coats about them. Their breath steamed in the frigid air.

As a plan formed in his mind, Luther leaned out the cab window from time to time to ensure the cab had not lost sight of the carriage. When it arrived and turned up the driveway to the mansion, Luther noted the location, then ordered the cab driver to take him back into the city.

He paid the driver and left the cab two blocks from his tenement.

He walked purposefully to his apartment where he packed his few belongings into a carpet bag. He loaded his short barrel shotgun and dropped a handful of shells into his coat pocket. With a final look around, for he would not be returning, he left carrying the shotgun in one hand and the carpet bag in the other.

By now, the intensity of the snowfall had increased and become a brisk whirling storm. With the carpet bag bumping against his leg at each step, he walked along the narrow streets guided by the glow of gas lights dimmed by the shifting white curtain from one corner to the next.

He pulled open the heavy entrance door just enough to slip inside the stable, dark, but for the small light given off by a kerosene lantern hanging on a nail. The warm fecund vapors of the horses in their stalls lingered in the barn air. The scruffy bearded man who minded the livery lay drunk asleep on his cot in a small room just off the center aisle. The coal burning in his stove was reduced to a pile of glowing white ash. His porcine body responded to the loss of heat with shivering and teeth chattering like a man in the throes of dying.

Luther placed his carpet bag and shotgun aside, then moved his black stallion out of its stall and tied him to a post near the lantern. He saddled and bridled the animal in the semi-darkness and strapped the carpet bag to the saddle. He led the tall horse along the aisle, pushed open the door, and mounted outside. With a slight pressure on the reins and a touch of his heel, he urged him into a slow trot down the center of the deserted street. His shotgun lay across his thighs.

Matias, Sophie, and Gustav shared an occasional quiet comment and lingered over their wine and the remains of a late dinner. Beth had finished her meal and retired to her upstairs room. The letdown after the emotional high of a performance left her weary. She soaked briefly in a hot tub, then went straight to bed.

Julie had eaten alone earlier and, in a state of half doze, was in the library working on writing her memoir.

Concealed by the darkness and shield of driving snow, the black horse and rider passed undetected from the street and maneuvered through the dormant gardens and shrubbery around the side property of the estate to the stable. He dismounted and tied the reins to a hitching post. Clutching the shotgun, he walked steadily toward the muted golden glow of lights from the ground floor dining room windows. He hesitated as a cook's helper came out through the kitchen back door of a ground floor cellar, threw a load of scraps into a barrel, and went inside.

Luther moved to the door and tried the latch. It was not locked. He pushed open the door and entered the kitchen. The back of the cook's helper was toward him, but the man turned at the sudden rush of cold air. Shock and fright froze his ability to move or speak at the specter of the tall bearded man in black aiming a shotgun directly at him. Trembling uncontrollably, he backed away as Luther approached him.

"Who, who are you?" he finally croaked. "What do you want? Food? I'll give you food."

"Don't want food and I don't want you." Luther swung the gun stock upward in a hard sweep to the man's jaw with a cracking blow that spun him into a spiraling void of unconsciousness. Luther waited and listened to see if the clatter and crash of falling pots and pans drew the attention of anyone. He waited with his gun leveled at the open archway at the bottom of a short flight of stone steps that led up to the dining room. No one appeared. He went up the steps and slowly pushed open a door revealing a long hallway. Barely discernable voices engaged in conversation came from another open door at the far end. He moved quietly toward the voices.

His onslaught left them no time to think or react. Matias had only a moment to recognize him as the shotgun blast obliterated his face and killed him instantly. The second blast cut off Sophie's soprano scream as her face disintegrated from the projectile's spreading impact. As Luther ejected the two spent cartridges and jammed in two more from his pocket, Gustav staggered toward him with a flashing steel carving knife. He saw the barrel rising to meet him. The single explosion threw him backward onto the table and his smashed brains spewed out of his shattered skull and mingled with the red juices of the beef eaten at dinner.

At the first muffled shot, followed by Sophie's scream and a second shot, Julie grabbed up her manuscript, leapt up from the desk chair, raced out into the adjoining hall, and sprinted toward the dining room as the third booming shot resounded from the ceiling and walls and set off an eerie tinkling of the large glass chandelier. She stopped in horror at the sight of Luther Baggot and the carnage across the room.

Luther charged toward her, but she was gone a split second before he fired and the shell smashed a large vase behind where she had been standing. Luther had to take a few moments to reload before he could pursue her, but his delay gave Julie just enough time to escape from the mansion through the massive front doors. Pushing one of them open created a further obstacle preventing Luther from reaching her. By the time he stepped out onto the sprawling stone porch, Julie had disappeared into the storm.

Fearing that Luther was following her, Julie ran on and on through the freezing snow into the night and into the city until she was exhausted and could run no more. She feared the risk that he might still be there should she go back. Then she remembered seeing Beth walk past the open library door on the way to her bedroom. Julie had waved at her and asked about the performance. Their exchange had been cordial and pleasant, one of the few of late. She hoped the assassin would leave without finding her.

Sound asleep deep in a fantasy dream, Beth heard nothing. With the exception of Julie's escape, Luther had accomplished his objective. He did not think there was any point in searching the rooms. He went down the back stairs to the cellar where the cook's helper still lay unconscious. Leaving the door standing open, he walked out into the storm across the back gardens to where his horse stood patiently waiting at the hitching post. He rode at an unseeing gallop along the dark streets, then slowed to a walk as he entered the city. There was one more person he needed to see.

Police Chief O'Neil had ordered the crime scene taped off limits to anyone except investigating officials. Newsmen hovered in the street just off the property. No one would answer their questions. The coroner had covered the three bodies and, with the help of his assistants, was preparing to transport them to the mortuary.

Early that morning, Julie had returned from Sister Pavalek's convent where she had spent the night. The storm had abated and sunlight glistened from the surface of new-fallen snow. She explained to the police officers at the gate that she lived in the mansion and had been there at the time of the murders and escaped from the killer. A policeman quickly escorted her inside to talk to the lead detective.

Jean disembarked from the late Pullman and hired a Hansom cab from the station. The New York train had been delayed three hours during the night by heavy snows that had drifted across the tracks in Ohio. When he arrived, he saw the crowd of newsmen, three patrol wagons, the coroner's wagon, police tape, and three bodies being carried on stretchers from the mansion. The blood rose in his head as he began to realize what might have happened while he was gone. He stepped over to the coroner wearing a full length black wool winter coat and derby hat.

"Can you tell me what happened here? Who are these people?"

The coroner removed the unlit cigar from his mouth. "Three murders. But I can't tell you anything. You have to wait for the detectives to come out. We can't say nothin' to the press."

"I'm not with the press. I'm a resident here. Can I see their faces?"

"Funny you should ask. They ain't got no faces. Shotgun took 'em clean off. Can't help you." He gestured with his cigar to his assistants. "Squeeze that last one in there. They'll all fit."

Jean walked over to one of the officers preventing entry at the gate.

"I'm sorry, sir, only investigators allowed inside."

"I just returned form out of town. I'm a resident. I have the right to go in. I have information. I know who did this."

"In that case, follow me. Tim, take over," he ordered his partner.

Jean's escort took him up the mansion steps and through the familiar doors. From where she and Beth were being interrogated in the living room, Julie saw Jean crossing the foyer. She jumped up from her chair and called out his name. He stopped and turned to take her in his arms as she rushed over to him. The tears she had been holding back gushed down her face in an unstoppable flood. Her body heaved with sobs.

"Weve got to get him," she finally gasped. "We have to find him and kill him."

The prim detective with a carefully clipped mustache approached them. "Excuse me, sir. I'm detective Owen DeLarey. And who might you be?"

"Jean Guenoc, a personal friend of the family. I've just returned from Europe on business. What has happened here?"

"Three people were violently murdered here last night, Matias Bauman, Sophie Augusta Rose, and an elderly gentlemen," he referred to his note pad, by the name of Gustav Weber. Do you know them?"

"Yes, they were all my dearest friends."

The escort officer stepped over from the foyer to speak to the detective. "He says he knows who committed the crime, sir."

"You know the identity of the killer?"

"Yes, both this young lady and I know him."

Owen raised his pad and pencil. "His name?"

"Luther Baggot. He's a bounty hunter."

"A bounty hunter. What did he want with these people? Surely they are not fugitives."

"He's a political bounty hunter. Someone in Germany wanted these people assassinated. That is why they came to America, to escape."

"And what is your relationship to this family?"

"I have been their protector. It is a misfortune that I was not here."

"Indeed. So you know the killer's identity. You know his name. What more can you tell me."

"I saw him twice in the city," said Julie, swiping at her dripping nose with the back of a wrist.

The detective quickly extended his handkerchief. "Where and when did you see him?"

"Once when I was a newsie downtown in the loop. The second time, he was a guard riding shotgun on a scab wagon during the garment workers strike."

"A guard, you say."

"Yes."

"That means he was working for Pinkertons. We can check with 'em as to his whereabouts. Must have gone rogue on 'em, especially this business. We can use Pinkertons to help us find and arrest him.”

“This young lady and I have a personal interest in finding him.”

“How’s that?”

“He killed her mother and father in the same way.”

“When was this?”

“About two years ago,” said Julie. “We lived on a farm in Minnesota.”

“A political murder?”

“Yes,” said Jean. “There was a list, but it was false, to mislead him, throw him off the track.”

Julie stared up at Jean in shock.

“The list could be evidence,” said Owen. “I would like to see it.”

“It’s in the safe in the library,” said Julie.

“Do either of you know the combination?”

Julie shook her head. Jean remained silent. He knew the access combination, but did not what the list to fall into anyone else’s hands. Its existence had prompted the deaths of five people it had been created to save.

“Until we talk to Pinkertons, we have nothing certain to go on,” said Owen.

“We can send out wanted fliers by rail to be posted in towns to the south, west, and north. Once we know where Baggot is running, we’ll hire Pinkertons to form a posse and hunt him down. Do you have anything further for me?”

Jean shook his head. “I’m sorry I don’t.”

“Do you have anything more for me, young lady?”

Julie shook her head.

"Then I thank you for your time and information." Owen shook Jean's hand. "Until you hear from us otherwise, the dining room remains a crime scene and may not be entered. Officers will be posted here on duty around the clock."

"We understand," said Jean. "Julie, shall we go? We have some things to talk about."

The detective turned away and walked back to Beth still seated immobile and withdrawn on the couch. "Just a few more questions, miss, then you can go."

"I have to get my coat," said Julie. "It's in my room."

Jean nodded. "I'll meet you in the foyer."

Fifteen minutes later, as they walked alone in the back gardens entombed under the snow, Jean controlled the intensity of his voice. "If we want to get to him before they find him, we can't wait."

"But how will we know where to go?"

"The detective said Baggot worked for Pinkertons. We'll start there."

"When?"

"We can't waste any time. Now."

"Shall we get the carriage?"

"Yes."

They altered their direction and headed for the stable.

"Yes," said, Clarence Rittenauer, the desk officer at the downtown Pinkerton's office. "We have 'im. He's right here." He pulled a card from his file. "We have 'im workin' on a special security assignment for Bill O'Riley, the garment company over on third. I placed 'im myself."

"Thank you, sir." Said Jean. "You have been most helpful."

"Glad to oblige. Have a good day."

"Have a good day."

"I'm from Pinkerton's," Jean lied to Bill O'Riley. "We're looking for Luther Baggot who I'm told works for you on a special assignment."

"Baggot, sure he works for me if he damn well came to work. Ain't seen him now for three days."

Julie tugged at the sleeve of Jean's coat. He glanced at her.

"I have to talk to you," she muttered.

"Would you please excuse us," said Jean.

"Sure, come back when you're ready."

Julie led him onto the elevated platform adjacent to O'Riley's office. "See that woman out there." She pointed down along the first row of the factory floor. "On the third loom."

"Yes," said Jean. "I see her."

"Her name is Hillar Kuznetsov. She attended the union meetings. One night, Conrad saw Baggot walking her home. He and Baggot got into a fight."

"We need to talk to her."

"Now?"

"Now, let's go."

As they walked out onto the floor, O'Riley watched them from his elevated office window. He stepped out onto the open platform and shouted at them. "Hey, you can't go out there! They're on the clock! They got work to do!"

Jean and Julie ignored him.

"Hey, you, I'm talkin' to you!"

They moved in on Hillar who glanced up at them once, but continued her loom operation.

"Hillar," said Julie. "You remember me, Julie Josephson, from the union meetings. We have to talk to you about Luther Baggot. We're trying to find him. He's wanted for murder."

"I can't talk to you now, but I will meet you after work. Outside at the end of the dock." Her shuttle did not miss a motion. Her eyes flickered at them, then focused only on the loom.

Red in the face, O'Riley came down from the platform and stomped over to them. "Did you hear me? I said you can't come down here. You can't talk to my workers."

"Thank you for your time," said Jean. "We're leaving now."

"That's a fine how'd do. Hope you didn't get what you came for."

Jean and Julie left by the side door and went down the steps of the loading dock. "We'll come back at five o'clock."

"How do we know she'll be done?"

"I saw the hours posted on the wall in O'Riley's office. They work a twelve hour shift seven days a week. She started at five this morning."

"What a god-awful life. The union was bargaining for an eight hour day."

"I'm sure they'll have it, some day."

Chapter 34

Ice

As they hurried along the snow encrusted streets with drifts pushed aside into long dikes marbled with dirt and grit, Julie noticed that horses pulling the teamsters wagons were shod with caulked steel to prevent slipping on the exposed ice which melted during the day and froze again at night with the departure of the sun.

She and Jean stood aside at the front corner of the factory near the loading dock and waited for Hillar Kuznetsov to appear. Shortly after the long whistle blew signaling the end of the work day, crowds of weary men and women streamed out of the building. Their sullen faces passed without noticing them.

Clutching her heavy coat about her and keeping a hand on the cross-slung strap of her purse, Hillar emerged from the tumult of shuffling bodies. At first, Julie did not recognize her because of the Russian fur hat she wore against the biting wind that sluiced along the alleys and avenues of the city. With temperatures dropping to 30 degrees below zero, people vacated the open spaces as quickly as they could.

Hillar motioned for them to follow her. She spoke as they walked side by side. Their leather boots crunched rhythmically on the snow. Their breath smoked in the cold air.

"I heard a pounding on the door late last night. My brothers and I were asleep. They did not wake, so I pulled on my coat and went to answer. I never expected it would be Luther Baggot. He was holding a shotgun. It was aimed at the floor. He had a strange look in his eyes, like his mind was somewhere else. That is the only way I can describe him. I feared that he had come to kill me. 'What do you want?' I asked. 'Why are you here?' 'I'm going home to Deutschland,' he said. His voice sounded flat and hollow. 'I want you to come with me.' I never suspected he had any feelings for me other than as an informer. I thought he was crazy and told him if he didn't go, I would have to wake my brothers. 'You have brothers?' he asked. 'Yes,' I said. "They're sleeping. It's past midnight. I cannot go with you.' He didn't say anything more, just turned away and walked off into the night."

Jean spoke. "Deutschland, that means he will be taking a train east to New York City to book passage on a ship to Europe. He's ahead of us by one day that has now become two. We have to find out when the next ship sails. Thank you, Hillar. You have been most helpful. We have to move fast, Julie."

"Goodbye, Hillar." Julie hurried to match Jean's rapid stride.

Enduring agonizing stops to pick up and discard passengers, they rode a crowded trolley to the Union train station between Van Buren and Madison Streets on the west side of the city. Leaving the trolley, they entered the massive building with its towering central edifice and checked the posted schedule of arrivals and departures to identify the most likely train on which Luther would be traveling. When asked, the uniformed ticket agent didn't recall a customer of Luther's description.

"I see a lot of people come through here. After a while, they all start to look the same. Sorry, can't help you. Train to New York City departed at seven this mornin'. There's a night train leaves here at ten. You want tickets?"

Jean pulled money from his wallet and pushed it across the counter to the man, who punched two tickets from his machine.

"Board thirty minutes before departure time. If you're late, next train leaves at seven tomorrow morning."

Jean pocketed the tickets. As they walked out into the terminal, Jean said, "It is too late to find a travel agent that is still open and we must eat. We have a short time to go back to the mansion and pack a bag to travel. Mine is where I left it. We won't see a shipping schedule until we reach New York, but I do know from my recent travels that the passenger steam ships take two weeks to make a crossing. The Cunard from New York to Liverpool is the most likely ship he would take. Baggot won't arrive in New York for one more day, but he'll book passage on the earliest departure."

"What if we miss him and he gets away?"

"He will never escape. I would follow him to Germany and find him."

After two days and nights traveling across the snow-covered farmlands of Indiana, Ohio, Pennsylvania, and New York in a Pullman sleeper, they arrived at New York's Grand Central at Park Avenue and 42nd Street in mid-town Manhattan. Julie felt disoriented following Jean through the world's largest train terminal with its 44 platforms and 67 tracks on two levels below ground. Among the thousands of people who swarmed about them and the millions more on the city streets, she despaired of ever finding Luther Baggot.

Jean wasted no time in hailing them a Hansom cab and urged the driver to keep his horse at a steady trot in rushing them to the harbor on the partially frozen East River congested with ice floes, masted sailing boats and long barges of all kinds and sizes and steam ships from different lands bearing signage of famous lines,

White Star, Red Star, Hapaag, Collins, Inman, and Cunard. Hurrying to keep up with Jean as they walked along the wharf, Julie took in the air, fetid with the smell of fish and ruled by flocks of screaming gulls whose hoarse cries competed with the shouts of longshoremen loading and unloading cargo.

They arrived at the Cunard Line warehouse and entered its cavernous interior. Having been there before, Jean went directly to the passenger agent and inquired about the next scheduled departure for England.

"Friday, two more days," the gray-haired man informed them.

"Is there a Luther Baggot on your passenger list?"

The agent scanned the manifest, ran his finger down the list of names, and nodded. "Right here, Luther Baggot. Ship boards in the morning at eleven and weighs anchor at two in the afternoon. No more cabins available. All are booked."

"We're looking for the man. Not booking passage."

"Passengers gather here for processing. Best place to find him."

"Thank you, sir." Jean turned and led Julie away back outside to the docks. "Two more days. We have time. We have no way of knowing where he's hiding now. We'll catch him here. We need to find lodging for ourselves. We'll stay nearby."

Considering that a sailor's inn would be too rough for a young girl, Jean found them a hotel a few blocks from the waterfront and booked them separate rooms. With little to occupy their time, Julie expressed her interest in seeing Ellis Island where she and Newt and her mother and father had entered the country as immigrants fifteen years ago.

She and Jean took a ferry out to the island and stayed part of the day watching thousands of new immigrants seeking a better life, their faces wreathed with hope and weariness, disembark from ships and process through the large brick buildings. Being quite young at the time she and her family entered the country in 1890, she did not remember much of what had happened, only the masses of muttering, coughing, spitting, men, women, and children who had made the two week journey in the unsanitary conditions of third class steerage, wearing the humble old country clothing of their homelands and carrying their meager belongings in soiled sacks and carpet bags.

Those who had purchased first and second class passage, were not subjected to the same degrading bodily inspections for ill health and disease, but endured only a cursory inspection while on board, then passed through customs without incident under the belief they would not burden the hospitals and jails as the sick and infirm or as felons. At the time, most came from England, Ireland, Germany, Sweden, Finland, and Norway. A few years later, people from the world over joined the immigrant flood tide battering the American shores.

Not wanting to risk that Luther would pass through the Cunard processing area undetected by them, Jean and Julie appeared on the dock next to the steamship, *Compania*, at the break of dawn. They carefully watched the arriving passengers disembarking from horse-drawn cabs and carriages as the morning fog lifted above the red black-tipped smokestacks of the luxurious waiting vessel. Jean was not concerned that Luther might instantly recognize them, since he would never expect to see them there.

Luther's quick long strides brought him into view. His black winter coat and bowler hat blended with what other men in the crowd were wearing. Standing a head taller than most, his height made him prominent.

"There he is," said Julie.

"I see him."

As he waited in the boarding process line, Luther suddenly noticed Jean and Julie moving toward him in the crowd. Shoving others aside, he bolted and ran across the warehouse and out again through an entrance door onto the waterfront streets. Jean chased after him, but lost sight of him among the confusion of wagon traffic and pedestrians.

Breathless, Julie lagged a few steps behind.

Jean continued to scan the sea of faces. "Now that he knows we're close, he will do anything to stop us."

"There!" Julie pointed.

"Stay with me."

Hampered by the crowd, they saw him climb into a Hansom cab that pulled away and blended with other cabs and carriages with the exception of a red ribbon encircling the crown of the driver's top hat.

Jean quickly hired a cab of their own to follow and immediately encountered a traffic jam where a Ford motor car and a horse and wagon had collided. The horse was down and thrashing in its harness. The cab driver maneuvered around the melee of shouting men and high pitched screams of the animal whose front legs were broken.

Through the cab window, Jean noticed from the myriad of intertwining tracks they were approaching another railroad center. "He's going to South Central Station. He's taking another train." He shouted to the driver to go faster. The driver whipped the horse into a choppy gallop that caused the cab to sway and buck tossing its occupants about. Jean and Julie clutched at leather straps to stabilize themselves.

Minutes later they leaped out of the cab at the station entrance and rushed inside. Searching frantically over the mass of people churning under the high central dome, Jean spotted Luther leave a barred ticket agent window and run toward one of the many boarding platforms where a Pullman idled preparing to leave.

"Stay close," shouted Jean. "We have to get on without tickets. We'll pay on board."

They heard the conductor calling the departure followed by the shriek of the train whistle and its clanging bell. Running along the platform billowing with hissing steam, Jean grabbed a guide bar and swung onto the loading steps of the nearest passenger car, then reached out to pull Julie in behind him.

They settled onto the first empty seats they could find. Jean was confident that Luther did not know they were on board the moving train and that would give them the element of surprise once they located him.

When the conductor came by for their tickets, Jean explained that they had been late with no time to purchase tickets and would pay him directly. Not wanting to reveal he did not know the destination, Jean asked, "What is the time of our arrival?"

"We reach Montreal tomorrow afternoon at three o'clock."

"Thank you."

When the conductor moved on, Jean muttered to Julie. "He hopes to leave the country by way of Canada. He could take a trunk line from Montreal to Quebec and book passage on another ship to England. I will take him before we ever reach the border."

After a moment of silence, Julie asked, "Are you going to kill him?"

Jean answered without hesitation. "Yes."

"I also want to kill him."

Jean nodded his understanding.

That Jean Guenoc had tracked him halfway across the country and prevented him from boarding the ship profoundly disturbed Luther. *Die Zieguner,* the gypsy, had told him he had special powers. Luther was confident he had not left any evidence, any trail that would tie him to the murders. Yet the man tracking him seemed to have powers of his own to know where he was going and, perhaps, the power to stop him.

His plan now was to reach Montreal, then transfer to a connecting line to Quebec. No one would know he had crossed the border. Quebec was a French speaking province. He would have plenty of time to find a ship to Europe, perhaps bypass England and go directly to France.

The snow was deeper and more widespread across mid and upstate New York. Luther had taken the precaution to book a sleeper cabin in order to remain out of sight. He had started the trip in a section with open seating for the general public. Upon punching his ticket, the conductor had told him the train would make brief stops at small towns along the way and Luther would have a few minutes to step off and stretch his legs. In his own mind, he wanted to reach Montreal without delay. He felt a strange unease that he was vulnerable and something could go against him at any time. After an hour of watching the passing snow blanketed countryside, he left his seat and started toward the back of the train and his private cabin.

Pausing in the vestibule to peer through the glass door into the adjoining car, a chill rippled up and down his spine at the sight of Jean Guenoc and the girl seated facing him halfway along the aisle. He quickly stepped back from view of the window. He had to leave the train. He would get off at the next stop. He turned and hastily made his way back to the first car.

His heart racing, he watched through the windows for signs of the approaching town. He heard the whistle and grind of braking steel against steel, and detected the train beginning to slow. He grabbed his carpet bag and left his seat to go stand hidden in the vestibule. At the first glimpse of the station platform, he pushed open the car door and leaped out onto the wooden planks before the train had come to a halt. The forward momentum caused him to stumble, but he regained his footing and continued to the door of the building which was not much more than a ticket office with an attached baggage storage warehouse.

Through his window, Jean saw Luther disappear inside the station. "He's off the train," he said to Julie. "I just saw him." Jean leaped up and, with Julie crowding him form behind, they made for the nearest exit.

Discovering there was no other access or egress to the station, Luther burst back out onto the station platform and clattered down the wooden side steps to the station property where he found himself knee deep in snow that hindered him all the way onto the narrow main street. He spotted a general store a short distance across and down the way and struggled through more deep drifts of undisturbed snow.

Jean and Julie had not been in a position to see Luther come back out of the station. As soon as the train stopped, they stepped off and ran toward the door of the small structure. Jean flung open the door and looked inside to find the interior empty.

"He's not here. Check the street."

Julie went in one direction and Jean the other where he saw Luther's bootprints and ragged trail. "He went this way," he shouted to Julie, who came around to his side. They went down the steps and, lifting their carpet bags high, ploughed their way through the snow to the street where Luther's clear trail continued to lead them in the direction of the store.

Inside, Luther grabbed an axe handle within reach and attacked the cowering proprietor behind the wooden counter, rendering him unconscious with a single blow to his bald exposed head that bloodied the side of his bewhiskered face and dribbled down his apron.

Luther snatched a shotgun and a box of ammunition from a display behind the counter and quickly inserted two shells into the chamber. Checking the street, he saw through the frost-coated window that Jean and Julie were following his tracks from the train station. He stepped out onto the porch and raised the shotgun.

Jean saw the flash of the barrel and in a single swift motion threw Julie to the ground and shielded her with his own body. Both shots passed over head, but the two loud explosions brought out nearby residents to see what was happening.

When Jean looked up, Luther was gone from the porch and nowhere in sight. "Stay down until I call you," he ordered and was up and charging through the snow toward the general store.

He followed the tracks a short distance around the side and to the rear of the store where they went off into a dense stand of forest. Jean returned to Julie and helped her to her feet. "He's running and we're in need of a gun."

Brushing the snow from her coat, she followed him into the store where they discovered the unconscious owner behind the counter. Jean bent down to the frail man. "He's still breathing. There's a pitcher and a basin over there. Bring that towel and some water." Moments later, he gently wiped away the blood from the man's scalp.

"We have to keep the pressure on Baggot. He has nowhere to go."

Jean stood and examined a rifle taken from the display that gave evidence the men of the town were hunters. Hoping he would need only a single bullet, in the event of a siege, he selected several rounds of ammunition and filled his coat pockets. He looked at Julie.

"I know you want to be in on this, but the danger is great. Too many lives have been lost. I don't want to put you at risk."

"I know how to shoot. My brother taught me back in Minnesota. I was better than he was."

"Have you ever killed anything?"

"I once killed a wolf. He was going after our chickens."

Jean handed her the rifle and lay six cartridges on the counter. Julie handled the rifle and inserted the loads.

"At a distance, these are better than his shotgun," said Jean.

"I know. I've always hated shotguns."

Luther stopped running and listened to hear if he were being followed. There was no crunch of snow or the snap of a twig, only the silence of the forest.

The moment reminded him of when he had been a young soldier back in Germany during the war with the French. He had been stalking an enemy insurgent in a snowy forest just such as this. His blood raced at the cat and mouse game they played that would end in the man's death, a young man no older than himself. They had exchanged fire an hour before, then nothing. Luther wondered if the other soldier had exhausted his ammunition. That would explain the silence. But the silence now was different. He was not the hunter, but the hunted.

He smelled wood smoke and followed its lingering scent to the stone chimney of a log farm house near a frozen river. A log barn that housed three milk cows and a team of draft horses was attached to the house by a worn path in the snow. An empty pig sty hugged one outside wall of the barn and hens pecked in the straw of the open doorway. Other than the rising smoke, there was no sign of a person. He crossed the narrow clearing from the edge of the woods to the front door.

With a single powerful kick, he pushed open the wooden plank door to discover two small children, a boy and his sister playing with poppet dolls in front of the fire. Their mother and father were nowhere to be seen. Luther knew they would be out in the barn feeding livestock and milking cows and would not be gone long.

The two children did not seem to be disturbed by him. They merely stared at him for a few moments, then continued their play as though he were not in the room. He took a chair opposite the open door and waited with the shotgun leveled at whoever would walk through.

He heard the mother's voice as she approached on the path. "Alice, Joseph, why is the door standing open?" She stopped in the doorway at the terrifying sight of the man wearing a black coat and aiming a gun at her. She dropped her pail and the milk it contained spilled and streamed out over the wooden floor. "My children," she started toward them.

"Don't move," Luther's deadly tone stopped her.

Her body stiffened. "Who are you?" she demanded. "What do you want with us?"

Luther slowly shook his head.

"If you want food, I'll give you food. Then you must be on your way. We lead a peaceful life here. You have nothing to fear from us. There is no sheriff in the town."

Luther remained silent.

"My husband will be coming from the barn. Just don't harm the children. What do you want us to do?"

At that moment, carrying an armload of firewood, her husband walked through the open door and nearly stumbled into his wife. Seeing Luther and the shotgun, he said nothing.

Luther noted that they were a young couple, like many of the young couples he had seen in German villages. He did not mean to do them harm, but he needed them in a different way.

Finally the man said, "There is no need here for a gun. Do you need food, a place to sleep, a blanket?"

"All of those and one more thing," said Luther. "Come in and shut the door."

The man used his boot heel to close the door. "Can I put these down?"

Luther nodded. The man carefully unloaded the wood from is arms into a kindling box next to a cast iron stove. Then he turned to face Luther who rose from his chair.

"We can talk. The gun is not necessary," said the husband. His face was raw and wind-burned. He wore a cap with ear flaps and a leather coat thickly lined with sheeps wool.

"A man is following me," said Luther. "He wants to kill me. He will come here."

"Then you must leave at once," said the husband.

"I will leave and one of you will go with me." Luther glanced down at the little girl.

"No, no, his wife cried out. You must go alone."

"If you have to take someone, then take me," said the husband. "Not a child."

"It's cold outside. Put warm clothes on the girl."

"No!" the mother shrieked. "No! You cannot take her!"

"If you get in my way, I'll kill you, your husband, and your boy. And then I'll take your girl."

"What are you going to do with her? What are you going to do?"

"I won't harm her. She is my hostage."

"What is going to happen?"

"The man coming after me will follow my tracks here to your house. He is not far behind. I'll be watching from the trees. You will invite him in. You will say nothing about me and your child. I will know if you do and I will kill her."

"We will do as you ask," said the father.

"Put warm clothes on the girl. Tell her to go with me and that I will not hurt her. Time is running short. Do it now."

Without further protest, the mother dressed her daughter in warm clothing and presented her to their abductor. "Alice," she said. "Go with this man into the forest. He will bring you back soon. We will be waiting for you."

Luther reached down and took her by the arm.

"Where are you taking her?" asked the father.

"We will be in the barn. Do as I say and no harm will come to her."

"We will do as you say."

The father and mother and the boy watched him lead the little girl out the door and along the well beaten path to the barn. Then the father closed the door.

A short time later, concealed by the thick trunks of spruce and pine, Jean and Julie stopped at the edge of the clearing and studied the farm house where smoke continued to rise from the chimney and Luther's tracks in the snow led to the front door. He noticed a few items of children's clothing hanging like frozen animal skins on a clotheslines attached between the house and a tall wooden post.

"He's inside," said Jean. "Whoever is there, he's holding hostage. We have to draw him out, but we can't put them at risk. Baggot is not expecting both of us to come after him and be armed. I'm going to draw his fire. If I'm hit and go down, he'll come out to see if I'm dead. Then you kill him."

"I don't want you dead."

"I'm just going to draw his fire. He telegraphs his moves. He'll miss, and I'll pretend to go down. Look at the clothesline."

Julie saw the children's clothing.

"You don't want anything to happen to them. That is most important. Remember that. Are you ready?"

Julie nodded once firmly.

Jean stepped out from behind the trees into the open and walked across the clearing toward the cabin. He stopped thirty yards away in plain view of the windows and door. "Baggot!" he shouted. "I know you're in there! This is the end of the line! I challenge you to come out and face me!"

Watching for the front door to open or a muzzle flash from the window, Jean did not catch the blurred movement from the barn. The double blast from both barrels destroyed him from his mid-section to his face. He fell thrashing to the snow and lay there unmoving."

Julie swallowed her scream and wiped the tears from her eyes so she could see clearly. She waited for Luther to come out of the barn. When he did, half-dragging and half-carrying the little girl in tow, she feared her aim would not be good enough. As Jean had told her, she did not want to risk any harm coming to the children. She would bide her time, be patient, and wait for the right moment that she knew would come.

As she watched Luther and the little girl walk to Jean's ravaged body, the cabin door opened behind them and the father stepped out. "It's over," he said. "Return our child. You said no harm would come to her."

Luther released his hold on the little girl's arm and she ran stumbling to her father who rushed out to scoop her up and carry her quickly back inside the cabin. He locked the door and received the rifle his wife handed to him. Then he heard a single shot fired from another rifle outside.

Luther twisted in surprise and anger as the bullet tore through his left shoulder. A second bullet grazed his hip and sent him running, staggering toward the forest on the other side of the clearing away from the hidden shooter. He cast a glance over his shoulder and saw Julie step out from behind a tree and walk purposefully after him through the snow. He ran on toward the river.

For a minute, Julie lost sight of him and realized he would be waiting for her to come into view. A spray of pine bark near her head followed by the delayed explosion from Luther's gun told her where he was.

Keeping thick trees, boulders, and dense brush between them, she circled around to approach him from behind. Her next shot bloodied his hands as his shotgun flew into the air and landed disappearing into the deep snow.

Julie stepped out from hiding. She saw current running under thin ice at the middle of the river. "Walk out there – on the ice," she commanded.

Luther stared at her.

She fired a shot, just missing Luther's head. "Get moving."

Clutching his mangled hands to his chest, Luther turned and stumbled and slipped on the ice. With some effort, he regained his footing and suddenly tried to run parallel to the bank and dodge back toward an exposed shallow gravel beach.

Julie fired a shot that penetrated Luther's boot and shattered his right foot. He staggered and fell, scrambling to get away as a third shot slammed into his other hip.

His movements edged him further toward the center of the river where the ice had thinned and weakened. He crashed through. His cry was smothered by the freezing water closing over him as the swift current pulled him under and carried him away to his death.

Epilogue

Barely able to raise and lower one sluggish step in front of the other, Julie followed the scuttled tracks in the snow she had traversed from the farm. She feared returning to what awaited her and wandered aimlessly until the cabin and barn came into view.

Unable to look at the dark form of Jean's crumpled body half buried in the snow, Julie slowly crossed the clearing to the cabin and knocked on the door, promptly opened by the father. He searched the loss and sadness that aged her young face, took the rifle from her that she still carried, placed a strong arm around her shoulders, and brought her inside to the fire. She stared back at the boy and girl whose wide-eyed sympathetic curiosity followed her into the room. The mother offered her a chair. Julie lowered herself onto the seat and stared into the flames.

Their mother had once told Julie and her brother that life was a great adventure and they should go out and experience it. "Let nothing daunt you," she encouraged in her intense energetic way of thrusting her blonde head forward so that they could see the taut cords of her neck. She was not a frail woman.

Their father had said that being married to their mother was the great adventure, at least for him. And, in many ways, it was for Julie and her brother, as well. Although their personal adventures were unexpected, she thought perhaps that was what adventures were intended to be.

"It's important for you to see many faces in many spaces," her mother had told them.

Julie thought the world seen through the eyes of a small child was quite astonishing. Everything was new and unexpected, because a child had no expectations but to be fed and nurtured. The tumultuous sights and noises of life were absorbed through all the senses and churned in a kaleidoscope in a miraculous brain that sorted it all out in a meaningful way. She had lost her sense of meaning.

Over time, Julie came to understand how different influences splinter that kaleidoscope in a multitude of directions with profoundly different results in how they lived their lives and the invisible forces that pushed and pulled at them. There were forces that she struggled against then and continued to do so during her later years.

The following morning, after breakfast, Julie watched the father build a coffin out of pine wood. She stared at the whorls and patterns in the wood that were once the vessels that carried nutrients from the soil up through the roots and trunk and out the branches to the leaves conversing with the sun and air, giving the tree its life. Just as with her mother and father, she thought it ironic that the now dead wood housed the body of Jean Guenoc, a man who protected and celebrated life.

She had been unable to look for long at his face, destroyed and distorted by the shotgun blast. A brief glance created the faces of her mother and father in her mind in a way she did not want to remember them. She did not need a reminder of the cruelties of life. She wanted to remember them whole and healthy and loving.

Julie told the father that even though Jean was a priest, he had neither believed nor disbelieved in the existence of a higher being. He would want an anonymous grave out there in the woods among creatures of the wild.

"I'll bury him when the ground softens at the thaw," he said.

He took Julie to town on a wagon converted to a sleigh by removing the wheels and attaching wooden runners, much like skis. Julie rode up on the driver's seat beside him. They did not speak to one another. At the station, he offered to come inside and purchase her ticket. She thanked him and said she would be okay from that point on. She watched him drive the sleigh back down the main street and return to the forest.

The sights of the countryside and the cities through which the train passed flashed by her window on her long journey home. She transferred lines once from the New York Central to the Chesapeake and Ohio, two of the railroads that wove the network of the new industrial society.

When she arrived in Chicago, she hired a horse-drawn cab to take her to the mansion. Newt, Beth, and Aaron solemnly greeted her at the door.

"Where is Jean?"

Julie shook her head and brushed at a sudden flood of tears. Newt took her into his arms. "He's dead," she gasped. "He's dead."

Julie wished she had a gun to shoot at a flock of raucous crows that descended to populate the barren branches of the massive oaks that grew in the cemetery where the mutilated bodies of Matias, Gustav, and Sophie Rose, were being laid to rest.

Horst Holtzman attempted to say a few words of blessing over their graves, but was drowned out by the crows, who, at the conclusion of the funeral, lifted off with a thunder of dark wings into the bleak winter sky and navigated over the city through the clouds of smoke and grit to the stockyards.

Newt and Aaron did not attend Harvard University as their mentor had planned. They remained in Chicago and continued to work in the manufacturing division of Bauman Enterprises, learning the realities of business and, with the help of their supervisors, kept the company in operation for five years until Kurt Wohlman sold the company to a conglomerate.

Julie became a journalist and continued writing her book in support of reform in business, politics and Government and of the middle-class. In 1911, she and Conrad Holtzman were married. They raised a family of five children, three girls and two boys.

Reader and Book Club Topics for Discussion

1. *The Revolutionist* chronicles powerful social, political, and economic forces at the turn of the 20th Century that affect the lives of all the characters in various ways and provide the foundation for the novel. From the very beginning and throughout her story, the protagonist, Julie Josephson, encounters situations where she must make difficult choices and react in various ways to survive. As you read the book, identify at what point in the novel she realizes she does not have to be a victim, but can resist and fight against those forces. What are the circumstances and what does she do to change her life?

2. From her childhood through young adulthood, Julie has a number of mentors during her coming-of-age experiences. As you identify them, how do they relate to and communicate with her? What are their influences and what actions does she take as a result?

3. The bounty hunter, Luther Baggot, is a threatening presence throughout the novel. How does he persecute Julie, her brother, and their friends and how do they retaliate?

4. How does Julie handle loss and grief?

5. What is Julie's first encounter with discrimination in the logging camp? How does she handle the situation?"

6. How does the intervention of the Bauman brothers introduce Julie, Newt, and Aron and Beth Peet into the social environment of class distinction? What are the events? How does each of them react? What personal discoveries are made?

7. How does the myth of Pygmalion figure in the novel?

8. What forms of news communication are used in the lives of the characters? What were the difficulties and obstacles? Compare those times to the effect of contemporary media and Internet technology.

9. The Revolutionist includes origins and contemporary parallels of ethnic prejudice, which is a major dramatic conflict Julie Josephson encounters. By definition, ethnic prejudice is the holding of negative opinions, beliefs, or attitudes about people who belong to a specific ethnic group. Ethnic groups are characterized by a distinctive culture, shared origin or ancestral history, and/or certain physical traits. Unique cultural traits include language, religion, marriage choices, food preferences, music, dances, literature, games, and occupations. Religion is one of the most significant traits of an ethnic group. How does Julie respond to ethnic prejudice?

10. The extent of discrimination against African Americans in the legal system motivates Julie Josephson to befriend Ophelia Robinson, an African American maid who is Julie's friend and confidant at the Bauman mansion. Bernard

Hutchins, an African American defense lawyer attempting to carve out a career in the racist legal system, confronts the prejudice of the court in attempting to exonerate a prisoner from a fabricated crime. Laws and politicians barred African Americans unless it was to prosecute them for crimes against white citizens. These were the cases that Bernard sought, Black defendants in the dangerous territory of white courts. How has the legal system changed today? How has it not? What are causes of discrimination?

11. During the early 1900s, waves of immigrants from Europe and Asia settled in major American cities. Met with hostility from native-born Americans in competition for jobs, they were forced into poverty-stricken ethnic neighborhoods and into dilapidated multi-family tenements. Witnessing such squalor in the Chicago slums plants the seeds of Julie Josephson's revolutionary fervor. Having come from an agrarian origin, her early life follows the transition of America into the Industrial Age and the struggles of men and women against their subjugation and exploitation by capitalists and corrupt politicians in the chaos of an emerging middle-class society. From an historical perspective, the recurrence of the lack of ethics, morality, racial prejudice, and of the lack of an appreciation for human value in modern times is an example of history repeating itself. What in your life and times is being repeated?

12. Among Julie Josephson's cultural influences, women's suffrage during the early 1900s plays a significant role in motivating her to fight against the inequality and discrimination that prevailed in society. Although the

challenges against misogyny continue to exist, Julie's character/persona represents many women at the forefront of changes that are steps to improve the lives of women. How does the movement against discriminatory, prejudicial, and outmoded beliefs continue?

13. Industrialists Then and Now

This, then, is held to be the duty of the man of wealth: First, to set an example of modest, unostentatious living, shunning display or extravagance; ... and, after doing so, to consider all surplus revenues which come to him simply as trust funds, which he is called upon to administer... to produce the most beneficial results for the community—the man of wealth thus becoming the mere trustee and agent for his poorer brethren, bringing to their service his superior wisdom, experience and ability to administer, doing for them better than they would or could do for themselves."

From "Wealth," by Andrew Carnegie, *North American Review*(1889). *"Law? Who cares about the law? Hain't I got the power?"*

Comment alleged to have been made by Cornelius Vanderbilt, when warned that he might be violating the law.

Over one-hundred years ago, through her association with the Bauman Brothers, Julie Josephson comes face to face with industrialist icons who embody both of the above differing points-of-view. How would you compare and contrast current political and financial personalities and philosophies then and now? Who would you say is like Andrew Carnegie? Who like Cornelius Vanderbilt?

14. The early 1900s heralded the invention of new manufacturing processes, steam power, chemical and steel production, and

the transition from hand to machine production and creation of factories. Julie Josephson becomes embroiled in the Industrial Workers of The World (IWW) as a union organizer supporting the rise of the working class striking for better wages and safe and healthy working conditions. The IWW promoted the platform of industrial unionism and workplace and economic democracy. Skilled and unskilled men and women and workers from all nationalities were welcome as members. During World War I and after, their influence ended with the imprisonment of 10,000 organizers and the deportation of many thousands as foreign agitators. What is your opinion of the evolution and necessary political role of unions today and partisan resistance?

15. How does the conclusion of the novel provide a sense of hope and redemption?

Characters

Julie Josephson – Teenage political activist intent on avenging the murder of her mother and father

Newt Josephson – Julie's brother, steadfast and heroic in looking out for her

Olaf Josephson – Father of Julie and Newt, a freethinker and political émigré from Sweden

Ingrid Josephson – Mother of Julie and Newt, a freethinker and political émigré from Sweden

Aron Peet – Close friend of Newt and Julie, supports them in their escape from the man who killed their parents.

Beth Peet – Close friend of Julie, has ambitions to become an opera singer

Luther Baggot – An assassin and bounty hunter tracking down political insurrectionists

Jack Moulton – Logging camp foreman

Charlie Brandt and Mitchum Hardie - Rivermen

Alfred Wohlman – President of a European rail and shipping transportation company, headquartered in Berlin. A secret poltical activist.

Anna Wohlman – Alfred's wife

Rudolf Palm – A sadistic highly placed officer in Chancellor Otto von Bismarck's secret police

Matias Bauman/Heinrich Wohlman - A university student from Vienna forced to flee from Europe because of his political activity.

Kurt Bauman/Kurt Wohlman – Heinrich's brother, a vice president in his father's company in Berlin.

Sophie Augusta Rose – A Viennese opera diva and lover of Heinrich Wohlman.

Horst Holtzman – A political organizer working for the Bauman brothers in Chicago

Conrad Holtzman – Horst's 18 year old son, a political organizer, body guard, and bare knuckle fighter

Liesel Holtzman – Conrad's 16 year old sister, a political organizer and sidekick of Julie Josephson

Dutton Koontz – Conrad's devoted friend with ambitions to become a pharmacist

Gustav Weber – Servant and family friend of the Baumans/Wohlmans

Jean Guenoc – A former Jesuit priest, family friend and protector and partisan of the French underground

Ophelia Robinson – A Negro maid at the Bauman mansion, becomes Julie's friend and confidant

Bernard Hutchins – A Negro lawyer attempting to carve out a career in a racist society

Bill O'Riley – Ruthless owner of a large mercantile company in Chicago

Jonah Delacroix – Negro sharecropper who joins strike breakers from Missouri

Orville Sampson – Jonah's friend, also in search of a better life

Francis Keely – Chicago ward alderman notorious for political graft and corruption

Maureen Keely – Francis Keely's wife, a progressive suffragette in conflict with her husband

Yang Wu Song – Chinese opium dealer

Henry Phillips – House of Morgan investment banker handling the Bauman brothers account

John Pierpont Morgan – Merchant banker, robber baron, and president of the House of Morgan bank.

Jacob Schiff – President of Kuhn, Loeb investment house and a rival of J.P. Morgan

Bibliography

"A Society Without A Newspaper is Like a Body Without a Head": Abbott, Karen, *Sin In The Second City*, New York, Random House, 2007.

Addams, Jane, *Twenty Years At Hull-House,* New York, Signet Classics, an Imprint of New American Library, 1961.

Address delivered in Sanders Theater, Memorial Hall, Cambridge, Massachusetts, Memorial Day, 1905.

African Chicago Politics, The Black Mafia: African-American Organized Crime In Chicago 1890 – 1960.

Akiyo, Yamamoto, *Reorganization of Gender Relations Among East European Immigrants In The United States: Realities and Representations*, Nagoya City University, Nanzan Review of American Studies Volume 30, (2008): 121-130, Proeedings of the NASSS 2008.

Albanians, University of California Library.

Avrich, Paul, *Anarchist Voices, An Oral History of Anarchism In America*, Edinburgh, Oakland, West Virginia, AK Books, 2005.

Beller, Steven, *Vienna and The Jews 1867-1938 A Cultural History*, New York, Cambridge University Press, 1989.

Big Business and The Much-Rakers, 1900-1910, History of American Thought, Exploring The Diversity of American Intellectual History.

Blau, Judith R., Thomas, Mim, Newhouse, Beverly, Kavee, Andrew, Bodnar, John, *The Transplanted*, Indiana University Press, First Midland Book Edition, 1987.

Boyer, John W., *Political Radicalism In Late Imperial Vienna Origins of The Christian Social Movement, 1848-1897*, Chicago and London, The University of Chicago Press, 1981, 1995.

Bray, Robert, *The Chicago Novel 1890-1915, Historical Research and Narrative*.
Bruce, Roscoe Conkling, *Freedom Through Education, Building and House History*, Minnesota Historical Society.

Candeloro, Dominic, *Mostly Melted/Still Connected: The Marchegiani in Chicago Heights 1893-1997*, Mayor's Office Chicago Heights Illinois.

Cather, Willa, *Song of the Lark*, New York, Penguin Classics, 1915.
Chernow, Ron, *The House of Morgan, An American Banking Dynasty and The Rise of Modern Finance*, New York, Grove Press, 1990.

Chicago Politics, History of Chicago From Trading Post To Metropolis, Roosevelt.edu.

Chicago Politics, Photographs From The Chicago Daily News, 1902-1933.

Chicago's Immigrant Workers And Their Press, Paper On Chicago Foreign Language Press Survey produced by a Work Projects Administration program administered by the Chicago Public Library.

Czologosz Trial, Website

Doctorow, E. L., *Worlds Fair*, Dreiser, Theodore, *Sister Carrie*, New York, Oxford University Press, 1991, 1998.

Du Bois, W. E. B., *The Souls of Black Folk*, New York, Oxford University Press, 2007.

Du Bois, W.E. Burghardt, Ph.D. and Dill, August Granville, A.M. *The College-Bred Negro American*, Atlanta, GA, Atlantic University Press, 1910.

Ethnic Buffer Institutions The Immigrant Press: New York City, 1820-1984, Historical Social Research, Vol. 23 — 1998 — No. 3, 20-37

Evans, Harold, *The American Century*, New York, Alfred Knopf, Inc., 1998.

Flexner, Eleanor, *Century of Struggle: The Woman's Rights Movement in the United States*, 1959, reprinted 1996 Belknap, Harvard.

Fraser, George MacDonald, *Royal Flash*, New York, Plume, Penguin Books, 1970.

Friedrich Nietzsche, Wikipedia, May 30, 1997, revision November 14, 2007.

Gaffney, Elizabeth, *Metropolis*, New York, Random House, 2005.

German Ethnic 1900, website.

Hill, Professor Thomas E., *The Essential Handbook of Victorian Etiquette*, San Mateo, CA, Bluewood Books, 1994.

Hudelson, Richard and Ross Carl, *By The Ore Docks, A Working People's History of Duluth*, Minneapolis, MN, University of Minnesota Press, 2006.

Ideology of Anarchism, www.geocities.com.

Italians In Chicago, 1850-1900, www.encyclopedia.chicagohistory.org/pages/115.

La Belle Epoque 1890-1914 Fashion History, Edwardian Era Files.

Larson, Amanda Wiljanen, *Finnish Heritage In America*, Marquette, MI, Delta Kappa Gamma Society, 1975.

Leidenberger, Georg, *Chicago's Progressive Alliance, Labor and The Bid For Public Streetcars*, Dekalb, Illinois, Northern Illinois University Press, 2006.

Lidtke, Vernon L., *The Outlawed Party Social Democracy In Germany, 1878-1890*, Princeton, New Jersey, Princeton University Press, 1966.

Logging (and Lumberjacks), Minnesota Historical Society.

Macfie, John, *Parry Sound Logging Days*, Toronto, Canada, Stoddard Publishing Co., Ltd., A Boston Mills Press Book, Erin, Ontario, 1992.

Macryan, Daniel, *Essay On Nietzsche*, www.geocities.com.

McClures Magazine (American Periodical) Encyclopedia Britannica Online.
McClures Magazine Mission Statement, The New York Times Published Noveber 23, 1901.

McClures Magazine, www.Learningcurve.gov.uk

McGerr, Michael, *A Fierce Discontent, The Rise and Fall of The Progressive Movement In America 1870-1920*, New York, Oxford University Press, 2003.

Meatpackers Strike Chicago 1904, Chronology of Illinois Labor History.

Meredith, Isabel, *Girl Among The Anarchists*, London, Covent Garden, W.C., Duckworth & Company, 1903.

Michels, Robert, *Political Parties Sociological Studies*, Kitchener, Ontario, Canada, Batouche Books, 2001.

Morris, Charles R., *The Tycoons, How Andrew Carnegie, John D. Rockefeller, Jay Gould, and J. P. Morgan Invented The American Supereconomy*, New York, Owl Books, Henry Holt & Company, LLC, 2005.

Morris, Edmund, Theodore Rex, New York, The Modern Library, 2001.

Music Chicago 1900-1910 (website).

Music Chicago, Chicago Theaters, The New York Times, Published: June 28, 1891.

Music Chicago, Opera, Theater Article, The New York Times, February 27, 1897.

Nasaw, David, *Andrew Carnegie*, New York, Penguin Books, 2006.

Nellie Bly, Norris, Frank, *The Octopus*, New York, Penguin Books, 1901, 1987, 1994.

O'Neill, Francis, *Chief O'Neill's Sketchy Recollections of An Eventful Life In Chicago*, Evanston, Illinois, Northwestern University Press, 2008.

Opium Smuggling, Website.

Palmer, Alan, *Twilight of the Hapsburgs*, New York, Atlantic Monthly Press, 1994.

Paxson, Frederick Logan, "Theodore Roosevelt", *Dictionary of American Biography* (NY: Scribner's 1934).

Perils of The New Land, Blackhawk Films Collection, 1996.

Polish in Chicago, encyclopedia.chicagohistory.org

Powers, Stanley, *Chicago Garment Worker's Strike*, The World's Work, Vol. 10, 1905.

Price, Matthew, *Making Love Pay In The Levee*, Book Review of Sin In The Second City, by Karen Abbott, September 2, 2007.

Riis, Jacob A., *How The Other Half Lives, Studies Among The Tenements of New York*, Stilwell, KS, Digiread.com Publishing Edit, 2005.

Rolvaag, O.E., *Giants In The Earth*, New York, Harper Perennial, 1927, 1991, 1999.

Schorske, Carl E., *Fin-De-Siecle Vienna Politics and Culture*, New York, Vintage Books, A Division of Random House, January 1981.

Shakeup in M'Clures Follows Dissension, Miss Tarbell, Lincoln Steffens, and R. S. Baker To Quit, The New York Times, Published May 5, 1906.

Shields, Jody, *The Fig Eater*, New York, Back Bay Books, Little Brown & Company, 2000.

Shpping Freight Business, Austro Hungary, 1800's.

Sinclair, Upton, *The Jungle*, New York, Modern Library, 2002.

Steffens, Lincoln, *The Shame of The Cities*, Mineola, New York, Dover Publications, Inc., 2004, unabridged republication of the work originally published by McClure, Phillips, & Co., New York 1904.

Stephens, Autumn, *The Essential Handbook of Victorian Entertaining*, San Mateo, CA, Bluewood Books, 2005.

Stieber, Wilhelm J.C.E., (Translated from the German by Jan Van Heurck), *The*
Chancellor's Spy, New York, Grove Press, Inc. 1979.

Sweden 1890-1914, World History at KMLA, November 8th, 2004.

Swedish Immigration, Swedish in Minnesota (website).

Synopsis Die Fledermaus & Der Rosenkavalier.

Tarbell, Ida M., *The History of The Standard Oil Company.url.*

The American Women's Dime Novel, Dime Novel Project Website.

The *Fight for Women's Suffrage*, America Free Thinkers.doc.

The History of Fashion: 1900-1910, Clothing 1900-1910 website.

The Shantyman's Life (Song), Life in a Lumber Camp

Timeline 1890-1910, Magic Dragon Multimedia.

Tuttle, Sam, *Manners & Morals of Yesterday*, Asheville, NC, Native Ground Books and Music, 1994.

Tye, Larry, *Rising From The Rails, Pullman Porters and The Making of The Black Middle Class*, Owl Books, New York, Henry Holt & Company, 2004.

Various News Articles, 1899.

Washington, Booker T., *Up From Slavery, The Autobiography of Booker T. Washington*, Secaucus, NJ, Carol Publishing Group, 1997.

Wharton, Edith, *House of Mirth*, New York, Penguin Classics, 1985.

Wharton, Edith, *The Custom of The Country*, New York, Charles Scribner's Sons, 1913, 1941.

Wheat Farms, Flour Mills, and Railroads: A Web of Interdependence, Teaching With Historic Places Lesson Plans.

William Jennings Bryan Article On Speeches, The New York Times, Published: October 11, 1896.

Wirth, Fremont P., *The Discovery and Exploitation of the Minnesota Iron Lands*, New York, Arno Press, A New York Times Company, 1979.

Woll, Kris, *Through the City, To these Fields: Eastern European Immigration, Religious Worship Chicago and U.S. 1890-1910.*

Zeublin, Charles, "The Chicago Ghetto," *Hull-House Maps and Papers: A Presentation of Nationalities and Wages in a Congested District of Chicago, Together with Comments and Essays on Problems Growing Out of the Social Conditions* (New York: Thomas Y. Crowell, 1895): 91-111.

About the Author

Rob is a graduate of the University of California, Santa Barbara and received his graduate degree in from the University of California, Los Angeles (communications).

Rob worked as a business and management consultant to advertising, and roles in corporate communications and media production companies; as well as many others. Now retired, he resides with his wife in Southern California where he devotes much of his time to writing. He is a recipient of the Samuel Goldwyn and Donald Davis Literary Awards. An affinity for family and the astute observation of generational interaction pervade his novels. His works are literary and genre upmarket fiction that address the nature and importance of personal integrity.

Follow his work at:

http://www.rmtauthor.com

Tell-Tale Publishing would like to thank you for your purchase. If you would like to read more by this or other of TT's fine authors, please visit us at:

www.tell-talepublishing.com